SHATTERED SIGHT

THE JACKSON DAVIS MYSTERIES
BOOK 1

LIZ MILLIRON

ISBN: 978-1-963705-05-8

Cover design: David Ter-Avanesyan https://ter33design.com/

Cover images: AdobeStock

Published in the United States of America by Harbor Lane Books, LLC.

www.harborlanebooks.com

To Dawn Dowdle, without whom this series wouldn't have seen the light of day.

CHAPTER
ONE

I stood in front of my open closet and shuffled through my tie selection. "Amy, have you seen my red tie?" I called to my wife.

No answer.

"Amy!"

She came into the bedroom, dark brown hair in a messy knot, stray strands stuck to her face. She held our six-month-old son, Christopher, over her shoulder as she rubbed his back. "What are you yelling for?" She glanced at the jacket on the bed. "I thought you only wore that suit to court."

"I need to look sharp today, which means I need my lucky red tie." I went over the ones on the rack for the third time. "The one with the dark gray pinstripes. It should be here."

"For crying out loud. Let me." She held Christopher out, forcing me to take him.

Before I could turn him around, he burped, a wad of spit landing on my chest. "Grab me a clean shirt, too." I didn't have time for this. "I need to make a positive impression today."

"Jackson, you're coming off desk duty, not starting a new job."

"All the more reason to look good. I need to remind the guys I'm an investigator, not a glorified secretary."

Whatever Amy said was lost in the rattle of hangers. "Here." She held out the tie. "It was with your other court suit, still in the bag." She tossed it, along with a clean shirt, on the bed.

I handed back our son. "You're an angel." I leaned over and kissed her. Even wearing an old T-shirt and jeans, she put any supermodel to shame. At least in my mind. If I hadn't been determined to be early, I would have demonstrated my gratitude with a little more emphasis.

"Yeah, yeah. Don't you forget it." She disengaged Christopher's hand from her hair.

I slipped into the shirt, buttoned it, and swiftly knotted the tie. Then, I shrugged into my jacket. I held out my arms. "Well, how do I look?"

She smoothed my lapel. "Like one of Niagara Falls Police Department's finest homicide detectives, which you are." Her voice was light, but I caught the worried glint in her beautiful, deep blue eyes.

"It's going to be okay, Amy. I'm ready to get back to work."

"I know." She kissed me. "Go get 'em, tiger."

———

I arrived at HQ and waved to the desk sergeant.

"Detective Davis, you going to testify today?" he asked.

"Nope. I'm back in the rotation, Herb."

He smiled. "It's about time."

I took the elevator up to the floor where the Criminal Investigation Division was located and went to my desk. As always, I avoided looking at the empty one facing mine. I briefly wondered how long that would last.

Hopefully for a while.

From across the room, a voice said, "Davis. You're here."

I looked up to see Captain Yannick striding toward me. Trailing him was an unfamiliar Black man. He was in his mid-thirties, close-cut hair, nice suit. A really nice suit. He held the largest size of coffee Starbucks sold in one hand and a cardboard box under the opposite arm.

I focused on the captain. "Morning, sir. You get the paperwork?"

"I did." The captain shook my hand. "I'm glad to have one of my ace investigators back in the rotation. I want you to meet Rodney Kirke. He's a new detective for homicide. This is his first day."

I nodded. "Welcome to the looney bin. I'd shake your hand, but it looks like they're full."

He put the box and Starbucks on the empty desk. "Captain Yannick told me all about you."

"Only the good stuff, I hope." I refrained from saying anything about his things on the desk. "Who'd you get partnered up with?"

It was Yannick who answered, pointing a finger in my direction. "You. Meet your new partner."

What the actual? I forced myself to remain calm. "Oh. You didn't mention anything on Friday before we left."

"And I apologize. I meant to, but the day got away from me."

I glanced at Rodney, then shifted my focus. "Captain, can I talk to you?"

"What about?"

"Nothing major. A few details and then I can get to work." Like how he'd forgotten to say he'd assigned me a new partner.

"Unpack and settle in." Yannick pointed to the new guy. He nodded toward me. "My office."

Once inside, I closed the door. "Sir, what the hell? A new partner on day one?"

"I understand you feel blindsided. I should have called over the weekend. Mea culpa." His expression told me he'd expected this response. "You had to know this was coming, though."

I did. But the speed unsettled me. "I guess I expected more notice. Not to walk in on Monday and be introduced to the new guy without even a hint. And I didn't realize Max was so easily replaced. I thought you'd take more time."

Yannick's gaze and voice held sympathy but firmness at the same time. "Her position has been open for six months. Kirke's recently passed the detective exam. You can show him the ropes." He leaned back. "I spoke to Kirke's commander from patrol, who said he's top-notch. I think you'll get on well together."

Seeing the empty desk every day had been hard. Having a stranger occupy Max's chair was worse.

Yannick seemed to read my mind. "Look, I can't

replace Max. Oh, sure. I can hire a new body. It won't be the same. I know. But give him a chance. You learned a lot from Max and she'd expect you to step up and pass it on. You two get the next call."

What a cheat. Problem was, he was right. She *would* expect it. "Yes, sir. I'll do my best."

———

I returned to the desks and assessed the man whom Yannick thought could fill Max's shoes. He'd unpacked the box and was arranging everything to his satisfaction. Strike one: he drank Starbucks. I couldn't stand the import from Seattle, much preferring Tim Hortons, the Western New York alternative. Max had not much cared about where the coffee came from as long as it was hot and black.

Strike two: he'd put a fancy brass nameplate in front of him, with a leather blotter and matching pen and pencil cup next to it. I hoped the attention to office supplies didn't mean anything except excitement for the new shield. Max had never bothered to have more than a jumbo calendar and her ever-present book of Sudoku puzzles on her desk. "Looks like you're ready to get to work."

His hand jerked and the cup of pens toppled over. "Just about." He straightened everything and looked around. Very few of the battered desks held anything as fancy as his desk set. "Guess I overdid it a little with the office supplies, huh?"

I heard a crash and clatter behind me. I spun, hand twitching toward my holster. Another detective had dropped his coffee mug, spilling hot liquid and scattering shards of ceramic over the floor. *Just a broken cup. Relax.* I took a deep breath, hoping no one had noticed my reaction. I turned back to Rodney. "How long have you had your shield?" I asked, willing myself to relax.

He watched me closely, so much so he had to be wondering what was up. "Two weeks."

That explained a lot. "I wouldn't worry about it. It's natural to be a little nervous, especially starting a new job like this." I sat down. "Where'd you come from?"

"Downtown. Spent a lot of time chasing pickpockets away from tourists." He unbuttoned his suit jacket and took his seat. "It's not very often you meet a white guy named Jackson. No offense."

It was what people said when they knew they'd been offensive. I could tell his clothes were new. The jacket and slacks were tailored and the tie shone like silk. "My mother was a horror fan and *The Lottery* was her all-time favorite short story. She loved it so much she swore to name her first child after the author. I'm lucky I wasn't a girl or I'd be called Shirley."

He laughed, but he stopped short. "I can't tell if you're joking or not."

I held up my hand. "True story. My father tried to get the nickname Jack to stick, but it never did. I've gotten used to it."

He shifted in his seat. "I, uh, heard about what happened to your old partner. Hope I can measure up. She sounds like she was quite the investigator."

The words were a knife in my chest. "She is." I had no intention of discussing Max with him. "Why'd you become a detective?"

If he noticed my use of present tense, he didn't show it. "It was time for a challenge. I also thought it would help in other areas."

I waited, but he didn't continue. "Such as?"

"What's the scoop? Did Yannick give you an assignment when you talked to him or something?"

He has things he doesn't want to discuss. We're equal there. "Not yet."

Yannick emerged from his office. "Davis, Kirke. Attempted bank robbery downtown. Get down there and take witness statements."

I stood. "On it, sir."

The bank incident didn't take long at all. I watched Rodney out of the corner of my eye while we interviewed bank staff and customers. He might have gone overboard with the clothes and desk supplies, but I couldn't fault his technique in the field.

At noon, we went to the nearby Niagara Falls State Park to eat lunch outside. In the Niagara region, where it wasn't unusual to wear snow boots in April, you took advantage of nice weather. Rodney and I grabbed a hot dog from a vendor in the mall outside the park entrance and wandered among the trees until we found an empty bench. The roar of the Falls was soothing, a natural white noise machine that calmed my nerves. The sun sparkled through the perpetual mist over the gorge. A few flowering spring trees gave a fresh, green scent to the air. Squirrels darted around, scrounging for food. Anyone visiting the park wouldn't believe that a few blocks away was crime, dingy buildings, and a stagnant economy.

I unwrapped my hot dog. "Tell me about yourself."

"There's not much to tell. I'm from New York City. Attended the University at Buffalo. Spent six years as a patrol cop and decided I needed a career change."

"Married?" He didn't wear a ring, but some guys didn't.

"No. You?"

A rather abrupt answer. "Married, two kids. My daughter is five, son is six months." I thumbed the wedding ring on my finger.

Rodney studied his hot dog with more attention than it deserved. "So, your son was born…"

"Right after the accident, yes." A muscle in my jaw spasmed. Would Max have done what she did if I hadn't been an expectant father? Probably. For the millionth time, I wondered how she felt. We didn't talk about that night. *Does she resent me? Or Christopher?* I bristled at the thought. What person would blame a baby? The thought brought on a wave of guilt. She had a right to be angry, not the other way around.

"How does it feel to be back?" Rodney asked as he peeled more foil from his hot dog.

"I never really left." I took care to avoid dropping relish on my pants. "I've been at a desk for six months. It's not like I've been on leave or anything. But if it had gone on much longer, I'd have gone batshit crazy."

"Good time to come back. Late spring, nice weather."

"Better than patrol duty in the winter."

He nodded. "Got that right," he said around a mouthful of food.

"You said you were from New York. What made

you stick around here?" I slathered relish on a second hot dog.

"I liked the area. You a native?"

"Born and raised." My sixth sense told me Rodney would have preferred to go back to the Big Apple. "Who was she?"

"What makes you think there was a woman?"

"Intuition."

"My ex-girlfriend." He focused on his lunch. "What do you think of the off-season for the Bills? I'm a Giants fan myself."

"I don't follow football that closely." Interesting. I needed to start a list of these forbidden topics.

I finished my hot dog and stared at the early season tourists. A few people roamed the park paths, but full-on tourist season, with its multi-language babble and proliferation of cameras, hadn't started yet. I could see the far side of the gorge and Ontario through the mist. I should take Madeline, my five-year-old daughter, to the Canadian park before the tourist crush started.

"Someone's having a rough day." Rodney nodded in the direction of a couple about five feet away. They stormed along the asphalt walkway between us and the railing.

Correction. She was storming; he was in hot pursuit. Both of them were dressed for a fancy lunch, not a walk through the park.

"Sylvia, wait. Please." The man grabbed her arm. There were damp patches on his shoulders and her shoes had bits of grass stuck to them. They'd been near the Falls. Near enough that the ever-present moisture hadn't dried in the sun. His expression told me this guy was on the losing end of an argument, and he wasn't happy about it.

She pulled away from him. "I told you, Keith, we're finished talking. At least I am. Feel free to carry on as I walk away." She spun and stormed off.

Rodney watched them. "You think we should break it up?"

"My advice? Stay out of it." I shuddered to think of the paperwork. I didn't need to get in the middle of a two-bit marital dispute.

"Sylvia, wait. Damn it, we aren't done here." He grabbed her again.

She pulled out of his grasp and cracked him across the face. "Yes, we are."

Rodney tossed his garbage in the nearby can. "Sorry, I can't let *that* go." He got up and approached the couple.

Shit. I understood his feelings. No one wanted a scene like this one to continue. But Rodney's reaction could open a huge can of worms. My best hope was to defuse the situation and get out of there.

Rodney had wedged himself between the couple and was attempting to calm them down, but he wasn't having much success. "Ma'am, you need to step back. Sir, you, too."

"This is none of your business," the woman said, glaring at the man I assumed was her spouse.

"Everybody take a deep breath." I showed them my badge. "Detective Kirke, is there a problem?"

"They claim it's nothing, but you saw the slap, same as I did. I was asking the gentleman if he wanted to file an assault charge." Rodney glanced from me back to the man, whose cheek was blossoming red where the woman had hit him.

An assault charge? "Let's back up a second. Sir, do you need someone to look at you?" *Please say no. Please say no.*

"I'm fine. I don't think we need the police." The man's gaze never left the woman's face.

She was pretty, even though the sparks in her eyes were intense enough to set dry grass on fire. "No, we don't. I might need a divorce lawyer, but not the cops."

"Ma'am, I witnessed you hitting your husband. I can't ignore that." Rodney glanced at me.

I respected Rodney's intent, but the guy did not understand the size of the tiger he'd grabbed. Niagara Falls still had the attraction for lovebirds. Which meant lovers' quarrels. Especially in the park, where the roar of the water often obscured the sounds. This squabble could turn into an administrative nightmare. "If neither of you wants to press charges, there's nothing for us to do here. However, I do have to ask you to take your argument somewhere less visible. I also advise you to keep it civil. As they say in kindergarten, keep your hands to yourself. Detective Kirke is correct. We can't stand by while one person physically abuses another. Can you two do that?" *Please say yes. Please say yes.* "Or do we have to get official?"

"Fine. I'm leaving, anyway." The woman spun and stalked off toward the park entrance, the angry click of her heels not quite masked by the sounds of spring and millions of gallons of rushing water.

Her husband's voice rose as the distance between them increased. "Sylvia, wait!" He rushed off.

Rodney watched him go, then faced me. "Why didn't you back me up?"

"I did." I heard the unspoken accusation in his words. Rodney thought I underplayed the situation. "I talked to the parties involved. I backed up what you said about not being able to sit back and watch a physical exchange."

The response didn't satisfy him. "But you let them go without making an arrest. Why?"

"We're detectives, investigators. Patrol cops get involved and you're not one any longer. If that's the work you want to do, you should've stayed where you were." I took in his affronted expression and softened my tone. "I know it's hard, but it's not our business. Nobody wanted to press charges. She slapped him. She didn't pull a gun, or a knife, or otherwise make a threat. We can't cuff everybody in Niagara Falls who smacks someone else, even across the face." I stared at the mist over the gorge, then turned to leave.

"You don't think it's worth the paperwork." He brushed some crumbs from his pants and checked his shoes, maybe looking for damp grass clippings.

"Go on. You can explain to Captain Yannick why one of his detectives is too busy handling a marital dispute to respond when the next homicide comes in." I waved my hand in the direction of the couple, who were now out of sight.

"You're right." He stared down the now-empty walkway. "All I'm saying is, there goes a man with troubles."

"But they aren't our troubles."

"I hope it doesn't come back to bite us in the ass."

I buttoned my jacket and walked off. "Let's get back to the office."

———

The afternoon passed without further incident. We helped a couple of the other guys who had open cases. Nobody needed to transfer anything. I debated stopping to see Max when I left. I hadn't gone to her place in a couple of days. Maybe she needed something, a grocery run or whatever.

On the other hand, my family was waiting. There would be too many nights when work kept me late. I needed to go home.

Max would call if she needed something. Wouldn't she?

Madeline's tricycle was out when I arrived. "Hey, I'm home." I tossed my keys in the basket by the door. "Madeline, why is your tricycle in the driveway?"

"I was afraid." She ran out of the living room. "It's dark. Will you come with me, Daddy?"

"One time. Tomorrow, put it away earlier." I walked her outside. I loved my kid's absolute adoration, but I wished she'd learn to put her things in their proper places. At least she still needed me to keep the monsters in the night at bay. The day was coming when that wouldn't be the situation.

Amy was stirring a pot of pasta sauce when I came back in. "Hey." I kissed her neck. "Where's Christopher?"

"Hey, yourself. He's sleeping, thank God. For now. How was your first day back?"

"Okay. No new dead people. New partner, though."

"How do you feel about him?"

"Please don't psychoanalyze me. I got enough of that during my leave."

"I only meant—"

"He's okay." I picked up a copy of *Buffalo Magazine* on the table and stared at the cover. "I recognize this woman."

"Mm hmm. Would you drain the spaghetti?"

"I saw her today in the state park."

"You mean Sylvia Bramley? There's a writeup on her in there. In an article about local businesses run by women. She runs some hoop-de-doo natural mineral cosmetics company."

"Do you use her stuff?"

Amy laughed. "God, no. A bottle of her foundation runs something like seventy-five dollars. I've got better things to spend money on." She pulled rolls out of the oven. "You say you saw her?"

"She was arguing with a man. Is she married to a guy named Keith?" I flipped through the magazine. It was the woman from the park. She looked more polished on the glossy pages, but it was definitely her.

"Yeah. It mentions him in the article. She talks about how supportive he is and how their solid relationship has enabled her to take risks in business."

"They didn't look too happy when I saw them." I skimmed the article. "What is it with women and expensive makeup?"

"What woman doesn't like to look—or feel—glamorous? Makeup is part of the look." She tossed the salad in a wooden bowl with some dressing. "The article says the company is considering expansion to an international market, but she's got quality concerns or something. I picked up the magazine for the pecan pie recipe in the back."

"Well, I do like pecan pie. But don't tell me if you start buying high-end cosmetics. Trash the receipts so I don't find them. Not that you need it. I think you're beautiful with no makeup at all." I swatted her butt.

She rolled her eyes. "Sure, no makeup and a shirt with spit-up staining the front. I'm ready for my *Vogue* photo shoot." She pointed at the pot. "Are you going to take care of the pasta, or do I have to do it?"

She didn't need to get snippy. Or was I imagining it? I could have kept talking while I helped her. "Give me a sec, I got it." I shrugged out of my jacket and pulled off my tie. Sylvia Bramley had definitely not looked like the happy, successful image she portrayed in *Buffalo Magazine*. But people couldn't be happy all the time.

And everybody had something to hide.

The next morning, I dallied with Amy a little before leaving. My semi-romantic interlude cost me the time I needed to stop at Tim Hortons. Maybe Rodney would bring a second cup.

When I entered the building, the desk sergeant, a middle-aged guy who looked hassled, was arguing with a man wearing the aggravated expression of someone who needed something and was being denied.

Keith Bramley, the man from the park.

"Sir, I understand," the sergeant said. "I told you, if you've called 911 and reported her missing, there's nothing else I can do."

I walked over. "Is there a problem?" Obviously, Bramley thought he had one, even if he didn't. The least I could do was help the desk with an unruly civilian.

The visitor wheeled at the sound of a new voice. "My wife is missing and this guy tells me he can't help." He blinked. "I saw you in the park yesterday. You're a cop. You've got to help me."

"What makes you say she's missing?"

"Aren't you listening? We went to dinner last night and she never came back to the casino."

"Calm down. This is the first I've heard your story." I took in the dark bags under his eyes. Something had caused him to lose sleep, whether it was Sylvia's disappearance or not. "The desk sergeant said you called 911. What did they tell you?"

"There was nothing for emergency services to respond to and I should contact the police to file a missing person's report."

"What's your name?"

"I'm telling you my wife is in trouble and you're asking my name?" He grabbed my shoulders.

I tensed and resisted the impulse to slap his hands away. "You need to take your hands off me. Now." He was distraught. I got it. But there was no need to manhandle a police officer. Maybe I didn't know how to balance my wife, a new partner, work, and personal responsibility, but I could handle an overwrought citizen.

The words and my voice snapped him into reality and he stepped back, mumbling what sounded like an apology.

I adjusted my jacket, smoothing the lapels back into place. "Before I can help you, I need your name. Remember, I'm hearing this for the first time."

"Keith Bramley." He ran his hands through his unkempt hair. "My wife is Sylvia Bramley."

I knew it. "Why were you at the Falls?"

"It was supposed to be a romantic getaway. We were

staying at the Seneca Niagara Casino. Not like the romantic part was working."

"What do you mean?" It was a leading question. I knew what he meant. I didn't have a notebook on me, but it didn't matter. I'd remember his words. I always did.

"We'd been arguing lately. We were trying to patch it up."

Unsuccessfully, from what I'd seen. "When was the last time you saw your wife?"

"Dinner. One last shot. We went to Top of the Falls. She left before dessert. When I got back to the hotel room," he swallowed, "she wasn't there. I figured she was still out walking. But she wasn't back when I woke up this morning. I called home, and she's not there, either. Our cleaning lady says her car is in the garage, so she didn't take an Uber home last night and leave again. You've got to help me find her."

"We will. Let's get you to the right department." I turned to the desk sergeant.

Bramley stepped forward. It wasn't the answer he wanted. The belligerent glint in his eyes said it all. "Why can't you help me?"

"I am helping you. I'm taking you to Missing Persons. I'm a homicide detective." I waited for him to process my words. "You don't want assistance from me in this matter."

"Why not?"

"Because if I'm working your case, it means your wife is dead."

———

I took care of things with Bramley, then headed to our office. Rodney hadn't brought a second cup of coffee. Well, that wasn't quite true. He'd brought a second cup and then some. All from Starbucks.

"You buying coffee for the whole department?" I waved at a carrier full of cups.

"Morning. I didn't know what you wanted, so I brought a variety." He pointed to each. "Dark roast, medium, blond, hazelnut, French vanilla. And," he dug into his pocket, "I brought sugar, Splenda, non-sugar sweetener, and two types of creamer." A small mountain of packets tumbled from his hand.

I laughed. One look at his face, with its affronted expression, made me stop. *Jerk. You were new once, remember?* Max whispered in my head. *He's trying to fit in.* I rushed to smooth things over. "Thank you, but I'm not complicated. Plain coffee, one cream, two sugars. No artificial anything." I pulled out the middle cup.

He looked at the full carrier and the pile of sweeteners. "What should I do with the extra?"

"We're in a department of police detectives. Put it in the break room. Someone will drink it." I sat, pouring cream and sugar into the cup.

He picked up everything, piling the packets on the carrier, and hurried off to deposit his goods.

Another detective stopped at my desk. "Hey, Davis, does your partner take orders?"

"He's new. I wouldn't expect this every day." I glared at the detective. "Don't you say a damn word." I remembered being the new guy all too clearly. Max hadn't laughed at me, not once. And Lord knows I'd goofed a lot in my first month. *Way to be the senior detective.* I stirred my coffee.

Rodney returned, a single cup in his hand. "Is everything okay?"

"Fine. Why do you ask?"

"You didn't mention you were going to be late. I wondered if something cropped up."

"It's all good. I actually walked in the building fifteen minutes early. I got sidetracked." I told him about seeing Keith Bramley downstairs.

"What did you tell him?" Rodney took his seat.

"I took him to file a missing persons report. That's about all he can do at this point. It's hard to hear, but she's an adult. There are a dozen legitimate reasons for her to take off."

He shuffled some paper and straightened his desk mat. "Did he say anything more about their argument yesterday?"

"No. And I didn't ask." At the sight of his confused look, I continued. "If she's been found and they called us, well, you get the picture."

He blinked. "Right. She wouldn't be in any condition to go home and work things out."

"Exactly. I realize murder is good for our job security, but let's not wish for the guy's grief, shall we?"

"Right." Rodney stared at me. "Still. Pretty loud argument for a public space. Must have been serious."

"I guess." I wasn't in the mood to speculate on the Bramleys's marital problems.

He looked at me. "No new cases. What are we going to do? Work a cold case?"

Normally, I'd have made a wiseass comment, but I

swallowed it. I'd already laughed in his face. I didn't need to make things worse. But hopefully this was a new-guy symptom and he wouldn't ask what we were going to do every morning. "We have a separate group for those. The Fraud guys have a witness coming in and they need help interrogating. Later this morning, the owner of a thrift store is coming in to make a statement about a theft yesterday."

"More paperwork."

I cracked a grin. "Did you think it was going to be dead people all the time? Relax. Things will heat up. Your entire detective career won't be spent typing forms. Well, it will be. But it won't be everything you do."

He reached for a pen. "Only most of it. At least I get to write them in a warm office instead of a cold patrol car."

I remembered those days. After I got my shield, I'd learned to appreciate the quiet times. He would, too.

———

Yannick emerged from his office around two-thirty. "Davis, Kirke. Dead body in the Niagara Gorge, a woman. You're up."

My mind flashed to Sylvia Bramley. What were the odds? Missing did not always equal dead. I got the exact location from Daniels and scribbled it down. "On it." I grabbed the keys to a car and glanced at Rodney. "Time to earn our paychecks."

We arrived at the gorge and threaded our way through the trees toward the water. The water down here was not quite as rough as above the Falls, but whitecaps still swirled and a twig thrown in the river would have been gone faster than you could blink. The mist didn't carry this far, but the rumble of the water was audible. They'd roped off a chunk of the hiking path. Looky-loos had gathered on the trails farther away from the river. Light glinted off phones held up. With the zoom capabilities now available on the cameras, everybody and their brothers were amateur newscasters.

Rodney cursed at every unstable step. His expensive loafers weren't the best footwear for the terrain. Neither were mine, but so be it.

She'd washed up on the edge, near the Whirlpool Rapids Trail, where the water lapped at the rocks and hikers often had to hop from boulder to boulder. Her legs were still in the water, her skirt floating around them. I stood back and watched the two deputy coroners remove the body from the river.

"Uniform is over there." Rodney pointed.

"In a second." I watched the deputy coroner work, wanting to take things in before we got started. I needed to settle my nerves. This wasn't my first death scene, not by a long shot. But I'd always had Max at my shoulder. I'd been riding a desk for six months. What if I'd lost my touch? What if I made a buffoon of myself in front of Rodney?

Despite my fervent belief, what if I couldn't do this job anymore? Who would I be?

Stop it. It's showtime. I recognized the deputy as Craig Fitch, someone I knew from working scenes with Max. I turned to Rodney. "Let's go."

We approached the uniformed patrol officer standing nearby. "Detective Jackson Davis, Homicide."

"Officer Pete Daniels. I responded to the call." He looked over at Rodney. "Hey, Rod. Long time, no see."

"Pete." Rodney looked like he'd developed a case of lockjaw.

"Nice shield. How's Rachel?" Daniels smirked. "Oh, shit, I'm sorry. I forgot."

Never mind the lockjaw. Rodney's face had been cast in cement. It didn't take a genius to see the animosity. Who was Rachel? I thought about Rodney's admission he'd stayed for an ex-girlfriend. There was definitely more to the story, but the universe had given me a second chance to show him I was on his side. I wasn't going to waste it. "I take it you two know each other." I kept my attention on Daniels.

Rodney jerked his head, and Daniels's smirk deepened. "Yeah. Rodney and me, we go way back. Don't we, Rod?"

"I'm glad to hear it. It's always easier for us when we can rely on the responding officer to be professional and competent. *Officer* Daniels, I'm sure you don't mind giving *Detective* Kirke the particulars of the call while I talk to the coroner." Technically, detective was an assignment, not a rank. That didn't mean a patrol officer got to be a wiseass. No matter what his history was.

Rodney had passed the detective's exam. This guy hadn't, if he'd ever taken it.

At my words, the smirk slid off Daniels's face. "Yes, sir. I mean, no, sir. I'd be happy to." He shot a look at Rodney.

"I'll meet up with you in a few." I nodded to my partner. The lockjaw had faded and I detected a glint of gratitude. *Don't take any shit*, I telegraphed to him. With any luck, Rodney's talents included telepathy. He and Daniels went up to the trail to talk.

As soon as Fitch and his partner had the body completely out of the water, I navigated my way through the woody terrain over to them. "What have you got?"

"Female. Late thirties, maybe early forties." Fitch didn't look up. He and his partner maneuvered the body into a bag, scooping up water and gravel with it. "Although with the bloating and physical damage, that's a pure wild-assed guess. No purse, no jewelry except a wedding ring. She has pierced ears, so she might have been wearing earrings and lost them in the gorge. One thing's for sure, she ain't dressed for hiking, so God knows what she's doing here."

I looked at the body. Her blonde hair was stuck to her face and the bluish-green eyes in the bloated face were slightly opaque, but there was no doubt in my mind. It was Sylvia Bramley. "Any obvious wounds? I mean, beyond the bruising I can see from here?"

I'd told Keith Bramley he didn't want my help. Looked like he was going to get it, anyway.

"No gunshot or stab wounds, and no ligature marks." He tucked the sodden hair into the bag, clearing any strands from the zipper.

"Drowned?"

"Until we do the autopsy, your guess is as good as mine." Body safely contained, Fitch looked up. "How's it hanging, Davis? Haven't seen you in a while."

Tight bands wrapped around my chest. "I've been on desk duty for the past few months."

Fitch nodded. "Is this your first call since the accident?"

I nodded and stuffed my hands in my pockets.

"I'm sorry." Fitch paused. "Max was a hell of a detective."

My response was swift. "She still is."

"You're right." Fitch shifted his feet on the gravel. "You still see her?"

"Yeah." I didn't want to talk about Max. "Can you tell me anything about the deceased?"

"She's pretty banged up." Fitch pointed to the bruising on the woman's legs, arms, and head, visible in the still-open bag. "There's a head contusion here. Ante or postmortem, I'm not sure yet."

"In other words, she could have gone over the Falls. As you said, this isn't a spot people wander into, and she's dressed for dinner out, not a nature hike."

"Could be a jumper. But that's your job, right? I'll tell you what didn't happen, and you figure out what *did* and how."

It was, indeed. *You got this.* I looked around the gorge. "American or Canadian?"

"My guess would be the American side. Hundreds of thousands of gallons of water bashing you against rocks the size of compact cars could easily do this kind of damage. Fewer rocks under the Horseshoe. If the bruising is antemortem, then someone worked her over pretty good."

"Then dumped her over the Falls."

"Or right here in the gorge." Fitch bagged the

woman's hands while his partner filled out the form to go with the body bag.

"Any signs of sexual molestation?"

"She's still wearing her underwear, so I doubt it. We'll look closer when we do the autopsy. Right now, I say no." They made sure everything was contained, then zipped up the bag. Fitch brushed a few random pieces of gravel off the outside and his partner readied the gurney for transport. "It'll take a while to get an ID on this one."

"No problem. I saw this woman yesterday. And her husband came looking for her this morning. Sylvia Bramley."

Fitch looked at me over his glasses. "I told you. There's no ID on the body."

"It's her. I'd bet the first round at Callahan's on it."

"I know better than to take any bet that involves your memory." He secured the body bag and popped up the gurney. "We'll see you at the autopsy. Same bat time, same bat channel."

"Tomorrow at nine." I waved at him. "You need help getting that thing over the gravel?"

"Nah, we'll manage." Fitch pointed at Rodney. "Is that your new partner over there? Has he ever seen an autopsy?"

"I don't know. Pretty sure this is his first scene as a detective, but it doesn't mean it's his first autopsy."

"If you're not sure, or he's not, tell him he might want to skip breakfast. I don't need to clean up vomit from the morgue. I have enough to do."

I nodded. Fitch and his partner manhandled the gurney and its contents up to the waiting van.

I trudged up from the edge of the water and met Rodney halfway to the car.

"Officer Daniels said the call came in from a couple walking their dog along the trail." Rodney checked his notes. "The dog went nuts, sniffing at what they thought was a bag of trash. Upon closer inspection, they saw it was a body and called 911. They didn't recognize her. No personal effects, so we don't have an ID."

"Sylvia Bramley. The woman from the park yesterday." I watched as the coroner's van pulled away.

"The wife of the guy you talked to this morning?" Rodney stared at me. "How do you know?"

"I recognized her. I've got an eye for faces. Hers was bloated and beat up, but I'm ninety-eight-point-five percent sure it's her." I looked around.

"Damn."

"Let's get a K-9 team and uniforms to sweep the area. Bramley said the last place he saw her was Top of the Falls. We'll search up there, too."

I stumbled over woodland debris on my way to the car. Not for the first time, I thought about how men's dress shoes were often completely unsuited to my line of work. *That's why you keep hiking boots on hand, you dope.*

"Big area."

"Yes." It was a big area, but there were only so many possibilities. Max would search everywhere between where the body was found and where she was last seen alive. Therefore, so would I.

Rodney's legs were shorter than mine, but he had no trouble keeping up with me, even over the uneven ground.

I glanced over at Daniels, who was getting into a city black-and-white. "You knew Daniels from patrol, I take it?"

"Yeah. We were buddies. I mean, sort of. Drinks after the shift, dart league on Fridays. You know. Right up until," he shrugged, "I passed the detective exam and he didn't."

A sore loser. It was natural for Daniels to feel some jealousy. However, based on the exchange, I doubted it was the whole story. "I assume Rachel is the ex-girl-friend you mentioned yesterday."

Rodney was silent.

What was I supposed to say? Max would have had words of wisdom. "Well, it sucks. But remember, you passed. He didn't. If the situation dents his ego, well, he should work harder."

"Right." Rodney finally met my gaze, his expression betraying a bit of embarrassment.

"We're done here, I think. Let's go to Seneca Niagara." I picked my way back to the do-not-cross line. I tried to shoo away the spectators, gave up, and headed to our unmarked sedan.

Rodney followed. "Why are we going to the casino? What's there?"

"Not what. Who. Keith Bramley. Call the station and get his contact info. Someone ought to tell him we believe his wife's been found, don't you think?"

CHAPTER
FOUR

We pulled up outside the casino, where I was lucky enough to snag a good spot without resorting to flashing the badge. "Room four-thirty-five, right?"

"It's what the missing person report said." Rodney stopped. "Before we go in, can I ask a stupid question? And please don't tell me there are no stupid questions because we both know that's bullshit."

It was the first thing to come out of his mouth that pulled a smile out of me. "Go ahead."

"How did you recognize the victim? We saw her in the park for five minutes. Maybe even less. You recognized her a day later, a bloated corpse?"

"My special talent." I shrugged. "Been doing it for years, going back to patrol. I can see or hear something and recall it on demand. Faces, facts, directions—you name it. Max once told me my mind was like a miser's bank vault. Stuff went in and didn't come out until I wanted it to." I buttoned my jacket. "We won a lot of bar bets because of my memory."

He paused. "It sounds like you two were close. How long did you work together?"

"Two years. And yes, we were. Spending eight hours together, sometimes more, investigating the seamy side of people, will make people tighter than spouses in some ways."

He gazed off down the sidewalk, hands in his pockets. "How long does it take? Getting close."

I shrugged. "As long as it does. Sometimes never." I read his expression, wondering if it mimicked my own on my second day. "Relax. We've been at this for less than forty-eight hours. It takes more than that. Max spent more time at our house than with her family." Spent. Past tense. One night had ended a lot more than a work partnership. Games of Monopoly, pizza night, and stories. Not from books, but ones Max made up herself.

Would I ever get it back?

My chest tightened and it felt hard to expand my lungs. *Breathe.* In one of my first sessions, my department-assigned therapist, Dr. Alverson, told me the anxiety attacks could be a symptom of PTSD. For that reason, I avoided talking, or even thinking, about the explosion. I was not going to allow head games to ruin my career. Or worse.

Rodney's voice interrupted my thoughts. "You don't look so good. If I need to cover the interview, I can."

"I'm fine." If I couldn't handle a simple death notification, I was hosed. "Enough chatter. Are we going to do this or not?" I hadn't intended to sound harsh, but judging from the way Rodney's jaw clenched, I must have. *Awesome. Way to be the senior guy.* So far, I'd laughed in his face, put him down in front of the other detectives, and dismissed what was most likely a genuine offer made out of concern. True, I'd stood up for him against Officer Daniels, but in my mind, it didn't even out.

I gave myself an "F" on this day so far.

When the elevator door opened, we got off and consulted the numbers on the wall for direction. Before we headed down, I said, "Sorry if I snapped. It's just," I paused, "I don't like talking about what happened. It's still raw. But as my partner, you deserve better."

He looked at me. "Apology accepted. Let's go talk to the husband." He walked off, forcing me to follow.

We reached room 435 and Rodney rapped on the door. "Mr. Bramley, Niagara Falls police. We need to speak to you."

Bramley didn't open the door, but we heard him call out. "Coming." Mumbled conversation was audible, even through the door, and we looked at each other. Was someone else in there?

Before either of us could say anything, the door opened, revealing a disheveled Keith Bramley wearing a stained shirt. His hair looked like he'd taken a high-speed ride down the Thruway in a convertible with the top down. I showed him my ID. "I'm Detective Davis, and this is Detective Kirke."

Rodney showed his own badge.

"You're the guys from yesterday." Bramley stared at us. "And you're the one I talked to at the police station this morning. The homicide detective." He gulped.

"Sir, I think it would be best if we continue this

conversation in the room." I looked around him. "May we come in?"

"Sure, sure." Bramley's face had gone as pale as new milk. He stepped back, closing the door once we were inside.

I surveyed the room, which had a sitting area as well as a bed. *A romantic getaway, but they didn't spring for a suite. Interesting.* A closed door led to what I assumed was the bathroom. Dirty dishes, maybe from a room service breakfast, littered the table. His clothes were on the floor. The half-open closet door gave a glimpse of a few dresses. A woman's jewelry box was on the dresser, open and empty. The strap of a bra was visible from under the bed. *Sylvia Bramley's or someone else's?* "Mr. Bramley, is anyone else here? We thought we heard you talking when we were in the hallway." The oversized flat-screen TV was on but muted, tuned to CNN.

Bramley started. "No, no one's here. I was on the phone."

"With whom?"

"My sister-in-law. I called her to ask if she'd heard from Sylvia since last night."

"Did she?" I faced him. "Hear from her sister?"

"She hadn't." Bramley's response was a shade too quick.

The door to the bathroom was closed. I went over and opened it. More mess, a shaving kit opened to show the jumbled contents, a few women's toiletries. He really was on the phone.

Bramley watched me. "Did you think I was lying?"

"Always best to be sure of one's surroundings." I returned to my post by the door.

He ran his hand through his hair. "She's dead, isn't she?"

I glanced at Rodney. "It's possible. I'm sorry to have to tell you this, but we retrieved a woman's body from the gorge earlier this afternoon. A formal identification is still pending, but the deceased matches your wife's description."

"You're saying it might not be her?" Bramley bit his lip.

Is he afraid it is his wife? Or afraid it isn't? "There was no ID found on the body." How many other women matching Sylvia's description had gone missing in the last twenty-four hours?

Bramley's hand shook as he poured himself a drink from the room's minibar. "Care for one?" He lifted the cut-glass tumbler, the only one that showed use.

"No, sir. Thank you. We're on duty." Rodney took a notebook from his pocket. "When was the last time you saw your wife?"

"Last night. We had dinner at Top of the Falls." Bramley pointed at me. "I told him earlier."

"You told Detective Davis you didn't leave together," Rodney said.

"Correct. Sylvia left without me. She wanted to get back here. I stayed to finish my dessert and pay the bill."

Rodney took notes. "What time?"

"I'm not sure. Maybe seven or seven-thirty?"

"Mr. Bramley," Rodney resumed the questioning, "were you and your wife on good terms? Meaning, would you describe your marriage as good?"

Bramley downed his drink and played with the empty glass.

"Detective Davis and I broke up a fight between you two yesterday. Your wife hit you, so it was intense enough to get physical."

Bramley shifted. "The slap meant nothing. Heat of the moment. Sylvia has, had, a temper. I mean, all married people fight occasionally. We hadn't had any major disagreements. Not like this."

"Like what?" Rodney looked up.

"Be honest. You're asking if we had a disagreement big enough for me to kill her." Bramley's chin jutted. "I'm telling you we didn't."

Rodney looked at me, and I shook my head slightly. We didn't know enough yet to press the issue.

He continued the questioning. "Why did your wife leave Top of the Falls without you?"

"I already told you. She wanted to come back and go to bed." Bramley's frustration had started to show. "She had a headache coming on or something. What is this? I've said all of this before. You trying to trip me up?"

We were, but there was no sense being antagonistic. I tried for a soothing voice. "We're trying to get the facts straight and be sure we understand. You should sit down. Make yourself comfortable."

"I'm fine standing." Bramley scowled. He refilled his glass and swirled it before taking a gulp.

"Was there anybody else she might have argued with? Perhaps, someone she might have run into last night after she left you?"

Bramley shook his head, his expression mulish. "I can't think of anyone, no."

Rodney remained calm. "When you and your wife went to dinner last night, was she wearing any jewelry?"

"I guess. Her wedding and engagement rings, obviously. She had a sapphire necklace I gave her for our fifth anniversary. She brought a whole damn box and it's mostly empty. She must have worn it." He pointed at the dresser and the open jewelry box. "Why do you ask?"

"We didn't find a purse or jewelry on her body." The box in question was not big. Amy had one about the same size, although not as fancy. She took it on overnight trips. Sylvia's was empty. I doubted she'd brought a lot with her. A single set of silver earrings and a matching pendant gleamed against the black velvet lining. *He calls something that small a whole damn box?* "What was she wearing last night?"

He blinked. "Other than her wedding ring? The necklace I mentioned and diamond earrings. I think she had a charm bracelet, too. She always wore it."

"It's all gone, except the wedding ring." I studied Bramley, looking for a hint of something, anything, that might nudge us in the right direction.

"Then, how do you know it's her? Maybe it's not." He looked from Rodney to me, finally settling on me as the man in charge and the one worthy of his attention.

"As I told you, she matches the description you gave this morning."

"Oh." He tilted his head. "Do you think she was mugged?"

It was possible. The purse and jewelry might have been stolen or it all might have been lost when she tumbled over the Falls. The water would have ripped away the earrings, bracelet, and necklace. Or had someone removed them after killing her to make it look like a mugging? But if so, why dump the body? Why not leave it where it lay? Muggers didn't usually dispose of bodies. And unless he couldn't get the wedding and engagement rings off, he would've taken them.

"Detective?"

I snapped back to the moment. "It's too early in the investigation to say. For now, we'll need someone to come to the coroner's office to confirm the ID. If you're up to it, we can do it now."

"Do I have to see her body?"

"No, we can show you a picture, if you prefer. You mentioned a sister when we arrived. If you decline to make the identification, we can call her."

"Sylvia had a purse at dinner last night."

Rodney answered. "We told you. We didn't find a purse."

Bramley frowned. "I don't understand why her body was found in the gorge if we were at Top of the Falls. How did she get down there?"

I couldn't decide if Bramley was upset his wife might be dead, she had been found, or we'd interrupted him. But he wasn't acting like the typical grieving spouse.

"We think she might have been swept over the Falls after falling into the river." Rodney closed his notebook. He avoided saying the words *pushed* or *dumped*.

"You think she jumped? No way. Not Sylvia." Bramley's laugh was filled with scorn. "I can't think of a person less likely to commit suicide. If she went over the edge, someone helped her."

Rodney didn't flinch. "We'll know better after the autopsy."

"But why—" Bramley's voice broke off. "Wait, did you say autopsy? What would you need one of those for?"

I couldn't quite put my finger on it, but Bramley was hiding something. He was either playing it cool, thinking we'd dismiss him as a suspect, or it was something else. But he was hiding *something*, and it put my investigator's sixth sense on high alert. He wasn't grieving, and although we hadn't mentioned it, he'd dismissed suicide out of hand. *Someone helped her*. Him? It could have been an accident, but I found it unlikely. "It's standard procedure for an unattended death. Otherwise, we can't be sure of the cause or manner of death."

"The manner of death." Sweat beaded on Bramley's forehead.

"Yes." Rodney ticked off the options on his fingers. "Homicide, accident, suicide."

"You mean, you don't know? Why are you investigating if you aren't sure she was killed?"

"Again, standard procedure." I took note of the wild look in his eyes. Like a cornered animal looking for an escape. "The death will be treated as a homicide until we know otherwise. You said someone else had to be involved."

He licked his lips. "Do I have to be at the autopsy?"

"No, you aren't required to attend. I recommend you don't, actually. I'll give you my card, and Detective Kirke will give you his." I handed Bramley a business card, as did Rodney. "We'll drive you to the morgue and get the identification over with, assuming you want to go. The sooner we do that, the sooner we can move to the next order of business."

Bramley had started to head to the bathroom after laying the cards on the table, but he stopped and turned. "What's the next order of business?"

I glanced at Rodney. "Finding out how your wife died and, if necessary, who killed her."

———

We drove Bramley to the morgue, where he made a positive ID of Sylvia. Then, we drove him back to the casino hotel.

He closed the back door and leaned toward the open passenger window. "When can I claim her body?"

I had gotten out to open his door, and I leaned on the car. "It depends on the coroner. He'll release it when he's done."

Bramley wiped his forehead. "And when will that be?"

"I don't know. The autopsy is scheduled for tomorrow. Someone will call you, but you can find a funeral home and start making arrangements. If you need recommendations, the coroner's office can help. Between those two, they'll know how to handle things." I started to get back in the car.

"Aren't you going to tell me to stay in town and not go anywhere?"

"They only say that on TV, Mr. Bramley." Rodney shook his hand. "As long as we have your address and phone number, which we do, you're free to leave whenever you like."

"But not free to take my wife home for burial." There was a twinge of resentment in Bramley's voice.

"I wish I could tell you otherwise, Mr. Bramley. I would release the body now, but it's not our call." I extended my hand. "We'll be in touch."

I got in, pulled away, and we left Bramley on the curb, the expression on his face resembling something between Madeline's scared and stubborn moods.

"What do you think?" Rodney asked.

"He looked and sounded rattled, for sure." I tapped my fingers on the steering wheel, navigating down Fourth Street. "Of course, if my wife had been pulled out of the Niagara Gorge this morning, I'd be rattled, too."

"You know, if you'd let me off the leash yesterday, maybe none of this would be necessary." He couldn't keep the note of accusation out of his voice.

"We aren't fortune tellers." I made the call at the time and I wasn't going to play the *what if* game. "*Maybe* is the operative word. For all we know, Sylvia Bramley's death had nothing to do with their argument."

"Yeah right. I'm new, not stupid." He stared out of the window.

Back at the office, I pulled out a notepad and started

a list. "We need background information on both Bramleys. And the sister."

"And the sister's name."

"Yes. Sylvia's Will. Personal financials. Records from her company. Background on other company officials. Anyone who might have been close to Sylvia. Get names and addresses for any other family."

"Criminal records?" Rodney looked over my shoulder.

"Yes. You start, and I'll push through a search warrant for the Bramley house. When did Grand Island say they'd send someone over to secure the house?" Oh, for the days when you didn't need a warrant for the search of the victim's home. Of course, I could ask Bramley for his permission, but since spouses were always the first suspects, I didn't want to give him time to get there and destroy any evidence. Better to leave him out of it.

Rodney glanced at his watch. "Should already be there."

"After we search the house, we'll go to Top of the Falls and question the staff. And get a better picture of the victim."

"You got it. I'll be ready to go in fifteen minutes." He headed off to start. "Do you need anything? Coffee? Water? Something to eat? I can get it while I put in the requests. Let me know."

"No, I'm fine."

"Are you sure? It's okay, really. I can do it."

"Seriously, I'm fine. Get the requests going before we lose more time."

Rodney hurried off.

I shook my head. So far, he had been smart and efficient. He seemed a little defensive at times, when he wasn't being a hard-charger. But he *was* new.

His only real flaw was he wasn't Max. *And whose fault is that?*

It didn't take long to get the search warrant approved for the Bramleys' house, which was located on Grand Island. We also got one for Sylvia's office at the Natural Wonders plant in Newfane. I called the local police in both towns to let them know we were en route and to secure the properties until we got there.

"We should get another team to help," Rodney said.

I didn't want to ask for assistance, even though it was logical. First case back, I wanted to keep things under my control. I didn't say anything, but the expression on my face must have done it for me.

"Why don't I go to the office while you take the house? Or vice versa?" Rodney crossed his arms. "It's inefficient to work it serially. The locals won't like being made to wait. They have things to do."

I liked the idea of splitting up even less. Not that I didn't trust Rodney, but it was his first homicide. Strike that. I *didn't* trust him. Not yet. We'd been partners for two days. At the very least, I didn't think he was experienced enough to run solo.

"You're the senior detective. Your call."

I was between a rock and a hard place. Asking for help might not look good to Yannick. Being unable to make the call definitely wouldn't.

"Tell Yannick we need another team to seize any evidence at the office." I tried to mask my reluctance. "You and I will search the Bramley house. We'll have to go back to Natural Wonders, but at least we'll have a leg up. We need to interview the staff at the restaurant, too."

"I can tell you aren't crazy about Plan A. We have options. I can run out to Top of the Falls, let the other guys handle the office, and you can take the house." Rodney waited a beat. "Or I'll take the house, and you—"

"Enough. You and I go to Grand Island. Send Dobrovski and Evans to Newfane. Then, we'll hit Top of the Falls. We'll keep the business until we sift through the evidence."

I could almost hear Rodney grind his teeth.

Warrant in hand, we headed to Grand Island ahead of rush hour traffic on the bridge. We knew the Bramleys had also had a home security system because the uniform at the scene called. While I drove, Rodney contacted someone at the firm to come disarm it and let us in.

I texted Amy to tell her I'd be late. At least my brain was functioning enough to remember to communicate with my wife.

We pulled up behind a marked Grand Island police

cruiser in front of the Bramley home, a newer house on a good-sized lot. A man wearing a jacket with the security company logo talked to the uniform at the door.

Rodney took in the grounds. "Nice digs."

I grunted as I parked. "You have the paper, right?"

Rodney pulled it out of his jacket pocket.

"Then, glove up and let's go."

We showed and read the warrant to the uniform and the security guy. The company rep unlocked the door, disarmed the system, and instructed us on how to lock up.

Inside, my first thought was I'd walked into a picture from one of the glossy home decorating magazines Amy loved to buy.

Rodney snapped on a pair of gloves. "Up or down?"

There was the dividing-up thing again. I hesitated.

"I get why you didn't want to split up earlier." He fixed me with an accusatory stare. "Keep it up and I'm gonna think you don't trust me. I've helped execute search warrants before. I know what I'm doing."

He'd read me like the proverbial book. And he had a point. Max hadn't babysat me. "All right. You take the upstairs. You know what we're looking for."

He dutifully recited the list. "Bills, records, correspondence, journals, calendars, checkbooks, computers."

"Cellphones. Remember, the victim didn't have one. Yell if you need me. Loudly. This place is huge."

He nodded and took off.

I started with the living room, which was decorated by someone who had expensive taste. Leather furniture that looked like it had come from the showroom floor hours earlier. A stone fireplace, but there were no charred stones, no ashes, no stack of logs nearby. Pricey built-in sound system.

Not a single picture. No personal knick-knacks. No magazines. A far cry from my own home, which was cluttered with pictures of Amy and me on our wedding day, the kids, and both sets of grandparents. Sure, the Bramleys didn't have children. But why wasn't there a single personal photo?

I went to the kitchen, another showplace. It brought to mind the slick displays at the home improvement store. *Amy would love this.* But as beautiful as it was, it was cold. No streaks or chips on the quartz counters. The cooktop was unmarked. No fingerprints or smears on the stainless steel. *Neat freaks or they ate out a lot.* Or they had a hell of a cleaning service.

The cupboards held plates in two different patterns, one formal and one for daily use. Wineglasses hung in military-straight lines. Not a mark on either set of plates. But there were spots on the glassware. The only full items were the wine chiller, the liquor cabinet, and the doo-hickey containing pods for the one-cup coffeemaker. The fridge held only a partially empty carton of half-and-half, some moldy cheese, and half a six-pack of fancy mineral water.

I opened the cabinets, most of which were empty. The drawers held gleaming flatware, a wine opener and silicone plug, and towels folded with edges so sharp I wondered if they'd ever been used. What I didn't see was the thing common to every kitchen—a junk drawer. Or as Amy called it, "the place unused things go to die." The cupboards held plenty of high-end cookware, but all of it looked like it had come out of the box minutes before I stepped in the room. But nowhere did I see any personal items or things for daily use. I didn't find any photos, notepads, or shopping lists in any of the drawers. The surface of the gleaming refrigerator was unmarred by a single magnet. Some of the cupboards were literally bare, devoid of cereal boxes, canned goods, or nighttime snacks. I wasn't getting the picture of a warm and comfortable home life for the Bramleys.

I looked in the full bath on the first floor. Towels hung neatly enough for a hotel, no clutter on the sink. The medicine cabinet was devoid of anything, including common items such as aspirin or vitamins. The accessories matched, but the toothbrush holder was empty and the soap dispenser was full. The stand for toilet paper was full, and the roll on it looked untouched. The drawers in the vanity were empty except for one stray pack of tissues. There weren't any common bathroom cleaning supplies under the sink. Not a water spot could be seen anywhere and a full dispenser of mini paper cups graced the wall.

The next room held a modern steel-and-glass desk and some dark wood file cabinets in addition to a twin-sized day-bed. A sleek silver computer took center stage on a leather desk mat. Not a paper clip was out of place and there wasn't a dust bunny to be seen. The full cabinets were the only sign this room wasn't a model office.

Sylvia's home office. One drawer of the cabinet was full of newspaper clippings. Another had folders with legal agreements and financial reports. I pulled those to take with us. Personal and business correspondence joined the pile on the floor. When I was done, I'd bag everything separately and box it.

On the corner of the desk was a dual frame, the first photos I'd seen. One side was almost empty. Only a torn upper corner remained, a piece of brilliant blue sky. *Who pissed her off enough that she ripped out the photo?* The other held a picture of Sylvia and a man, but not Bramley. This was a stocky guy with salt-and-pepper hair, the backdrop a sunset over Lake Ontario. He and Sylvia held up half-full champagne flutes. I noted the position of his arm around her waist. A lover? A business partner? Whoever he was, he and Sylvia had a close relationship. One she didn't mind displaying in public.

In the bottom desk drawer was a leather-bound journal. "Finally." I tried to open it. *Who locks their diary these days?* Wasn't that a teenage girl thing? Did teens even keep diaries anymore? I tossed it in the pile.

I turned my attention to the laptop. Password protected. "I couldn't be lucky enough for it to be unlocked," I muttered under my breath. No matter. It would go with me. The boys in the tech division would make short work of breaking into it.

No desk calendar. No Rolodex. Everything must be on the computer. No cellphones, either, although I did find a wireless charging plate. She hadn't tried to unplug during the weekend and left it at home. It was probably long gone, adrift somewhere in the Niagara Gorge or pounded into pieces by the Falls.

I gathered up my pickings, bagged and tagged them, and put them in a box. The last thing I checked was the closet, but there was nothing there except a few reams of paper for the printer. One of the advantages of being extremely tall—I didn't need to stand on anything to inspect the shelf. But Sylvia hadn't squirreled anything away in the shadowy corners.

Rodney was already in the foyer, a box of goodies at his feet. "What did you find?" He nodded at my cache.

"Financials, correspondence." I waved at the box. "A password-protected laptop and a locked journal. What about you?"

"Not sure." He nudged the box with his foot. "Bramley's office was upstairs. Got his laptop, also password protected, and a bunch of letters. Some alumni magazines from Buff State with mentions of him and the wife. It's what I didn't find that puzzles me."

"What?"

"Personal items. This place is a mausoleum. I use the word only half-jokingly." He waved his hand, taking in the hallway. "It's clean enough to be a model home. You could do a photoshoot in the master. Nothing is out of place. If the toothpaste wasn't half used, I'd swear no one went in the bathroom."

"Same down here. One of them is a clean freak. Or they pay a service to make it look like no one lives here."

"Not Bramley. His office is the only room that looks lived in. Trash in the basket, doodles on the desk calendar. And this." He held out a picture frame. "Bramley, Sylvia, and another woman. She looks like Sylvia, so it's possible she's his sister-in-law. But notice where Bramley is standing. Not next to his wife."

I couldn't miss the innuendo. "Funny how both

Bramleys are so cuddly with people who aren't their spouse." I told him about the picture I'd found.

Rodney shook his head. "Not a single picture of Keith and Sylvia, the two of them. Not even a wedding photo. Yet, they both keep pictures that could imply illicit relationships?"

I looked around the sterile hallway. Shoes lined up on a rubber mat. Umbrellas in a stand. Model home, indeed. A model of what?

"No art from nieces or nephews," Rodney continued. "Luxury decorating, but no personal touches. Bramley's drawer contents are messy, but Sylvia's clothing is arranged by color."

"She kept his mess where she couldn't see it."

"Over-controlled husband snaps and kills his wife? We saw the hotel room."

"The idea would make more sense if we'd found her in the hotel or at home. In the gorge, not so much."

"Let's document all this stuff, write out the receipt, and take the boxes back to the evidence locker. After, we'll go to the Top of the Falls? Speaking of which, I'm famished. Want to grab something to eat?"

I glanced at my watch. "It's only four-thirty. If you're hungry, get something to go. My wife said she'd hold dinner for me."

He picked up the box at his feet. "I should have thought of that. Naturally you'd want to go home."

I should have invited him to dinner. It would help build the partnership, but I was hesitant. Amy was concerned enough over me going back to full duty. Bringing a new partner for dinner on my second day— before she'd had a chance to meet him—would be a step too far. "Let's get this stuff back and head to Top of the Falls. Still plenty of time before the dinner rush."

"Sure." Rodney followed me out.

We completed the bagging and tagging and I left the receipt in clear view on the kitchen counter where Bramley would find it upon his return. On the way out, I reset the security system and locked the door as instructed, dismissing the Grand Island patrol officer.

All the way back, I second-guessed myself. Was Rodney insulted that I turned down eating with him? Or that he hadn't gotten an invitation? After all, he was a single guy. Who was he going to eat with? He didn't act insulted. Was I making something out of nothing?

I knew what Max would tell me.

———

Dobrovski and Evans were still in Newfane. After dropping off the evidence from the Bramley house, we headed to Top of the Falls. The spectacular view of the Horseshoe Falls made it a popular spot for dining. This close to the water, the mist hung in a thick layer, sparkling in the sun, and the foamy water chased itself over the edge of the gorge. We showed our badges to the hostess, and I asked to speak to the manager. "Or the most senior person who was here last night."

"I'll get her." The girl hurried off.

A few minutes later, a graceful Black woman with short-cropped hair walked up. "Tanya Clarkson. Jill said you were looking for me."

"Yes, ma'am. NFPD." I took out a picture of Sylvia

we'd found online for ID purposes. "Were you here last night?"

"I was."

"Do you recognize this woman?" I held out the picture.

Tanya took it. "Mrs. Bramley. I seated her and her husband around five-thirty, maybe five forty-five. I don't remember exactly."

Rodney lifted his eyebrows. "You knew her name?"

"Yes, because of the recent *Buffalo Magazine* article. In fact, I asked if she would sign it for me. I like seeing women succeed in traditionally male areas, like corporate leadership." Tanya's gaze was challenging, as if she expected two men to argue with her.

I wouldn't dream of it. My wife had been a damn good accountant before she decided to stay home with the kids, and I'd worked with a kick-ass woman as a partner. "Did she? Sign?"

"Oh yes, she was very gracious about it. She even let me get a picture with her."

Rodney jumped in. "Mr. and Mrs. Bramley, were they in a good mood?"

Tanya paused. "He, Mr. Bramley, didn't look happy when I asked him to take the photo. He wasn't angry, but he wasn't pleased, either. My impression was that he resented it. But maybe he was hungry and wanted to eat. It's hard to say."

"What about Mrs. Bramley?"

"Tense." Tanya bit her lip. "She looked like she wanted to be somewhere else." She handed back the photograph.

I pocketed it. "Did you hear them talk over dinner?"

"It was very busy last night. I checked on them once, and they were the same as when they got here. I didn't see them leave. I'm pretty sure their server is working now if you'd like to speak with her."

"Please," I said. "We'll wait here."

She left, returning a few minutes later with a college-age girl wearing black pants, a white shirt, and short hair that looked bleached. "This is Janice. She may be able to help you further. If you need me again, just ask." Tanya left.

"Ms. Clarkson said you were police and had some questions." Janice looked from me to Rodney and back. "Could you hurry? 'Cause if I don't get the customers served quick, I'm gonna lose tips."

I didn't take her semi-challenging tone personally. Young people talked to everyone like that. I handed over the picture. "Do you remember this woman? She was in here last night with her husband. You would have waited on them around six."

"Yeah, I remember." Janice sniffed and handed back the picture.

"From your tone, I take it not in a good way." Rodney took out his notepad and clicked open his pen.

"When I took their orders, they were quiet. Barely spoke to each other. Neither looked very happy, you know? Anyway, they were arguing when I brought out their food. I set the plates down and they didn't even notice me."

I put the picture away. "Did they have anyone else in their party?"

"Not that I saw, unless the other people took one look at them and decided they didn't want lousy company." Janice giggled. "When I served them, they were busy being mean to each other. I guess they kept going after I left, because one of the other servers had to ask them to quiet down so he could hear the people at his table."

"Shouting?" Rodney studied her.

She shook her head. "Not quite that loud. It was pretty clear to me they were pissed at each other. At least, she was really mad at him."

Her story tallied with what we'd seen in the park. It made me wonder why they came to dinner together at all. Had they planned to join friends who didn't show? "Did you hear what they were arguing about?"

Janice's cheeks flushed. "I tried not to eavesdrop. Ms. Clarkson would get mad, and I need this job too badly to do something that could get me fired."

"But you couldn't help it," I cajoled her. "It's okay. We're not looking to get you in trouble."

She bit her lip. "When I refilled their water, I swear they were talking about a divorce. She said something like, 'Don't forget, you signed the prenup. So, keep your dick in your pants or else I'm going to cut it, and you, off without a penny.' Maybe not those exact words, but pretty close. They definitely talked about a prenup."

I glanced at Rodney, who was taking rapid fire notes. As for me, I wasn't likely to forget these details. "Anything else?"

"She left in a hurry. I think it was a little before seven. They ordered cheesecake for dessert, but by the time I brought it out, she was gone."

"Gone where?" Rodney asked.

Janice shrugged. "I don't know. The husband told

me she had a headache and had gone back to their hotel. And to get a box 'cause he'd take the cheesecake back. But…"

I pounced on the pause. "But what?"

"Maybe she did like he said, but to what hotel? There's nothing real close. The casino's not far, but it was darkish. It's a twenty-minute walk. You'd have to go down the road to the bridge or cross the pedestrian bridge at Green Island. And she was in heels. Seems kinda dumb." She raised an eyebrow. "The bus wasn't around, and good luck getting a taxi. I thought he was covering his ass, trying not to look like a loser who'd been dumped."

I held out my phone. "And you're sure these were the people you waited on?" I swiped so she could see both Sylvia and Bramley.

"That's them." She looked from Rodney to me. "Do you want anything else? I've got tables to take care of."

"Yes, thanks. If you think of anything else, please give us a call." I handed over a business card. So did Rodney.

Her eyebrows shot up. "Homicide detectives? Is one of them dead? Wow."

I buttoned my jacket. "Thanks for your time."

Despite her protests that she had tables, Janice stood and stared at us as we walked out. I guess dead customers were more interesting than tips.

CHAPTER
SIX

Outside, I walked the few yards to Terrapin Point, which offered a whole line of those quarter-fed cameras that let tourists look at the water up close and personal. It also provided a great opportunity to let the mist hit my face, clearing my head. The rapids weren't quite as intense as above the American Falls, but the water still moved at a good clip. The rumble of the water tumbling nearly two hundred feet to the bottom of the gorge intensified, as if it had the power to carry away every-thing in the world. It probably did.

I heard Rodney speak behind me, but I couldn't catch all of the words. I turned. "Say again?"

He was standing several feet behind me, out of range of the water. He raised his voice. "Are you even listening? It can't be that loud."

"It is over here. Speak up or come closer."

He shook his head. "I'll get wet."

"It's only mist. Feels good. Fresh." Droplets sparkled on my jacket sleeves, and I felt a trickle run down my cheek. For the first time in two days, I didn't feel like an overtightened guitar string.

"If it's all the same to you, I'll stay dry. This is a new suit." He brushed his lapels. "Think she went in here?"

I thought about it, then shook my head. "I doubt it." I joined him, deciding I was damp enough.

"Why not?"

I looked around and waved. "It's too public. Even around seven, there would be people around. She'd be in full view of the restaurant. I'd think it would warrant a phone call, a woman jumping over the edge. Or being pushed."

"You have a point."

"Besides," I started to walk toward the car, "Fitch said the injuries to the body were inflicted by the fall, which was more indicative of the American Falls, not the Canadian."

"What makes them so different? Isn't water, well, water?"

I paused, a little stunned he didn't know. The Niagara Falls were a big deal, literally and figuratively. How could he not know New York geography? On the other hand, it often seemed like people from New York City barely knew Western New York existed. "There's more rock debris under the American Falls. You can see it. It's not the same under the Horseshoe Falls. I think it's why most of the daredevils—folks who shoot the Falls—try the Canadian side. Water cushions the impact."

"Not by much, I'd imagine."

"I wouldn't want to try to prove it." I started toward the parking lot and he followed.

"Quite a view, though."

"One of the Seven Wonders of the Natural World. You should see the water, and hear the noise, from the Hurricane Deck at Cave of the Winds. Now, there's a sight. You can reach out and touch it. If it wouldn't rip your hand off." We reached the lot. "Let's walk a bit more," I said.

Rodney shrugged. "Where to?"

"Janice told us Sylvia left early. Her statement tallies with Bramley's statement. He said she walked back."

"But according to Janice, Sylvia was wearing heels. Those aren't shoes for long distance walking."

"If a woman wears those all day, maybe it isn't such a big deal. Question is, which way did she go?" I walked through the lot toward Goat Island Road, maybe twenty-five yards from the restaurant. The sound of the river was still in the background but muted, allowing us to return to normal conversation volume.

"Doesn't this road go over a bridge to the other side of the river?" Rodney indicated the cars passing us.

The bridge wasn't far, less than a football field away. "Yes. If Sylvia had left by car, that would have been the best route back to the casino."

"She could have gone in the river at the bridge. Plenty of rapids, no boats. She'd be over the Falls in minutes."

"Still too much traffic. People going to Top of the Falls or Terrapin Point. People coming back. Again, it's a visibility problem."

He frowned. "How else could she get there?"

"There's a pedestrian bridge that crosses from Goat

Island, which is where we are, to Green Island and through to the other side. Both places are right over the rapids. You come out in the park." It was popular, but at night?

"Low light, fewer people, close to the rapids. Hell, right on top of them."

Exactly what I was thinking. And probably less than a hundred yards to the park entrance, maybe another hundred to the casino. Sylvia might have thought it would be walkable.

"K-9 and patrol didn't find anything when they searched. They lost her scent here at the road."

I waved my hand. "We can still look."

We walked down to the pedestrian bridge to Green Island. The path through the island was wide. Not enough for a vehicle bigger than a golf cart, but several people could walk abreast. In the middle of the day, there was a fair amount of foot traffic, but there was also plenty of tree coverage only feet from the path.

After less than a quarter-mile, we reached the other side of the island and the bridge leading to the main area of the state park. The river tumbled by under our feet with a dull roar, water thick with froth betraying the rocky riverbed—Hell's Half Acre, the roughest patch of rapids before the edge of the American and Bridal Veil Falls.

"Looks like a good place to dump a body." Rodney inspected the area. "It's a good ambush spot. Trees, low light. Maybe she was mugged on the way back."

"But would a thief throw the body in the river? It would be faster to leave it." And would that actor commit murder? Why not grab the purse and jewelry, and run? Sylvia wouldn't have been in any condition to chase him.

I shouldn't have been shutting down ideas this early. Max would have yelled at me. But the scenario felt wrong. I couldn't explain it, it just did. Rodney was fresh off patrol, but he had to have instincts. Didn't he? I had. At least, I thought I had.

"Panic? Maybe he killed her by accident and dumped the body without thinking." He glared at me. "You've got to admit it's possible." His chin jutted.

What would Max do? Easy. Not only shouldn't I reject ideas at this stage, I also shouldn't shut down my rookie partner. "It is." I didn't see any signs of an altercation, but I wasn't doing an exhaustive search. "What's also possible is she was killed elsewhere and dumped in the gorge. She never went over the Falls at all."

"But how would that have happened? You can't drive a car down there, and it would be too hard to carry the dead weight of a body along those trails, whether she was unconscious or dead."

"She caught a taxi on the other side, she ran into a friend, maybe she met up with a lover after she left Bramley, maybe she didn't care and walked all the way down." I ran a hand through my hair, still damp from the mist.

"You don't believe the last one, do you? Walking to the gorge? Was she batshit crazy?"

"Unlikely, yes. Impossible, no." I thought. "Bramley told us he stayed to finish dessert."

Rodney flipped through his notes from the interview. "Yeah. She left, he stayed."

"But Janice at the restaurant said Bramley asked her to box the cheesecake."

"Maybe only hers."

"We'll go back and ask." The permutations swirled around to beat the rapids as we recrossed the bridge. "Then, let's head for the barn."

"For what?"

"Dobrovski and Evans should be back. And maybe some information is in. I feel in dire need of some cold, hard facts right about now."

———

Janice hadn't been happy to be interrupted again, but she was adamant. Bramley had requested both desserts be boxed and he hadn't stayed to eat his. In fact, she was pretty sure he'd left not ten minutes after his wife had.

"That contradicts his statement to us." Rodney looked over his notes.

Thank you, Captain Obvious. "I know." I didn't need notes. I took them for trials, but I had no problem remembering Bramley's statement.

"We should go back to confront him."

"Not yet. Background first."

Information had come in while we were out. It was piled on both our desks, but fortunately each pile contained something different.

"We have criminal background checks, public records on Sylvia's company, and background information on Bramley and Sylvia." Rodney sorted through the piles. "What do you want? Maybe the financials? I'll take the personal stuff, it's simpler. Or if you—"

It doesn't matter. I snapped my fingers. "Give me the personal results." I understood his not wanting to step on my toes, but this was ridiculous.

Rodney's indignation was obvious, but he pushed the piles toward me.

Maybe I should have felt bad. I didn't. Instead, I sat and started reading. Sylvia and Keith Bramley, married seven years. She was thirty-eight, he was thirty-nine. Both originally from Western New York. No kids. Getting bank records would take more time, but the property records showed the mortgage and taxes as current. However, the payment had been late nine of the last twelve months. Never late enough to incur a charge, though.

I wondered who paid the bills. My gut said it was Sylvia.

She had a business degree from Niagara University. Bramley had a biology degree from Buffalo State College. He'd worked as a drug rep until three years ago. Two cars, both newish and expensive: a Mercedes and a Lexus.

I skimmed through what we had. "Bramley doesn't work. Left his job three years ago." Neither had any outstanding warrants either in New York or other states and no convictions. Sylvia had one younger sister, a woman named Gwyneth Walsh. I made a note to get Ms. Walsh's address and number so we could schedule an interview.

"Probably because that's when Sylvia's company

exploded." Rodney handed me a piece of paper covered in numbers. "Right here." He pointed.

I looked at the column. "Seems like it was a successful business."

He nodded. "Double-digit growth the last three years. She must have cashed in on the natural mineral makeup trends."

"And started raking in the money." I wasn't a financial genius, but I knew enough to know the numbers were impressive. "Is that sustainable?"

"Maybe if you go international." Rodney slid over a photocopied article from *The Buffalo News*, dated six months ago. "Representative of the company, a Bert Guenther, is quoted saying it was the next logical move. He's the company's vice president."

"Do the financials support it?"

"Hard to tell from these. We'll have to wait for the warrant. Guenther thought they did." He riffled through some papers. "I assume Sylvia did, too. It's her company."

I gnawed on the end of a cheap ballpoint. "The waitress, Janice, said she heard the Bramleys talking about a prenup. I don't suppose your pile contains legal papers."

"No. Still waiting on it, same as the bank records. I wonder how the private financials stack up. How much money did the agreement cost Bramley?" He looked at the clock. "How long is your wife going to hold dinner?"

"Shit, what time is it?" I checked my watch.

"Almost seven." Rodney looked up. "Are you sure you don't want to grab some Chinese or something?"

"I should go home. It's only my third day back, and I'd like to keep Amy happy." The autopsy was tomorrow. Bank and legal records always took more time than the publicly available stuff. "If we don't have the info, there's no use staying."

"You're sure?" Rodney's expression fell.

I shrugged into my jacket. "If you want, we can set another place at the table." I wasn't sure how I felt about the invitation. I knew what Amy would say.

"No." He shook his head. "I haven't met your family. It would be weird. See you at the morgue tomorrow."

"See you." Max had come over for late dinner lots of times. Why didn't I push it with Rodney? Because I wasn't comfortable with him yet?

Had to be. Max knew all my warts. I still had to act the role of lead detective for Rodney.

At least, that's what I told myself as I headed for home.

I pulled up outside my house, a Dutch colonial in the DeVeaux area of the city. The sun was going down and I narrowly missed the overturned tricycle in the driveway.

I braced for impact as I entered. "I'm home."

"Daddy!" Madeline crashed into me, hugging my knees with fierce joy.

"Madeline, please." Amy emerged from the kitchen. "Dinner's almost ready. Go wash your hands." She wiped her hands on the towel at her waist. "You mind grilling the steaks? I'm desperately trying to get Christopher to take a little nap while we eat."

"Absolutely. Sorry I didn't text a second time. Got caught up. New case." I leaned over and kissed her cheek. "It won't happen again."

"Don't make promises you can't keep."

I pulled back. "Since when don't I keep my promises?"

"That's not what I said and you know it." She brushed hair from her forehead. "I admit it's been nice having you home at a regular hour these past months. But you don't work a job where you can always be home by five." An infant howl came from the kitchen, and Amy rushed back.

As I hung up my jacket, I looked at my daughter. "Hey, Madeline. What have I told you about your tricycle?"

"Put it away?" Madeline looked at me, the words coming slowly.

"Then, why is it in the driveway?"

"But it's dark, Daddy. I'm scared."

"I think I told you to put it away before the sun went down. Didn't I?"

"Yes, Daddy." Her lip trembled.

I sighed. "I'll go with you, but this is the last time. I mean it."

I followed my daughter outside and watched as she put her tricycle in the garage. I gave her a high-five and we went back inside, where I looked at Amy, who was working at the stove while simultaneously jouncing Christopher on her shoulder.

I leaned over and kissed his fuzzy head. "Let me get changed. I don't want to grill in a suit and tie."

I changed into a T-shirt and jeans, and returned to the kitchen. "Steaks in ten minutes." I grabbed the platter and went out back.

The grill had been heated to the perfect temperature. I laid the meat on the rack, closed the lid, and waited. While I did, I let my thoughts wander.

Amy's voice floated out of the house. "Jackson? Potatoes are ready. How are the steaks coming?"

"Checking now." Still buried in my musings, I opened the lid to the grill.

Flames rushed out with a whoosh. I blinked and backed up. I was surrounded by heat, flames, and noise. The wail of sirens filled my ears and I smelled chemical fumes. Someone was yelling. Me? I couldn't tell.

I slid to the ground, knees pulled up to my chest, shaking. I was in my yard. At my house. I had to be. But there was a lump beside me. It was Max, crumpled after tackling me to the ground. I covered my ears to block the noise and squeezed my eyes shut to block out the sights of the flames and my injured partner. Heart pounding, I fought to take a breath with lungs that were crushed under the pressure of the surrounding air. It was hot. So hot. Dark and not dark at the same time.

"Jackson? Jackson! Are you hurt? Answer me. Open your eyes. Breathe, honey. Come back to me."

I felt hands on my face, and I blinked. Amy had dropped the lid on the steaks, cutting off air to the flames. Sweat trickled down my face and slithered down between my shoulders. "I'm fine. The grill. It flared." I closed my eyes again.

Next to me, I felt Amy move. "Madeline, go in the house."

She doesn't want our daughter to see me. I willed my heartbeat to slow and took measured breaths. I didn't want her to see me, either. Not like this. No one should see me like this.

"Is Daddy okay?"

"Yes, he's fine. Go inside and check on your brother." The door slammed.

"Dinner is wrecked, I'm sorry…" I started to speak, but stopped.

"Forget dinner."

I opened my eyes. Amy's were filled with worry. I didn't think she was worried about physical injury. Well, maybe she was a little, but that wasn't her main concern, I was sure of it. "The flames, it was like being back there." I choked on the words.

"I know." Amy brushed my forehead with the towel.

"It's been six months, for God's sake."

"There's no set time for healing."

"There should be. It should be back to normal by now." I closed my eyes. Dr. Alverson had said the same thing. How much time did the universe think I had?

"Have you ever thought maybe this is a part of who you are now?"

"Then, I hate it. I want my old life. You, me, the kids. Max coming for dinner. A job I like."

Amy sat beside me. "I begged you not to rush into things." She grasped my hand.

"I need to work. What am I supposed to do? Stay home and sell insurance, like your brother?"

"Connor makes a good living. You shouldn't knock it."

"I'm sure he does. It's just not for me." I looked at the smoldering grill. I'd screwed up. Again. Missed the signs that would have kept the flames at bay. My failures had already cost Max everything. What if I blew it with the Bramley case? With Rodney? What would I do?

I rubbed my eyes, telling myself the tears were from soot, knowing I was lying. "There must have been drippings on the bottom of the grill that caught fire. I opened the lid and fed the flames. I should have cleaned the grill. I should have paid more attention. I should have—"

"You don't have to apologize." Amy leaned over and kissed my forehead.

I couldn't speak. All I could do was cry.

CHAPTER
SEVEN

I met Rodney at the morgue at eight forty-five the next morning. He walked in holding a Starbucks tray with two cups and a bakery box.

He didn't bring coffee for the entire staff. Progress. I chose to focus on that and not the fact he still brought Starbucks. "Morning."

He held out the tray. "Black, one cream, two sugars."

"Thanks." I took the cup. Sooner or later, I'd buy coffee. When I got Timmies, maybe he'd get the hint. "What's in the box?"

"Doughnuts." He handed it over. "Didn't know if you'd get breakfast. There's Boston cream, plain, sugared, glazed, jelly-filled, custard, powdered sugar, chocolate iced, and coconut." He shrugged. "I didn't know what you'd like."

From coffee for twelve to doughnuts for an army. *Good grief.* "Thanks. Plain glazed is fine. Peanut is my favorite. But," I set my coffee and the box on a table outside the door, "we'll wait until after. Don't want to contaminate anything." And I didn't want to munch on breakfast while staring at Sylvia's innards.

"Oh, yeah. Right." He set his cup next to mine. "Should have thought of that." He looked away and focused on making sure the box wouldn't topple off the table.

"Don't sweat it. Water over the Falls." We hadn't gone in yet and his dark skin looked a little pale. "I probably should have asked you this yesterday, but have you ever seen an autopsy live?" Better to find out now. Not only could the procedure be tough to watch, the somewhat mordant humor of the pathology staff was tough to handle for new detectives.

He crossed his arms. "I'm not squeamish. I've seen dead bodies."

"I'm not saying you are. Autopsy is different than dead."

"How?"

"It's unnatural to see the insides of a human body. The smell is distinct. Pungent. Some detectives like to do their first autopsy on an empty stomach." I had. Max always had. Everybody was different.

"I'll be fine." He waved me off.

"If you say so. But if you think you're going to puke, it's okay to leave. No one will think badly of you." I pushed open the door to the autopsy room, and Rodney followed me in.

Sylvia's body was on a stainless table. Fitch was setting up the camera. The coroner, David Wilke, stood off to the side, starting the report. Wilke looked as though he could have played linebacker in the NFL. His bald head gleamed like a bowling ball in the fluorescent lights.

"Morning, Dave."

"Jackson Davis. How the hell are you?" Wilke stuck out a hand and I shook it. I'm sure he didn't mean to crush my fingers. "Haven't seen you in a dog's age."

"Been on desk duty for the last few months." I didn't need to say more. Wilke knew all the details.

Wilke looked over at Rodney, who was hanging back from the table. "This the new guy?"

"Rodney Kirke, David Wilke, Niagara County coroner." I waved Rodney forward. "And this is Dr. Pete Kwasniak, one of the pathologists."

Dr. Kwasniak, a thin man who could blend into anything, waved.

Rodney took Wilke's massive hand and his eyes widened. "Nice to meet you." He extricated his hand and shook it out. "Good grip."

Wilke laughed, a deep baritone roll. "You a virgin?"

"I beg your pardon?" Rodney looked from Wilke to me, eyes narrowed.

"An autopsy virgin." I slapped his shoulder. "One thing you should know about coroners: they're all a little warped. I think it's in the job description."

Rodney's face cleared. "If you mean is this the first autopsy I've attended, yes."

"I assume Davis here explained rule one." Wilke tugged on a pair of gloves. "If you need to hurl—"

"Head for the doors. Got it." Rodney paused. "I wasn't nervous before. But now…"

"You'll be fine." I pulled him toward the table. "Morning, Fitch. You remember Rodney Kirke?"

"From the scene. Yep." Fitch made a final adjustment to the camera. "Ready when you guys are."

They started with photographs of Sylvia's clothed form from every possible angle. Wilke narrated. "Severe bruising on the extremities. Nail beds blue, fingernails torn from the third and fourth fingers of the right hand. No visible blood or tissue under the remaining nails."

I looked at him. "Washed away by the water?"

"Probably," Wilke said. "But the nails are torn, not snapped. She snagged them on something."

"Or someone." I checked on Rodney, who was holding steady but even paler than before. I refocused on Wilke. "Thoughts on the bruising?"

"Inflicted before death, or very close to it. I can tell by the coloring." Kwasniak examined the marks. "Judging by the pattern and distribution, I think it was the rapids. Not beating with hands or an object like a stick or a pipe."

Wilke and Fitch proceeded to strip the body. The bruising continued onto Sylvia's chest, big flat areas turned purplish blue. Fitch took another thousand or so pictures as Wilke narrated his observations. "Let's open her up." Wilke nodded at the pathologist.

Dr. Kwasniak made the Y-incision and peeled back Sylvia's chest cavity to expose the contents.

Next to me, Rodney choked. "For the love of God."

I glanced at him. He'd turned a dark shade of green. "Door's over there."

"I'm okay." He swallowed. "Pictures don't do the smell justice."

No, they didn't. I'd warned him, but it was the difference between reality and mere words.

Kwasniak and Fitch cracked the rib cage. Rodney flinched at the sound. The pathologist began removing and weighing internal organs, Wilke keeping up a steady narration of observations. "Water in the lungs." He took a sample.

"Then, she was alive and breathing when she went in the water." I tapped my foot. "Ribs broken?"

"A couple of them, but that could be from bumping over the rocks." Wilke pointed at the cracked bones. "Organs are normal weight and color, no visible abnormalities." He moved on to the stomach and intestines, taking a sample of the stomach contents. Fitch ran the gut, rinsing water through the intestines.

Six weeks of admin leave had not made me forget the unique smell of death. Next to me, Rodney gagged.

They moved on to the lower organs, which Kwasniak pronounced of normal size and weight. Then, they moved up to Sylvia's head.

"There's a contusion on the left occipital region." Wilke indicated the area with his finger.

I looked. "Skull cracked?"

Kwasniak probed the area. "Not soft. We'll know when we remove the brain."

This was always the hardest part for me—the noise of the saw as the coroner's team removed the top of Sylvia's skull and her brain. I gritted my teeth against the sound of metal on bone and the burning smell. My brain knew nothing was on fire. No one could make my nose believe it.

"Oh, shit." Rodney staggered toward the door. Guess his nose wasn't convinced, either.

Fitch laughed. "I love being at a detective's first

autopsy. You can always tell the guys who enjoyed dissection in biology. You didn't flinch, Davis."

"Not on the outside." I looked at the door. *Later.* "What about the contusion?"

"No sign of fracture." Kwasniak continued his exam. "No damage to the brain. I'd say the blow was perimortem."

"Enough to stun, not enough to kill." I mulled the information over.

Kwasniak weighed the brain and took a sample. "Enough to disorient her."

"You're sure it wasn't caused by the rocks in the rapids?"

Wilke shook his head. "I think the force of that would have at least fractured the skull, if not completely broken it."

"Time of death?"

Wilke thought. "Hard to say. Cool water messed with the body temperature. The water itself will muck with everything else."

"She was seen alive between seven and seven-thirty."

"We'll get a better estimate when we analyze the stomach contents." Fitch glanced at me. "They aren't completely digested. But this one will be less exact than usual."

Like TOD was ever exact. Another downside of water deaths. It was hard to narrow in on a window.

Wilke turned on the recorder again, leaving Fitch to replace Sylvia's brain and skull cap. "Cause of death, drowning. Manner of death, undetermined."

I rubbed my face. Of all the possibilities, undetermined was the worst because it meant there wasn't enough evidence for the coroner to make a call. Sylvia might have been thrown into the water or she might have jumped. It would be up to me to determine what happened. "You're sure?"

"Positive." Wilke set down his recorder and stripped off his gloves. "You'll get the full report, but for now, finding out how this happened is all on you."

———

I found Rodney in the hallway leaning against the wall.

He was sweaty, but his breathing had returned to normal. "Are they done or are you coming to get me? I hope it's the former."

"I warned you. The visual plus the smell." I clapped him on the shoulder. "They're done. Pretty fast. It's only a little past eleven."

He closed his eyes and grunted.

This had been Max's least favorite part of the job. I sympathized. "Want a doughnut? Another coffee?"

"Coffee, yes. I'll pass on the doughnuts." He sagged against the wall. "I blew it, didn't I? I didn't think it would be that bad."

"You aren't the first guy to bolt from an autopsy, and you won't be the last. Come on, let's get a pick-me-up."

We hit the drive-through at Tim Hortons. Rodney accepted the brew and drank it black. I hoped he'd noticed where I stopped.

Back at the office, I selected the glazed and sugar doughnuts and put the others on a tray in the break room. Dobrovski entered as I was leaving. "Not a word," I told him when he opened his mouth. I headed back to my desk.

"Eat this." I set the plate down.

"I don't think I can." Rodney sipped the coffee. "Shit, this reeks of death." He sniffed his jacket sleeve, trying to be subtle and failing. "Do I smell of death?"

"You don't smell." I watched him continue to sniff. "Eat. You'll feel better. The scent of sugar and coffee might get the stink out of your nose." I waited until he selected the sugared doughnut, then took the other.

"New guy's first autopsy?" Dobrovski called over, the Boston cream in his hand. Then, he turned to a couple other detectives, and they chuckled.

Rodney stared at his desk, fists clenched.

"Hey, Dobrovski." I looked up, wiping glaze from my fingers. "Remind me. Who barfed all over the table at his first autopsy?"

The others laughed harder, but now it was Dobrovski's turn to be red-faced. He sat down without responding. At least, not that I could hear, which meant Rodney couldn't, either. Which was the important thing.

Rodney reached for a stack of paper, shooting me the briefest glance. "Does the smell get better?"

"No, but you get used to it. Or not. Let's get to reading." I didn't mention the other guys, and I suspected Rodney was grateful.

After an hour or so, I looked up. "You find anything? Because my eyes are crossing."

"Not really. This is Sylvia's expense account record." He tossed out his coffee cup. "The most interesting thing here is that she ate at Seneca Niagara a lot for lunch. If she's expensing it, they were for business."

"Or she's cheating on her husband and using it as a cover."

"Possible."

"Business lunches at the casino." I flipped through the stack of paperwork until I found what I was looking for. "The company headquarters is in Newfane. Not exactly close."

"And?"

"I'm sure there are restaurants in town. I know there are in Lockport, which is a lot closer to the business than the casino."

"Your point?"

"If she drives to Niagara Falls from up there every day, or every other day, she's making quite a trip for a business lunch." I consulted a map and measured the distance. "Thirty miles. I'd bet it's at least forty minutes from Natural Wonders' headquarters to the casino. Maybe longer with traffic."

"Whoever she was meeting liked the casino." Rodney clearly thought I was barking up the wrong tree.

Maybe his lack of curiosity was because he was new. Max had taught me odd behavior always warranted questions. "People don't drive two hours to go to lunch. Not three to four times a week." A quick look at Sylvia's expense report told me how often she had these alleged business lunches at Seneca Niagara.

Rodney took the map. "Maybe she gets free lunches. You know, a perk."

It was a possibility. But it was a lot. And for doing what besides being CEO? "Did the tech guys unlock Sylvia's computer yet?"

He sifted through the piles of paper until his desk surface looked as though someone had upended a paper recycling bin on it. "I don't see any reports, and no messages."

Of course he didn't see a report. How could he through the piles? I glanced at my phone. The message light was dark, so no one had called me. "Let's check at Seneca. If the tech guys haven't gotten in touch by one, we'll call them." I stood and pitched my empty cup.

"Are they open? The restaurants?" Rodney's face told me he thought it was crazy, but he stood, too, trying to make a neat pile out of the mess of paper.

"That's the beauty of a casino." I spread my hands. "It's open twenty-four-seven. Go get the keys to a car and meet me out front." He walked away, and I looked at the mess of paper on his desk. Max had been disorganized, but this was ridiculous.

Where to get coffee and what doughnuts I liked, I could teach him. Organization, well, he'd have to figure that out for himself.

I drove. Max had never let me behind the wheel. Mostly because she liked to control the radio. Now, it was my turn.

I wasn't fast enough, though. In the car, Rodney flicked the station from classic rock to a sports talk show without even asking my preference. I gritted my teeth. Five minutes of listening to some talking head discuss major league baseball moves left me wishing for opera.

"The Mets are going to suck this year." Rodney continued scanning stations. "You don't mind sports talk, do you? I could go back to the classic rock station. Or oldies. Maybe you're a jazz guy?"

We were almost to the casino. "Max and I had a rule. The driver gets to pick the radio station."

"Driver? That doesn't make sense."

I didn't have the strength to argue.

The casino wasn't busy at this time of the day, but there were people around, several of whom were already parked in front of the slot machines. I surveyed the floor.

"Should we split up? We'll talk to more witnesses. I guess we'll have to cover the gaming staff, which could take a while." Rodney pulled out his notebook and started making a list. "This doesn't include those who aren't here. Then, there are the bartenders, wait staff for the floor—"

"Slow down," I smothered a sigh. Did he really think we were going to interview every person in the building? Rodney wasn't a new cop, but he was a new detective. He'd be a go-getter. Eager to show he could do the job. Flash his gold shield every opportunity he got. Impress the new boss. I didn't remember being like that, but maybe I was looking at the past through selective lenses.

"Splitting up will save time. But you might catch something I miss. And vice versa." I thought back to the expense reports. "The receipts came from Three Sisters. Let's start there."

He tugged at his collar. "Are they open?"

"Twenty-four hours."

"Should we check the other places, too?"

"Come here." I led him over to a sign advertising all of the eateries in the casino. "La Toscata, Koi, and The Western Door all open too late for lunch. We can eliminate them. At least, for the first pass."

He frowned at the directory.

"It's possible she ate at the other two casual places and paid cash, but the expense reports all say Three Sisters. Let's not overcomplicate things. Yet." If he was trying to make up for his behavior at the morgue, he was overdoing it. Or he was hyped up on sugar.

"Of course. Stupid." His crestfallen look would have been comical in other circumstances. "This is my first case as a detective. I don't want to screw it up."

"Relax. You know your stuff or you wouldn't have the shield. Got the picture?" I was okay with him bringing five dozen doughnuts and several gallons of coffee from wherever he wanted as long as he remembered the basics.

He patted his breast pocket.

Three Sisters was cafeteria-style. Put your order in at the window, get your food, pay, sit, and eat. Perfect for those looking for a quick bite before going back to the lights and the one-armed bandits. But it was too casual for a business lunch. At least, it was in my opinion.

There weren't a lot of patrons and the focus seemed to be breakfast. I stopped a passing worker. "Is there a manager here? Or have you ever seen this woman?" I gestured to Rodney, who pulled Sylvia's picture out of his pocket.

Her eyes narrowed. "Who are you and why do you want to know?"

"NFPD." I flashed my shield.

The girl shook her head slowly. "I don't know her. But we get a lot of diners. I'll get Todd. He's the manager on duty. He might be able to help you."

We waited until a middle-aged man, paunchy and balding, walked up. "Todd Conroy." He shook my hand. "Lisa told me the police were here. Hope no one's in trouble."

"No trouble, sir," Rodney said. "We're Homicide."

"Homicide?" Conroy's face paled and his eyebrows shot up. "Did someone die?"

I'd have to speak to Rodney about how to introduce himself. Something else with new cops and detectives—they wanted everybody to know who they were. "Someone died, but not here and not today. We're looking for information. Have you ever seen this woman?" I held out the photograph.

Conroy took it and stared, his tongue sticking out slightly as he bit it. "Yeah, I recognize her. Comes in a lot around lunch time. Never got her name. You'd have to check with the staff." He handed it back.

I pocketed the picture. "We know her name."

"Then, why are you asking?"

"Tell me, was she usually alone or did she eat with someone? In general."

"Interesting. Let me think." He tapped his foot. "Every time I remember seeing her, she was alone."

I glanced at Rodney, who shrugged. "Did she come in off the street or from the gaming floor?"

"Not sure. But the last time I saw her, she definitely left here and went to the casino. I heard her when she paid her bill."

"Oh?" Rodney asked.

"Yeah. Joanie said 'good luck' and the woman made a comment about it being well past time for some luck. Or something along those lines." Conroy sounded confident.

I looked around. "Is Joanie working today?" If Sylvia had been claiming business lunches, why had she been alone? And why was she going to the casino floor?

Conroy pointed to a woman in her forties standing at the cash register. "That's her."

"Thanks." I waved to Rodney, and we went over. "Morning." I was determined not to let Rodney blurt out our department. "You recognize this woman?" Once again, I held out the photo.

"Oh yes, Mrs. Bramley. She's one of our regulars," Joanie said after a quick glance.

"How regular?" Rodney took out pen and paper.

"Three, four times a week? Usually midday." Joanie waved us aside. "You're blocking the line."

A customer behind me humphed, and I moved out of the way. "Alone or with company?"

"Oh, alone." Joanie focused on her cash register. "Always alone. I guess misery doesn't always love company."

I leaned against the register. "What do you mean, misery?"

"I got the impression she lost a lot." Joanie finished ringing out the customer and looked up. "Based on our conversations. Although," she chuckled, "she must have hit it big, oh, maybe three weeks ago."

I looked at Rodney. "How do you know?"

"She came in here all giddy and insisted on giving me a hundred dollars. For listening to her sorrows, she said. 'I hit the jackpot, Joanie. Figured I would celebrate by sharing.' She handed me a nice, crisp bill." She chuckled. "Crazy, but sweet of her. They usually only tip at the bar and on the floor. Not at the fast-food checkout."

"Did she do that often? Eat lunch and go to the casino?" If Sylvia was a gambler, it would be another piece in the puzzle.

"Only if you consider every time she ate here often." Joanie turned her attention to the next customer in line. "Why else would someone come in? Most of our guests are going to or coming from the gaming floor." She paused. "I don't think her marriage was happy, which was why she played so much."

If the Bramleys had been in town to rekindle their romance, probably not. I picked a toothpick from the container. "How so?"

"I admired her engagement ring once. A big, beautiful stone, it was. Pure white. She said something about how it was the only beautiful thing she had from being married."

"Was she ever in here with a man?"

"I never saw one." Joanie rang up a third customer. "I asked once if her husband came with her. She said no. I think gambling was her thing, not his." The customer left, and Joanie peered at me. "Is Mrs. Bramley okay? Why are you asking these questions?"

I hesitated. Joanie wasn't family, but she did seem genuinely concerned. "I'm afraid Mrs. Bramley is dead. You mentioned the engagement ring. She ever talk about divorce?"

Joanie shook her head. "Poor, poor woman. Bless her soul." She crossed herself. "I did ask once. She brushed me off. I had the idea she thought it would look bad. A failed marriage. Weird, but I guess there are still women out there who think that way." She sniffed, letting me know what she thought of those women.

Sylvia had fought with Keith at dinner. Had she

rushed out of Top of the Falls for a jaunt to the casino, without her husband, before heading back to their room? Gambling could have been her solace if her marriage was on the rocks. "Thanks very much, Joanie."

We left. I stopped in the hallway and stared at the blinking lights.

"Back to the office?"

I shook my head. "I'm thinking the casino manager knows something."

If Sylvia had been as regular a customer as we thought, a manager might remember her. Or seen her the night she'd died. Either way, it was worth a shot.

———

As we walked down the hallway, Rodney stopped in front of a large poster. "Take a look at this." It was an advertisement for the casino's Player's Club card. "Think she had one?"

It was a good idea. "We'll find out."

Inside the casino floor, we asked to see the manager. While we waited, I looked around. The crowd wasn't huge on a weekday, but it wasn't small, either. Lights flashed everywhere. Little old ladies sat at slot machines. A few middle-aged guys dressed in everything from button-down shirts and slacks to jeans and T-shirts played table games, mostly poker and blackjack.

"I wonder how long they can sit there?" Rodney leaned against the hostess stand and nodded toward the flashing lights.

"All day, I'd imagine. As long as they have money." I returned to studying the gaming floor. Was it sad or pathetic, all these people inside throwing their cash away on a gorgeous spring day? I couldn't decide.

After a few minutes, a stocky man in a well-tailored suit approached. "Irwin Cole." He extended his hand. "Manager on duty. You wanted to speak to me?" He was built like a fullback, broad shoulders, thick neck, solid waist. His teeth gleamed against dark skin. His hair was cut close to his scalp and his deep brown eyes were wary. But his handshake grip was strong and confident.

"Detective Davis, NFPD." I showed him my badge. "This is Detective Kirke."

Rodney, who'd passed the time flirting with the hostess, pulled himself away to shake Cole's hand.

"Police? I hope nothing has happened." Cole lowered his eyebrows.

"Not here at the casino." I pulled Sylvia's picture from my jacket pocket. "You recognize this woman?"

Cole studied the photo. "Can't say as I do. We get a lot of people in here. Did you ask Clarisse?" He gestured at the hostess.

"In a minute." I played with the edge of the photo. "We've talked to people who put her here often."

Cole shrugged. "We don't keep tabs on the guests. If she was here, she was never involved in an incident requiring my attention." He waved Clarisse back to her station. "What's she done?"

"She's dead." Rodney fixed him with a piercing look.

"Dead?" Cole's eyebrows went up. "Was she murdered?"

Rodney didn't move. "Why do you ask?"

Cole's shoulders twitched. "Why else would the police be involved?"

I definitely needed to have a word with my partner. "We don't know yet. We were hoping you recognized her. She was a frequent visitor. Or so we've been told." I studied Cole's reaction. Surprise, yes. But my gut told me he was telling the truth. He didn't recognize Sylvia.

"The poster outside." Rodney jerked his thumb over his shoulder. "The one for the Player's Club. How's it work?"

"It's like a frequent shopper's club." Cole removed a pamphlet from the inside of his charcoal-gray jacket. Nearby, a slot machine erupted in a series of whoops. "It's free to join. It tracks how much you've gambled, and players earn rewards. You can get free food, free hotel rooms. Stuff like that."

I read the pamphlet. "How many visits?"

Cole shook his head. "It's based on money. We don't follow players' visits or their movements."

Rodney took the pamphlet from me. "How do you keep tabs on the wagers?"

"Two ways." Cole chose to focus on Rodney. "We've got a slot-only and table-only card. Slots are easy. The player slides the card in the machine and it records play. For table games, she gives the card to the pit boss, who notes the number."

"You know exactly what's wagered?" I looked around again. *All these tables, talk about quite a job.*

"Not individual hands." Cole grinned. "It's a calculation. Average wager, number of hands, number of players. It's good enough."

I frowned. Too bad they didn't swipe when they entered. "Can players see their activity?"

"They can log in online and see a complete win-loss statement at any time. As well as the number of points earned."

"Can you tell me if a Sylvia Bramley had a card, and if she does, show me her statement?"

"I'm sure I could." Cole's faint smile was tinged with a bit of complacency. "As soon as you show me a warrant."

Smart man. "It was worth asking," I said.

"Of course." Cole's eyes gleamed with amusement. "Anything else?"

"Yes." Rodney held his pen over his pad. "How do you pay out winnings?"

"Cash." Cole shrugged. "Players can request a check, but only if the payout is four thousand dollars or more. Most of our payouts are cash."

Which also meant New York and the IRS were easier to cheat. But Cole seemed to read my mind, because he shook his head and smiled. "We issue tax statements where required. We can't control whether people pay, but we do send them." He looked from me to Rodney. "Anything else I can do for you, gentlemen?"

I thought about it. Until we got some financials or this win-loss statement, probably not. "No. Thank you, Mr. Cole. Here's my card. If you think of anything else, please call."

On the way out, we showed Sylvia's picture to

Clarisse. She didn't recognize our victim, either, but it was worth a shot.

Outside in the sunshine, I gazed at the parked cars. This far from the river, the sounds of traffic masked the roar of the rapids. I missed it. The sound of rushing water helped me relax.

Rodney came up beside me. "What are you thinking?"

I looked at him. "We need to push on a warrant for Sylvia's bank records and legal papers. And find out if she had a Player's Club card." It would be easier if we had her purse or wallet, but hey, we couldn't have everything.

"I'll call from the car. I assume you're driving." He walked off, forcing me to follow.

Yes, I was. And it was time I stopped to see Max.

NINE

Since there was nothing to do at the office except continue to pore over existing information and review our notes from the afternoon, I left exactly at five. The office felt constrictive, anyway. I called Amy from the car. "I'm going to stop and check on Max. You need anything?"

"Mmm."

It was an indeterminate noise. "What do you mean?" Amy didn't make indeterminate noises.

"Are you stopping because you need advice, or because you need to check on Max again?"

"I want to talk to my friend and former partner. Why did you say *again*?" The fact I'd be there, able to take care of anything that might have come up, was extra.

"I'm not going to discuss it on the phone. I'll keep a plate warm for you." She clicked off.

I shook my head. What did she mean by *again*? She said it as though it was a bad thing. I'd stopped a couple of times since the accident. It wasn't like Max had tons of people to rely on. She'd chosen to stay in Niagara Falls, a blind woman living alone.

And I owed her.

Max's usual parking spot was open since her car had been sold. I wondered if the neighbors kept it free for visitors.

There was no answer when I knocked on her apartment door, but I heard the familiar operatic musical sounds. I knocked louder. "Max, it's Jackson. Is the door open?"

Still no answer. Where would she have gone? Or was she ignoring me? As I was about to knock again, the door flew open.

"It's almost dinner time. If you aren't working, why aren't you at home?" Max wasn't holding her cane, but we'd been very careful not to move the furniture so she could get around without it. She wore a faded T-shirt and sweats. It was a far cry from the perfectly pressed suits she wore to the office when we worked together. It was even a step down from her usual weekend attire. The only time I'd seen her approach this level of casualness was when we went to the gym together to work out. For a woman who had a different power suit for every day of the week, it was quite the change.

"It's me, Jackson." I leaned on the doorframe. "I figured I'd stop by and see how you're doing. Can I come in?"

"I know. Not only did you announce your name, I recognized your voice. I'm blind, not deaf." She didn't invite me in, but she didn't tell me to leave. She felt her way back to the living room.

I interpreted it as an invitation and followed. "How's it going?"

"Things are fine. I'm fine. The same as I've been the last dozen times you've dropped in." She sat, and her tuxedo cat, Leroy, jumped into her lap. "Are you and Amy fighting?"

I dropped onto the couch opposite her. The room was immaculate, the exact opposite of her desk. She'd said once she had enough chaos on the job. I knew she'd worked with an occupational therapist and they'd made a few minor adjustments, but everything looked pretty much the same to me. The only difference was the stack of puzzle books by her chair had been replaced by a tablet. "We're fine. Why do you ask?"

"Because we both know how precious family time is in this job." She stroked Leroy, who regarded me with an indecipherable green-eyed stare. "Especially if you're off desk duty. If you're here, something's wrong."

"No, it's not. I wanted to see how you're doing."

"For the hundredth time, Jackson, you don't need to check on me every day."

"I am not here every day."

"But you call. Or text." A ghost of a grin flitted across her face, and she fixed me with a stare that was no less intimidating for all the milkiness of her once-hazel eyes. "I'm not a child."

"I know. Remember, you're family, too. Or pretty damn close." Hers lived on the other end of the state. We'd adopted each other. "Madeline misses you."

"How is the squirt?"

"Growing like a weed. But she needs to learn to put her stuff away."

"She's five. She'll get there. Be patient." The ghost came and went again. "They give you a new partner yet?"

"First day back. Yannick didn't even ask my opinion." I told her about Rodney.

"Police work isn't a democracy." She leaned back. "He reminds me of another fresh, eager new detective."

"I knew how to get coffee."

"You had other foibles."

I tapped my thumbs together. What had I expected? Max hadn't coddled me when she was on the job. She wouldn't now. Why had I come? She clearly didn't need anything from me.

But I need her.

Awkward silence reigned for a long second. She flipped open the glass on her watch and fingered the time. "It's late. As you can see, I'm hunky-dory. Unless there's something else on your mind, you should get home."

Amy and I had bought her the watch when we asked her to be Christopher's godmother. She'd turned us down for the godmother role. Told us family was more suitable. But she'd kept the watch. "I was cleared to return to duty on Monday. Caught a new case the next day. Sylvia Bramley."

"The makeup company woman?" Leroy leapt down and Max crossed her legs.

"The same. Autopsy was this morning. Drowning, undetermined. Before you say I should still be at the office, I hit a wall for the moment. It's another part of the reason I came to see you."

No response.

"She could have been pushed over the Falls, could have jumped, or could have gone to the gorge with someone. Maybe she went over the pedestrian bridge on Green Island. I suppose she could have gone over at Terrapin Point. She and her husband had dinner at Top of the Falls last night. But there are so many people there. She would have been seen. Her injuries are more consistent with a trip over the American Falls. Witnesses and the husband say she walked, but—"

Max cut me off with a disgusted snort. "You still do it."

"Do what?"

"Overcomplicate the shit out of things. Didn't I teach you anything? Make a list, cross off the things that are totally impossible. Stop getting so stuck in the damn trees. Look at the forest for a change." She sighed and rubbed her eyes. "You really ought to be discussing this with Kirke. He's your partner."

"I did. I wanted your take on it."

"I don't know why."

Because I need to know I'm doing it right. Max and I never talked about the night of the accident. It was too uncomfortable for both of us. There was so much I wanted to say, but I didn't want to hurt her more than I already had. It was better to move on. "I thought you'd be interested."

"A little. But not enough for you to make special trips." A strange expression came over her face. Pity? No, that couldn't be it. Definitely some form of sadness, though. "Go home, Jackson. Eat dinner. Tomorrow, sit down with this new guy and do your job."

Leroy came over and put his paw on my knee. Max clapped her hands and he immediately scampered over to her.

I'd failed her. Again. I didn't know how, but I had. "Why don't you come over one of these nights? Madeline's been asking about you." Maybe if I got her to come home with me, I could make up for whatever I'd done. Make her realize we still needed her. Wanted her around. Let Madeline work her five-year-old magic. And Max would get a decent meal. I hadn't missed the spotless range when I came through the kitchen, which meant she wasn't cooking much. Nuked frozen meals were no substitute.

"Not tonight. I'm tired." She refused to look in my direction.

I'd always been good at reading her emotions, but this time I drew a blank. Had we changed so much? "You're sure?"

"Yes." She fingered her watch again. "Tell Amy and the squirt I said hi. Tomorrow, talk to your partner and work your case. Act like a damned lead detective. It's your turn now." She leaned back and turned on some opera, her favorite. It was a clear dismissal.

I stared at her. When she didn't say anything, I stood. "Have a good evening."

Back in the car, I slammed my door. The visit hadn't gone the way I wanted. Why wouldn't she talk to me?

Not like you're talking to her, a little voice whispered in my mind. It was one I'd heard often in the last six months, almost always in the recesses of my mind. It was familiar, but I couldn't quite place it. *That makes two of you.*

———

I was cranky when I arrived home. Finding the damn tricycle in the yard did not help and I admit I was a bit snappy with my daughter. It didn't inflate my self-respect, which in turn soured my mood even more.

"I thought you were going to remind her about the trike." I focused on Amy and tried not to shout over two wailing children. Because, of course, Madeline's cries had set off Christopher.

"I did, but I can't follow up on her and deal with a baby at the same time." Amy held out Christopher. "Take your son. I'll be back."

I held Christopher face out in an attempt to minimize the drool deposited on my suit. Then, I retreated to the living room, gently bouncing him while his refreshing baby scent soothed me. Never mind those fancy candles that smelled like either a bakery or a hothouse. The person who figured out how to bottle the smell of a clean baby would make a fortune.

I was still sitting there, eyes closed, a burbling Christopher on my lap, when Amy walked in.

"Now, tell me." She crossed her arms. "Who peed in your Post Toasties? If this is the way being a lead detective is going to make you—"

"Leave it. Please. Long day. I'll apologize to Madeline later." I didn't need a lecture about the effects of my job. It wouldn't put me in a better mood. I heard Amy's sigh and imagined her look of frustration. Something else I didn't want to see.

"I'll go warm up your dinner. No, don't get up. Stay there and relax." The sound of footsteps on carpet receded and I knew it was just us guys. At least Christopher wouldn't offer a comment on my behavior. He was gumming my tie and I should have stopped him, but right then, I didn't care.

I'd mostly let go of the day's frustrations by the time I'd finished eating. Madeline accepted my apology with the kind of enthusiasm only a child could display, although I'd had to promise an extra bedtime story in the process. While I ate, Amy fed Christopher and put him in his crib.

"Get Madeline to bed while I clean up." Amy took my plate after I'd finished.

"You sure?"

"Yes." She squeezed my hand. "I think some quiet time with her will do you good."

I went to my daughter's room.

Madeline's eyes lit up. "Time for my stories?"

"Sure. Pick one out."

She clapped her hands. "You said two stories, Daddy. Two stories."

I picked her up and swung her around. "How could I forget?"

Two stories turned into three. With droopy eyes, Madeline tried to argue for a fourth, but I shut her down. "Save some for tomorrow night." I kissed her forehead. "Night, Squirt."

I closed her door and went to my bedroom,

intending to change into sweats. It was only eight, still early.

"Thought you could use this." Amy appeared in the doorway, glasses of wine in her hands. During story time, she'd changed into a shimmery pink nightgown with a matching robe. She'd pulled up her hair, exposing her neck, and the thin fabric showed off breasts that held up pretty well after two kids and nursing.

I dropped the sweatpants I'd been holding, walked over, and took the wine glasses. "I could. And I don't mean the wine." I set the glasses on the dresser and kissed her, my hands sliding over the slippery fabric and untying the belt at her waist.

We stumbled back and fell on the bed. She ran her hands under my T-shirt. They felt cool against my skin. I grabbed a fistful of nightgown and slid my other hand underneath over her warm, soft skin.

Between childbirth and the aftermath of the accident, there hadn't been a lot of alone time for us. Amy touched me and I shuddered. The remaining stress of the day melted as we kissed like two horny teenagers. Problems? What problems? The past year hadn't happened. I was a normal guy with a loving wife, two kids, and the world at my fingertips. Normality was in my grasp.

The baby monitor crackled, and I heard Christopher whimper. *Come on, kid, give your old man a break.* If he started crying, the evening was over before it started.

Amy paused, but I pressed on. "He's fine." I kissed a path down her neck to her chest.

The whimper turned into a thin cry.

She pulled her head back. "I should check on him."

"He's all right. Or he will be for a few minutes."

The cry turned into a full-fledged wail.

"I can't have sex to the sound of a crying baby." She tried to pull away, but I held her fast.

"Then turn the monitor off." I tugged on her chin to get her to look at me. "Please, Amy. Ten minutes. He'll be okay for ten minutes. You can't leave me like this."

"Sorry." She pushed herself away and stood, straightened her nightgown, and tied her robe. "He's six months old. You're a grown man. I have to put him first. Maybe later." She left, and moments later I heard her on the monitor, soothing Christopher and settling in to nurse him.

I pounded the bed. There'd be nothing later. The moment had passed. *Grow up. You think you're the only disappointed one?* the voice whispered. *What about Amy? Are your needs more important than your baby's?*

I got up, pulled on my sweatpants, and grabbed my glass. At least no one had taken my wine.

CHAPTER
TEN

My goodbyes the next morning were brief. I'd spent most of the night alone. Amy hadn't slept much and stood in the kitchen bleary-eyed, guzzling coffee. I had a lot to say, but it didn't look like now was the time to say it, so I gave her a quick peck on the cheek. Madeline couldn't pull her attention away from whatever ridiculous cartoons were on at seven in the morning. Christopher was busy throwing Cheerios on the floor. I tried not to crush them underfoot. Making more work for Amy wouldn't help my cause.

I stopped at Tim Hortons for two cups of coffee. As predicted, Rodney had brought some. Starbucks. I placed my cups down. "We need to come up with a schedule or we're both going to have the shakes."

He looked up. "Tim Hortons?"

"I like their medium roast."

"Why didn't you say something?" He looked at the two cups in front of him. "Not like we won't drink it."

Because I didn't feel right complaining out loud. "Do we have any new information?"

He shook his head. "Nothing."

"Then, we're off to Newfane." I considered the cups. Remembering Max's admonition of the previous night, I took the Starbucks.

We drove to the Natural Wonders headquarters in Newfane. A quick call confirmed Bert Guenther was in the office and didn't have any appointments. When we arrived, we were immediately ushered into an office filled with expensive antique furniture on a plush, deep red carpet. Guenther was not there, although the secretary assured us he would return shortly.

Rodney examined the office. "Makeup is good business."

The desk was massive, made of solid dark wood. A minibar against the wall held top-shelf booze and cut-glass tumblers. Heavy gilt frames were on the shelves. Some contained photographs, others held awards. I picked up one photo of a middle-aged couple against an azure sea. It was the same guy from the picture in Sylvia's home office, but a different woman. His arm was around her waist. She had to be at least ten years older than Sylvia with perfectly waved silver hair. An elaborate set of rings was on her left hand, including what I assumed was an engagement ring and wedding band. A wife. So, what was with the other picture?

Someone bustled into the office behind us. "Sorry for the delay, gentlemen. Emergency on the production floor."

I turned to see the man from the picture in Sylvia's

home office. Bert Guenther was probably pushing fifty with the stocky but trim figure of someone who worked out a lot. His graying hair was cut close on the sides. His eyes reminded me of a shark's, dark gray and dead-looking. He had the air of a man used to getting his own way.

"Detective Davis, NFPD." I waved at Rodney. "This is Detective Kirke. You're still operating?"

"Sylvia's death is tragic. But she would want us to carry on. After all, business waits for no one." Guenther didn't attempt to shake my hand. "Marcy didn't say what division. Theft, fraud?"

"Homicide." I watched his reaction.

His gray eyes widened slightly. "They told me the police were here yesterday, but no one mentioned homicide."

"You weren't at the office?"

"I had a meeting in New York. I didn't think the police investigated suicide."

"Who said anything about her killing herself?" I studied him. His boss had died. Where was the reaction?

"The word I received was her body was found in the gorge and speculation was she'd gone over the Falls. How else would she get there?"

Rodney spoke up. "Mr. Bramley was very adamant. His wife was not suicidal or depressed."

Guenther managed to turn a laugh into a cough. "Excuse me for saying this, but Keith's opinion of Sylvia's state of mind is hardly reliable these days."

Rodney's expression hinted at his confusion. "But he's her husband. Wouldn't he know?"

This time, Guenther did laugh, although it was a

delicate sound. "I see no one has informed you of their private lives. Their marriage was—"

"On the rocks." I interrupted him to keep the conversation focused. "Yes, Mr. Bramley mentioned it." I unbuttoned my jacket. "They haven't issued a ruling on the manner of death. In those situations, it's routine for Homicide to investigate until the facts are known." I gestured to a chair. "Mind if we sit?"

Guenther acknowledged the question with a mute agreement.

"When was the last time you saw Mrs. Bramley?"

"I saw her last Friday." He moved to the bar in the corner, forcing us to twist in our seats to watch him. "I don't suppose I can interest you two in joining me." He added ice to a glass and poured three fingers of bourbon on top.

"We're on duty," I said.

He stared at us and frowned, sipping his bourbon. After a moment, he sat in the leather swivel chair behind the desk. "I didn't get a lot of details yesterday. If she didn't jump, could it have been an accident?"

"We aren't sure." I leaned back. Given she'd been returning from dinner, I found the possibility of an accident remote unless she'd struggled with someone and fallen into the rapids. Which might have been accidental, but it didn't fit my definition of *accident*.

"We only know she drowned." Rodney flicked an imaginary piece of lint from his slacks.

Guenther took a healthy drink. "Tragic. So successful. So young. Relatively speaking, of course. I almost can't believe she'd kill herself."

"You keep mentioning suicide." I folded my hands

in my lap. "What makes you go down that path?" This guy was as cool as a cucumber. Regardless of how Sylvia died, I would have expected more emotion. Instead, he was dispassionate as though it had been a stranger and not the woman he worked for. I got the feeling an announcement Natural Wonders failed to meet their sales goals would elicit more response.

Guenther leaned back and swirled his bourbon. After the small reaction to our introduction as Homicide detectives, composure had returned to his face. His eyes were predatory. "Perhaps, it wasn't obvious to others. However, I'm afraid Sylvia, although she put on a good face to the world, was not a happy woman."

"Why not? From the looks of things, business was good."

Beside me, Rodney started taking notes.

Guenther sipped his drink. "Business *was* good. Perhaps, too good. I don't think Sylvia was prepared for the stress of running a company with this level of success. We had reached a point where decisions had to be made. Ones Sylvia didn't want to make. And, of course, there was her home life."

Rodney didn't look up. "Tell us about the business."

"We need to expand." He crossed his legs, resting his glass on his knee. "We're big locally, but if we want to continue to grow, we need to increase operations and sales. Definitely within the US. Possibly internationally."

"Canada?"

"And Europe." Guenther sipped his bourbon.

I was glad Rodney seemed comfortable scribing. It

left me free to focus on the interviewee. "Was that the topic of your New York meeting?"

Guenther nodded.

"I take it Mrs. Bramley wasn't in complete agreement with you," Rodney said.

Guenther hesitated. "Sylvia had concerns. Not unfounded, of course. We rely on natural components—minerals and such—for the cosmetics. She was worried increasing production would mean needing to buy more supplies, which would cost more and lead to price increases. She also thought making the products stable for shipping would dilute quality."

This cold, calculating recitation did not match the celebratory air of the photograph I'd seen in Sylvia's home office. "You didn't share her concerns."

"I believed they could be addressed." Guenther drained his bourbon.

"How intense was the disagreement?" Rodney asked.

"It started mild, but grew to be fairly volatile." Guenther shifted in his seat. "This is going to make it sound bad for me, but it had reached a point where I threatened to resign my position if Sylvia did not agree with my expansion proposal. As the majority shareholder, she had the final say."

"It's not entirely her company?"

"No. At one point, she was the sole owner. Now, the company stock is held by a few people, myself included. But Sylvia controlled corporate direction. Our last discussion resulted in quite the argument. I regret to say, we were shouting at each other. I tell you this because I know you'll ask the employees. Someone is bound to have heard us."

I paused over my next question. "How are you compensated, Mr. Guenther? Salary, bonus, dividends?"

His eyebrows drew together. "I get a yearly salary as well as annual dividends, although we're not traded on any exchange. Bonuses are awarded to all employees. The amount depends on the company performance for the fiscal year."

"Would this expansion mean a bigger bonus?" Rodney's thoughts were along the same lines as mine. "Maybe you'd have to go public with your stock?"

"Possibly. Or borrow, or get additional investments." Guenther's eyebrows beetled some more. "Assuming the expansion succeeded according to my projections, we'd all get more money. What are you getting at?"

"Nothing." I tilted my head. "Now that Sylvia Bramley is dead, who is in charge of corporate decisions?"

Guenther paused. "I am." He sounded like he'd rather not admit to it. "Until a new CEO is appointed."

"Would you be a candidate?" Again, Rodney and I were in sync.

"It is possible it could be me. But the majority stock ownership will pass to her husband, or whatever beneficiary is listed in her will. I'm not privy to the exact details." He steepled his fingers.

Which meant Bramley had a powerful financial motive for murder. But so did Guenther. How heated had their disagreement been?

I eyed him. "You could pull the trigger on this expansion. As acting CEO, I mean."

Guenther's expression cleared. I didn't like the cunning look I saw. He leaned back. "I see where you're going. Correct. I could go ahead with the expansion. Keith Bramley has no standing in the company outside of the inheritance." Guenther's expression showed feigned reluctance. "However, Sylvia's body is not yet cold, so to speak. I don't want to malign her memory."

Liar. It was something everybody said, but nobody really meant. People loved to dish dirt on the deceased. "We're conducting a homicide investigation. Whatever your feelings, we need to know."

"We have problems in the back office." He paused.

I waited, but had to prompt him. "Such as?"

"Someone is embezzling money from Natural Wonders. I believe it was Sylvia, and the true reason she didn't want to expand was that her actions would be exposed."

Rodney looked up. "Why would she steal from herself?"

Guenther gave us a condescending smile. "She was a little too fond of the gaming tables."

"Didn't you say it's her company? Couldn't she draw whatever money she wanted?"

"Yes, but it must be reported." Guenther's tone bordered on patronizing, a teacher explaining to an underperforming student. "And the reporting has been, shall we say, erratic."

Interesting word. "Erratic how?"

"Some irregularities have been reported from finance." He pushed a button on the intercom. "Marcy, send in Anthony Dellafiore with those papers he and I discussed. He'll know which ones." Letting go of the buzzer, he added, "Anthony is our accountant. He originally identified the problems and brought them to my attention."

"Why not Mrs. Bramley?" Rodney sounded curious.

"He thought it better to talk to me."

I eyed him. "How did he know you weren't behind the missing money?"

"He didn't. But Sylvia was difficult to talk to at times. She'd been moody and reclusive lately." He leaned forward and placed his hands on the desk. "As I told you before, she spent a lot of time at the casino. I think she was compensating for an unhappy home life."

"You've mentioned this before. How bad could it have been? She was happily married, had a nice house. Add two kids and a dog, and it would be the stereotypical American family." I watched him. A new emotion had crept into his face. Glee.

Rodney paused in his note taking. "According to Mr. Bramley, they had a decent marriage, even considering their recent troubles."

Guenther chuckled. "Far from it. He wanted kids. She didn't. Also, she believed—in fact, knew—her husband was having an affair."

So much for Bramley's assertions, but I couldn't say I was shocked. I wasn't going to give away my thoughts to Guenther, so I kept a calm face. "Did she know who the woman was?"

"Oh yes." Guenther leaned back, a sly smile spreading on his lips. The cunning look came back. "Keith was sleeping with Sylvia's younger sister."

CHAPTER
ELEVEN

There was a pause, during which another man entered the office. "Anthony." Guenther waved him forward. "Close the door. These gentlemen are from the Niagara Falls police. I'd like you to show them the reports you showed me."

My first impression of Anthony Dellafiore was of a ferret. A pencil-thin neck rose out of a shirt too big in the collar. The brown hair was combed over an expanding bald spot, and the eyes behind the glasses were sharp, though a muddy brown color. His shoulders were hunched, maybe from working over a computer all day.

"You called the police?" Dellafiore fingered the manila folder in his hands.

"We invited ourselves." I grasped his hand. Dellafiore's grip was dead-fish limp. "Homicide."

"Homicide? Who's been murdered?" Dellafiore's eyes grew wider.

Rodney cleared his throat. "Possibly Sylvia Bramley. We're investigating."

"Mrs. Bramley committed suicide."

Rodney twirled the pen in his hand. "Oh?"

"I mean it's obvious, isn't it?" Dellafiore glanced at each of us, settling on his boss. "At least, that's what everyone is saying."

"Everyone may or may not be right." I leaned back. "Which is why we're here."

"Why do you want to see me?" Dellafiore's gaze flicked from us to Guenther, and he licked his lips.

"The reports, Anthony." Guenther snapped his fingers. "Please tell these gentlemen what you told me."

"Yes. Yes, of course." Dellafiore jumped, then laid out the papers in the folder. "When I was balancing the monthly books, I noticed some discrepancies in the totals. By comparing monthly income and expenses, including inventory, salary, and—"

He was going to go into a lengthy financial discourse. I cut him off. "Mr. Dellafiore. I realize you want to be thorough and I appreciate your efforts. For now, conclusions are sufficient."

Dellafiore flinched. "There's money missing. Not a lot in each transaction, but it can't be explained by the balance sheets. Someone is going in and skimming off small amounts of money per grab. Done repeatedly, it would add up to a nice sum."

"How much?"

"Fifty thousand dollars, give or take." Dellafiore looked at me for the briefest moment before looking away.

Not a lot of money for a major corporation, but

Natural Wonders wasn't a big operation. "How long has this been going on?" I took the paper from his hand. The columns of numbers meant nothing to me. They'd have made sense to Amy, in her former life, but only the presence of red digits and underlines told me something was wrong.

"At least six months. That's as far back as I've gone right now." Dellafiore fidgeted and picked at a torn cuticle on this thumb.

I handed the paper to Rodney. "What makes you suspect Mrs. Bramley?"

"It had to be someone with access to the accounts." Dellafiore fussed with his tie. He shot a look at Guenther. "Senior management, mostly. Given Mrs. Bramley's behavior over the past few months, naturally I couldn't help but wonder."

"What about her behavior?" Rodney passed the report back to Dellafiore.

"She was erratic. At least, I thought so. There was never any doubt she was in charge. But she seemed distracted. Not as attentive to detail as she usually was. I thought she was hiding something."

There's that word again. "It's her company." I kept my voice bland. It was the same point I'd made to Guenther, but I wanted Dellafiore's answer. "She can take anything she wants."

Dellafiore swallowed. "Mrs. Bramley routinely took money for petty cash. Usually less than a hundred dollars. These amounts are bigger."

"How big?" Rodney asked.

"Several hundred to a thousand at a time." Dellafiore nodded toward the paper. "It's in the report.

Plus, any such withdrawals have to be documented, which the petty cash is. In this case, whoever is responsible is clearly trying to hide it."

"Clearly, they haven't been successful." I glanced at Rodney, who had his attention riveted on Dellafiore.

Dellafiore fiddled with his tie again. "The coverup would stand up to a casual glance, but not a careful look."

I nodded. "You brought this to Mr. Guenther."

"As VP and COO, it seemed to be the most logical move. I trust him. Mrs. Bramley didn't want to hire me in the first place." Dellafiore's gaze locked on me for a moment, before he looked at Guenther.

Why would Sylvia Bramley care about a low-level accountant? Unless she was indeed the person filching from the till. "Who hired you?"

Guenther broke into the conversation. "Sylvia made the hire based on my recommendation. My insistence, really. She was doing the bookkeeping herself. Not something that can continue as a company expands."

In my memory, I scanned the reports from Dellafiore. If Sylvia was handling the books, it would be easier to cover any withdrawals and any illicit activity. Guether may have had another reason for wanting Sylvia to give up the accounting. He was the embezzler. If Sylvia was so attentive, she'd have caught on, at least eventually. "If you expand—go public, have to get loans, whatever—wouldn't that trigger an audit?"

"It would." Guenther folded his hands. "And yes, I'm sure it would also find this discrepancy."

Again, I reviewed the reports in my head. It didn't make sense. If Guenther was the guy pushing for expansion and he knew he'd get caught in an audit, he wouldn't be embezzling. Probably. Unless he also thought he could co-opt another employee into his plan for a coverup.

"Which would explain Mrs. Bramley's suicide." Dellafiore glanced between Guenther, Rodney, and me. "She knew she was going to get caught."

"It might." They wanted me to keep talking, I could tell. Truth was, it was also a motive for murder if Sylvia knew about the theft. Either by the person responsible for the fraud, or by a person eager to keep her crime a secret until the expansion was a done deal. But I wasn't going to share my thoughts. Not yet. I wasn't completely buying the suicide story, either.

"You went to Mr. Guenther because you trusted him." Rodney looked at Dellafiore. "Since he went to bat for you in the hiring process?"

"Yes. Isn't that a good enough reason?" The skinny man lifted his chin a little. Then, he looked at Guenther. "Are we done, Mr. Guenther? I'm in the middle of the monthly revenue reports."

Guenther looked at Rodney, who looked at me. I shrugged. There would be time to dig deeper into Dellafiore's allegations. Our own forensic accountants would have a look at the Natural Wonders books. "Yes, thank you." I handed Dellafiore a business card. "We'd like your home address and phone number. In case we have further questions."

"I have to return to work. If you talk to Human Resources—"

Rodney cleared his throat. "We'd rather have it straight from the horse's mouth, so to speak."

"Oh." Dellafiore rattled off an address on the north side of the city and a telephone number. He looked at Guenther, then me. "May I get back to work now?"

Was he an aggravated employee or trying to escape? "We're good for the time being. We'll be issuing a warrant for the company financials for our own accountants to review."

He blinked some more. Was it an act? "Is that necessary? I'd be happy to share my findings in a full report. With Mr. Guenther's permission, of course."

"We appreciate your willingness to be helpful, but we prefer to get our own interpretation." Rodney smiled.

"Of course. Well, excuse me. Mr. Guenther." He bobbed his head toward his boss and hurried out of the office.

Once the door closed, Guenther faced us. "Poor Sylvia must have been at the end of her rope." He sighed. "I wish she'd have talked to me. There would have been consequences, but we could have handled it. I could have gotten her some help."

"You and Mr. Dellafiore are convinced this is a suicide." I crossed my legs. "I still don't understand why I'm not hearing this from other people."

"She never talked about it explicitly, you understand. She never threatened to kill herself." Guenther leaned back. "But her change in attitude, the affair, the gambling, the embezzlement—what else could it have been? Perhaps others, such as her husband, were too caught up in their own lives to notice." He spread his hands. "Or are you suggesting—"

"We aren't suggesting anything. We're gathering

information. If you'd agree to give us a copy of those financial records, it would be helpful. If we need to, we'll get it through formal channels."

"I'll have one made for you."

"We appreciate it. Thanks for your time." I stood. "We can show ourselves out."

"Yes, and call us any time if you think of anything." Rodney handed over his business card.

We walked out. I had no doubt we'd been fed a load of bullshit. The question was, why? Had Sylvia really been the cause of the missing money? Or was someone using her death to sidestep the blame?

———

Outside, Rodney put on a pair of sunglasses. "Talk about unexpected."

We were headed back to the office after the conversation with Guenther—me driving, Rodney reviewing notes in the passenger seat. "I wonder who Sylvia thought committed the bigger betrayal." I thought about the torn corner of the photograph in the empty frame. Finding out your sister was banging your husband would definitely cause that kind of rage.

"Husband or sibling?"

"Or whoever was stealing from her company." It was all very convenient. Everything in Sylvia's life fell apart and she threw herself over the Falls? Only in the movies.

The silence went on, and finally he broke it. "What do we do now?"

"Let's get court orders for the financial records for

Natural Wonders. I don't trust Guenther to give us shit. Check on financials for Sylvia and Keith Bramley." I parked in the lot and got out. As I did, I swept the street with my gaze, a prickly feeling on the back of my neck.

"What's got you so uptight? There's nobody around." Rodney's eyes narrowed.

I forced myself to relax. "Nothing. My back hurts from the seats in the car. Get general background information on Guenther and Dellafiore."

He seemed to accept the lame explanation because he went back to business. "Why both of them?"

"Guenther argued with the victim. Dellafiore may have exposed her criminal activity. Just do it."

"If you insist."

The implication I was wasting his time rubbed me raw. He wasn't going to last long as a detective if he automatically reached for the easy answers. Max had hammered that home to me. Maybe if I gave Rodney enough tasks, he'd get the hint. "I do." *And I shouldn't have to*, I thought. He didn't need to be as smart as Max to know this. "When you're done, get a phone number and address for Sylvia's sister, Gwyneth Walsh. I'd love to get her financial information, but I don't think we can. Yet. I want the contact info by the time I get upstairs."

"Are we ignoring Bramley?" The stiffly polite tone of Rodney's voice did not cover the implication he thought I'd gone off the rails.

"No, but we know where to find him." I parked in the station lot. "Call the casino hotel and see if he's checked out. The romantic getaway is over."

"If he has?"

"We go to his house. We'll see him after we talk to Walsh. I'll be up in a minute."

Rodney opened his door and paused. "Where are you going?"

"I'm going to clear my head."

"You wouldn't have to if you didn't insist on making this more complicated than it needs to be."

"What do you mean?" *Since when was being thorough a bad thing?*

"Her husband was having an affair. He argued with her. He lied to us. And he was the last one to see her alive. Pretty straightforward, if you ask me. I don't know why we aren't bringing him in for a talk."

Everything Rodney said was true. I wasn't ignoring it. But how was I going to make him see the simplest solution was not necessarily the best one, or even the right one? *Only by sticking to my guns*, I decided. This wasn't patrol work, where you got to hand off the dirty work of digging.

"I told you, we'll get to him. I'm sorry if you find the work an inconvenience, but this is how you run a homicide investigation."

He gave me a patronizing look that really pushed my buttons. I understood he wanted a quick end to his first case. He wanted to look good, prove he was up to the shield. But not at the expense of good police work. Neither kissing up or being pig-headed was going to impress me. Or Yannick.

"I'll pretend I didn't see your face." I pointed. "You've got things to do."

"Yes, sir." He slouched into the building.

Outside, I inhaled a lungful of air and immediately

coughed. One of the administrative staff stood off to the side, smoking.

I hadn't had a cigarette in five years. Not since Amy announced she was pregnant for the first time. I'd quit cold turkey and never looked back. Suddenly, I wanted one more than anything. "Got a spare?"

The young guy pulled a pack from his pocket and shook one out. "Need a light?"

"Please." I put the end of my cigarette to his and pulled. The sweet rush of nicotine flooded my system. My mind cleared and my nerves relaxed. Why had I ever given this up?

Because you and Amy agreed, the insidious voice whispered. *She didn't force you. You said it would be better for her and the baby. Now, look at you.*

I tried to ignore it. Amy didn't need to know.

You're a pathetic liar, Jackson Davis. A dirty habit won't fix what's wrong.

I shunted the voice into a corner of my mind. With everything else going on, I didn't need to be hearing voices. Besides, it was only this one. That's all I needed. Was it so wrong to put my needs first for a change? One cigarette wouldn't kill me.

Bramley was a strong suspect, particularly in light of the fact of his affair and inheritance of Natural Wonders. But I couldn't ignore this new information because it made things more complicated. I wasn't being pedantic. It was solid police work.

I took another drag and exhaled. Smoking soothed my raw nerves and calmed me down. Too bad it couldn't make those around me see everything my way.

CHAPTER
TWELVE

My spirit was significantly less ragged when I got off the elevator. I'd found a piece of stale gum in my pocket and chewed it. Thank God for the thin blue line. If Amy learned I'd had even a single cigarette, she'd have kittens.

And she should, the voice whispered.

Go away, I responded.

I found Rodney at his desk, hunched over a stack of paper.

"Status?" I leaned over to look.

"Background checks are running. Here's contact info for Gwyneth Walsh." He handed me a sheet, not meeting my gaze. "We've got the Natural Wonders stuff from Guenther. It may be bent, but he coughed it up."

"What about the warrants?"

"Those I haven't started yet. Decided to pull stuff off the web first." He sniffed. "Your breath smells like tobacco. Overlaid with spearmint. I didn't know you smoked."

"Heard anything about the laptops?" I sat down at my own desk.

He glanced at me. "Got a message from the tech guys. Still working, but they had some news. Lots of personal stuff. Letters, shopping lists, a few attempts at what look like household budgets."

"Deleted items?"

"They're focusing on the files that are there."

"Email? Web history?"

"She was still logged in to her social media accounts, but her last post is months old. A few pictures. Web history is a lot of news in the natural makeup world." He paused. "They also found a bunch of online gambling sites and searches."

"Really?" Seneca Niagara was not the only place Sylvia played. "What kind?"

He picked up his notebook and read. "Things like online Texas Hold 'Em. She sucked. Tech said the losses are staggering. The wins barely put a dent in what she owed." He handed me his notes, a list of websites and numbers showing the amounts wagered, lost, and won.

"Not only an in-person gambler, huh?"

"Her account has been suspended in three places for failure to pay her loss amounts. Up until she died, she logged on to these sites every day without fail. The sign-ins are usually in the evenings, between nine and eleven."

"Have we requested her records from Seneca Niagara?"

"Part of what is next." Rodney sipped from a cup of this morning's coffee.

I wasn't much of a gambler, but even I could tell

Sylvia hadn't had a good run. The amount of money wagered and lost boggled my mind. How did she afford a house on Grand Island when she was losing money like this? "She went to Seneca in the daytime. Looks like she gambled online, or elsewhere, at night." I scanned the notes. "This is serious money. Sylvia had a gambling addiction."

"I think you're right." He gave me another sheaf of paper. "I tried to rush the request on bank records for the Bramleys. First Niagara won't budge. We'll have to wait."

"It's only been two days." Friggin' bureaucrats. "I don't suppose Bramley will hand over his bank statements, huh?"

"I didn't even waste time asking. This," he waved at the stack in front of him, "is stuff from Natural Wonders. The info Guenther gave us."

"How likely is it to be correct?"

"Depends. Guenther told us the evidence of embezzlement came from in-house. It might show something."

I tapped my fingers on my desk. "Not if he's the culprit."

"I guess he could have said something to appease Dellafiore, but then why bring in the accountant? Or why not say he had it audited and Dellafiore was wrong?" He rubbed his eyes.

I shuffled the papers. "This make any sense to you?"

He shrugged. "I can barely balance my checkbook without a computer. I studied criminal justice, not accounting."

I took the paper and scanned the columns of

numbers. They didn't make any magic sense to me, either. "What about Bramley and Walsh?"

"Bramley is still registered at the casino hotel." Rodney consulted his notes.

"Weird." Why not go home? Unless he thought it would look suspicious if he did.

"I talked to him. Said he was staying until arrangements could be made to transport his wife's body."

"The autopsy was yesterday." I drummed my fingers on the desktop. "Sylvia's body should be released and arrangements aren't complicated. Call a funeral home. Why stay?"

"Dunno. But he is." He paused to drain the cup of what had to be stone-cold coffee. "I called Walsh's workplace. They say she's on vacation in Florida and won't be back until Monday. However…"

I looked up. Rodney had a smug look on his face. "You don't believe them."

"I think she's holed up with Bramley. I heard a woman's voice in the background when I called."

Talk about a good reason to stay. Hotels were safer and more anonymous than your house. Especially when your wife may have been murdered. Anybody might drop by to leave condolences. "What about Dellafiore?"

"No prior convictions, no outstanding warrants. He graduated magna cum laude from Buff State with a degree in accounting. Been with Natural Wonders about eight months. Address is an okay part of town. Car is five years old. Still working on past employment history."

My gut had a nagging feeling about Dellafiore. Max

would tell me to listen. "Get his financials. Let's ask someone to help. Maybe Dobrovski."

"I'm not sure why Dellafiore would be on our radar. He's only worked for the company for a few months, and he's the one who discovered the embezzling." Rodney leaned back. He thought I was nuts. It was in his eyes.

Maybe I was, but I didn't change my mind. "His story bugs me. I want more information before I cross him off the list of suspects."

"You suspect everybody. There's no evidence he's involved."

I pointed at him. "Lesson number whatever-this-is: All information is valuable. You follow it. Evidence will appear, or it won't. Closing off possibilities this early will tank the entire investigation."

It was a lesson I'd learned the hard way. By over-looking something and getting burned. I could try to help Rodney avoid the same thing. If he was smart, he'd listen. If not, he'd learn the hard way, too.

I stood and checked my watch. It was one. Plenty of time to file those warrants and make an unexpected visit. "Instead of going cross-eyed over numbers, I suggest we check and make sure Mr. Bramley is comfortable."

"See if he's got company?" Rodney stood and grabbed his jacket. "Should we call first?"

"And warn them we're coming? Don't be insane."

———

Upon reaching the casino, we proceeded to room 435. Rodney raised his hand to knock, but I stopped him. "Listen." I pressed my ear to the door.

There were two people in the room. One of them was female.

Rodney gestured toward the gun in his shoulder holster, but I shook my head. Whoever Bramley was with—and I had a pretty good idea—busting in with guns drawn was not necessary. Not that the situation didn't call for a healthy bit of caution.

I rapped on the door. "Keith Bramley. NFPD. We need to speak to you."

"Uh, be there in a minute." Bramley's voice came through the door, followed by hushed conversation, rustling, and the sound of an object, maybe a table, being knocked over.

I glanced at Rodney. He'd been right. Gwyneth Walsh was not in Florida. *Everybody lies*. The question was not why cops were so cynical, it was why everybody else wasn't.

When Bramley opened the door, he appeared to be the only person in the room. "Detectives. I wasn't expecting you. Please, come in."

We entered, and I scanned the room. It was a cluttered mess. A small table was out of place. It must have been what we heard knocked over. The pointed toe of a woman's shoe and the silky sheen of pink lingerie peeked out from under the bed. The air had a faint hint of citrus and musk. Perfume, not cologne. The bathroom door was closed.

"Where's your company?" Rodney watched Bramley while I surveyed the room.

Bramley played innocent. "Company?"

"We heard a woman's voice."

"TV." Bramley rubbed his chin. A convenient response. Flat-screen TVs didn't emit the warmth of the old, bulky sets. No way to check the veracity of the statement.

I put my hand on the bathroom door.

Bramley jumped forward. "I wouldn't go in the bathroom. I haven't cleaned up after my shower."

Bingo. "Then, it's pretty rude of you to shove your guests in there." I opened the door.

Standing inside the bathroom was a young woman wearing a hotel robe, no makeup, and tousled platinum blonde hair.

I recognized her from the pictures I'd seen. "Greetings, Ms. Walsh. Your boss said you were in Florida." I waved her out.

She stamped over to Bramley and glared at Rodney and me. "How'd you know I was here?"

I smiled. "You weren't exactly stealthy. Besides, a quick question to the kitchen would have told me they delivered room service for two." I pointed at the tray of plates on the table.

Rodney muttered under his breath. All I caught was the word "stupid." His opinion of them, or their opinion of us? Didn't matter.

Walsh tossed her curls and crossed her arms.

"You didn't call first." Bramley picked up a glass and put it down.

Rodney's voice was flat. "No, we didn't."

In addition to the scent of perfume, I detected the odor of cigarette smoke. An ashtray with a pile of butts was on the bedside table. From the lipstick stains on the filters, I gathered they were Walsh's. "When did you get back from Florida?"

She shot a look at Bramley. "Last night. Keith called to tell me about Sylvia. It's awful. Throwing herself in the river, going over the Falls."

"You spent the night here?" Rodney asked.

"I couldn't get a room," she responded, stone-faced.

Like we wouldn't check airline schedules. I looked around some more. No doubt she had only spent one night in the same room as her brother-in-law. At least, recently. But not because she had been out of state. More likely because her sister had been here. Bramley was prolonging the romantic retreat, but not with his wife.

"Sylvia always went for the dramatic." She tugged her robe closed, but not before I noticed she wasn't wearing anything underneath except a bra and panties.

My gaze settled on the couple. "Who said she threw herself in the river?"

Bramley flushed a brick red, but Walsh maintained an innocent look. "How else would she end up in the gorge? I assumed—"

"Naturally." She was right, but those details hadn't been released.

"Keith told me she drowned." She looked at us through narrowed eyes.

"Yes." I refused to break eye contact.

Her blood-red nails stood out on the white robe as she clutched the sleeves. "I didn't think the cops investigated suicide."

I kept my voice conversational. "We investigate any unattended death."

She glanced at Bramley.

"Until we determine it isn't homicide." Rodney's expression could've competed with any professional poker player.

Her blue eyes snapped to him. "Homicide? You mean murder?" She snorted. "Who'd want to kill Sylvia? Silly question. Lots of people. But who'd actually do it?"

I raised an eyebrow. "Her cheating husband? The sister who was sleeping with him?" I rocked on my heels. The smell of the room made me slightly sick, yet I craved a cigarette at the same time.

Rodney spoke up. "A spouse who wanted cash for a new wife?"

"I'm not cheating on Sylvia," Keith said at the same time Walsh burst out with, "We are not having an affair."

Rodney turned his head and uttered a stream of words that were audible, if not understandable.

I pinched the bridge of my nose. "Cut the shit."

Bramley and Walsh stayed silent.

"Sylvia knew you two were sleeping together. My partner and I showed up this morning to find you, Ms. Walsh, in a robe and not much else, in your brother-in-law's room when we've been told by your employer you are on vacation."

More silence.

"This room smells of cigarettes and perfume." Rodney pointed at the ashtray. "Cigarette butts with lipstick on them. Mrs. Bramley didn't smoke."

"More than I'd expect to see from a single night, unless someone's a serious chain smoker." As a former smoker, I'd know. "I doubt Mr. Bramley wears lipstick. I don't think he smokes. You, Mr. Bramley, said this was an attempt by you and your wife to *patch things up*. Right now, I've got my doubts."

Bramley glanced at his lover and licked his lips.

"We can go get a warrant for the hotel to tell us whether or not Ms. Walsh is registered here."

"You can't do that." Bramley's voice was full of false bravado.

"Watch us." Rodney put his hands in his pants pockets.

"Or you can save us the trouble and be honest. I don't care much. We'll find out either way." I continued as if no one else had spoken. "Who you two sleep with is not my concern. Finding out what happened to Sylvia is."

We stood in silence, staring at each other. It was true. I didn't care if Walsh and Bramley were having an affair unless I found out it was connected to Sylvia's death. It would be much better for them if they'd come clean, but I wondered if the realization would occur to them.

Rodney broke the silence. "So, Ms. Walsh, when did you get back from Florida?"

Walsh tossed her hair and strutted to the bed, where she tapped a menthol cigarette out of its pack. "I never left." She lit it up. "I bought the ticket, told everyone I was going, but never got on the plane. I came here, took a room on another floor under a fake name, and waited for Keith." She blew out a cloud of smoke and held out the pack. "Want one? You look like you could use it."

I shook my head. "When did you arrive at the casino?"

"Last Saturday night." She took another drag. "I holed up in my room and waited for Keith to call. I didn't want to run into Sylvia, so I stayed off the gambling floor. I knew it would be the first place she'd go."

Out of the corner of my eye, I noticed Rodney had taken out a pen and notebook, so I kept asking questions. It was becoming a pattern. "What made you think your sister would hit the casino first?"

She snorted. "You've got to be kidding me. You know Keith and I are screwing each other, but you don't know about Sylvia's gambling habit?" She flicked the ash off her cigarette.

"Sylvia had a problem." Bramley went to the mini-bar. "At least, I'm pretty sure she did. She spent way too much time down here, and our checking account used to get regular hits from sites I assumed were related to gambling."

"You said it used to." I shifted to look at him. "Maybe she quit."

He sighed and sat on the edge of the bed. "About six months ago, I told her she needed to get help. We argued. Afterward, she set up a separate checking account in her name. The suspicious withdrawals stopped coming out of our regular account, but there were regular transfers out. I think she was funneling money into the second account. For her gambling."

"You think." Rodney looked up from his notes. "You don't know? How could you not know?"

"Sylvia controlled the money." Bramley poured two

fingers of scotch. "She did almost everything online. I know the money went out. I couldn't tell exactly where it was going."

"You could have gone to the bank." I thought it was early to start drinking, but I wasn't being interrogated. "If your name is on the account, they'd have told you what was happening. You didn't try very hard. After all, you had what you needed in terms of money, right?"

He looked at me and nodded, then stared at the floor.

I glanced at Rodney. "When did you two start having your affair?" I asked Bramley.

"Around the same time." Bramley talked to the floor. "Right after we argued, Sylvia banished me to a second bedroom. Not that it mattered. We hadn't had sex in quite a while. We barely talked."

"Keith met me for drinks one night." Walsh picked up the story. "We started out talking about Sylvia, her problems, their problems, and ended up at my apartment." She stubbed out her cigarette. "I'm sure you can figure out what happened next."

I paced a bit. "Mr. Bramley, on the night you and your wife argued—the last time you saw her—when did you leave Top of the Falls?"

"I told you, Sylvia stormed out." Bramley swirled the scotch. "I stayed to finish my dessert. I didn't look at the clock before I left. Eight? Maybe a little later."

More freaking lies. Max had loved this game. It drove me crazy. "Try again. The waitress boxed both desserts, yours and your wife's. You left right after her. You didn't even wait ten minutes." I paused and took in

Bramley's mulish silence. "Mr. Bramley, where did you go after you left Top of the Falls?"

The silence stretched on until Walsh broke it. "For God's sake, he came to my room. We talked, had sex, and he went back to his room around eleven. Sylvia wasn't there. This whole *getaway* was more about the two of us having some time together than Keith and Sylvia making nice. Happy?"

It was an alibi of sorts. I didn't think it was unrealistic Bramley would come and see his mistress in his wife's absence, but an alibi from a mistress wasn't worth a lot. I played like I accepted it. Appearing to go along might elicit additional information. "What was in it for you?"

"Excuse me?" Her eyes narrowed, glinting like ice chips.

"You slept with your brother-in-law. Had a six-month affair with him." Rodney eyed her. "Are you in love? Did it to spite your sister? Or just for kicks?"

"You're a young, attractive woman," I added. "Why steal your sister's husband?"

She laughed. "At the start, it was fun, I suppose." She looked at Bramley, who sighed. "The satisfaction of taking something from Sylvia."

"And now?"

"Turns out Keith and I have a lot in common. And I still get to take something from my sister."

Rodney lifted his eyebrows. "Sounds like not a lot of love lost between you and Sylvia."

She stood, tossed her hair again, and cocked her head. "Love? I'm sure you don't need a wah-wah story about how I'm broken up over my sister's death and some bullshit about how devastated I am. You want the truth?"

Rodney and I exchanged looks. He shrugged, and I answered. "It would make things a lot easier."

"Then, here it is." She pulled the sash on her robe. "Sylvia was a lying, manipulative bitch. Always had to be first. Be perfect. She deserved everything she got and more. I'm not at all sad she's dead." She lifted her chin. "I hated my sister, but I didn't kill her. Although I'd love to shake the hand of the person who did and buy him a drink. Because that guy? He's my freaking hero. And that, detectives, is God's own truth."

CHAPTER
THIRTEEN

The first thing I did when we got back to the office was instruct Rodney to make sure our warrant affidavit included all of Sylvia's financial records, not only the joint accounts with her husband. "Get financial records for Walsh, too. See if anything pops."

"Got it. I'll check to see if Bramley has anything he hasn't told us about." Rodney grabbed a form. He stopped writing and looked up. "Guenther and the accountant say suicide. Sister mentioned suicide, but then jumped to murder. By the way, do you believe her? She didn't kill Sylvia?"

"She was pretty emphatic." It had been a masterful performance if it was a lie. Did Walsh have that kind of bravado in her? Of course, she'd snuck around with her brother-in-law. Not hidden from Sylvia, true. But her actions had more than a bit of bravado. The same attitude could be used to claim innocence of murder.

"Bramley didn't seem on board with suicide, though. At least, to me."

I sat and drummed my fingers on the desk. "Who knew Sylvia the best?"

He tilted his head. "Normally, I'd say family. Why do so many people assume it's suicide?"

"If someone's body is found in the gorge, and you think she went over the Falls, the first instinct is that she jumped or it was an accident." For normal people, at least.

"An accident?"

Right, Rodney wasn't a local. "Daredevils. People trying to go over the Falls in a barrel. Standing on the guardrail to pose for a picture. All kinds of stupid shit. Live here long enough, nothing will surprise you."

"Detective Davis? These came for you." Our department admin assistant handed me a thick manila envelope. "Records from Natural Wonders. A copy was sent to the forensic accountants, but they also brought a copy for you."

"Now, there's a fast turnaround. Thanks." I took the envelope and removed a stack of paper. Leaving Rodney to finish his requests, I got a Coke from the vending machine and sat at my desk to start reading. Too bad smoking wasn't permitted in public buildings these days.

While I nominally knew what I was looking at, the significance of it stayed hazy, at least on the surface. "I hate numbers." I pushed aside the paper and rubbed my eyes. "What the hell did we do before accountants? This shit might as well be in ancient Greek."

Rodney reached over and picked up the top sheet. "It's a balance sheet. The business equivalent of your checkbook register."

I snatched the paper out of his hand. "I know. I'm not an idiot." I stuffed the paper and the rest of the stack back in the envelope. "I know what I'm looking at. I don't know what it means. Money comes in and money goes out. Whether or not it's going or coming the way it's supposed to, well, damned if I know." I stood, put on my jacket, and grabbed the envelope.

"Where are you going?"

"Home. It's five o'clock. I've got a headache." I briefly entertained the idea of stopping at Max's again. But she had made her opinions pretty clear yesterday. I wasn't in the mood for another lecture, either about work or my resumed habit. I was sure she'd ferret that out with those super-senses she had.

But what if she needed something? Her place wasn't out of my way. Stopping wouldn't even make me late.

Piss on it. I'm going home.

I retrieved my keys from my desk drawer. "Maybe these numbers will make more sense when I have a whiskey in my hand. See you tomorrow."

He started to speak, then stopped. After a moment, he said, "See you tomorrow."

Poring over the financials with a beer was how Max and I would have finished the night. I'd have called Amy to tell her I'd be late, and we would have banged this out. I didn't feel the same sense of camaraderie with Rodney. Not yet. I wanted to trust him. *You should. He's your partner.* Max's voice rang in my head. I got the nagging sense I'd failed another test of a senior detective, but I'd already committed to going home. Too late to change course now.

I grabbed the envelope and headed for my car. What

was wrong with me? Sure, I'd always been the overly analytical one, maybe even too much so, but I'd always had a pretty good grip on what I wanted to do. Had it been because of who I worked with? Max had always seemed so cool and confident. I doubted she'd ever second-guessed herself.

But Max wasn't here, and it was my fault.

My hands were cool and clammy. All I could see was the car in front of me. A curtain had dropped around my vision, focusing it into a tunnel. My heart pounded against my ribs as I took rapid, shallow breaths. Bands tightened around my chest. The air around me was cool, but sweat ran into my eyes.

I put my hand on the car door, focusing on the cold metal, and inhaled as deeply as I could. I couldn't drive through a panic attack. I closed my eyes. *Not now. Please, St. Michael. Not now.*

The moment passed. Who had seen me? I twisted my neck, trying to see everywhere at once. There was no one around. No one knew.

But I did.

———

"I'm home." I tossed my keys in the basket and kicked off my shoes.

"Daddy." Madeline came running out. At least someone was happy to see me. "Yuck. You smell funny."

"I'm sorry. The people I was with today smelled, too." True enough, but it wasn't the only reason. I pushed the thought aside. "Where's your mommy?" I gave her a brief hug. The last of the panic attack had faded on the drive home, but I needed a hot shower to wash away the smoke and tension. Afterward, maybe I could talk Amy into resuming our interrupted alone time.

"I'm right here." Amy came into the hallway. "Madeline, go wash your hands."

Madeline scampered up the stairs.

Amy leaned in for a kiss, then made a face and backed off. "Ugh, you stink." She pushed me. "You quit smoking five years ago. We talked about this, didn't we?"

"Amy, please. Let me explain."

"What the hell is wrong with you? When did you start again?" She kept her voice a low hiss so Madeline wouldn't hear her, but the acid lacing her words was unmistakable.

"Nice to see you, too, dear." I slapped the envelope down on the hall table. "For your information, I was interviewing a woman at her hotel today for the Bramley investigation. She was smoking, not me." I started to hang up my jacket but decided it needed a trip to the dry cleaners. I chucked it down the stairs.

Amy said nothing.

"They were menthol cigarettes. You know I hated those. I appreciate your trust and confidence. Really, I do." The little voice started, but I immediately silenced it. Now wasn't the time. I was filled with too much righteous indignation to listen.

Amy bit her lip and some of the red receded from her cheeks. "Jackson, I'm sorry. I assumed." She reached out a hand.

I pulled back. "You know what they say about assuming."

"I said I was sorry."

I yanked off my tie as I headed up the stairs. I recognized the pressure building in my head and chest. If I stayed, I'd say something I'd regret, which I didn't want.

Yes, I'd had a smoke earlier. Yes, I had technically broken my promise. If Amy's reaction had been a bit more sympathetic, I'd have 'fessed up. Not now.

Steps behind me let me know Amy followed. *Damn.* The darkness pushed in again, and I pushed back. *Now's not a good time, either*. This wasn't going to work. Every little stressor could not make me freak out. It was a sure way to deflect conflict, but it would raise other issues, ones I really didn't want to deal with.

I shut the door to the bedroom and removed my shirt and slacks. I'd take them straight to the laundry. I didn't want them in the room. Behind me, I heard the door open and shut.

"Jackson, I'm sorry. You're right. I judged without knowing the facts and I was wrong."

"Not now, Amy. Please. Let me take a shower." I didn't face her. I couldn't bear it.

"Yes, now. We'll get distracted later. You have to see it from my view."

I tugged off my socks. "What's your view?"

"I don't know."

"Great. How do you expect me to respond?" *Don't say anything. Nothing good can come of this.*

"I want to help you."

"Jumping to conclusions doesn't help me." I

stripped off my T-shirt and faced her, wearing only my boxers. In days past, this would have led to interesting places, but I didn't think we were going there now.

"The last six months have been difficult. You haven't been the same." She tucked a strand of hair behind her ear.

I opened my mouth to reply, but she cut me off.

"I know what you're going to say. I'm not unsympathetic." She blinked, fighting back tears. "You're tense. Irritable. You go to see Max, but that doesn't make you happy, either. I don't know what to do."

"I am not irritable." *This is making me tense and irritable.* I threw my T-shirt in the hamper. Why didn't she understand?

"Yes, you are. You never would jump all over Madeline for things like leaving her trike out before. The only time you're at peace is when you're holding Christopher."

Because he doesn't talk. It was easier to relate to him and his simpler needs. "Speaking of which, she did it again. The tricycle. One of these nights, I'm going to hit the damn thing." Either on purpose or by accident. I wasn't sure which.

"See?" Amy threw up her hands. "I know how it goes. Kids, cops, wife. I get it. Max has said the exact same things to you I have."

"How do you know?"

She played with her hair again. "I just do. You piss her off to no end."

"Have you and Max been talking about me behind my back?" What was this, high school? I ran my hands through my hair. After everything I'd done for her, Max thought it was okay to gossip about me to my wife, of all people? The one person I thought always had my six. Turns out, I was more alone than she was.

"It's not how you're making it sound." Amy's eyes shone with unshed tears.

"Feels like it. I'll give you Rodney's phone number. The three of you can have a good time discussing me and my behavior." There it was. Exactly what I wanted to avoid: words I couldn't take back. The priest at our pre-cana conference had warned us about trying to talk before we'd taken time to cool down. We hadn't listened. Not this time. And look where it got us.

Amy hugged herself tightly. "Listen to yourself. This isn't you, Jackson. You're better than this."

I sank onto the bed and buried my face in my hands.

"Maybe if you go back to Dr. Alverson. Maybe—"

It was out of the question. I needed to be strong. I needed time, and I could get a handle on everything. "I do that, and I'll find myself back on desk duty. Or worse."

Amy didn't say anything.

"You think I'm bad now? Try me after another few months of doing nothing except answering the damn phone. I'll go out of my mind. The department won't put a detective who is in counseling on the streets." I wasn't sure of much these days, but I was sure of that.

The room was thick with silence. After a minute or so, I looked away. "Go downstairs. I think we've said enough, don't you?"

"I want my husband back." Amy's voice was barely a whisper.

My tension dissolved, leaving me feeling like a wet

dishrag. "Go eat. I'll be down after I shower. You're right. I smell like an ashtray. Let me unwind. We can talk later."

I walked to the bathroom. Behind me, I heard the door open and shut as Amy left without another word.

My anger bled out of me as fast as air out of a punctured balloon. *Great job. Way to be a good husband. You made your wife, the woman you love more than anything, cry. You asshole.*

I turned the shower water on as hot as I could take it. Having other people critique my behavior was difficult. Listening to myself? That was damn near intolerable.

———

If it hadn't been for Madeline, dinner would have been horrible. The gift of early childhood. She had the ability to be so self-absorbed, she didn't notice the overly polite behavior other people used to mask tension, so the fact her parents were treating each other like porcelain didn't faze her at all.

She and I cleared the table after dinner. While Amy tended to Christopher, I gave Madeline a bath and read a bedtime story. "Night, Squirt." I kissed her head and snapped on the princess night light.

"Night, Daddy. I love you."

"I love you, too." I blew my daughter one last kiss. Snuggled down in her pink sheets and bedspread, she returned the gesture. I pretended to snag it out of the air and place it on my cheek. Then, I shut the door. Why couldn't everybody be as accepting and understanding as my five-year-old daughter and infant son?

Downstairs, I retired to the den with a beer and the envelope of papers. I wanted something stronger, but we were out of bourbon. I don't know how long I sat there, but my eyes were glazing over when Amy appeared, wearing silky blue pajamas.

"How's it going?" She hesitated in the doorway.

I didn't need to be a trained investigator to see she was afraid of me. *Swallow your pride, you idiot.* I figured an apology would only make things worse, so I decided to act as though nothing had happened. "It's not going anywhere." I set down the papers and rubbed my eyes. "No matter how hard I stare, they're sheets of numbers. I don't know what I hoped to figure out. I should wait for the pros, but looking made me think I was doing something."

She sat beside me. Her hair was damp and she smelled like baby powder. "Let me take a look." She reached for the stack.

I handed it over. She'd been a tax accountant pre-kids. Her education had been one of the things that helped her to get along so well with Max. "Be my guest." I applied myself to the rest of the beer, an activity much more satisfying than studying numbers.

I studied the light glinting off Amy's hair, made even darker by the water. It was rather mesmerizing. I set the bottle aside and stroked the soft brown length. "I've always loved your hair."

"You're weird." She smiled as she flipped to another sheet. "So is this."

I stopped. "What?"

"What's the corporate structure at Natural Wonders, public or private?"

"Private. Sylvia was the majority shareholder. Other shares were divided, including some to her COO, Bert Guenther." I leaned over to look at the reports.

"Okay." She pointed. "Here are line items marked petty cash."

"Sylvia. It's her company. She can do that."

"Yes, but it has to be justified. Go back several months and it looks like the withdrawals were always less than one hundred dollars. Then, they get bigger. Up to a thousand. Here." She pointed again.

I looked. "Is it a lot?" My arm brushed Amy's shoulder as I reached for my drink.

"Yes." She flipped the sheet. "It's her company and she can take money. But you said they were looking to go public."

With my mouth full of beer, I nodded. Then, I swallowed. "Or something. Guenther told us they were looking at expansion that would require some sort of infusion of capital."

She flipped another sheet. "If I were conducting an audit, I'd want more details on this *petty cash*. Too much, too frequently. It might be legit, but then again, maybe not." She started muttering, doing calculations in her head.

Right. This type of transaction wouldn't be used for major business expenses, like new equipment, because those would need documentation for tax purposes. So, why was Sylvia taking so much cash?

"Then, there's this." Amy tapped the page. "Not cash withdrawals. Still playing with the numbers, but in a different way. This is a balance sheet. Expenses in this column. Income here. I'm not using a calculator, but I'm getting a different set of numbers when I do the math. Was Natural Wonders losing money?"

"Not according to their annual statements. They were making it hand over fist." I sat back. It didn't make sense. Why would the public statements show a profit, but the sum of the details not match the overall total?

Amy was comparing against the bank statements. "The bank balance isn't matching the operating statements."

This was why I wasn't a finance guy. My head hurt and I hadn't done anything except look and listen. "What do you think it all means?"

"Someone's skimming. I'd have to do a more thorough audit to be absolutely sure." She handed me the papers.

"How easy would this be to hide?"

"Depends on who's looking. How knowledgeable is the person? It's a lot of comparisons. If you're lazy or numbers make your eyes glaze over, it's easier." She poked me in the side.

I finished my beer. "If they were expanding?"

"It would be spotted easily. Hell, I saw it. You go public, the SEC starts looking. You try for a loan, the bank does the same." She pulled her legs up under her and the nightgown bunched over her thigh.

"Could it be more than one person?"

"Maybe. It's odd. Numbers shouldn't be odd, which is what I loved about them. The consistency. When they got inconsistent, that's when I knew there was a problem."

I set the papers on the side table. "When we interviewed Guenther, he said he suspected embezzlement at the company. We talked to one of their staff accountants who had the same story. He was the one who brought the issue to Guenther."

"Was it Sylvia Bramley?"

"According to them. And Guenther thinks it's the reason she was fighting to keep from expanding into new markets or going public." I scratched my chin.

"Because going public would mean an audit of the company finances. Any discrepancies would be found and investigated—"

"She'd be busted. Or whoever is at fault would be." I told Amy the background about Dellafiore's hiring and how the financial irregularities supported the suicide theory. If this had been going on for months and Sylvia hadn't spotted it, it didn't say good things about her abilities.

Amy rubbed my leg. "You don't sound convinced."

"Because I don't have the information. It's at least as good a motive for murder as infidelity."

"Sylvia found the money problems, knew who it was, and threatened to turn him, or her, in."

"Or she was about to be exposed. At least you've corroborated Dellafiore's story." I stretched out my legs, brushing Amy's thigh.

"Does that make you more or less likely to believe him?" She gazed at me, the skin of her face luminous without makeup.

"Neither. I'll have to wait for her personal financial

records. Money coming out has to go somewhere, right?" I laid my arm across her shoulders. Talking like this, I could almost pretend things were like they were before the accident.

She ran her hand up my leg. "You are incredibly sexy when you're being all detective-like." Her hand traveled higher and I twitched. She gave me a sly grin and leaned over to nibble at my neck.

"Amy." My voice was scratchy and I felt myself get stiff. "Don't wind me up like this unless you intend to wind me down, too."

"Who said I didn't intend to wind you down?" She breathed on my neck and nipped at my ear.

Her breasts brushed my chest and I grabbed her hip. She'd complained about the extra curves from child-bearing, but they were okay by me. "About earlier, I shouldn't—"

"Let's not talk about it."

Hey, I'd tried. If she wanted to drop it, who was I to say otherwise? I ran my hand through her damp mass of hair. "The last time we were at this point, Christopher interrupted."

She ran her tongue down my neck. "I just put him down." Her breath was hot against my cheek. "He should be asleep for a few hours at least."

I gripped her hip a little tighter. All thoughts of work, Max—hell, of anything other than my desire —evaporated.

CHAPTER
FOURTEEN

I slept better than I had in months. The good feeling lasted through the next morning, right up until I parked outside the office. With what I knew, what was the next step? As soon as I walked in the door, I'd be expected to have answers. To know exactly what to do.

What if I didn't? The bands tightened around my chest.

I took deep breaths and got out of the car. I'd figure it out. I had to. Max wasn't there to have one of her *a-ha* moments.

My hand was on the building door when Rodney's voice came from behind me. "Jackson. Wait up."

I turned to see him striding over. He held two cups in a Tim Hortons carrier and a bag. "I think I got it right this time. Medium roast, one cream, one sugar. One peanut stick. Yes?"

I accepted the coffee and bag. "Sorry. Didn't occur to me to stop and get coffee this morning."

"No sweat. I don't mind going first." He swirled his coffee. "You go through those reports last night?"

I nodded. "My wife used to work as an accountant. She agrees. Something was wrong."

"Then, we believe Dellafiore."

"On the surface." I fished the peanut stick out and tossed the empty bag into the trash by the door.

He shook his head. "You're a suspicious son of a bitch."

"Like it was any different on patrol. The shifty guy loitering in front of the convenience store was waiting for a bus. My ass." I brushed peanuts from my jacket and looked around at the parked cars. "Someone was filching money. Got it. Who? Was Sylvia killed because she was doing the taking or she threatened to shut down the taker?"

"The records indicate she made the withdrawals."

"True." I took a few steps toward the lot, turned, and walked back to the door. There was a detail there and I was missing it. "What about this?" I summarized what Amy and I had discussed the previous night. "Thoughts?"

"Kind of complicated. What's wrong with the simple conclusion Sylvia was embezzling? Husband was cheating. Husband killed her to one, get her money, and two, for the new woman."

"Nothing wrong with it. Only—"

A car backfired down Main Street and I nearly jumped out of my skin. Darkness pressed around my vision. The sounds and smells of that night crowded out Rodney's voice. I could smell acrid chemical smoke. Felt the heat on my skin.

"Jackson. Snap out of it."

I blinked and came back to reality. Hopefully, I could gloss over my reaction. Pretend nothing had happened. One look at his face told me, *fat chance.* I tried, anyway. "Sorry, got a little distracted running over the possibilities. Bramley has means, motive, and opportunity. So does Walsh, if you think about it. Now the question is—"

"Stop." His eyes narrowed. "You still having problems? Was that the start of an attack? Can I call someone for you?" He took a step back. Distancing himself from the leper.

"No." I took a deep breath. I didn't need Rodney believing he had a defective partner. Even if he did. "I'm fine. Not enough sleep, too much caffeine. Bramley and the sister."

He studied me, but I couldn't read the look in his eyes. Or his expression. Both obscured what he was thinking. "A random mugger. An unidentified person at Natural Wonders. Anyone else you want to throw in the mix?"

"Smart-ass. We need to start whittling the list down. Let's follow the information, see where it leads before we do anything." My cellphone rang. From the caller ID, I knew it was someone in the department, hopefully someone with a lead.

"Detective Davis, it's Tom Farraday. We've finished with the computer you brought in. You want to come down, or should we send you a report?"

"We'll be down. Type up the report for reference." I ended the call. "Tech guys have the dirt on Sylvia's laptop. I'll get some keys and we'll go."

"Screw that." Rodney put his hand on my chest to stop me. "I'll get the keys. I'm not letting you behind the wheel." He walked away.

I bent down to look at myself in the side view mirror of my car. "Holy shit." I looked like a fresh corpse. No wonder Rodney didn't want me driving. I brushed my hair back, wiping sweat from my hairline. "You are on the fast track to an insurance job, so get your shit in order." Did I have time for a quick smoke before Rodney returned?

"You say something?"

I flinched. Rodney had come up behind me unseen. He must have taken the stairs three at a time, or I'd been staring in the mirror for longer than I realized. "Nothing important. We've got a computer to see."

We headed over to City Hall, where the tech division was located. Rodney was silent on the drive. I had no idea what he was thinking, and it worried me. Was he planning to talk to Yannick when we got back? I'd let him drive for the rest of eternity if I could prevent that.

Before we went inside, I stopped him. "About earlier. Don't say anything. I don't want to end up back on a desk. Or worse. You don't want it, either."

"Why not?"

"Because you'd get a new partner. If I had to guess, it would be Dobrovski."

He shuddered. "I'll keep quiet. But Jackson, if you need help—"

"It won't happen again." I hoped it was the truth.

Farraday was a skinny guy who had as much hair on his face as he did on his head. He waved and led us back to a desk. I recognized Sylvia's computer, and he touched the pad to wake it up. "I've opened all the relevant sites on different browser tabs. You can look, but here's the gist. Internet history shows multiple visits to several online poker sites, which she visited two or three times a day."

"Stop there." I pointed at the screen. "I thought online gambling with real money was taboo?"

"You were misinformed. You can still find services that do real money gambling online. Some of them even have apps for your phone."

"How do you get the money in?" Rodney asked.

"Credit card, debit card, PayPal, funds transfer." Farraday shrugged. "Lots of options."

I clicked the first tab and saw it was signed in to her account. "You hacked her login?"

"Didn't need to. She used password management software. Which was good for her, because it can generate strong ones and she'd only need to remember the master."

"Good for us, too. You only have to break one," Rodney said.

"Exactly." Farraday pointed to the screen. "She lost quite frequently. As you can see, the sums aren't pocket change. At least, not any kind of pocket change I'm used to carrying. We're talking four and five figures."

I scanned down the page. "As long as they get their money, no one will care how much she lost."

"Exactly. Most of these were tied to the same credit card." He handed over a printout with a few highlights.

"Her name only. She paid the bill online, according to the history. She only got in trouble a few times."

I scanned the rows. Farraday was right. Not pocket change. "Looks like she exceeded her limit on the card."

Farraday sat. "Yep. Charge denied. Pay down the card, wait a couple days, charge clears."

"Payments to Wild Diamond, LLC. Who are they?"

"Wild Diamond runs a variety of online gambling sites." He handed over some paper. "Written report."

I handed the papers to Rodney. As soon as we got the final analysis from the forensic accountants, we'd compare it to what Farraday found. "That all?"

"Nope. She wasn't very good about deleting emails. There's a lot there, but I printed the ones that'll probably interest you the most." Farraday handed a stack of paper to Rodney.

He started reading and whistled. "Listen to this. 'You little whore. I suggest you stay away from my husband, bitch, if you know what's good for you.' Here's another, dated months later. 'Gwyneth, you've always been second to me, and you always will be. I gave you a shot and you blew it. I suggest you find yourself a new job. Take my pathetic excuse for a husband, if you want.' No love lost is putting it mildly. These two hated each other."

I scanned the printouts as Rodney passed them over. "Where does Walsh work now?"

Rodney handed me another sheet. "The makeup counter at Macy's."

"From this, I take it she worked for Natural Wonders at some point. We'll have to ask her." From a corporate job to a department store makeup clerk. Talk about a bump down. How much bitterness had that caused?

Rodney continued to flip through the emails. "Her sister isn't the only one Sylvia argued with." He paused. "Here's one to the VP. 'You heartless bastard. Screwing me is one thing. Screwing my company is another. If you won't settle this quietly, I guess the next person you'll hear from is my attorney. I'd pack your office if I were you.' Guenther didn't mention this conversation, did he?"

I reached for the page. "When is it from?" *Pack your office* sounded a little more threatening than a dispute over expansion.

"A week ago today."

"Right before Bramley said they left for their getaway." I skimmed the email. "When she talks about screwing her, what did she mean?"

"Literally or figuratively?" Rodney finished.

My thoughts exactly. I stood. "Anything on the work computer?"

"The personal one had the juiciest bits. She was smart enough to keep her personal stuff off the corporate system." He spun in his chair. "However, her browser history shows she visited the same gambling sites, once in the morning and again in the middle of the afternoon. I'll write up a full report and send it over to you later today. Monday at the latest."

"Thanks." I headed outside to the car. "Call the office. See if the legal papers have come in."

"Right." He pulled out his phone.

"When we spoke to the waitress at Top of the Falls,

she said she heard something about a prenup. I'd like to know what those details are."

Rodney shook his head. "If they aren't there already, I hope we'll have them Monday. Where to next?"

"I think we need to pay Mr. Guenther another visit. But first, let's get some lunch."

"Want me to drive, or are you good?"

I unlocked the doors. "I'm good. Driving will help me think. Besides, you need to call on those papers." If I had to concentrate on traffic, I'd be less likely to think about anything that would trigger another flashback.

The computer records were, indeed, facts. But for me, they asked more questions than they answered.

Lunch was fast food. Not my preference, but Rodney was right when he said we didn't have time for a leisurely meal. And since he'd agreed to keep quiet about this morning, I figured I owed him the decency to let him pick where we went.

We ate in silence for a few minutes. Then, Rodney piped up. "Idea one. Sylvia takes the money, tries to cover it. Someone discovered it and killed her."

I opened a ketchup packet. "Not suicide."

"It feels wrong. If that were the case, why hasn't Bramley said something about her mental state? Estranged or not, he is her husband." Rodney unwrapped his hamburger. "Here's what bugs me, though. Let's say Sylvia's stealing from the company. Why kill her? It's hers, right? So, she's ripping herself off. Turn her in, she goes to jail, problem solved."

"Yes, but remember, Guenther wants to go international. If Sylvia ruins the financial standing of the company and its reputation, she puts his plans at risk. He might find bumping her off and doing some damage control a viable option."

"Here's another question." He pointed a fry at me. "Clearly, the Bramleys had a subpar marriage. The sisters hated each other. So, why didn't either Sylvia or Bramley get a divorce?"

It was a good question, one for which I had no answer. Yet. "Couple options on why Sylvia was killed. Next question. Where?"

He sucked on the straw. "The dogs lost the trail near the footbridge to Green Island. No scent in the gorge. Must have gone in at the bridge."

I took a bite and thought about it. "Not necessarily. She could have gone in there, true. But she could've gotten in a car, or a bus. Or the dog lost the damn scent. It proves nothing."

"Shit, you aren't going to give me an inch, are you?" He shook his head. "Skip where she was killed for a minute. Who?"

"Bramley. Means, motive, and opportunity. He was with her when she was last seen, and he knew where she was going. He was cheating on her and doesn't hide the fact the marriage was on the rocks." I shook out a few fries. The spouse was always the primary suspect in a death. It sounded like a fictional cliché, but the stats backed it up. It didn't mean we should limit ourselves, though. That would be sloppy.

"Gotta put Walsh in the same column. She was at the casino waiting on Bramley and could've seen Sylvia leave. Plus," he took a bite, "there's the email."

The first one, maybe, but the second email made it

sound like Sylvia was all too happy to get rid of her spouse. "I really want to see the prenup. How much do you want to bet Bramley got almost nothing?"

Rodney's mouth was full, so he nodded.

"How long do you think Sylvia knew? I mean, if she was as uptight as everyone claims, why'd she put up with it?" I finished off my burger, wiped my fingers, and turned my attention to the remaining fries.

"The spouse, or significant other, is always the last to know." Rodney wiped his fingers. "That's the way it was for me."

A piece of the puzzle that was Rodney Kirke clicked into place. "Rachel *was* your girlfriend, wasn't she? And she cheated on you with a brother officer." The woman Daniels asked about at the scene. If I was right, it would definitely explain the tension between Rodney and Daniels that day.

He focused on his lunch. "Who said anything about her?"

"I remembered her name from the day we found Sylvia. It's—"

"I meant I would have been the last to know. My mother always told me I was too trusting."

Talk about evasion. But the question made me think. Would I know if Amy was cheating on me? Or did I have the same blind spot as every other married man? Despite being a detective. Hopefully, I'd never have to find out.

Rodney stuffed the burger wrapper in the empty fry box. "Anyway, it's one idea. Personally, I like it. You have other candidates?"

"Someone at Natural Wonders."

"The email with Guenther. The picture of them at the Bramley house. Another set of lovers? Maybe she dumped him in addition to wrecking his plans to go public." He sucked on his straw, but the resulting gurgle told me nothing was left in the cup.

"But did he know Sylvia was at Top of the Falls?" I started cleaning my own trash. "We don't know Sylvia was the culprit. Amy's conclusion was Sylvia might have been set up—someone piggybacked on her petty cash withdrawals or something."

"Who else would steal?" Rodney got up and went to the trash.

I followed him. "Guenther? Dellafiore? Someone else?"

Rodney snorted. "Dellafiore? Tell me you're not serious. He doesn't look like he could crush an ant, much less throw a grown woman over a railing."

"We're spitballing here. He's possible until the facts say he isn't."

"Then, we also have to include a mysterious mugger." He grinned. "It's possible until the facts say it isn't."

It was a juvenile, rookie tactic. Throwing my words back at me. But since he was technically right, I kept my mouth shut. I tossed my trash and headed for the parking lot.

He followed and paused by the car. "My money's on Bramley. He's got the trifecta. Why we aren't bringing him in for questioning is beyond me."

I opened the door. "Let's wait until we get the prenup."

Rodney muttered under his breath. I wanted to

demand to know what he said, but I could imagine it. Something along the lines of overcomplicating things. Max had tweaked my nose about the same thing quite often.

I was being pedantic. But if I wanted to keep the attention off my mental issues until I got them under control, I needed to keep the focus on Sylvia, which meant exhausting all possibilities. And if that made me a stubborn son of a bitch, there were worse things to be.

———

Rodney was downright sullen on the drive to Newfane. I parked and looked at him. "What's your problem? Don't tell me nothing."

He looked around, maybe thinking of what to say. "Why are you blowing me off? I'm new. I get it. That doesn't mean I don't have ideas."

"I'm not blowing you off."

"I want to know why we don't have Bramley in an interview room, grilling him within an inch of his life. And there's one other thing."

Here it comes.

"I can't figure you out. You're okay, then you're not. I don't know how I'm supposed to respond."

I got the feeling there was a lot more he wanted to say, but he didn't. "First of all, I am not ignoring you. Let's say we do bring in Bramley. Then, we find out his prenup gives him a big settlement. There goes his motive. Right now, as far as we know, Sylvia was more valuable to him alive, unhappy marriage or not."

Rodney looked away.

"I promise, if it turns out Bramley was better off with Sylvia dead, we'll bring him in. We don't know enough. Yet. As far as stiff-arming you…" I rubbed my chin. "I don't mean to. Honest. If I have, I'm sorry. I'm finding the return harder than I expected. Now," I opened the car door, "are we going to interview Guenther, or are you going to fume in the car?"

He glared at me and got out.

Max, what am I supposed to do?

Silent inspiration didn't strike, so I went into the building, trailing behind Rodney. The stiff posture told me he was still pissed. He'd have to work on that. It couldn't all be on me. I was right. At least, I thought I was. Of course, if I was wrong, I'd never hear the end of it. And not only from Rodney.

I leaned against the receptionist's counter while Rodney inspected the paintings on the wall. Now that we were inside, he had dropped the indignation. Or, at least he'd covered it well. "Are these originals?"

I wouldn't have known originals from paint by numbers. Rodney had some art knowledge in his background. *From Rachel?*

"They are." Guenther had entered the lobby unseen. "Sylvia was lucky enough to purchase the Miller and the MacRae in February on my recommendation. They were among her favorite pieces."

"American artists." Rodney looked at me. He turned back to the paintings. "Nice."

I took his word for it, seeing as my own art experience was currently comprised of the crayon drawings from my daughter. "Mr. Guenther, we have a few additional questions for you. Is now a good time?"

"Not really, but I get the impression you'll only come back, so we might as well talk now." He made a show of checking his watch.

"I think it would be best if we go to your office." I waved toward the hallway. "We'll follow you."

Guenther stared at us. For a moment, I thought he would refuse, but he turned and headed down the hall. Rodney and I followed.

Once inside, Guenther sat behind his desk, as though it might protect him from our questions. "I have an appointment in a few minutes, gentlemen, so I'd appreciate it if we could hurry this along."

"Certainly. Mr. Guenther, were you having an affair with Sylvia Bramley?" I sat and crossed my legs, studying his face.

Guenther, who had been drinking from a bottle of water, choked and began coughing. "I beg your pardon?"

"I think it was a pretty simple question, don't you, Detective Kirke?" I was pretty proud of myself, actually. The surprise question was an old trick of Max's, one I'd seen her pull off a number of times. I flattered myself by thinking she'd be proud of me, too.

"Indeed," Rodney said. "Unexpected, maybe, but simple."

"Mr. Guenther?" I focused on Guenther, whose face had become blotchy.

"I am a married man, Detective Davis."

"Which has nothing to do with whether you had an affair. Married people cheat on their spouses all the time. Keith Bramley did."

"I think you two should leave." Guenther stood.

"The city of Niagara Falls has spent enough money investigating a suicide, and you have wasted too much of my time."

Neither Rodney or I moved. "I find it fascinating you are determined this is a suicide." I put my elbows on the arms of the chair. "There's no evidence. Mrs. Bramley was not depressed. She didn't leave a note, didn't give away her possessions. She did nothing typical of a woman contemplating killing herself."

Guenther breathed heavily through his nose but said nothing.

"Such an insistence kind of makes us wonder." Rodney's voice sounded innocent. "Almost seems like you want to brush this under the carpet. Why?"

Guenther's eyes narrowed. He sat, folded his hands, and rested them on the desk mat.

"We've recovered some emails between you and Mrs. Bramley from her computer," Rodney continued. It wasn't good-cop-bad-cop, but the tag-teaming felt right. "It doesn't put you in the best light. You may want to take the opportunity to clear things up now, rather than wait for a more formal occasion."

"You have no right looking through her private correspondence." Guenther's gaze looked flat, almost predatory.

"We're investigating her death." Rodney's expression was calm. "We have every right."

"These emails talked about you screwing her and the company." I handed him a copy. "Naturally, we'd like to know if she meant literally or figuratively. Which is it?"

Guenther puffed up. "I don't have to answer that question."

"You're right, you don't. At least, not at this moment." I folded my hands. "Of course, if we determine Mrs. Bramley's death was murder and this goes to court, I'm sure the district attorney will put you on the stand. Once you're there, you'll either answer or be held in contempt."

"Are you threatening me?"

"No, I'm explaining how it could go." I leaned back. "I know this is a delicate question. If you answer and it has no bearing on Mrs. Bramley's death, or if it helps us determine no crime was committed, it need not go any further than this room."

The silence felt like it lasted forever. Suddenly, the fight went out of Guenther and he sagged. "There are things you need to understand. My wife and I haven't lived under the same roof for several years. She got tired of Western New York. She spends her time in Florida in the winter and New York City in the summer. I make money, Katharine spends it."

"Convenient." Rodney shot me a look.

"It cuts down on the fighting." Guenther sat back. "Sylvia was an intelligent woman. I could talk to her in a way my wife could never appreciate. It started out innocently enough, but after a while it became more. I think the tipping point came when she learned her husband and her sister were carrying on together."

I raised my eyebrows. "You were okay being a means of revenge?"

Guenther shrugged. "I knew Sylvia's motives were

murky at best. I'd been apart from my wife long enough it didn't matter. I was glad of the company."

"You had an affair?"

"Yes, damn it. We did. Satisfied?"

"I am." I straightened. "Why would she say you were screwing her company?"

The color returned to his cheeks. "Detective, I have no idea. I cut off the relationship with Sylvia a couple of months ago." He straightened his desk mat and fussed with the pencil cup. "It was not due to any sense of guilt. I thought it was unhealthy to encourage Sylvia's revenge on her husband. We also had a rather violent argument, after which things were rather strained."

"How violent?"

"Yelling, shouting." Guenther waved his hand. "Not physical, if that's what you're getting at."

"What was the argument about?" I leaned forward.

"Her gambling. I thought it was becoming problematic for her."

I thought about the information I'd seen. *Problematic* was an understatement.

"And you thought she was embezzling from the company to pay her gambling debts," Rodney said.

"I'm not seeing where any of this would make Mrs. Bramley think you were screwing her company." I didn't want to give Guenther time to make up another story, so I tried to keep the conversation going. "You wanted to make it more successful, not less."

"I don't know. Maybe in her anger and denial over the affair she concocted some idea I was out to ruin her and her company. She did build Natural Wonders on her own, with little help and starting from nothing. I came on about two years ago as growth was taking off." He looked at his watch. "I'm sorry. I'm late for my appointment."

I didn't move. "Where were you last Tuesday between six and midnight?"

Guenther frowned. After a lengthy pause, he answered. "At home, by myself. I ate dinner and watched a movie. I didn't even order out. I cooked, so there's no one to back me up. It's a terrible alibi, but it's the truth."

"What movie?" A nice question on Rodney's part. Guenther could have checked the TV listings, or been watching another way, but being able to name a movie would give his alibi more weight.

"It was a John Wayne marathon. *The Searchers*. Not one of my favorites." He looked at his watch again. "Now, I'm really late. I'd be happy to continue this conversation another time, although I'd appreciate it if you'd make an appointment. And I would like to have my lawyer present."

"That won't be necessary." I nodded at Rodney and we stood. "Thank you for your time. What is this meeting about?"

Guenther paused. "It's a discussion with representatives of a small cosmetics company in Europe about whether we could conduct a merger, which would benefit both our organizations."

Which would accomplish his goal. Especially now Sylvia was out of the way.

Guenther rocked on his heels. "This company is five hours ahead of us. I must get on the call. So, if you'll excuse me, I have work to do."

"We'll get out of your hair." Rodney straightened his jacket.

As we left the office, Guenther drummed his fingers on his desk, a crease in his forehead.

Outside, I leaned on the car. "Talk about illuminating." I pulled out my phone.

"What are you doing?"

"Checking the TV listings from Tuesday night." A few taps and I had what I wanted. "Well, he was either watching TV or he made sure he could name a movie. *The Searchers* was on the night of Sylvia's death between seven and ten." It would have been much more convenient if Guenther had been flat-out lying.

"Not helpful. What about the affairs? Doesn't anyone sleep with their own spouse?" Rodney snorted in disgust. "He killed her to get her out of the way for the merger. Or he's a jilted ex-lover. I still like Bramley better."

"I know you do." I slipped my phone back into my pocket. "It's entirely possible for Sylvia to have been embezzling from her company to fund her gambling addiction, but there's another possibility here."

"You think that's what Sylvia meant by screwing her company." Rodney aimed a finger at me. "Guenther was the one embezzling money, maybe to fund his ambition. And he tried to pin it on Sylvia. She found out, and over the Falls she went."

I waited a beat. "What's wrong with the idea?"

"It's elaborate and I don't quite buy it, but what if Guenther planned it all?"

I frowned.

"He wants to get Sylvia out of his way. He kills her,

frames her for embezzling, tries to convince everyone her death was suicide, and blames it on her gambling."

"And you're criticizing me for having complicated theories." However, it was an option other than Bramley. Still. So many possibilities. Too many. I needed them to start dropping away or we'd be at this forever.

We returned to the office to put in the subpoena for Guenther's financials.

Rodney stood by his desk and faced me. "I want to bring in Bramley."

I shuffled the papers on my desk. "I don't see a prenup. What are you going to ask him that we haven't asked already?"

He slammed down a folder. "Screw you. I don't know, okay? Maybe if we get him in a room, he'll fold."

"Or he'll call a lawyer and refuse to say anything." We didn't have any new information. We'd be talking from a position of weakness. Rodney started to argue and I cut him off. "I know you don't like it, but we have to wait until we have something to work with, to challenge him on."

"Because you say so, and you're the senior detective." His voice was scathing.

"You know it's the right decision. Think about it. We can't rush. We might only get one swing at him." He was new, but he was smart. If he took the time, he'd realize waiting was the right play.

He scowled. "Damn it, I wanted a quick resolution."

"Have patience. It'll happen. See you Monday." I left without saying another word. On a Friday, we should have been going out for a beer, but the day hadn't inspired camaraderie.

I should have spent some time on the weekend reviewing the case. Rodney wasn't the only one who wanted another crack at Bramley. But putting him in a room, shining a bright light, and pounding him with the same questions for hours wasn't going to work. Good TV, bad policing.

My weekend was booked, anyway. Saturday, I tackled my "honey-do" list. I also promised Madeline we'd go to the aquarium, something she reminded me of by jumping on me in bed at six-thirty Sunday morning. Off to the aquarium we went.

By three-thirty, I'd seen enough penguins, dolphins, and fish to last me for the next three years. Madeline loved it. I don't know what Christopher thought, but he stayed pretty happy through it all. Amy and I managed to not fight for the entire day. Nor did we discuss work or my mental health, which was probably why we didn't fight.

I did get dirty looks as I continually checked my phone and responded to texts from Rodney, who was at the office.

"Can't you put it away for one afternoon?" Amy hissed at me, our conversation covered by the aquatic show.

"Not when I'm in the middle of an investigation." I

focused on the leaping seals. "Be happy I was able to get away for a day in the first place."

Amy's lips moved, but I couldn't make out her words, which was almost certainly better for both of us.

"Pizza for dinner, Daddy," Madeline sang as we pulled in the drive at home. "You promised. Pizza for dinner." She scrambled out of the car.

I stared after her. "She remembers the fact I promised her pizza two weeks ago, but she can't remember to put her tricycle away."

"That's kids for you." Amy lifted Christopher from his car seat. Her smile faded as my cellphone rang. "Work?"

"Max." I answered the phone. "What's up?"

Amy sighed and got out of the car.

"Hey." Max's voice was hesitant. Something had happened to make her call me on a Sunday and she wasn't happy about it.

I ignored Amy to focus on my partner. "Is there a problem?" It was the only explanation for her tone.

She swallowed. "I didn't want to bother you on a weekend. You're probably with Amy and the kids." She paused. When she spoke again, her voice was low and rough. "There's water coming out from under the kitchen sink. I called the super. He instructed me to put down towels and he'd look at it Monday. Not an emergency."

I got out of the car and followed Amy into the house. I shook my head at her questioning look. "And?"

"It's soaking the towels. I'm afraid I'll slip. I'd rather not call a plumber."

"A weekend job will cost a fortune." I finished the sentence. If it was a simple leak, I might be able to fix it, or at least patch it enough to last until tomorrow. If it was serious, I could let Max know she should call and demand someone look at it tonight. "I'll run over and take a look. We just got home. It'll give Madeline time to unwind. Besides, we have to wait for the pizza to get here."

"Jackson, I'm sorry. I mean it." Another awkward pause. "On second thought, never mind. I shouldn't have bothered you. I'll figure something out."

"It's not a problem. I'm here to help. Be over as soon as I can." I ended the call, went inside, and found Amy in the living room. "That was—"

"I heard." She'd put Christopher in his swing in the dining room. I could hear Madeline singing in the TV room, some commercial jingle.

"Water leak. Building manager says it's not an emergency, but he didn't even look." I touched her arm. "I owe her, Ame."

Christopher squawked and Amy fetched some Cheerios. "You promised your daughter. Max wouldn't want you to ditch her. and I'm sure she said as much."

"I promised we'd go to the aquarium. We did."

"Where you spent the whole day texting your partner."

I ignored the accusation, and not just because it was true. "I told her pizza, and we will. Think of it as a useful way of killing time." Amy's expression cut me. I thought we were on the same page on this. Apparently not. "I can't ignore Max. Who else does she have?"

Amy shook her head. "Go. I'll order. Try to get home before the pizza is cold." She picked up the phone.

I retrieved my toolbox from the garage. I understood how Amy felt. My job did take a lot, and family time was something to be protected when possible.

Max was family. Especially after everything that had happened.

I saw Madeline's face pressed against the window as I pulled out. *I'll be back before the pizza even gets here,* I told myself. I could make good on my promise to my daughter and take care of the person who'd made it possible for me to keep doing what I needed to do.

I'd figure out the Sylvia problem. I'd get my panic attacks under control. I'd make up with Amy.

Superman had nothing on me.

———

Determined to prove to Amy—and myself—I could do it all, I may have broken a few traffic laws driving to Max's apartment. Instead of wondering why the spot in front of her unit hadn't been claimed by another tenant, I was grateful it was free.

I knocked before opening the door. "Max? It's Jackson."

"In here." Her voice floated out of the kitchen.

I found her groping for wet towels and laying down more. A fine sheen of water leaked from under the sink and covered the floor. Leroy watched the action from the countertop.

"I can't slow it down. It soaks every towel within

minutes." Max stood and leaned against the counter, fists clenched, her voice a low growl.

I laid a hand on her shoulder. "Let me take a look. If I can't fix it, I'll get you taken care of until Monday." I made sure she made it safely to the table before dropping to look for the leak.

"Sunday night and you're here." Max ran a hand through her hair. "Damn it, I'm sorry. How was the aquarium?"

Everything stopped for the job, but no cop wanted to pull a partner away from family, especially when family involved kids. "Same as usual. Amy understands. It'll be okay. Madeline and Christopher won't even know I'm here." I shone a light under the sink. Sure enough, a steady stream of water was issuing from the cold water line. "I'm sure she went right back to the TV and he's—"

"A baby." I could feel Max's gaze on me. Blind or not, it was a powerful force. "Did I totally screw your day?"

I reached in and twisted the connection with a wrench. It didn't move. "No. Seriously, no. Where's your water shut off valve?" I looked over at Max's defeated figure, slumped on the chair, head in her hands. "You don't look like you've had a good day."

"Utility closet." She waved her hand down the hall. "It hasn't been one of my better ones."

I went and shut off the water, then returned to the kitchen. "Anything I can do?"

"Not really. New washers and dryers. Front loaders, very snazzy. All LED indicators I can't read. Had to ask

Mrs. Dockerty to help me. Imagine needing to get laundry help from a woman almost twice your age."

I could hear the anger and frustration in Max's voice. "We'll figure something out." I forced cheer into my voice. I'd never seen her like this. Dejected. Not even over a stubborn case.

You made her this way, the little voice hissed.

I applied more force to the wrench and was rewarded with movement. The plumber's tape on the threads was almost gone. I retrieved a roll from my box and wrapped new tape. That should slow the leak.

She shook her head and leaned forward. "Let's talk about work. Catch any more dead bodies?"

The conversation had gotten a little too close to things we both would rather not discuss. "Nope." I mopped up the remaining water and laid down a dry towel to see if the pipe still leaked. "I don't need another. This one is proving to be a royal pain in the ass. Hold on a sec." I headed back to the utility closet.

"What's the problem with it?" Max called after me.

The puzzle aspect had always been her favorite part of the job. "We still don't know murder or suicide." I reopened the water valve, then returned to the kitchen. "The VP of Natural Wonders is gung-ho on Sylvia killing herself, yet no one close to her has said a word about her being depressed."

"That makes you suspicious." She drummed her fingers on the table.

"Rodney wants to bring the husband in and grill him."

"Motive?"

I told her about Keith's affair with Gwyneth,

Sylvia's gambling addiction, and the missing money from Natural Wonders.

She continued to stare at me, fingers twirling Leroy's tail.

"I suppose Sylvia could have gotten into trouble over the gambling, although there's no evidence. Or her husband wanted her out of the way. Or maybe the VP was angry—"

"Stop."

I blinked. It almost sounded like the Max I knew, and I expected her to launch into a lecture. She did, but it wasn't what I wanted to hear.

"Didn't I teach you anything? You're spiraling. Focus on one possibility. Eliminate it and move on. Forest, trees." She stood and waved in the general direction of the sink. "Is it fixed?"

"It's good enough for now. Leave a towel underneath the sink. You've got the occasional drip, but it should hold you until the morning." I put away the wrench and tape. "I need you."

"No, you don't."

I looked at her. "You were always the smart one."

"Oh, don't be stupid. You're as smart as I was. Am." She rubbed her forehead. "You're right, I miss the job. Hell, it's all I've ever done. I have to find something new."

Apologize, the voice whispered. I opened my mouth, but the words stuck in my throat. What good would it do to bring it up? It was a night we both wanted to forget had ever happened.

As if we could.

"It's not important." She stared out the window. She

sniffed and cocked her head. "Why are you smoking again?"

I sniffed my jacket sleeve but didn't smell anything. "I'm not." If she'd been able to see my face, she'd have spotted the lie.

"Liar." She crossed her arms. "Does Amy know?" She didn't even wait. "Of course not."

"It was one, maybe two. A moment of weakness. It won't happen again."

"Mmm hmm."

I slammed the toolbox on the table. "Knock it off."

She didn't move.

"The fix should hold overnight, but make sure the super comes tomorrow. If he doesn't take care of it soon, it'll only be worse." I picked up my things and headed for the door.

Max's voice stopped me in my tracks. "You're better than you think you are, Jackson."

"Goodnight."

I left, my unsaid apology dead on my lips and my conscience kicking me in the back of my brain.

You're better than you think you are.

Max's words were more of a lie than anything I'd said to her, or anyone, in the last six months.

The next morning, I rummaged in the basket for my keys. I felt like I'd had one too many the previous night, which I hadn't. I wanted a cigarette, but I was determined to prove I had a handle on things.

As I searched, Amy came into the hallway, arms clasped around her middle.

"You seen my keys? I'm gonna be late." *Where the hell are they?*

She lifted a hand to show my keyring dangling from her finger. "These?"

"Come on, Ame. This is no time for games." I reached for the keys, but she jerked them out of reach. "Seriously? You're doing this now?"

Her chin lifted. "You want your keys. I want you to ask about more counseling."

My wife was blackmailing me. "I've been cleared. I fail to see—"

"You had a nightmare last night." Her stare challenged me.

I had no response. My dreams had been troubled. Had it been a reaction to the conversation with Max? It had been as close to talking about the accident as we'd ever come. My subconscious had replayed the explosion, people dragging Max's limp form away from a cloud of chemical fumes and into an ambulance. It was all my imagination. I'd been unconscious for that part of the evening, but it must have been what had happened. I hadn't woken up, but I must have cried out if Amy knew about it. I could cover up panic attacks. *How do I hide something subconscious?* "Yes. My dreams were a little unsettled. It happens to everybody. Please give me the keys."

"It was more than a little. You were practically crying." Her hand tightened around the keys. "If you won't do this for yourself, do it for me. For Madeline and Christopher."

She was bringing the kids into it? Low blow.

"You think Madeline doesn't notice when you're in a mood?" Her voice trembled. "You need help and you won't take it from me. Why won't you admit it?"

I clenched my fist and stared at the keys dangling in front of me, yet out of reach. Like normalcy. "If I go back to therapy, they'll kick me back to desk duty. Or worse. People are relying on me. You, the guys at the office, Max. How am I supposed to support you if I'm not doing the job?" If I wasn't whole, I was broken.

"Which is precisely why you need help. You don't have to do it all alone." She sniffed and tears welled in her eyes, but she wouldn't let them fall. "For us, Jackson. If you love us. Promise me."

She wasn't going to give up those keys until I

relented. "I'll ask. I don't know how much more the department will cover, but I'll ask. Please. Give me the keys. I've got to go."

She let me take them, but she clutched at my hand as I did. "We love you. You know that, right? I want you to be like you were. Or as close to it as possible."

Didn't she know I was trying? It seemed like the tighter I held on, the less control I had. How much more did the universe expect me to do? "I *do* know, Ame." I squeezed her fingers. "I'm trying. Give me time." I brushed a kiss on her cheek, which was now damp and salty. "I'll see you tonight. Give the kids a kiss for me."

I rushed out the door. I had barely enough time to stop for coffee.

What do you want from me, God? I'd done the therapy. I was back to work. I balanced family, job, and Max. What more? I was doing it all and it still wasn't enough. What cosmic wrong had I committed that meant I was forced to watch myself fail those who mattered most over and over and over?

I gripped the steering wheel. A car behind me honked. The light had turned while I was lost in thought. *Stop being a cop,* Max had said. But I couldn't. It was who I was. I was fine. I needed time, space, and patience. My kids understood. Why couldn't everyone else?

"Davis. My office, please." Captain Yannick beckoned as I entered.

Shit. I was late. More than a little late, too. He was

going to bust me for that, and for the lack of progress on Sylvia. "Yes, sir." I followed him and sat on the edge of the chair he kept for visitors.

"Close the door." He cracked a smile. "Relax. For God's sake, you look like my kid when he's been caught sneaking candy."

I breathed a sigh of relief. "You can't blame me. You aren't big on casual conversation." I sipped my coffee. "What's up?"

"It's been a week since you got back. How's it going? You need anything? I know it can't be easy, so I wanted to check in with you." He looked at me, eyes intent.

I tensed. "It's good. I'm fine. I don't need anything." I paused. "Rodney's a typical newbie. Eager beaver. But I'm working on it." *You promised Amy*, my conscience nagged me. "I do have a hypothetical question for you."

"Shoot."

"If I said I needed to go back to the shrink for another conversation or two, what would be the deal?" I studied him over the rim of my cup.

His eyebrows pulled together. According to him, I'd been half of his best team. Of course he was concerned. "PTSD is no joke, Davis."

"It's only a question. My wife, well, you know how spouses worry. She asked me and I didn't have the answer." I sipped my coffee, trying to stay calm.

He leaned back and folded his hands. "Are you requesting additional counseling?"

"Not at all. I'm fine, sir. Hell, the only problem I have is solving Sylvia Bramley's murder." My response was fast, probably too fast from his expression.

"You know I got a final assessment from Dr. Alverson."

I nodded. *Shit.*

"Her conclusion was cautiously optimistic. You showed significant improvement, enough for her to return you to full duty. But she said to be alert for relapses." He fixed me with a look that could have cut through Ontario limestone. "I need you to play your A game, Davis. Do you need additional therapy?"

My career flashed in front of my eyes. I was determined not to fail, not to tell him I wasn't up to the job. And I couldn't let Amy leave the kids and return to work. We'd made an agreement years ago. I brought in the money, and she took care of the kids. I would not renege on my promises.

My heartbeat thundered in my ears. I was sure it would give me away. I kept my face still. "No, sir. Sure it's a little work adjusting, but it's nothing I can't handle."

His expression didn't change, but there was a sympathetic glint in his eye. "How about a compromise?"

"Sir?"

"You go back for two sessions. We leave you on duty. Get the doc's assessment. Regroup."

I thought about it. It left me on duty, at least temporarily. But it was still a risk.

"Davis?" Yannick's stare was piercing, like he could see right through my soul. "I don't think you would have asked if you weren't at least a little concerned. I urge you to take me up on the deal."

"Can I, uh, think about it?"

"You've got until the end of the day. Dismissed."

————

I high-tailed it back to my desk. Rodney was already there, with stacks of paper cluttering his desk.

He looked up at my approach. "Morning." He frowned. "You look like shit. Are you okay?"

I put down my coffee, the paper cup clunking on the desk. "Of course I am. Why does everybody think otherwise?" I looked around and threw out my arms. "Hear me, people? I'm fine. Leave me the hell alone."

"Hey, Davis," Dobrovski called from across the room. "Are you okay?" He and his buddy broke into laughter.

I flipped them off then sat at my desk, adjusting my jacket in the process. "Where's the stuff they seized from Sylvia's office?" I pawed through the stacks. What a friggin' mess.

"Right here." He pushed some paper toward me and lowered his voice. "Anything I should know about?"

I shook my head. Rodney hadn't earned the right to know my personal affairs.

"Weekend okay?"

I kept shuffling papers, not meeting his gaze. "Why wouldn't it have been?"

"Jackson. I know I'm not Max, and it's pretty obvious I haven't covered myself in glory in your eyes. But," he paused, "I want to do the right thing here."

I closed my eyes. *Breathe. Count to ten.* Taking out my frustration on Rodney wouldn't help. I'd only feel worse. I opened my eyes and focused on the paper. "It gets a little old, being asked if you're okay all the time."

There was no response.

I glanced up at him. He was studying me like I was a particularly interesting science specimen, one eyebrow raised. I grunted again.

His voice remained low. "From what I can see, you've got a lot going for you. Career. Wife. Kids. Don't self-destruct."

"I appreciate the concern, but I'm not going to self-destruct. I need people to let me do the job. Now, can we discuss the case? Please?"

For a moment, I thought he was going to keep on me, but then his shoulders jerked in a mini-shrug. "Whatever. I want you to know if you need to talk to someone, I'm here."

I barely knew Rodney, but his words shamed me. "Anything new come in on Sylvia over the weekend?"

His voice returned to a normal volume. "Not really." He sorted through some paper. "I haven't found anything interesting from her desk. She was compulsively neat. Even sorted her paperclips by size." He handed over the inventory of items taken from Sylvia's office at Natural Wonders. There were no personal papers, no random love letters, no intimate details. The interesting things were on her computer.

I scanned it. "Did the guys who inventoried the office talk to anyone?"

"Only in the most cursory fashion. They were interested in the stuff. Left the people to us." He looked through another couple of piles.

"Now I'm the one with the question." I pointed at

the mass of paper. "How can you find anything? Wouldn't it be easier to, like, categorize or something?"

He waved at my desk, which was immaculate except for the papers I'd been reading. "Let me guess, Max was like Sylvia."

No, I was the one who sorted paper clips. Max's system could be generously described as *controlled chaos*. "No. I never understood her, either." I straightened the nameplate on my desk. "I can't work with clutter. Things should be put in their proper place."

"Well, let's say I'm somewhere in between the two of you. It works for me." His lips twitched. "We still need to find the crime scene, too. Where Sylvia actually went in the river."

We did. But I had no idea how to do that. We couldn't comb every inch of ground from Top of the Falls through the state park.

I stood and buttoned my jacket. "First, let's see if we can find someone who can give us a fuller picture of Sylvia. She doesn't come off too well from her husband, sister, or VP. Someone had to like her. It would give us a better idea."

Rodney followed my example, snagging his jacket from his chair. "Are you sure you're okay to drive?"

"Get in the car."

Before we left, I printed out some information. Then, we made a short stop. The Niagara Gorge, where Sylvia's body had been found.

"I don't know why we're here." Rodney stood by the car. "All this has been searched already."

It had. But I had to satisfy my curiosity. I picked my way down to the shoreline, paper in hand. *You're wearing the wrong shoes. Again.* This time, it was Max's voice I heard, critical but amused at the same time.

The day was clear, the sky a perfect blue. At this distance, the sound of the Falls was merely a background rumble. Clouds of mist rose to my left. The sun meant a clear rainbow. If I'd looked, I'd have seen the Rainbow Bridge, with cars shuttling between Niagara Falls, NY, and Niagara Falls, Canada. But I was focused on other things.

I consulted the paper in my hand. Then, I looked at the water. It moved, swirling gently as it headed east. Bits of wood and bracken caught in nooks and at the shore. Down here, away from the cascade of water, there was less of the scuzzy foam. The river was calm enough it was virtually silent. A few weekday hikers walked behind us. All of them slowed briefly to watch but thankfully did not stop for photos.

"What the hell are you looking at?" Much more careful of his footgear, Rodney had come up behind me.

"Current patterns for the gorge." I looked at the paper again.

He looked around and tugged at his jacket. "There's a current?" He waved at the still water in front of us.

"Okay, I know you're not from here, but surely you studied New York history."

"In seventh grade. Re-educate me." He took a step, the debris from winter crunching underfoot.

I gestured to illustrate my points. "Short version. Lake Erie flows into the Niagara River. Over the Falls, down the gorge, into Lake Ontario. So, yes, there's a current. Not as strong, but it's there." I shook the paper at him. "This describes the patterns. I'm trying to figure out if Sylvia was dumped here, or somewhere else and this is where she ended up."

I went back to studying the water, trying to visualize. If I was the killer, what would I have done? I'd have pushed the body further out, where it would have been caught up and landed somewhere else. Not here.

Rodney took the paper from me. He must have come to the same conclusion. "I don't think she was killed in the gorge. A smart killer would have made sure she washed up downstream…or whatever the hell you call it."

I nodded and pulled a cigarette from the pack in my

pocket. I'd picked one up earlier with my coffee. *To keep at work.* I lit up and used it like a pointer. "Agreed. She floated here. Our scene is up top." Still a big area, but we'd cut it down. There were only so many logical entry points.

"I didn't know you smoked."

"I don't, not really." I mashed the cigarette on a rock. A couple puffs had been enough to stave off my building headache. "Let's head out to Natural Wonders. Searching the entire park isn't efficient. Maybe someone there can give us a clue as to where Sylvia might have gone after leaving Top of the Falls." I avoided his gaze as we made our way back to the car.

At Natural Wonders, we parked in a visitor's spot and surveyed the building. For a company all about natural mineral cosmetics, the office was terribly modern: glass, chrome, and harsh angles. It reminded me of the "flash cube" building near the state park entrance, cold and severe. Maybe the bushes around the front would soften things once they'd finished their spring flowering.

"Looks new." Rodney scanned the building. "It's very stark. I wonder if Sylvia designed it."

"No clue. Let's go in." We entered the building and approached the receptionist. "We'd like to speak to members of the staff." I held out my badge. "Sylvia Bramley's personal secretary, if she had one. Any other people who interacted with Mrs. Bramley on a regular basis."

The receptionist frowned.

"We're trying to put together a picture of Mrs. Bramley's life." Rodney leaned on the desk and flashed a smile. "Especially her last days."

"Did you talk to her frequently? What was she like as a boss?" I leaned on the counter while Rodney took out a notepad and pen. Our standard routine.

The girl—Marcy, if the nameplate was right—bit her lip. "She was pretty nice. I've definitely had worse. It's hard being a female CEO, I guess. Natural Wonders was her company, her baby. She was very proud. But it made her touchy."

"How so?"

"Demanding." Marcy thought. "For example, she insisted the front lobby be immaculate, even if we weren't expecting guests. Fresh flowers every couple of days. If they looked wilted, she'd be furious."

"What else?" There was more. I sensed it. This was the beauty industry. Appearance was everything. I was sure Sylvia hadn't stopped at flowers.

"She once sent me out for a manicure because I hadn't had time to take care of my nails in a while. She was known to offer makeup tips and free samples to the female admin staff. She even did a consultation for Helene, her personal secretary."

Rodney scribbled notes. "Doesn't sound good."

Marcy tilted her head. "Oh, no. It wasn't like that at all. I mean," she chuckled, "yeah, keeping up with the flowers was a pain. God forbid I show up with chipped nail polish. And nobody likes being yelled at. But Mrs. Bramley was really kind. My boyfriend broke up with me, by text, in the middle of the day last summer. I was devastated because I thought he was going to propose. Mrs. Bramley was right there with Kleenex, chocolate, and kind words. She let me leave early. Later, I got a gorgeous flower arrangement and a box of company cosmetics. 'The best revenge is looking beautiful,' was written on the note."

"Was she like that with everyone?" I asked.

"Oh, yes. I'll buzz Helene, you can talk to her. I've worked for other companies. Honestly, now that I think about it, Mrs. Bramley was the nicest boss I ever had."

"Thanks. If Helene has a few minutes to talk to us, it would be very helpful." I continued to lean, but Rodney inspected the flowers. They did look fresh. Amy would love them. *You should get her some callas.* The thought flitted across my mind. *Later*, I promised myself. When the investigation was over. The least I could do was show my appreciation.

"These are expensive arrangements." Rodney moseyed over to me. "I bet Sylvia plunked down a few hundred dollars a week in flowers."

"Welcome to the beauty industry." *All style, no substance?* A woman in her thirties, wearing an elegant silk blouse and linen skirt, rounded the corner. Her face was flawless and her hair was pulled back in some sort of knot at the base of her neck.

I held out my hand. "Detective Davis. This is Detective Kirke. You're Helene?"

"Helene Montgomery. Marcy said you wanted to speak to me?" Helene arched a perfectly groomed eyebrow.

I introduced myself. "If it's not too much trouble. We can talk here or in an office. Your choice."

She waved a hand that looked like it had never

known manual labor. "Here is fine. What can I help you with?"

Rodney took out his pen and pad again. "You were Mrs. Bramley's personal secretary?"

"Yes."

"For how long?"

"About five years."

Helene was not going to offer any details. No gossip for her. I changed my tactic. "How did you come to work for her?"

"I was the receptionist for a construction company." Her smile was faint. "I saw the opening in the paper and thought it might be interesting to work for a beauty company instead of with men covered in plaster dust. I'm afraid I didn't give Mrs. Bramley a very good impression. She hired me, but the first thing she did was send me for a full-day session at a local spa."

Rodney's expression was mildly surprised. "Kind of rude, don't you think?"

"Oh, no, it was wonderful. I'd never be able to afford such an indulgence on my own." Helene smiled. "All expenses paid. I'd never felt so pampered. We are a beauty company. Mrs. Bramley was very insistent about looking the part."

"Marcy," I nodded at the receptionist, "said Mrs. Bramley could be very demanding."

"Yes." Helene folded her hands. "This was her company. No doubt about it. Things were done her way or not at all. But you mustn't think badly of her." She looked from Rodney to me, her gaze very earnest. "Mrs. Bramley rewarded the people around her very gener- ously and was always there when you needed her. She was especially sensitive to relationship woes." Her voice trailed off.

"Yes?" I prompted her.

"She didn't say much, but I gathered her own marriage was difficult." Helene had warmed up enough to talk, but not enough to be comfortable with what she considered gossip. Especially if it would paint her former boss in a bad light. "There used to be a lovely picture of her and Mr. Bramley on her desk. I think it was taken on their honeymoon. Several months ago, I came in and it was gone. She said she dropped it and broke the frame, but I got the feeling she was fibbing."

"She didn't elaborate?"

"No, Mrs. Bramley was a very private person regarding her own affairs."

Rodney's turn. "Did she ever mention a sister?"

There was no hesitation in her answer. "Gwyneth? Oh, yes. She used to work for Natural Wonders."

I thought of the email. "In what capacity?"

Helene paused. "Marketing. She had a degree from Niagara but had trouble breaking out on her own. Mrs. Bramley hired her for a time."

"Gwyneth doesn't work here anymore?" Rodney held his pen over the pad.

"No." Helene blushed. "Mrs. Bramley let her go this spring. She didn't say why."

Right around the time the picture disappeared. No wonder Sylvia fired her sister. Who wants to work with the woman who's sleeping with your husband?

I switched gears. "Were you aware Mrs. Bramley spent a lot of time on online gaming sites? Did you ever see her on those?"

Helene shook her head. "No, never. I mean, I knew she went to Seneca Niagara pretty frequently for lunch. She never talked about it. Never asked me to go with her or for money. I think I'd recognize signs of a problem."

Maybe, maybe not. "We've been told Mrs. Bramley may have been embezzling to fund her gambling. Her depression led her to take her life."

"That's preposterous." Helene's face reddened and her body stiffened. "This company was Sylvia's entire life. She didn't have children. She devoted her time to her business and her employees. The idea she was stealing from it is ridiculous."

Rodney spoke up. "But you agree with the assessment she was controlling?"

Helene looked from Rodney to me. Then, she nodded as if making up her mind. "I think you gentlemen need to come with me and see something. Another side of Mrs. Bramley."

I glanced at Rodney. "What other side?"

"You're getting a very warped picture." Helene stood. "This way."

———

Helene led us down the executive hallway, past plushly decorated offices and meeting rooms. The door at the end led to a stark hallway that ran along the back of the building. A bank of windows allowed us to look out on a garden showing signs of flowering. I thought I recognized a dogwood tree in early bloom, shading a wrought iron bench. Daffodils and tulips were clustered around the space. A small fountain splashed next to the bench.

I slowed my steps. "Pretty space."

Helene didn't look outside. "A quiet spot to take a break or have lunch. Mrs. Bramley thought it was important to be able to retreat a little during the work day, if necessary."

We passed an alarmed fire door, then another door leading to a covered walkway. At the end of the walkway was a squat building, one story and decidedly less glamorous than the main building.

Rodney waved. "What's over there?"

"Our production floor." Helene held open another door. "The covered walkway protects from rain or snow, and this back hallway allows people to get from there to the lab or offices quickly."

The building wasn't a flash cube. It was a square doughnut.

The hallway beyond wasn't as decorated as the executive suit, but it wasn't as stark as the one we'd come through. Through the windows on our right, we could look out over the grass. The rooms on the left looked like labs. Soapstone counters, oversized sinks, beakers, and burners. I hurried past. Flames meant sparks. Sparks could mean fires or flare-ups. Like my grill. I didn't need to have an incident during an interview.

"What do you do back there?" Rodney jerked his thumb toward the labs.

"Experimentation for new products. Here." Helene pushed open a door at the end of the hallway.

The room beyond looked like a cross between a

doctor's office and a spa. Bright lights, but the walls were painted in a soft green. Little tables with lighted mirrors. A couple of women were seated and dressed in shabby or well-worn clothing. A few others stood by, wearing the smocks worn in labs. Open makeup was everywhere. Against one wall were a row of chairs with blow dryers, all mercifully silent.

"What is all this?" I asked.

"This is our makeover studio." Helene held out her arms. "All of these women are here for makeovers. Color consultations, haircut and color, waxing. The works."

I looked around. I wasn't entirely sure how much this all cost, but I knew it couldn't be cheap. "Nice side business."

Helene shook her head. "No, Detective. None of them pay for anything. It's a service."

I looked at Rodney, sure his expression mirrored mine. What kind of service?

"These clients," Helene gestured, "are all low income. They're either trying to re-enter the workforce or escaping from abusive homes. Mrs. Bramley knows it's important, especially for older women, to look the part when they are trying to get a job. She provides makeover services using company cosmetics for free. There's even a selection of clothing available to choose from for interviews. All employees are encouraged to donate unused items to the closet."

Rodney looked around. "No men?"

Helene sniffed. "Not to disparage men, but Mrs. Bramley was more focused on women. She always said everyone deserves a second chance, but it was harder for women to grab one. She was trying to help. She couldn't educate or provide skills." Helene's sweeping gesture took in the room. "It's hard to feel good about yourself when you look like crap. Mrs. Bramley understood that. It was something she could do."

I took in the scene, paying extra close attention. Yes, these were women who'd seen the harder side of life. A few bore marks I was sure had come from a fist. The people in the smocks gave makeup and hair tips, how to hide lines or bruises, or how to highlight good features while downplaying others. The subjects' eyes all shone with the same emotion. Hope.

It must have been my week for insight. Sylvia wasn't much different than me. We were both damaged on the inside. She tried to paper over her flaws with makeup and gambling. Tried to present a picture of happiness, confidence, and success she may not have always felt. I was doing the same thing. Trying to convince the world I was whole. Except I wasn't using makeup to do it.

"Ms. Montgomery." I faced her. "If Mrs. Bramley had been upset, what do you think she would have done after leaving her husband at Top of the Falls? For example, would she have taken a walk, taken a taxi back to the hotel or even back to her house?"

Helene tilted her head. "I'm not entirely sure. I think it depends on if she'd made up her mind or not. If she was still considering what to do, she might have gone for a walk. But if she'd decided on a course of action, I think she'd have gone straight back and packed her things."

It wasn't entirely helpful, but it did narrow down

the options to two. And the scene in front of us put a whole new light on Sylvia's character. "Thank you. This has been very helpful. We can see ourselves out." I jerked my head toward Rodney.

Helene caught my jacket sleeve. "You understand now, Detective? However Mrs. Bramley wound up where she did, seeing what I've shown you, do you really think she committed suicide? Do you honestly believe she was a thief?"

No, I didn't. I looked at Rodney. I didn't think he did, either. The only questions to answer now were how and why Sylvia had been killed. And who was responsible.

After leaving Helene, we stopped to ask if Anthony Dellafiore was in. Upon learning he was working from home, we decided to pay him a visit.

As we drove, Rodney spoke. "Do you think all those women were abuse victims?"

"Dunno." The visit had left me with a new opinion of Sylvia. Controlling, yes. Determined, absolutely. But also generous when it came to helping women in unfortunate situations. Maybe because of her own.

"Who knew makeup was so important." Rodney shot me a look. "You're married. Did you know?"

I thought about Amy. Pre-kids, she'd always been polished. Lately, it hadn't seemed to matter. But was that entirely true? On the couple of occasions we'd been able to get out alone, she'd put a little more effort into looking good. It didn't matter to me. I thought she always looked good. But it seemed to matter to her.

But appearances did matter. Even for me. "I hadn't given it much consideration, but yeah. You and I don't come to work in jeans and a T-shirt, and there's a reason. When you were on patrol, did you care what the uniform looked like?"

"Of course. Sloppy uniforms don't give people a good impression."

"Same thing, I guess." We'd reached Dellafiore's apartment and I parked. "No reason a woman wouldn't feel the same. Makeup is part of the outfit, I guess." Did Sylvia feel the same? Her life had been a mess on the inside, but she tried to help those around her. Did she have the same sense of inadequacy and fear of letting people down I did?

"Wow. Deep thoughts by Jackson Davis." He grinned, which took the snark out of the comment.

"Wise-ass. Let's go." I exited the car and headed inside, Rodney in tow. The neighborhood, on the north edge of the city, was drab, but clean. Not the projects, but not upscale, either. The streets were clear of litter, but the cars parked alongside the curb were modest, most of them a few years old. Chevys and Fords, not Cadillacs and Lincolns. Exactly the type of neighborhood a mid-level accountant would live in.

Dellafiore's apartment was on the fourth floor. After waiting a few minutes for what must have been the city's slowest elevator, I decided to take the stairs. Mistake. By the time I reached the right level, I was puffing. Time to dig out the running shoes again. *Smoking won't help*, my conscience said. I ignored it.

We knocked on Dellafiore's door. While we waited, I took in the surroundings. Harsh fluorescent lighting. Plain, dark carpet. Not threadbare, but not luxurious. Nondescript, bland paint, but relatively fresh. The doors along the hallway weren't fancy, but they weren't battered, either. The brass numbers were shiny. I couldn't decide if it was depressing or not.

Rodney knocked again and pressed his ear to the door. "Can't hear anything. I thought they said he was working from home. Late lunch?"

"Maybe." I was about to scrap the visit when the door opened. "Mr. Dellafiore. We were about to conclude you weren't home. May we come in?"

He'd not been expecting company. That was clear from the sweats and faded shirt. Dellafiore's hair stuck up at the back and his feet were bare. He blinked and gripped the door. "I guess. I'm working, though, so it'll have to be quick."

The first impression I had when we stepped inside was I'd walked into a giant bowl of oatmeal. Everything was some shade of tan. The carpet. The walls. The furniture. Even I would have used more color, and I was no great shakes at decorating, as Amy always teased me. Either Dellafiore's landlord didn't want to invest money in interior design, or Dellafiore himself was spectacularly uninspired.

"What can I do for you?" Dellafiore gave an exaggerated look at the clock on the wall. A brown clock, naturally.

"We won't be long," I brought my attention to the milque-toast man in front of me.

Dellafiore ran a hand through his already messy hair. "I'm not sure what more I can tell you. I didn't know Mrs. Bramley well, meaning outside of the company. I'd have no idea why she'd decide to walk back to the hotel. And that direction, too. Or why she might kill herself."

"Quite all right, Mr. Dellafiore." I gazed around the apartment. "We're no longer considering Mrs. Bramley's death a suicide."

"You aren't?" He wrapped his arms around his chest. "Then what, an accident?"

"No, we're treating it as a murder." I thought I saw a glimmer of fear in his eyes, but it was gone before I was sure. I glanced at the furniture. It didn't look very comfortable, so I chose to stay standing. "The suspected embezzlement. How did you first notice it?"

Dellafiore glanced at both of us, settling his gaze on me. "We covered this."

"Tell us again," Rodney said.

"It was about six months ago." Dellafiore chewed his lip. "The numbers weren't adding up on the monthly balance sheets, as I told you. Not a ton of money, but a steady deduction. More than historical figures. So, I went to Mr. Guenther."

"Why not Mrs. Bramley?" I put my hands in my pockets, a show of being relaxed. Next to me, Rodney had taken out his pad and pen, ready to take notes.

"I had reservations."

"What kind of reservations?"

"More of a weird feeling than anything." He shifted, swallowing so the Adam's apple in his pencil neck bobbed. "She was standoffish, if you get my drift. Her attitude didn't inspire confidence."

"She hadn't wanted to hire you." Rodney read from his notes. "Did that influence your decision?"

"Uh, well, yeah." Dellafiore squirmed and adjusted

his tie. "She might think I was fussing over nothing." He bit at a ragged fingernail.

"But she was the CFO?"

"Yes."

It was more or less the same story. He wasn't changing his facts. But his claims didn't jell with my updated image of Sylvia. A woman who had been meticulous with the way her office looked. Her employees. Even total strangers. I doubted she'd dismiss the observations of any employee. Helene and Marcy had painted a much different picture, one I believed to be more accurate. Perhaps, Dellafiore had not worked there long enough to understand his boss. Or maybe he was uncomfortable around women, especially confident ones.

I pressed. "How long had this money problem been going on?"

He blinked. "I beg your pardon?"

"Did it start six months ago, or is that when you noticed it?"

Rodney must have understood my point because he added to the question. "In other words, did you go back to prior months to check?"

Dellafiore must have forgotten my partner was there because he twitched. "Oh. I see." His forehead puckered. "It hadn't been going on long. Yes, I went back two more months and it started about then."

"About the time you started working at Natural Wonders." I drew his focus back to me.

He nodded.

"Who kept the books before you got here?"

"Uh, I believe it was Mrs. Bramley." Dellafiore's

forehead still showed creases. "At least, there wasn't another accountant when I arrived and the workspace looked like it hadn't been used for a while. And she trained me."

"Mrs. Bramley kept her own company financials. Did Mr. Guenther review them?"

"I couldn't tell you. They never discussed it with me."

Rodney and I exchanged a look. If Sylvia kept her own books, she would have known someone was embezzling and reported it. Unless, of course, she was the culprit.

———

Dellafiore did not walk us out and we didn't ask him to. Once in the sunshine, I leaned on the car and studied the building. What we were learning didn't make sense. I may not have been setting the world on fire with my lead detective performance, but I could see that much.

"You're thinking." Rodney opened his door but didn't get in. "About what?"

"I'm wondering whether Dellafiore's role goes further than a snitch."

Rodney looked back. "If he was taking the money, why would he alert Guenther?"

"To divert attention? Or to frame someone? Maybe Dellafiore and Sylvia argued, and he was trying to set her up." The idea felt wrong, but I couldn't dismiss it. Dellafiore rubbed me the wrong way. Maybe it was the odd combination of being twitchy and sneaky in his manner.

Rodney snorted. "Don't you think a guy who was skimming money from his employer could afford a better suit? If Sylvia was so concerned about her employees' appearances, why not give him a makeover?"

A male makeover? "Perhaps, she tried and he's a lost cause."

"When we saw him at work, his suit looked like he bought it off the Goodwill rack and it was made for a guy twice his size." He adjusted the silk tie on his own shirt. Rodney dressed himself well for a homicide detective. Much better than me. Who was he trying to impress? I thought briefly of Rachel. Why *did* she leave?

It was a curiosity, but not relevant to the matter at hand. "Back to Dellafiore. If he's taking money and he's smart, he wouldn't go splurging on items that made him look like he's living beyond his means." I opened the car door and climbed in. "But it does raise a question for me."

Rodney got in the passenger side. "What?"

"If Sylvia wasn't embezzling, where was she getting the money for her gambling? It had to come from somewhere."

"I find it more interesting that Keith was having an affair with Sylvia's sister. How many kinds of stupid is he? Her husband cheats on her with her sister, she's got a gambling addiction, she's been caught stealing from her own company—I'm finding the prospect of Sylvia throwing herself in those rapids more and more likely. No matter what her assistant said, she was a hot mess and didn't see another way out, plain and simple."

"She's allegedly stealing from her company. Remember, Helene and Bramley say no way."

Rodney snorted. "People with addictions do weird things."

"You don't find it curious only Guenther and Dellafiore say Sylvia was suicidal?" I started the engine. "There was no suicide note. Sylvia didn't give away all her possessions. She never talked about death. You say you studied psychology. What do you think?"

"Fine, she doesn't sound like the stereotype of someone who is suicidal. There are outliers." His voice betrayed his reluctance to admit anything of the kind as he fastened his seat belt.

"Let's run a background check on Dellafiore, subpoena his bank records, and see what's come back on Walsh." I pulled away and pointed the car back toward the office.

"If suicide is really out of the picture, I still think Bramley wanted his wife out of the way so he could get her money and move on to a woman who appreciated him. Or at least move on to somewhere he could get laid."

Rodney's solution felt as wrong as Dellafiore framing Sylvia, but the details swam in my head. I needed to get rid of the clutter.

"Unrelated question. When are you going to let me drive?"

"Are you kidding? And give up control of the radio?" It was childish, but with everything else in my life spiraling away, I needed to control something.

CHAPTER
TWENTY

Amy waited until Tuesday morning to confront me. "Did you talk to Yannick?"

"Yes." I adjusted my tie in the hall mirror, trying to ignore the sudden pounding of my heart and light-headed sensation. I could not let Amy see me falter. A panic attack now would be as good as a verbal admission of my weakness. *Stay strong.* My inner voice mumbled something about real strength was being able to accept help. I smothered it with a virtual pillow.

"And?"

"It's possible." I didn't mention the proposed compromise. By some miracle, I'd been able to avoid Yannick since he'd offered it. "But, Amy." I faced her. "I feel good. Better each day. Give me a little more time." I could hear the pleading in my voice and hated it. I sounded like Madeline, begging for an extra cookie.

"I won't wait forever, Jackson." She kissed my cheek and walked away.

I spent the entire drive sure I was having a heart

attack. Once I arrived, I barely spoke to anyone, convinced doing so would be a dead giveaway of my near-breakdown mental state.

The full background check on Gwyneth Walsh arrived later in the morning. I scanned through it while Rodney checked his messages.

"I'm starved." He hung up his phone. "Can we read and eat?"

It wasn't my preferred way of working, but it was almost noon. "Sure. Let's grab something and sit at the park. Nice day for it."

"Last time we did, we saw a murder victim."

"I think the odds of it happening again are slim. Besides—"

"You can have a smoke." Rodney looked at the pocket where my contraband was hiding. "Aren't you worried you won't be able to quit again?"

I headed for the door.

Rodney muttered under his breath, but I ignored him and he was smart enough not to repeat it. Yes, I knew the words were a sign of a problem. But I'd take smelling like an ashtray over heart palpitations.

The park was nice. It was hard to have a panic attack in the early May sunshine, the roar of the water in the background. The perfect white noise. The ever-present mist hung over the gorge, a faint rainbow visible through it. I felt myself relax without resorting to the nicotine rush. We snagged a semi-secluded bench far enough away from the rapids we didn't have to shout at each other, unwrapped our lunches, and started read-ing. "Gwyneth Ann Walsh, born 1981." I held my food away from the paper.

"Four years younger than her sister." Rodney took a bite of his club sandwich.

"Degree in marketing and communications from Niagara. Employment history is spotty. Currently working part-time at the Clinique counter at Macy's."

"Prior convictions?"

"Nothing. No outstanding warrants. She's got an apartment here in Niagara Falls." The address wasn't the greatest neighborhood, but not the worst. About what I'd expect a cosmetics counter salesclerk to afford.

There was silence while I read and Rodney ate. Eventually, he piped up. "How long did she work for Natural Wonders?"

I kept reading, careful not to drip hot sauce on the pages or my pants. "She was there for about eight months before Sylvia let her go." I wiped my fingers. "Bank account is skating near zero. Looks like she gets paid, spends it, and is practically broke by the next payday. She has very little in the way of savings and I can't imagine the 401(k) at a makeup counter is so great."

"Tell me," Rodney sipped at his Coke, "what makes a guy like Bramley—who's got an attractive, wealthy, successful wife—have an affair with a mostly-broke salesclerk?"

"Mind-blowing sex?" How should I know? I was happily married. Well, mostly happily. "The people at Natural Wonders said Sylvia was demanding and controlling. Even Helene. Maybe her attitude extended to the home front. Bramley could have been looking for someone who let him wear the pants in the relationship. Figuratively speaking. Remember the house." It made sense. No man wanted to be constantly told he was second-rate.

"A magazine could've done a photo shoot in their place." He crumpled his wrapper and stuffed it in his bag. "Think she was as controlling at home as at work?"

"Maybe. Yes, she offered makeovers to disadvantaged women, which is great." I stared at the mist. "However, you could argue doing so is another form of control. I think Sylvia desperately wanted to *look* like she had it down precisely because she felt the exact opposite." *Just like me.* The thought was uncomfortable, so I did what I always did. I shunted it aside for later. At the rate I was going, there'd be hell to pay when *later* showed up.

"Take your trash?" He stood and I handed him my bag. When he returned, he had a copy of Sunday's *Niagara Gazette* in his hands. He flipped through it, scanning the pages. "Holy shit."

I looked up. "What?"

Rodney handed over the section he'd been reading, folded over to the bottom. He tapped a story in the corner of the column titled *Engagements.* "Talk about something I didn't expect."

I read it. *Keith Bramley and Gwyneth Walsh are pleased to announce their engagement. No date set as of yet.* "His wife isn't even in the ground, and he's getting engaged to her sister?"

"What possible reason could they have for moving so fast?"

I stood. "I can think of a very good one."

He blinked. "Walsh is knocked up?"

"Okay, two. But not what I was thinking. What

happens if they get married, and one or both of them gets charged with Sylvia's murder?"

"Neither can be forced to testify against the other. Shit." He stood.

I slapped the paper against his chest. "Let's go and hope they haven't changed their minds and opted for the quickie route. And call the office. I want details on the Bramleys' prenup. Now."

———

A quick call confirmed Bramley had checked out of the hotel, so we sped to the house on Grand Island. Bramley's Cadillac CTS occupied the garage. Another car, a dark blue Chevy Malibu that was a couple years old, was parked in the drive. Sylvia's car was nowhere to be seen.

"Walsh's?" Rodney jerked his thumb at the Malibu.

Probably. I scanned the front of the house. Unlike last time, the curtains were open. I started to notice other differences. A vase of wildflowers in the window. The doormat was the same, but it was off-center and smudged with mud. Used, not for show. *Because there's a new woman in the house, or is it Bramley breaking free?*

The door was opened almost immediately in response to my knock. "I heard a car." Bramley wore jeans and a golf shirt that had seen more than a few washes. Well-worn sneakers. "Didn't expect you, though."

"Keith? Who is...oh." Walsh, clad in similarly comfortable clothes but sans shoes, had come up behind Bramley. "What the hell do you want?"

"Gwyneth, please. Come in, detectives." Bramley pushed open the door.

Once inside, there were more signs of change. Shoes jumbled by the door. A coat thrown over a chair in the walkway. A few days' worth of newspapers on the hall table. I could see into the living room, where an afghan trailed on the floor. The fireplace door was open, a pile of wood in front of it. The last time we'd been here, the thing had been unused. Bramley was making some changes. No more mausoleum.

"You're here for a reason, I take it." Bramley leaned on the back of the couch.

Rodney handed over the paper, folded to showcase the engagement announcement. "Congratulations. I think. Awfully fast, don't you agree?"

"Ah." Bramley didn't even look. He handed the paper back to Rodney. Walsh had already stalked off after cussing under her breath. "Please, come in the kitchen. We're having lunch."

We followed him. I spotted a coffee ring on the counter. Several pods missing from the coffee holder. Dishes were askew in the cabinets, and what looked like sauce was spattered on the stovetop. It made the place look lived in. Better, more attractive, at least to me.

Bramley waved at the barstools near the island. "You want to sit down?"

"We're okay standing." I took the paper and tossed it on the counter. "Care to explain that?"

"We're getting married." Bramley moved to take Gwyneth's hand. "It's been in the works for a while. With Sylvia's death and everything going on, we're going for low key, but Gwyneth wanted an announcement."

"Define *a while*."

"We've been discussing marriage for at least three months." Bramley got out a cup. "Would you like some coffee?"

I shook my head. Rodney didn't give any indication he'd even heard the offer.

"Your wife isn't even buried yet. Don't you think you're moving a bit fast?"

Walsh tossed her head. "No." She grabbed her cigarettes and lit up. She blew out a cloud of smoke. "Who gives a rat's ass about propriety? No more waiting for a divorce. We can do it and move on."

I'd smell like smoke again when I got home. *It'll cover your own sins.*

Bramley put the cup back. "Anyway, this shouldn't be a shock. I was upfront about the affair. If you've spoken to anyone who knew Sylvia—"

"We have," I said. "You were only upfront after we caught you."

He ignored me. "Do you know what it does to a man? To be constantly reminded he's completely dependent on his wife and she can turn him out on a whim?"

Not being in such a situation, I could only imagine. "You could have gotten a job. Had your own money."

He shook his head. "The prenup was complicated, Detective. It limited how much control I had over finances. Even if I'd had a job, Sylvia held the purse strings. It's one of the reasons I quit working."

"What else did this prenup say?" Rodney looked at me.

Bramley sighed. "I'm sure you can get a copy, if you haven't already. The biggest issues were financial control and what would happen if we got divorced. I'd get a payment of ten thousand dollars. Not a dime more. No alimony."

"Even if she's the one who cheated?" Rodney's tone was full of disbelief.

"Yes. It was part of the discussions between Gwyneth and I." Bramley grasped his mug. "Did we want to continue our affair, or suck it up and take the financial hit? I'm sure you've determined Gwyneth doesn't have a high-paying job."

"I can get one." The light in her eyes shone hard.

Bramley sipped his coffee. "You're a married man, Detective. Could you live like that?"

I rubbed my chin. We would definitely check the facts, but I was inclined to believe Bramley was telling us the truth. It would play well with what we'd learned of Sylvia's personality. Wanting to control the image of her life, even if it wasn't the truth. "Pardon me for asking, but why the hell would you sign such an agreement? It would never work to your advantage."

"Unless, of course, something happened to Sylvia," Rodney added.

"If you are implying I killed my wife to get out of an unfair, ill-advised legal agreement—"

"I'm not implying anything." Rodney began to turn, then stopped. "Wait. That's exactly what I'm implying. You've got to admit, you're not exactly making it look like an impossibility that you and your fiancée collaborated in the scheme."

"Me?" Walsh's eyebrows shot up. "What would ever make you think I'd be involved?"

I fixed her with a stare. "You admitted you didn't like your sister. You slept with her husband."

Rodney tapped the engagement announcement. "I'm sure the legal benefits of marriage in a trial situation are completely coincidental. And you'd both profit financially."

Walsh tutted, her face scornful, but Bramley was sober. He set down the mug. "Detective Kirke, I know how it looks—"

"I'm not sure you do."

"—but such is not the case. Gwyneth and I did not conspire to get rid of Sylvia. In fact, we'd decided I should file for divorce, take my meager settlement, and leave." He moved and put his arm around his fiancée.

It was unlikely, but possible. If it was a lie, these two were putting on a great act. I had to hand it to them. "You haven't answered my question, Mr. Bramley. Why sign such an agreement?"

"Because I never thought it would be an issue." He stared straight at me. "When Sylvia and I married, we were insanely happy and very much in love. Tell me, did you go into your marriage ever considering you'd be less in love than you were at that moment?"

It was not the time to think about my own marriage.

"I'll take your silence as a no." Bramley set down his coffee. "I signed it because I loved her. But as the company grew, she changed. Got harder, more controlling. Everything needed to be perfect. Her, me, our marriage, the house. I didn't feel cared for anymore. I was an accessory, not a partner. She took to gambling. I'm not sure where the desire came from. And when I tried to talk to her, she shut me out. After a while, I moved on. I'm not proud of it. But neither was I willing to continue to be a trophy."

I understood. I did. His story still painted Sylvia in a harsher light than Helene's, but that didn't make it a lie. How hard had he tried? As hard as Amy was trying with me? Was I turning into Sylvia, determined to have things my way?

Bramley continued. "I don't know how things went so bad so quickly. But I am absolutely sure of one thing."

I glanced at Rodney, then moved my focus back to Bramley. "What?"

Bramley held my gaze, his face still as rock. "I did not kill my wife. And neither did Gwyneth."

Rodney cocked his head. "You don't think she committed suicide?"

Gwyneth snorted, but Bramley shook his head emphatically. "No, I do not. Sylvia was a lot of things. Controlling, demanding, and troubled. But not suicidal. Someone killed her. But it wasn't me."

———

We drove back to the office mostly in silence. As we walked to our desks, Rodney asked, "Do you believe him?"

I picked up a thick envelope from my desk. "I don't know. If I do, it's not because he said so."

"Why do you suppose Sylvia started gambling?"

"It made her happy?"

"Nobody close to her says she was depressed."

"Happy might be the wrong word. She was losing control of her life and gambling felt controllable. Or she liked the thrill of the game. I don't think we'll ever know for sure."

"Are we sure it was really her? What if someone was using her computer?"

"Home and business? Remember all those payments to Wild Diamond? I'm betting it was her. No pun intended." I looked up. "Anything in that pile of paper about a Player's Club card?"

He shuffled through some papers. "We got a letter from Seneca Niagara." He scanned it. "Sylvia didn't have a Player's Club card. Not surprising. You don't need promo materials mailed to you if you're trying to hide your habit."

Which meant we had no idea how much she'd won or lost. I slipped the contents out of the envelope. "Finally."

Rodney looked up.

I unfolded the papers. "The Bramleys' bank records, including Sylvia's private account."

"Took long enough." Rodney slung his jacket over his chair and sat.

"A week?" Was he kidding? It was a fast turn-around. I sat and began to read.

After a moment, he spoke. "Are you going to send those to the accountants?"

I flipped a page. "Eventually. I want to look at them first. See if anything pops."

Of course, it didn't. The columns of numbers stayed columns of numbers. Money in, money out. I checked my watch—quarter to five. "I'm taking these home. Guess I'll see you tomorrow." I stood and slipped a cigarette out of the pack. I could smoke it quickly before I got into the car. Maybe it would take the edge off the pounding behind my eyes before I got home.

"You want to grab a beer?" Rodney followed me.

The idea of a beer with my partner appealed to me, which made my response hard to give. "I can't. Things are tense at home. I owe it to my family to spend time with them."

"You don't want to disappoint them."

I swallowed against the rock in my throat.

He looked around the nearly empty squad room. "Can I give you some advice?"

"Sure."

He pointed at the cigarette. "Give those up. You say you don't need the shrink. You don't need those, either."

I stared at the cigarette.

"Trust me, a relationship built on lies won't work. Tell your wife the truth, then quit. Otherwise, you're kidding yourself that you're in control."

I was in control. I was not Sylvia. "Thank you, Dr. Phil."

He shook his head. "See you tomorrow." He left me standing by my desk, holding the pack.

I smoked my cigarette before I got into the car. One more, then I'd quit. I arrived home more relaxed than when I'd left the office. A stick of gum took care of any aftertaste. Much to my gratification, Madeline's tricycle was not in the driveway.

"I'm home." I tossed the keys in the basket, hung my sports jacket on the banister, and followed my nose to the kitchen. "Smells good." I leaned over and kissed Amy on the cheek. "I know, I smell like smoke. Same witness, different day. I'll shower later. But if I take over dinner, will you look at something for me?"

She handed me a basting brush in exchange for the stack of bank records. "Baste the chicken with the sauce in the bowl. What am I looking at?"

"More bank statements. This pile is the Bramleys' shared account. This one is Sylvia's slush fund. At least, I think it is. Here are her credit card accounts. Pay particular attention to the one from Chase." I swirled the brush in the glaze and pulled the chicken out to brush it. "Is there anything there to make you suspicious? Deposits, withdrawals, whatever."

As I basted the bird, Amy leaned on the counter, studying the sheets. She chewed her bottom lip as she murmured under her breath. It sounded like she was doing addition. "See anything?" I shut the oven door.

"I'm not sure." She flipped another page. "This is all so general. I mean, there's a lot of money flowing, but that's not really unusual these days. If you're looking for evidence, it's going to take a lot more than me eyeballing bank statements before dinner."

I almost swore, then remembered Madeline might hear and caught myself. "Thanks. It was worth a shot."

She checked the chicken. "Go wash your hands and tell Madeline to do the same."

I pushed away from the counter.

"Jackson."

I turned.

"I know you could have stayed at work. I know you could have gone out with your new partner. Thanks for coming home. And for helping with dinner." She pulled the chicken out of the oven. "It's as normal as things have been in a while."

She was right, and it felt good. I had been right, too. All I needed was time to get back on my feet.

TWENTY-ONE

After dinner, Madeline and I cleaned up the dishes, and then I sent her upstairs to her mother for a bath. In the meantime, I retired to our room to discard my shoes and tie, and take a quick shower. I'd gotten through an entire evening without arguing, yelling, or panicking. Things were looking up.

I was unbuttoning my shirt when I heard Amy's voice behind me. "Jackson Lee Davis."

Shit.

I turned to see her standing in the doorway, my sports jacket in one hand, a crumpled cigarette pack in the other. Damn. I'd forgotten to leave them at the office. "I can explain." I held up my hands.

"You lied to me." She threw the pack at me. A few cigarettes fell out onto the floor. "You said you weren't smoking."

"I know, but listen—"

"Were you lying about interviewing a witness?"

Anger fought embarrassment in my chest. "I was telling the truth. If you want, you can call Rodney."

"How long has this been going on?" She pointed at the white sticks on the floor. "If I hadn't picked up your jacket to hang it up and felt the pocket, I'd have been clueless. Or was that the point?"

Deep down, I knew I deserved every word, but it didn't stop anger and resentment pushing their way to the top. My face grew warm. "A week. I swear. It's only since I've been back to full-time. I only bought one pack. You can see there's more than half of it left."

"Why? Why didn't you tell me?"

"I wanted to, but I knew you'd react this way."

"Don't you dare try to blame me." She crossed the room and slapped my shoulder. "I wouldn't have been this angry. Disappointed, yes. But it's like we tell Madeline, the act doesn't make me as angry as the lie."

"I was going to quit."

"You were? You're not going to quit now?"

"I didn't mean that. Shit." Why hadn't I told her? *You idiot. Not even smarter than a five-year old*, the voice said in a disdainful tone. I tried again. "I cannot begin to describe these last few months. The pressure, the stress. Sometimes, I feel like I'm going to blow apart at the seams."

"Same old story, isn't it? You were a homicide detective for two years and didn't act like this. Don't tell me it's because the job was less stressful."

I rubbed my face. "I'm trying, Amy. I am trying so hard."

"That's the problem. I think you're trying too hard

to do it all yourself." She paused, still angry but with a smidge more compassion. "You need help. There's no shame in admitting it."

"I am not going back to the damn psychologist." The words came out in a hiss. "You, Rodney, Max—all of you won't leave it alone. I'm trying to figure things out and you won't let it be."

"Because we care. Jackson. You are a man. A human being. You ask too much of yourself. God." She wiped tears from her eyes. "It's too much."

Her words hit me like a two-by-four. "What's too much? All of a sudden, I'm too much?"

"That's not what I said and you know it."

"Then, what is it?" I waited. "What's *too much,* Amy?" But she didn't tell me. Maybe she was afraid of the answer. I wanted to hear it, but at the same time I didn't. What if the answer *was* me? I knew deep in my gut hearing those words would blow the fragile pyramid I'd constructed of my life to smithereens.

I picked up the fallen cigarettes. I needed to clean up. Clear my mind. The peace of dinner was a million years ago. How could I have thought things were looking better?

She grabbed my arm. "Your daughter is waiting for you."

"I haven't showered."

"You'll have to wait. She wants a story and only Daddy will do. We can talk later."

I looked at her, taking in her pale face and the tears in her eyes. The anger ebbed away, leaving me hollow. "Amy, I'm sorry. I didn't want to let you down."

"Then, you should have told me the truth." She turned and walked out, leaving me with a handful of bent cigarettes I no longer wanted.

———

Madeline was ready for story time with her favorite book of fairytales on her lap, cheeks pink from scrubbing. "Sit here, Daddy." She patted the bed next to her. I sat, and she clambered into my lap. "You smell funny again."

"I know. I'm sorry. But your story is more important than smelling nice." I looked at the book. "This one? Are you sure you don't want a new one?"

"No, Daddy. This is my favorite. Do the funny voices, please?"

I started to read, and she snuggled into my chest. The scent of baby shampoo was calming, and it was relaxing to have Madeline's simple, accepting warmth leaned against me. She giggled at all the parts where I changed my voice to be the dwarf, the troll, or the woodland fairy. She laughed especially hard at the fairies. Hearing a grown man mimic a tiny fantastical creature must have been hilarious. At least I could still make my daughter smile. "And they rode away, perhaps not happily ever after, but happily enough for now. The End." I closed the book, set it aside, and hugged her.

"You do the best stories, Daddy." Madeline snuggled up to me. "Even better than Mommy."

"I'm sure Mommy does a fine job." I squeezed her. It was nice to get a compliment.

She squeezed back, then sat up and placed her left hand on my cheek. "Daddy, why is Mommy mad at you?"

She'd heard us despite our best efforts. "She isn't mad at me."

"Yes, she is. I heard her." Her face scrunched up. "Did you leave your toys outside?"

I laughed and stroked her cheek. "Kind of. I've made a lot of mistakes lately and your mommy is tired of it."

"Don't make mistakes, Daddy. You have to try your best."

Oh, if only it was so easy. "I can't seem to stop. I don't know why."

She put her right hand on my other cheek. "I know why you're making mistakes, Daddy."

"Oh, you do, do you?"

"It's because you're sad all the time." Her voice was solemn. "Why are you sad, Daddy? Did Mommy or I do something bad?"

Talk about a sucker punch to the gut. "It has nothing to do with you or Mommy. You, Christopher, and your mommy are the most important people in the world." I pulled her close in a bear hug and kissed her still-damp head.

"Daddy, you're squishing me." Her voice was muffled, and I relaxed my hug. She sat up and pushed hair out of her face. "Is it because of Auntie Max? Is that why you're sad?"

Out of the mouths of babes. I stroked the soft wisps of dark brown hair. Hair like her mother's. "Like I said, it's kind of complicated. Now, it's time to get into bed."

Madeline scrambled off my lap and burrowed under her covers. "I wish Auntie Max would come see us." She blinked those blue eyes framed by long lashes. "Maybe if I called her, she'd come. Then, you wouldn't be sad and make mistakes."

"Maybe. But right now, it's sleep time. Your mother and I will try not to keep you up." I kissed her head.

Her voice made me pause at the door. "I love you, Daddy."

"I love you too, Squirt. To the moon and back. Goodnight." The sight of her, a small lump under the covers, her tiny features full of absolute trust, tugged at me like no lecture ever could. To Madeline, I was still Super-Daddy, capable of anything. The thought was reassuring and frightening at the same time.

———

Amy was reading in bed when I returned to our room. I shed my socks and pants. After a quick shower, I slipped into bed. It was hours before I usually called it quits for the night, but maybe the extra sleep would do me good. I reached out to stroke her arm.

She pulled away. "Kiss and make up won't work. This problem is too serious to be solved with sex."

I let out a slow breath. I deserved her response. Still, it hurt.

"Jackson."

I pushed up on my elbow. She had put her book down and was fingering a business card. I instinctively knew whose card it was, but I played dumb. "What is it, Ame?"

She cleared her throat. "I want you to call Dr. Alverson tomorrow and make an appointment." She handed me the card.

I didn't take it. "You're right. I should have told you about the smoking. I'm sorry. But I don't think—"

"I told you. I'm not angry about the cigarettes. I'm angry you lied. That you felt you had to lie. And it hurts me you think you have to be this superhero figure who goes it alone. You were never like this before."

I didn't know what to say. For once, I did the smart thing and kept quiet.

"I'm sure your behavior makes sense behind your thin blue line. Those guys don't have to live with you. I do. I love you." She continued to hold out the card. "It's clear to me you're still struggling with what happened, and I'm sure it's obvious to everyone else around you. Maybe they think you're doing fine. I don't. You don't have to agree with me, but don't bother to deny it. You're too smart not to see what's going on. The more you try to hold on to control, the more it slips away." She dropped the card on the bed.

I picked it up and stared at the crisp, black letters on the white stock. I wasn't solid. I didn't have to go deep for the realization, but the thought of returning to coun-seling terrified me. *You're broken,* an insidious voice in my mind hissed. *Unfit to be a detective. To be a husband. A father. You make that phone call and everyone will know. You can't hack it. You've failed them.* "I don't know."

"I do." Her gaze challenged me. "You say you don't want to let me down. Then, call her, Jackson. Tomorrow. I'm not asking you. Don't make me take more drastic steps." Conversation over, she returned to her book.

I rolled over and put the card on my bedside table. Again, I studied the elegant script. Some things were too true to be said in the daylight, but I could admit it at night. I needed help. Whether Dr. Alverson could offer it remained to be seen.

CHAPTER
TWENTY-TWO

Thursday morning, I sat at my desk, staring into space. It had been a week and a half, and we hadn't learned a lot. I had a collection of information I couldn't make sense of and enough suspects for three murders, but no hard proof of anything.

Not a great way to start my career as a lead detective.

I tapped Dr. Alverson's business card on my desk. The edges were bent from all the times I'd pulled it out only to stuff it back into my wallet. I'd even dialed the number a couple of times but never completed the call. I might have been ready to admit defeat last night, but it was harder to do in the daylight.

The coroner had released Sylvia's body on Wednesday. There were viewings at ten and four today. I turned the card over and over in my hand, trying to decide whether I wanted to drop in on Alverson unscheduled. Yannick approached, and I slid the card under a stack of paper. I didn't need him to see it.

He stopped at my desk. "Davis, got a minute?"

"Uh, sure." Like I could say anything else. "What's up?"

"You've been ducking me. Thought about my compromise?" He looked me over. "You look frazzled."

Talk about an understatement. I'd slept, but I didn't feel rested. The tightness in my chest was happening so frequently I was beginning to wonder if I needed to see a doctor for a heart check. Which only made me panic more. I was sure I'd seen Rodney studying me when I wasn't looking, probably trying to decide if I was coming apart at the seams. He hadn't said anything, but he was almost certainly deciding how long he was going to stay hitched to a train threatening to go off the tracks.

Yannick's gaze softened. "You're scared."

It was easy to underestimate his deductive abilities, but Yannick had been a detective. He could read people. I nodded.

"Understandable. There's no reason to be." He gave a slight laugh at my reaction. "We all, me included, want the best for you."

"I know." I drummed my fingers on the desk. *It's just a phone call. A conversation. How bad could it be?* Bad. "Give me one more day."

"One day." He raised an eyebrow. "What's the status on this case? We're tight on resources. I can't have you and Kirke spinning your wheels if Sylvia killed herself." Yannick crossed his arms and sat on the edge of my desk.

Relieved to move the focus of our conversation to work, I handed him the financial information we had from the case. "We don't think it was suicide. It doesn't mesh with what we've been told by people who ought to know. Even her sister says no way, and they weren't on the best of terms."

He took the papers.

"We're still waiting on legal stuff. Hopefully, it will come soon." I pointed at the stack. "Also waiting on a thorough analysis from the money guys. I'd bet my next paycheck somebody was up to something."

Yannick flipped the pages. "Sylvia?"

"Somebody. She had a gambling problem. I don't know whether the two are connected. Again, the people closest to the victim say no way Sylvia would steal from her own company."

"You're sure it's murder." He handed back the papers.

"Murder feels more right than suicide. Until someone is able to prove to me that Sylvia threw herself into the Niagara River, I'm keeping at it."

"Fair enough." He tipped his head. "Suspects?"

"Husband, sister, VP. There's even a possibility it's a random mugger."

"Motive?"

"Bramley and Gwyneth Walsh have announced their engagement. They were having an affair."

"He could have filed for divorce."

I shrugged. "He says he gets nothing in a split. He'd get a lot as a widower."

"Same motive for the sister. Free up the boyfriend and money." Yannick thought for a moment, then nodded. "Motive for the others?"

"Sylvia had an affair with her VP. Jilted lover? Or he

was the one actually behind the embezzlement and she threatened to turn him in. Or she *was* embezzling, despite what everyone thinks. She threatened his plans for expansion, so he killed her."

"What does Kirke say about all this?"

"He thinks it's Bramley."

"You?"

"I'm not sold. Then, there's Sylvia's jewelry, which still hasn't surfaced."

Yannick tapped his foot, eyes narrowed. "It could have been ripped off in the water."

"Autopsy didn't indicate any physical damage that would be associated with a forceful removal."

Yannick didn't say anything, but he indicated I should continue.

"We've given a full list to all the pawn shops and jewelry resale places in the city, but no bites yet." I could see I wasn't impressing my boss. The tightness in my chest returned. A week and a half, almost two, and all I had was a pocketful of conjecture. Max and I'd had an excellent close rate on our cases. What if it had been because of her, not me? "That's where we are. Not as far as I'd like, but we'll get there."

He stood and smoothed his tie. "Keep me posted. And let me know about the other thing."

My heart pounded against my ribs. At the same time, it felt as if my lungs were having trouble expanding. Had someone turned up the heat, or forgotten to turn on the A/C? "I will. Thanks for understanding."

"Don't make me regret it." Yannick walked away, nodding to Rodney as he approached with two coffee cups.

Rodney set down a Starbucks cup in front of me. "Line at Timmies was insane. You'll have to deal with inferior coffee." He grinned, but it faded quickly. "What's wrong?"

"What makes you think anything is wrong?"

"Because you look like death. Paper white and you'd think it was a million degrees in here with the way you're sweating." He studied my desk. "What are you hiding?"

"Nothing." I reached for the coffee cup, leaving my left hand in place to cover the business card. It meant I had to reach across my body to get the cup, which was awkward. "I'm getting used to Starbucks."

He lifted my hand, then picked up the card. "Nothing, huh? Looks like you've been worrying at this for a while." He handed it to me, then sat down at his desk.

"It's something to play with. I'm fine."

"Unless you're using the definition of *fine* from the old Aerosmith song, I don't think you are."

F'ed up, insecure, neurotic, emotional. Yup. "When did you become a shrink?" I cringed at the snap in my voice.

"Calm down. Go have a cigarette. It's what you do, isn't it?"

"I threw them away. Wife caught me."

"That explains it." He sipped his coffee, eyes thoughtful.

I took a drink myself. "What the hell do you mean?" I put the cup down with a little more force than necessary, and coffee splashed onto my desk. Growling, I grabbed some napkins to mop up the mess before the paper was ruined.

"It explains why you're especially snarly this morning. Don't tell me you aren't." He set down his coffee cup. "Are you gonna use that card, or worry it to pieces?"

"I don't need a psychologist." I was careful to keep my voice low. I didn't need the rest of the guys hearing me. "We need to make some damn progress on the Bramley investigation. I was thinking we'd go to the viewing. We might learn something."

He tossed his empty cup in the trash. "Jackson, are you sure you're okay to go? I can handle it, if not. I told you I'd keep quiet about the panic attack—"

"They aren't panic attacks. I'm a little stressed."

"They? You've had more?" He sighed. "You're going to get yourself killed. Worse, you'll get me killed."

"Thank you for the vote of confidence."

He mumbled and shook his head.

"Shall we?" I was tempted to give in and make the phone call, if only to end the almost constant state of tension.

Rodney stood. "I wore my dark suit today. Let's roll."

————

We pulled up outside the Cantore Funeral Home. Inside, we checked the board in the lobby. Sylvia was laid out in Room C, at the back of the building. I fiddled with the doc's card, which I'd stuffed in my pocket, as we walked down the carpeted hallway. *I can't call now. I've got people to question.*

It was about two-fifteen in the afternoon. The room

wasn't crowded. I saw Bramley in a somber charcoal-gray suit, white shirt, and maroon tie. Walsh was close by in a black dress. I checked her left hand, where a modest diamond solitaire glittered. My gaze automatically went to Sylvia's crossed hands as she lay in a casket lined with white silk. Her engagement ring was on her left hand. Walsh and Bramley weren't hiding their relationship, but at least the man had gotten a new ring.

"See anyone interesting?" Rodney scanned the crowd. "Should we sign the guest register?"

"No, but check the signatures. There probably aren't many, but let's see who's stopped by so far."

He moved away as I looked around. It was sparse, mostly women in fashionable clothes. Bert Guenther stood by the fireplace, deep in conversation with a woman who had short silver hair. I didn't see anyone who set off alarm bells.

There was a tap on my shoulder. It was Rodney. "Check this out."

"Did you look at the register?"

"I did. No names popped out at me." He tugged me around, "But look who walked in."

Standing at the door, looking lost, was Anthony Dellafiore. I frowned. "Is it me or does he look like a fish out of water?"

Rodney shook his head. "Should we grab him?"

"At a funeral home? No. Scoping out the guest register is one thing. Interrogating someone is tasteless. We can wait."

We hadn't been noticed, so it was the perfect time to beat it. Out of the corner of my eye, I saw Dellafiore approach the casket. He knelt briefly, then went over to Bramley. "I am so sorry." Dellafiore shook Bramley's hand. "Your wife was a wonderful woman. So kind and generous. And so few people saw it."

Why the sudden switch in opinion? When we'd talked to him before, he'd sounded down on Sylvia, even a tad bitter. As a homicide detective, I didn't like unexplained changes. Max had taught me to be suspicious of them. I tapped Rodney on the shoulder and jerked my head toward the door.

We made it out without notice and loitered on the sidewalk. Dellafiore couldn't stay in there long. He didn't know anyone, or at least, I didn't think he did. Sure enough, he emerged from the funeral home about five minutes later, blinking in the sunlight. "Mr. Dellafiore." I walked toward him. "Nice to see you."

"Detectives." He shuffled his feet. "What are you doing here?"

"Still investigating Mrs. Bramley's death." I gestured a little ways down the sidewalk. "Can we talk?"

His gaze darted around the street. "If you insist."

"Nice of you to come to the viewing." I put my hands in my pockets. "I wasn't under the impression you and Mrs. Bramley were particularly close."

"The entire company was invited. Mrs. Bramley was a nice lady. She did give me a shot."

Talk about a one-eighty. "You've told us—twice—Mrs. Bramley wasn't enthusiastic about hiring you, and you suspected her of embezzlement."

"No hard feelings."

Rodney might have thought the same thing. "Will you be part of the cleanup? At the company?"

"No. I gave my notice at Natural Wonders this morning."

"Really?" I looked at Rodney. From the look in his eyes, he was as suspicious as I was. "A rather sudden decision, isn't it?"

"With Mr. Guenther taking charge, I don't think it's the right place for me." His gaze skittered around the street. Anywhere but us.

It didn't make sense. I stepped toward him. "You brought your suspicions regarding Mrs. Bramley to Mr. Guenther, but you can't work for him?"

"Mrs. Bramley was a lady with a problem. I had to talk to someone. Believe me, if it could have been anyone other than Mr. Guenther, I would have. I don't approve of taking advantage of people with problems."

Rodney put his hands in his pockets. "How was Guenther doing that?"

Dellafiore licked his lips. "Did you know he had an affair with Mrs. Bramley?"

"I did. He told us it was over." I watched him. "Said he ended it."

"He didn't."

I glanced at Rodney. His expression mirrored mine when Madeline changed her story three times about who broke the living room lamp—squinting, eyebrows raised, a small frown. "What do you mean?"

"Mr. Guenther wasn't the one who broke off the affair. Mrs. Bramley did." Dellafiore finally looked at me.

Interesting. "Is this something you know or something you suspect?"

"I heard them. I'd gone to give Mrs. Bramley some paperwork. Her office door was closed, but they were shouting at each other, so it was easy to hear." Dellafiore's throat bobbed.

"What did they say?" Rodney had taken out a notepad and pen.

I concentrated on Dellafiore.

"I only got the end of the conversation. I don't remember the exact words, but she said something about betraying her trust and turning out like everybody else in her life. I think it had something to do with the art." Dellafiore fidgeted a little.

"The art?" I looked at Rodney for clarification.

"The Miller and the MacRae. In the lobby." He focused on Dellafiore. "Are those what you're talking about?"

Dellafiore twitched some more. He made me antsy looking at him. "Yes. I'm not sure they're real."

Rodney jotted down this new information and waited for Dellafiore to continue.

"I know a little bit about art." Dellafiore scuffed his shoe against the pavement. "Mr. Guenther brokered the sale. I think it's possible he sold her fake paintings because she broke off their affair. Then, he thought embezzling was a better route. Or the other way around."

She broke off the affair because she found out Guenther was embezzling, and he sold her fake paintings as revenge? I couldn't quite believe it. What bullshit was this?

Rodney's question gave voice to my thoughts. "Why

would she buy paintings from a guy who stole from her company?"

Dellafiore shrugged. "It's only an idea I had."

I glanced at Rodney. "You said you suspected Mrs. Bramley of the embezzlement."

"I did. At least, originally. The more I think about it, maybe Mr. Guenther is a better candidate. He wanted to take the company public, and Mrs. Bramley refused. It could be another reason he sold her fake art. It was a way to get money he thought was his." He shot a nervous glance between us. "I should go, Detectives." He hurried down the street, not looking behind him.

When Rodney spoke, it was clear he shared my disbelief. "Now, Guenther is the embezzler. And what's with the whole fake art thing?"

"Weird, I know. But we should check and see if those paintings are genuine."

Embezzling, gambling addiction, infidelity, and now art fraud. This case needed to start making sense. And fast.

I didn't see the tricycle in the driveway. But I heard the crunch, and felt the jolt, when I hit it. I got out of the car and looked underneath. Sure enough, the trike was firmly wedged in the undercarriage. Swearing a blue streak under my breath, I wiggled it out.

One look told me it was toast. The cheap metal frame would never stand up to being straightened. I wasn't a good enough metal worker to do it, anyway. Now, I had to buy my kid a new bike. Eventually.

Dropping the mangled tricycle in the garage, I went in the front door. "Madeline Jane," I called.

She slunk into the hallway. "Yes, Daddy?"

"Where's your tricycle?"

"In the driveway, Daddy. I'll move it." She started toward the door.

I stopped her. "Don't bother. I hit it with the car. It's in the garbage."

Her bottom lip trembled. "The garbage? Why?"

"Because it's broken."

"Will you fix it?" A tear slid down her cheek.

I didn't want to shout. Shouting would not help. "No. I can't fix it. Don't give me the sad eyes and the boo-boo lip. You left your toy out, and it got wrecked. Just like I told you."

She sniffled. "Will I get a new tricycle?"

I smushed down a surge of anger. "Not until you prove to me you can take care of it."

Another sniffle.

"That won't get you a new one." I threw my keys in the basket.

"But I'm sorry, Daddy."

"Not good enough this time." I stared at her tiny, quivering mouth and willed myself not to buckle. It was easily the hardest thing I'd ever done, or ever would do.

"I'm sorry." She ran up the stairs, howling.

Amy came out of the kitchen, wiping her hands on a towel. "What was all the noise about?"

"Our daughter left her tricycle in the driveway. I hit it with the car. I only told her a dozen times to put the damn thing away." I ran my hand over my face. *Stay calm.*

"Okay, but why did she run upstairs bawling?"

"Because I told her I wasn't going to fix it or buy her a new one. And saying *I'm sorry* wasn't good enough." *You said you'd remind her.*

"Did you have to make her cry?" She clenched the towel.

Wait, *I* was wrong? "What, you think I should have let it slide? How does that help?"

"It doesn't but—" A fresh howl came from upstairs, this time accompanied by one from downstairs. A howling duet. Amy closed her eyes. "Great. She woke up the baby. *Exactly* what I was trying to avoid. You go take care of him. I'll get her." Amy rushed up the stairs without another word.

I found Christopher in his portable bassinet in the den, his tiny face resembling a squashed tomato as he let the world know of his discontent. I picked him up and bounced him. "I know how you feel, bud." I did.

After a few minutes, Christopher quieted down, lapsing back into slumber. At about the same time, Amy entered the den. Her face was drawn, with pale purple smudges under her eyes. I could tell she'd had a long day. I didn't want to pile anything more on, but I would not be the bad guy in this scenario.

"He okay?" She waved toward me.

I nodded. I set him back in the bassinet, hoping the lack of bouncing wouldn't wake him. It didn't. We went to the kitchen to continue our argument. *Conversation* was too mild a word, but *fight* was too strong. For the time being.

Amy leaned against the counter and closed her eyes. "Jackson, I understand where you're coming from. Really. But it was a forty-dollar toy, not a Ming vase. Christopher has been cranky all day. I think he's teething. Then, you come home, set Madeline off, and bam, two crying kids."

"Amy, let's hope her stupid forty-dollar *toy* didn't break something under the car. You know, the car I need to go to *work*. To earn *money* to keep a roof over this family's head. I told her to put it away. She didn't. Now, she has to face the consequences." I grabbed a beer from the fridge.

"Couldn't you have delivered the same message in a softer tone?"

I took a long pull of the beer. "Didn't you remind her? Like you promised you would?" I tried to keep my tone non-accusatory.

From the way Amy's eyes narrowed, I didn't quite succeed. "Fine. If you want to play that game..." She took a deep breath. "I forgot to talk to her, and yes, I did say that. My mistake. But you promised you'd do something for me, too. Did you call Dr. Alverson?"

I wasn't the bad guy with the trike, but I was busted on the shrink. I took another swig of beer. "No." There was no justification, so I didn't offer one.

She threw the towel in the sink. "What is it going to take to get you—oh, never mind. I didn't want to, but I guess there's no other way." She stormed out of the kitchen, wiping a hand across her eyes.

What the hell is she talking about? I set down the beer. I didn't know what Amy meant, but I had a suspicion I'd find out.

CHAPTER
TWENTY-THREE

After the fight, Amy had retreated to the den, where she carried on a lengthy phone conversation. A conversation that paused when I walked in and started again as soon as I left. I wasn't a moron. She was talking about me. To whom? Probably her mother.

She hadn't been in bed when I fell asleep. She wasn't there when I awoke. We didn't talk before I left.

When I showed up to work, Rodney was already there. "I started making a list of local art dealers, and I dug up the one who sold Guenther the Natural Wonders art."

"Good. Any leads?"

He shook his head. "The locals aren't open yet. The phone number associated with the dealer who sold the Miller and MacRae is out of service. I'll keep at it."

"Good. While you keep on that line, I have to see someone." I headed for the door.

"Who?" It wasn't a question. More like a challenge.

"A friend."

"Max?"

"Yes."

"Why don't I go with you?"

I stopped at the door. "Be reasonable. I have to talk to her. You'll be checking the art angle. This way, we're both moving forward."

He glared. "That's an excuse. And not a good one."

I didn't say anything and left.

————

I headed to Max's apartment. It was only nine, but she was an early riser. I wouldn't wake her.

After a minute, she opened the door. "What are you doing here at this hour? You should be at work."

"Can I come in?"

She walked back to the living room and sat in her usual chair. The lights were dim and she'd drawn a set of translucent curtains against the morning sun.

I followed and sat down across from her. "I need to run a few ideas past you, see what—"

"Stop." She shifted in her chair and looked away from me.

Now what?

"I am not your crutch, Davis. I'm not your mother. If you expect me to sit here, listen to your self-pity, and tell you how mean the other kids are, think again."

She couldn't have hurt me more if she'd slapped me. "What the hell are you talking about?"

"It's time to be a grown-up, shelve your pride, and do what you should have done weeks ago." Leroy leapt up into her lap. She ran her hand over his back. "Why are you here?"

"To ask your advice."

"No, that's not it. What do you want from me?"

I want your forgiveness, I thought. *I want you to tell me it's not my fault, or at least that you don't blame me. I want to know I didn't let you down.*

Staring at her unflinching expression, the words wouldn't come. Daylight filtered through the curtains, leaving her face in a half-light. Put a blindfold on her, give her a sword and some scales, and she could've doubled for the statue of Lady Justice. She seemed as cold and remote as the blinded figure of the Greek goddess.

After a moment, she spoke. "I thought so."

My voice came out as a croak. "Thought what?"

"You don't need me to tell you what to do. You know damn well. You're too cowardly to admit it."

The one solid rock I'd been standing on cracked. "Are you freaking kidding me?" The frustration and anger I'd been carrying around for the last six months boiled over, a metaphoric, stinking pus. "Do you know —can you understand—what it's like, going in every day without you?"

Her stony look didn't falter.

"I walk into the office every day feeling like someone cut off my right hand and I've got to learn to write with my left. Except, I don't know if I can. Because it's weird and awkward, and I never think I'm in control. I can't function. I'm breaking apart." It was the first time I'd admitted it to anyone. I couldn't admit my weakness to the world. But I could say it to her.

"Then, do something about it."

"I don't know what."

She slapped the arm of the chair. "Yes, you do! Stop being a child. You know *exactly* how to fix this. You're too afraid to do it. Grow a pair, will you?"

We stared at each other for a long minute. I'd opened myself up to one of the two people I trusted most, and this was what I got? How could I expect better from a relative stranger like Dr. Alverson?

"Go, Jackson," Max said. "Do what you know you should do."

Leroy hissed at me.

I fled.

———

Rodney was at his desk when I came in. Not trusting my voice, I sat, hitched my chair forward, and picked up a random piece of paper. He stared at me as I did. Eventually, it got intolerable. "What?" I could hear the snap in my voice.

"Things didn't go well with Max." He tapped his pen on the desk.

"You can grasp the obvious. Bravo."

He continued to twiddle the pen and stare.

I was already hot under the collar from my run-in with Max. Being studied like a bug under a microscope didn't help. After a minute, I looked up. "You got any information?"

"Nothing more than I had when you left."

I grunted and looked back at the papers in front of me.

"You look like someone killed your dog. And that someone might have been you. I've been thinking. As much as I need to look out for my partner, I have responsibilities."

I looked up. "To whom?" I didn't even try to keep the dangerous edge out of my voice. Now was not the time to push me. If he couldn't see it, he wasn't paying very close attention.

"To myself. You are a basket case, to put it mildly."

"What the hell do you mean?"

"I don't trust you not to lose it under pressure." He stood and buttoned his jacket. "I'm going to ask Yannick for a different partner. I don't care if it is Dobrovski." He glanced at Yannick's door, but the captain's office was dark. "First thing in the morning." He walked away without another word.

———

The suitcase in the entry was my first clue things were wrong. *Strike one.*

The fact it was the one I always used told me things were disastrous. *Strike two.*

"I'm home." I pitched my keys in the basket. No rushing Madeline. *Strike three.* "Why is my suitcase out here?"

Amy came out of the kitchen. "I thought you might need it."

"Am I going somewhere?"

"That depends on you." She crossed her arms across her chest. She was pale, but her voice sounded like she was discussing the weather, not throwing her husband of seven years to the curb.

I stared at the suitcase. "You're kicking me out?"

"I'm giving you a choice."

"What?" This was unreal.

"You haven't called Dr. Alverson." She held up a hand to cut off my response. "You think you're in control. You're not."

The rock of my life had cracked when I spoke to Max. I felt it widening, and I could hear the roar of rapids underneath. I was precariously close to falling in.

"You told me you'd talk to Yannick," she continued. "Get more counseling."

"I did." I hadn't promised to call Alverson. Had I? I couldn't remember.

"What exactly did he say?"

I licked my upper lip. "He offered a compromise. Stay on duty. Go back to Alverson. Reassess." The edge of the rock crumbled under my feet.

"You didn't take him up on it." Amy's eyes glinted. It was more than anger. In fact, the hard shine I associated with her anger wasn't there. This was pure disappointment.

Now look what you've done. I stood over my personal Hell's Half Acre, barely holding myself steady. "What do you expect from me?"

"To be the man I married." She hugged herself tighter.

Her words pushed me further toward the edge.

A tear leaked out of her eye and trailed down her right cheek, but she jerked her head away when I tried to wipe it. "Jackson, I understand in your job, you have to be hard. You can't do what you do without putting on your tough guy mask. You used to take it off when you came home."

"Leaving isn't the answer." One corner of my mind wondered why I wasn't raging. I reached for her, but she moved half a step away. "I know things are a mess," I continued. "I'm sorry. I've had a bad day. Hell, I've had six months of bad days. Give me a chance. I can turn it around." It was hard to talk around the lump in my throat.

"You've had six months of chances, too. You've walked past every one of them."

The words hurt, but she was right. I'd had them, and I'd thrown them away as surely as tourists threw pennies into the river. "If I leave, what are you going to tell Madeline?"

"I'll say you're away on business." Amy's smile was watery. "I hear what's in your words, I do. But it's not working. Time for an intervention." She nodded at the suitcase.

"Where do you expect me to go?"

"Get a hotel room, go stay with Max, go to your brother's. You've got choices." She turned away.

"Amy, I love you." I'd imagined a lot of things for us, but not this. Never this.

She faced me and the tears were flowing freely. "I love you, too. Why do you think I'm doing this? I didn't want to, but what other choice have you left me?"

The rock crumbled and I fell.

TWENTY-FOUR

I drove aimlessly after leaving the house.

I didn't want to go to a hotel. I wouldn't check in alone. I'd be with my buddy, Jack Daniels. I didn't think he was the company I needed.

I couldn't go to my brother's. He and his wife would side with Amy. And they'd be right.

Without thinking, I found myself parked behind Top of the Falls. I got out, the roar in my head and the smell of water from the mist surrounding me. A clean smell. Full of possibility.

I went down to the bridge and over to Green Island. I imagined Sylvia storming down the path, fresh from another fight with her husband. Her situation was not unlike mine, both of us trying to hang on to an image too perfect to exist with reality.

I should have been focusing on my personal life. However, that's not what occupied the forefront of my mind. Solving this murder was inextricably linked with fixing everything else. And, at the moment, thinking about Sylvia was less painful.

What had possessed her to walk back to the casino hotel? Why not call a cab? What were the thoughts in her head?

Before long, I'd crossed the island and stood on the bridge connecting it with the main side of the park, overlooking Hell's Half Acre. Even in the dark, I could see the whitecaps from the river rushing over the rocks below. It was angry and jumbled. I'd always believed the water could carry away anything. The ultimate symbol of strength. Now, they were a mirror of chaos.

Infidelity, embezzlement, a gambling addiction, and forged art. It was too much. I would have completely understood if Sylvia had paused on this bridge, jumped, and decided to let nature determine her fate. I was tempted myself. But she hadn't jumped, and neither would I.

The key to getting out of the rapids was staying calm, working step by step until you were on solid ground again, in safe water. The more you fought the flow, the worse it got.

I chose to focus on the case, which was the easier problem to solve. There were too many threads, too many possibilities. They couldn't all be true. I leaned on the mist-covered railing and stared at the foam. This was the part I'd never believed I was good at, picking one thread and pulling it until it came loose and ended or led to something else. Identifying the solid ground that led to safety, the stable rocks amid the loose shale.

Now, I had to be.

It was more than personal observations swaying my

opinion. Something else was wrong. An observation in the autopsy made me instinctively dismiss the suicide angle. Before we'd even started interviewing people. What had it been?

I closed my eyes, visualizing the text of the report. This was my strong suit, memory. Max had always said my recall of faces and facts was second to none.

Severe contusion on the occipital region of the skull, occurring perimortem. Occipital—that was the back of the head. Perimortem meant the blow had occurred near the time of death. The injury had not been consistent with striking the head as the result of a fall. Someone had hit Sylvia, hard, from behind. *With what?* There were plenty of trees around. Most likely the suspect had used a large branch. It would be easy to toss it aside, maybe even into the river where the water would sweep away the evidence.

I opened my eyes to look at the rapids below. I could see the edges of the rock. It was easy enough to believe they'd inflict a serious wound if someone pitched off the bridge. But on the back of the skull? More likely the front or the top, caused by jumping or falling head first. The only way the injury made sense in a suicide scenario was if Sylvia stood on the railing and fell backward into the water. I found it as unlikely as the idea that she'd gone hiking in the gorge, or climbed the railing like some tourist seeking a cool vacation picture and slipped.

Helene and Bramley were right. This wasn't suicide. The autopsy report proved it.

I crossed Green Island again, this time stepping off the path to look in the grass. My shoes sank in the soft earth. The dark made it nearly impossible to see anything. Moving back to the sidewalk, I looked up and down the asphalt. No people, and only a few lights. The perfect place for an ambush.

My argument with Amy demanded attention, but I ignored it. It was satisfying—invigorating, even—to be reconstructing events, pieces of an elaborate puzzle. I needed to start with Sylvia. Solving her puzzle would be my first step back.

I had no physical evidence to back up my belief, but I was sure. This was where Sylvia had met her death. Or, at least, where she'd been beaten before her body was dumped into the maelstrom of Hell's Half Acre. Never mind the K-9 team hadn't traced her here. Facts were all well and good—and necessary—but a top-notch investigator never ignored his instincts.

All I needed was one shred of evidence. One small puzzle piece, and it would fall into place. The odds of finding it here were low, but I would come back with Rodney tomorrow—assuming he hadn't asked for and obtained his reassignment. But first, I needed help untangling the mess in my personal life. I had to find the next stable bit of rock.

For that, I needed a friend. All I could do was hope she wouldn't throw my ass out without a fair hearing.

———

It was ten-thirty by the time I parked outside Max's apartment building. I sat in the car, afraid to move. I knew I had to. I couldn't stay where I was. Amy had been right about one thing; she couldn't help me, but I couldn't help myself, either.

The window was dark, but I figured Max was awake. She'd always been a night owl. I got out, but I left my suitcase in the trunk. Best to find out if I would be welcome before I took the trouble of hauling it up the sidewalk.

I paused for a moment outside the door. I could hear music. I knocked. "Max." My voice cracked, and I cleared my throat. "It's me."

Footsteps. "I told you not to come back." Max's voice sounded from the other side. She had come to the door.

I rested my forehead on the door. "It's either here or Motel Six. I don't have any other options."

The door opened, but she'd left the safety chain on so the gap was only an inch or so wide. "Options for what?"

"Somewhere to sleep." At least she hadn't told me to get the hell out and then slammed the door in my face. "I don't deserve it, but I need another chance. I want another chance. Please."

Max didn't say anything, but the door shut and I heard the safety chain being unlatched. The door opened again, this time wide enough to admit me. "Don't you dare track mud in my apartment."

I looked at my shoes. There was dirt caked between the soles and heels. "How do you know my shoes are muddy?"

"You smell like water and dirt. It's not raining, so you've been walking by the Falls. Take off the damn shoes."

I stepped inside and took off my shoes, placing them on the mat. I'd clean them later. Then, I went to the living room.

She was in her usual chair, Leroy at her feet. Max switched off the stereo and pointed at the couch. "Sit."

It didn't occur to me to disobey.

"Talk. I better like what I hear."

Instantly, I was seven years old, telling my mother a story she already knew. If my version varied outside a reasonable tolerance, I'd find myself outside without a drop of sympathy. Without the music, I could hear the faint rush of the river through the open window.

Leroy leapt onto my knees and butted his head under my hand. He'd never done that before, and the velvet feel of his fur was soothing. I spoke, and I didn't spare any details. Everything of the last two weeks poured from me, culminating in Rodney's threatened transfer and Amy's final ultimatum. "If I go to a hotel, I'm going to get shit-faced drunk, which won't help." I was empty of righteous anger. Only shame remained. Shame I could only show Max. "I really bolluxed everything up."

"That's one way to put it. A complete cluster—"

"Don't." I snuck a look at Max and read the emotions on her face. Tightness in her jawline and around her eyes. Anger, sure. Disappointment, absolutely. But what else?

Pity. The woman who'd lost her job and her sight pitied *me*. How ironic. I'd been pitying her. But she wasn't in trouble, I was.

The set of her face was unforgiving, but her voice was soft. "You dumbass."

"I need one night."

"It's not all you need, but it's a start." She stood and went to the closet. "Get your suitcase."

I sagged with relief.

"You'll get your one night." Her voice was patient. "We'll talk again in the morning. Chain the door when you get back in."

I complied, fetching the luggage from my trunk. Once I was inside, Max pointed to a corner. "Set it there. You get the couch. Here's a pillow and blanket." She tossed them at me.

"Couch is fine. Thanks." I licked my lips. "Max, I need to say something."

She held up a hand. "Save it for later. Right now, you need to sleep. There will be time for everything else. Not like I'm going anywhere." She disappeared down the hallway, and I heard the door to her bedroom shut.

After a moment, I stripped down to my T-shirt and boxers. Then, I laid down on the couch. It was too short for me, but I was grateful not to be at a motel. I pulled the blanket around me and closed my eyes.

A soft, but heavy, thump near my chest made me open one eye. Leroy had curled up next to my chest. With feline solemnity, he licked my nose with a sandpaper tongue, then set his head down, green eyes blinking. His purr sounded like the motor of a Coast Guard vessel.

I closed my eyes and slept.

———

I expected to dream. I always did after episodes of intense emotional stress. Yesterday had definitely counted. But my slumber was deep and dark. Maybe it was the cat.

"Wake up." Sunlight streamed across me as Max yanked the curtains back. She had a soft yellow robe around her, and her hair was damp from the shower.

I blinked. "Thought the light hurt your eyes." Leroy was still curled in front of my chest. He got up, stretched in a way only a cat can stretch, and leapt down to run to the kitchen.

"It does. You need to get up. There's time to shower, get dressed, and eat something."

I rubbed my face. "I thought you wanted to talk."

"We can talk while you eat." She paused. "What are you waiting for?"

I glanced at the blanket. My plan had been to be up and dressed before she made her appearance. "I'm not wearing pants."

"For God's sake. I can't see you. Your modesty is safe."

I obeyed. Amy had packed a full shaving kit, not one but two extra suits, and plenty of underwear. I hung a coat and slacks in the bathroom where the shower steam would take care of any wrinkles. In the kitchen, I picked up my shoes. The mud had dried, and I dislodged it from the heel. It fell apart, leaving a pebble in my hand. I brushed off the dirt. "I need a baggie."

"What for?" But she handed me a sandwich bag.

"Something on my shoe." I put the stone, a

diamond, in the bag and zipped it. Then, I sat at the table. The diamond could wait.

Max pushed a plate with two perfectly toasted slices of rye bread and a bowl of Raisin Bran in front of me. A cup of coffee finished brewing and she put the mug down as well. "Those one-cup jobs don't make as good a brew as a French press, but they're certainly easier for me to operate." She eased down into the chair opposite. Leroy jumped into her lap, and she scratched him behind the ears.

I poured some milk over the cereal.

"I'm going to talk. You're going to listen." She continued to rub Leroy's head. "Good news. I've decided to help you out."

"Max, thank you. I—"

"Shut up. You're listening, remember?" She tilted her head. "You said if you could change things, you would." She paused, blinking. "I wouldn't."

I didn't know if she wanted a response, so I kept my mouth shut.

"What happened, happened. I don't like it, but that's not required. I made my decision and I'm not sorry."

I almost spoke but held back, sensing she wasn't finished.

"Last night showed maybe you're ready. I'll help you the best I can."

I finished the cereal and took a swallow of coffee. I'd been right. Had I not told the whole story, I wouldn't be sitting here. "Thank you."

"On one condition."

Condition? *Shit.* "What?" But I knew without asking.

"You will call Dr. Alverson and make an appointment. Right now. You will see if she can fit you in later today. If not, you will take her next available appointment."

I knew that would be it. I found myself tired of fighting. In fact, the idea held a sort of comfortable attraction. I'd lost everything already. There wasn't anything left to lose. And so much to gain. "Max, what I wanted to say last night—"

"Save it. You aren't ready. I want you to think long and hard before you tell me anything."

Part of me was relieved. Was this her way of saying she didn't want to talk about what happened beyond the generalities?

"I didn't save your body so you could piss away your life. It's time to shelve your pride, stop being an asshat, and get the professional help you need." She leaned back in her chair. "I know all about what happens behind the thin blue line. Enough with the noble-hero-suffering-in-silence bull." She removed my cellphone from her robe pocket and pushed it across the table. She must have filched it while I slept. "You want my help, make the damn appointment. Or pack your stuff, get out, and don't come back."

I stared at the phone. This was it. I claimed I wanted a second chance. Max had thrown me a rope. Was I willing to grab it?

I picked up the phone and dialed.

TWENTY-FIVE

Alverson's office staff managed to shoehorn me in at four-thirty. "Pick me up at four," Max said when I hung up.

"I'm not a child. You don't need to go with me."

"Like you were so willing to do it before now. Pick me up at four."

The irony was not lost on me. I needed a blind woman to get me to an appointment.

When I got to work, I stopped at Yannick's office. "Captain, got a second?"

"Certainly." He waved me toward a chair, but I didn't sit.

"I want to take you up on your compromise. With the doc." I waited for his response.

He leaned back, studying me. "First appointment is when?"

"This afternoon." I shuffled my feet. "How many before you make a decision?"

He cracked a grin. "More than one. I don't expect

miracles." He paused. "I'm glad you came to your senses. What made you change your mind?"

"I'd rather not talk about it." I nodded at him and returned to the squad room.

Then, I snagged Rodney. "Can we talk?"

He didn't look at me. "Nothing happened overnight. I'm still waiting on information about the paintings." His voice was clipped.

"It's not about that. Let's go to the supply room."

He looked up, eyes narrowed, but he followed me.

The supply nook was out of the way enough that I didn't think we'd be overheard, but not so far that we looked like we were hiding. I took a deep breath. "I want to apologize. I've been—"

"An asshole?"

I bit back a retort. That's exactly what I'd been. "Have you talked to Yannick yet?"

"Yes."

I was too late. I held my breath.

"He said no. Wants me to finish this case, then ask again." Rodney's voice was neutral, but the glint in his eye told me he wasn't happy with Yannick's decision.

I exhaled. "Good. I was hoping I'd get another shot."

"A shot at what?"

"Being the partner you deserve." I held out my hand. "I'm sorry. I'll do better. I promise."

He jammed his hands in his pockets, but at least he didn't storm away.

I glanced around, but we were still alone. "I've made an appointment with a psychologist today at four-thirty. Give me this case. If we get to the end of it and you still want a new partner, I won't stand in your way."

He still didn't answer.

"Come on. What more do you want me to say? You're right. I was an asshole. I had a lot going on, but that's no excuse. I could stand here and recite chapter and verse on what I should have done, but it won't change anything. I'm asking for a second chance. I don't deserve it, but I'm hoping you're a better guy than I am, than I was."

He stared at me, his face unreadable.

"If you really want out, I'll talk to Yannick myself. But I'd like the chance to prove myself." The silence stretched between us, shorter than it felt, I'm sure, but long enough I started to worry. "Damn it. Say something. Screw you, go to hell, anything. Speak."

He glanced at my outstretched hand, then looked me straight in the eye. "I'll work with you. For now. I'm not making any promises about later."

I closed my eyes, relief washing over me. "Fair enough. I'm going to put things right."

He walked away.

————

I got a refill on my coffee and joined Rodney at our desks. Contrary to TV stereotypes, we didn't have bad coffee. It wasn't the same as a fresh cup from Tim Hortons, but it was better than mediocre.

I decided the best way to proceed was to keep it business as usual. "I went back to Green Island last night, trying to clear my head." I handed over the baggie. "Found this in my shoe this morning."

He turned the baggie over in his hands. "Looks like a diamond." Rodney must have come to the same decision.

"Maybe from an earring."

He held it up. "Sylvia's?"

I flipped through the file. "Here. Bramley said Sylvia was wearing dangly silver earrings with diamonds."

He gazed at the bag.

"I think it's worth considering."

"We've been over the area already and didn't find anything." He twirled the pen in his fingers.

"So, we look again. Maybe we missed it the first time. Also, Sylvia's injuries." I told him what I'd thought about while staring at the rapids.

"Makes sense. What about Dellafiore and Guenther? They insist it was suicide. Hand me a pen." He pulled out his notebook.

I gave him one from my desk. It was dented from where I'd chewed it.

"Disgusting. Do you have one without teeth marks?"

I scrabbled in my desk drawer.

"Never mind." He got up, left, and returned with a handful of ballpoints. He sat again and started making notes. "Diamond from the earring. Injuries from the rapids. Two people say suicide, two don't."

I took back my pen and gnawed it. It *was* gross. It also helped me think. "What does your gut say?"

"Say again?"

"Knowing what you know, what do your instincts

tell you? You've been a cop long enough to know it's not only about facts."

"She was murdered." He kept writing. "And it's not like we don't have motives or suspects."

"Speaking of motives, we need to add Dellafiore to our list."

"I don't see him as our killer. He discovered the embezzlement."

"So he says. I can figure it happened in one of two ways. He knew Sylvia was embezzling and tried to blackmail her. Somehow, it went south, so he killed her. Or, more likely, he was the one with his fingers in the cookie jar. Sylvia found out, confronted him, and he got to her first."

"I still don't think he looks like an embezzler. Or a killer."

"Neither did Jeffrey Dahmer." I rubbed my chin. "Dellafiore's financial records in yet?"

"No."

"Damn."

He stood. "Let's go check your bridge." He jabbed a finger at me. "I'm driving. Got it?" He walked off without a backward glance.

―――――

Being out and busy helped keep my mind off the afternoon. We parked in a lot off Main Street and crossed from the far side of the bridge, where Sylvia would have turned to head for the casino had she made it that far. Then, we donned gloves. "Look under any leaf debris, in bushes, under trees," I told Rodney. "I don't expect to find much on the bridge itself, but maybe we'll get lucky at the ends this time."

"I know how to do a search." He walked away.

Going slow, we looked under every leaf and twig. The city-side efforts yielded nothing except a few empty plastic bottles, crushed cans, gum wrappers, cigarette butts, and other trash.

I called over to him. "Find anything?"

"Garbage. The stone you found was in dirt. Let's check the island." Rodney started across the walkway without waiting for my answer.

The well-traveled, paved walkway was devoid of evidence. I paused to study the whitecaps at Hell's Half Acre. They didn't look as threatening in daylight, and the sound was powerful but not ominous. *Too bad we can't check the riverbed.* Anything that had gone into the water would be at the bottom of the gorge by now. The current was too strong. Even if something was lodged in the rapids, I wasn't sure anybody short of the Navy SEALs would be able to make an underwater recovery.

Rodney had already reached Green Island and was combing the ground under the trees, so I sped up to catch him. As I reached the edge, he straightened, holding something in his hand. "This was smashed in the dirt under the garbage can. I don't know how they missed it the first time."

It was an earring. Dangly and silver. "It's a lot of ground. You said it was under something." I could see the gap where one diamond was missing. "I think this is it." I checked the post. The earring had a hinged closure. "The clasp is shut."

He brushed some leaves off his slacks. "You think the killer stripped her jewelry and dropped this one?"

"I do. He was trying to make it look like she was mugged."

"How'd the stone come loose?"

"Don't know." I took the baggie out of my pocket. "Looks like it might fit. Maybe he stepped on it in the dark, dislodged the one diamond. Or someone else did. I was lucky to step in the same mud."

"Let's get a tech team back down here." He headed back to the parking lot, removing his gloves. "Where'd the rest of the jewelry go?"

I bagged the earring and filled out the custody information. "It'll turn up. We have to get Bramley in to identify this."

"After we handle the scene." He pulled out his cellphone to call for the crime scene folks. "I'll take care of it while you talk to Bramley."

In other words, he'd do the field work while I took care of the administrative details. At least he was still talking to me.

———

The tech team didn't find anything else, but I wasn't surprised given the amount of elapsed time. Bramley hadn't answered the first time I called, so I tried again on the way back to the office. This time, he answered.

"I can come on Monday." Bramley sounded harassed. "Or can you send me a picture?"

"Mr. Bramley, either you come to us or we come to you." This needed to be done today.

"Fine. I'll be there later." He hung up.

"You'd think I asked him to do something hard, not identify an earring." I slipped my phone back in my pocket. If Bramley delayed his arrival, I might not be there. *Don't think about that.*

"What can I say? He's familiar with your winning personality." Rodney didn't look at me.

"If he comes after I leave, you'll have to handle it."

"I think I can do one simple thing." He shot me a glance, and a bit of the hard edge in his eyes faded. "How much does the earring help?"

"It identifies our murder scene." I studied it through the bag.

"What if we're wrong and she did jump?"

"If you're going to commit suicide, why would you take off your jewelry first? Wouldn't you either keep it on or leave it at home?"

He grunted. No snarky comeback. Progress.

When we arrived back at the office, the forensic accountant's report of the Natural Wonders financials awaited us.

Rodney looked over the contents of the envelope on his desk. "The Bramleys' information is here, too."

I dropped the bag on the desk and made sure the paperwork was filled out correctly. We'd send it to the evidence locker as soon as we got a positive ID. "What does it say?"

He muttered to himself as he read. "Someone *was* skimming from Natural Wonders, but the money wasn't going into any known account of the Bramleys. Neither of them."

"Not all that convenient." I reached up for the report.

He jerked it out of my reach and kept reading. "It wasn't going to Guenther, either. Does it mean they're off the hook?"

"Don't know. May I see?" He handed over some pages and I scanned the summary. "One of them might have an account we haven't found yet."

Rodney looked over another sheet. "Sylvia had investment accounts. Hers, not with her husband."

I looked up. The fact was promising.

"That might be where the gambling money came from, at least some of it." He held out the sheet, pointing. "Compare these dividend payouts to the amounts of the cash deposits in her bank account."

I looked. "I see a couple of matches, but it doesn't account for all the deposits."

"The rest could be the so-called petty cash. Or winnings from Seneca Niagara. Or both. It doesn't have to be from the company."

We spent the next hour and a half reading the report from the forensic accountant and looking for hidden accounts for Bramley, Sylvia, or Guenther. Every time I looked at the clock, I was reminded of where I would be later, so I tried to stare exclusively at the paper in front of me.

"It's three thirty-five. Don't you have somewhere to go?" Rodney jerked his head toward the door.

Bramley had not come in yet. "Let me know about the earring. And if you hear about the paintings."

"Sure. And Jackson?" He toyed with the paper in his hand. "I mean this sincerely. Good luck."

CHAPTER
TWENTY-SIX

I was a few minutes late getting to Max's, but we still arrived at the doc's office in plenty of time. Concentrating on driving kept my panic at bay. Once I parked in the lot outside the nondescript brick building, it broke free, paralyzing me.

"You getting out?" She opened her door.

My grip on the steering wheel was white-knuckled. "What if she tells me I'm a lost cause? I'm beyond hope?"

"Knock that shit off. Right now." Max grabbed my chin and forced me to look directly at her hazy eyes. "You are not a lost cause. I would not be investing the time and effort to get your ass back on track if I believed you were. Get out of the car."

I met her on the sidewalk, and she laid a hand on my arm. We started toward the building, but after three steps, I stopped. *Nothing to be scared of. Just your life on the line.*

She gripped my arm. "Don't freak on me. Walk."

Inside, I signed in and sat in the waiting room. I supposed the earthy browns were supposed to be soothing. It didn't do anything for me at the moment.

"Detective Davis?"

I jumped out of my seat like someone had electrified it. Dr. Alverson stood there, her reddish-brown hair tied back in a professional ponytail and kind eyes behind rimless glasses. "It's good to see you." She looked at Max and extended her hand. "You must be Detective Simon."

"Ms. Simon these days." Max shook her hand once.

"Ms. Simon, good of you to come. Moral support is important."

"He's still my partner." Max looked at Dr. Alverson. Even with her milky eyes, the look couldn't be described as anything but direct. "Our boy here is in bad shape, doc. Think you can help him out?"

"We'll certainly try." Alverson gestured to her office. I followed her.

"Have a seat." Alverson shut the door and waved toward an easy chair, the same one I'd always sat in when I visited before. In the distance, I could see the mist off the Falls. The leaves on the tree outside unfurled in a translucent green. I took it as a good sign. A sign of rebirth.

I sat, my insides both leaden and as jittery as if I'd mainlined pure caffeine. I pulled at my tie, the collar of my shirt tight around my neck.

Alverson sat across from me. "Detective Davis—"

"Jackson."

"Jackson." She inclined her head. "If you need to

take off your tie, go ahead. Unbutton your collar. Whatever makes you comfortable."

I hesitated, then pulled off the tie and loosened my collar. It didn't make breathing any easier.

"Talk to me about what's going on." She placed a pad and pen on the table in front of us but didn't write anything. She crossed her ankles and waited.

"I—" I stopped. "I need to move. I'm going to jump out of my skin sitting."

"If you wish."

I sprung up and started to pace like the caged lions at the Buffalo Zoo. I talked, the words coming slowly at first, but soon they tumbled over each other like water at the lip of the Falls. I told her everything. I spilled every bit of guilt, anger, and the crushing responsibility I'd felt for the last six months. "I'm scared shitless." I rubbed my hands on my legs. "Every freaking second of the day."

"Of what?"

"What if I can't make it? Will someone tell me? Or will they let me fumble along?"

Alverson said nothing, but she motioned for me to continue.

"Will I get my new partner hurt? Or killed? What about my kids? My wife? Can I take care of my family?" I rubbed my face. "I screwed up. Lost concentration. Look what it did to Max. I can't let everyone down again. I know next time, it'll be worse. I don't know how, but it will be." I collapsed into the chair, out of breath, but the weight had disappeared from my chest. Who knew emotions were so heavy?

"I think I've spoken to you about this before, but have you and Max ever talked about what happened?"

"She doesn't want to hear it."

"How do you know if you haven't asked?"

"I don't have to. I know." I looked at Dr. Alverson. "You saw her out there. Would you want to be reminded of the thing that made it impossible to do the job you loved? I wouldn't. As for me, I don't need to remind myself of my screw-ups and the consequences. I live with them every day."

"Yet, she came here with you today. Is it possible you're projecting your fears onto her?"

I ran my hands through my hair. "I don't think apologizing is going to solve my problem, doc."

She leaned back. "Oh, not completely, I agree with you there. But I think it's an important start."

"Why?" I was already in one painful conversation. Why start another?

Her voice was soft. "Because you're feeling a tremendous amount of guilt, Jackson. I can see it in your eyes, hear it in your voice. The words you use are very telling. You don't want to let people down *again*. Which means you think you've done it before. Has your wife said anything to you?"

"Amy? Never."

"Your commanding officer?"

"No."

"Do you think they're lying to you?"

Amy loved me too much. Yannick was honest to a fault. "No, I don't."

"And if you've never spoken to Max, how do you know what she thinks? Are you psychic?"

If only. "We don't need to talk about it."

Dr. Alverson fixed me with a piercing gaze, as though she'd seen it all before. She was an official psychologist for the NFPD. She probably had. "Oh, I think you do, Jackson. Yes, I think you do."

———

I exited Dr. Alverson's office forty minutes later, my insides a lot less jumpy than they'd been when I went in. "Thanks."

"You're welcome." She smiled. "Remember what we talked about. I understand you're in the middle of an investigation, but I want to see you Tuesday. Same time. Schedule it before you leave. Or I have a group session Monday morning."

I shuddered. "No groups. I'm not ready to talk to a bunch of strangers."

"Then, I'll see you Tuesday, and we'll pick up where we left off."

We walked back to Max. She must have felt us approach because she took the earbuds out of her ears. "Well, doc? How's our boy?"

Dr. Alverson chuckled. "The prognosis is good." She cast a calculated look at Max. "You know, Ms. Simon, if there's anything I can do for you, don't hesitate to call."

"No worries. I'm fine. I'm not just saying that. I really am, doc." Max stood and grasped her cane. "I had my come-to-Jesus moment. It may not have been as painful as Jackson's, but it happened. Eventually." She tilted her head toward me. "You ready?"

"Let's get some pizza and beer."

"And wings. I want wings." She turned to the door and grasped my proffered forearm. "Onward."

I guided her out of the office and back to the car.

Onward.

Max ordered while I drove. We loaded up on the toppings, something I never got to do at home. We also stopped to pick up a six-pack of beer. While we ate, I brought her up to date on the investigation. "Kind of thin, huh?"

"You've worked with less."

"True." I took a drink. "What do I do about Rodney?" I tossed down a bone. "He's pissed at me. With good reason. But I meant it when I told him I wanted another chance. He's not a bad guy."

"You apologized to him, right?"

"This morning."

"Then, it's up to him. If he's as decent a person as you say, he'll give you a second chance. Quite honestly, I'd like to meet him."

"You would? Why?"

She smirked. "I want to know about the guy who's going to have to put up with your sorry ass."

I decided Mark Twain was right when he talked

about fools and speaking, and I kept my attention on the food.

After a while, she pushed away her plate. "God, I'm stuffed. I haven't eaten like that in months."

"Seriously?" Pizza, wings, and beer had been a late-night staple.

"You don't order a large pizza and twenty wings for one person." She wiped her fingers. "Well, you might with your freak-of-nature metabolism. I don't."

I chuckled. "I'd better call Rodney."

"After you call your wife."

Should I? I stared at my plate.

Ever the partner, Max read my mind. "Don't be stupid. She wants you to call."

"She probably thinks I'm at some flop-house."

Max started clearing the table. "She doesn't."

An intervention, Amy had said. Then, it dawned on me. She hadn't been talking to her mother. "What are you not telling me?"

"A lot. Go call your wife."

"Yes, ma'am." I was glad Max couldn't see my grin because she'd have smacked me. Which is why I was shocked when she reached out and gave me a light slap across the chin. "What was that for?"

"For laughing at me."

I blinked. "What the hell? You couldn't possibly see me."

"No, but it's something you would do." A sly grin curled her lips. "Besides, you confessed."

It was a trick I'd seen her pull in dozens of interviews, and I'd fallen for it hook, line, and sinker. Maybe introducing her to Rodney wasn't such a good idea. I didn't need another partner with her habits.

———

My call with Amy was brief. Enough to let her know I was working on getting back to where I was better, if not perfect. She didn't seem at all surprised when I told her I was at Max's, which strengthened my suspicions. I asked after Christopher, and then Madeline got on the phone. "Goodnight, Squirt."

"When are you coming home, Daddy?" Her voice sounded a little forlorn.

"In a few days. Tell you what, I'll read you one story for every night I'm gone, okay?" The promise perked her up. Then, I called Rodney.

"Didn't expect to hear from you until Monday. How'd it go?"

Alverson and I had talked about the word *fine*. "Better. I didn't want to wait until Monday."

"Wait for what?"

"I know I apologized this morning. Look, I'm not good at this, but I wanted you to know—"

"Bro, what do you think I am? You said your piece. I don't need to hear it again. I've been thinking."

I waited.

"You remember the officer from the gorge? When we found Sylvia's body? Of course, you do."

Officer Daniels. "The one who ragged you about Rachel?"

"Him. Truth is, she didn't leave me. I was the one who walked out."

I'd been right earlier, when he'd slipped and said he'd been the last to know. "She cheated on you with Daniels. How many times?"

"It had been going on for months." His voice was glum. "See, I worked a lot of graveyard shifts when I was on patrol. Daniels was on day shift."

"She wanted someone to warm her bed, and he was it. How'd they even meet?"

"I introduced them at a Christmas party. I thought it was cool she got along so well with the other guys. I thought it meant she'd understand the job." He let out a bitter laugh. "Joke was on me, huh?"

"Man, that sucks."

"At least I found out before I bought the ring. When I saw him at the Bramley scene, well, it all came back."

It was a tiny act of confidence, but I appreciated it. "Why're you telling me now?"

"Because while you have been a supreme asshole, I could have been more understanding. Guys always tell me how they can't imagine walking in with a dozen roses to find your girl shacked up with someone you thought was a friend." He paused. "For as much as others feel sorry for me, you've had it ten—no, a hundred—times worse. I'm sorry."

I wasn't sure if the phone made the silence more or less awkward. Time to get back to work. "Anyway, did you ID the earring?"

"It's Sylvia's. Bramley didn't hesitate. Seemed to me like he couldn't wait to get out of here."

I frowned. "I find the man's lack of concern about locating his wife's killer disturbing."

"I agree. I mentioned it to him, in fact."

"What did he say?"

"That it was our job to figure it out. He paid enough in taxes to fund our salaries, so we should do our jobs. Those were his exact words, by the way."

I sighed. The refuge of the public: *I pay your salary.* "What about the paintings?"

The rustle of paper came over the line. "My local contact called. He doesn't handle those artists but gave me names of galleries that do. I've got messages out."

At some point in the conversation, Max had entered the room. "Ask if his contact knows if the paintings are on the market."

I tapped the speaker icon. "Since you've been eavesdropping, why don't you ask him?"

Max flipped me off.

"Not offhand." Rodney spoke over more paper rustling. "All we have is Dellafiore's assertion they're fake. However, I did trace the payment for purchase."

"The place with the defunct number?" I asked.

"It's an LLC. A shell, as far as I can tell. Local guy said he'd never heard of them. So, I did more digging on the LLC, trying to find out who owns it."

"Did you?" I looked at Max.

"I did." There was a note of satisfaction in Rodney's voice that told me he was pleased with the result. "The owner of the LLC is listed as one Bertram Guenther."

I whistled.

"Guether owns the art gallery that sold the paintings? Not suspicious at all." Max's voice implied the air quotes.

"My thinking exactly," Rodney said. "I don't expect

to hear from the NYC dealers until Monday. But where there's smoke—"

"There's fire." Max sat back. "Nice work."

"Thanks. Max, we'll have to go out for drinks and you can tell me how you put up with Jackson for two years."

She laughed. "Don't give up on him. He grows on you. Like fungus."

I gave her a hard look. "Can you two not talk about me like I'm not sitting right here?"

"Max, first round's on me. We can talk about him behind his back. Catch you later." He ended the call.

I slipped my phone in my pocket. "Really? A fungus?"

———

I brushed my teeth and slipped into a pair of sweatpants. Blind or not, I was not going to appear in front of Max in my boxers again. A man had to have some dignity.

I returned to the living room. She had put the pillow and blanket on the couch for me. "Are you going to steal my cat from me again tonight?"

"It wasn't my idea. He picked me." I sat on the couch.

"Typical feline. Goodnight." She turned off the light.

Dr. Alverson's words from earlier ran through my head. "Max, wait." The full moon outside gave enough light to make out the details of the room. I twisted in my seat.

Max had paused in the door to her bedroom. In the

twilight, her eyes were darker, almost enough to think they'd returned to her normal hazel. "What do you want now?"

The words stuck in my throat again, but this time I forced them out. "I wanted to tell you I'm sorry."

"What the hell for?"

I'd started, which helped. Plus, it was dark. I didn't think I could have said it in the light of day, but the moonlight blunted the edges of the world and made it easier to say things I should have let out months ago. "For that night. For what I did."

"What is it you think you did?"

"I should have let him go. The runner."

She moved to her chair in the living room. The light from outside illuminated her eyes, revealing their milky whiteness.

I kept talking. "We knew who he was. We could've collared him at any time. Or radioed for another unit to watch the exit, or sent someone to his apartment or something. But I had the bit between my teeth and my adrenaline was up. I chased him where I had no business going." I stared at my hands. "It's not much of an excuse, but it's all I have."

"You were being a cop. I know how hard it is to rein it in under those circumstances. It doesn't explain why you're sorry."

She wasn't dense. I looked at her. "I made you follow me. If I hadn't done that, the explosion might have happened, but you wouldn't have been affected. You'd still be on the job. I took everything away from you. I'm sorry. I don't deserve your forgiveness, but I hope I have it. I'll spend the rest of my life making it up to you."

The silence went on for so long, it became painful. Her face was in shadow, her expression unreadable. "You colossal dumbass," she whispered.

"I beg your pardon?" I'd unburdened my soul, and this was what I got?

"Jackson, you didn't make me do a single thing." She reached out and laid her hand on my knee. "I followed you because you're my partner and that's what partners do for each other. Okay, maybe for a moment I wished you'd stop. But you didn't, and I wasn't going to let you run onto the Occidental Chemical grounds alone, at night, in pursuit of a possibly armed suspect."

"Right, but—"

"What if I hadn't followed? Yes, I'd still have my sight and maybe I'd still be on the job. Maybe I'd have been at your funeral, watching your pregnant wife accept a flag from a thankful police department. Maybe I'd be the one in therapy, wondering how I'd make it up to you, to your family, because I'd let my partner run off into God-knows-what without me. Do you really think I'd prefer it if things had turned out like that?"

I stared at the carpet. "No."

"At least, you know me." She sat back. "We haven't talked much about what happened. It's as much my fault as yours. As cops, we don't do well with the touchy-feely things."

Talk about an understatement.

"You don't owe me an apology, Jackson. There's nothing to make up for as far as I'm concerned. I told you before, I made a decision and I'm not sorry. Yeah, I miss the job. But if the choice is to have you and no job, or be on the job without you, well, it's an easy one to make."

I felt wetness on my cheeks and was glad she couldn't see me. How embarrassing. Crying in front of my partner. "Thanks." I could see her own cheeks gleam in the light. Maybe it was best that neither of us could see well.

She stood up. "Right. Good talk. Now, go to sleep. There's work to be done in the morning."

TWENTY-EIGHT

On Monday, I picked up two coffees on my way to work. I also grabbed a couple of breakfast sandwiches. Sort of a peace offering. And I was hungry.

True to form, Rodney was at his desk when I arrived. "Morning." I held out a sandwich. "Breakfast?"

He looked up and squinted. "Are you trying to bribe me?"

I shrugged. "Thought you might be hungry. If you don't want it, one of the other guys will."

He snatched the sandwich out of my hand. Then, he set it down to unwrap it.

I kept my face expressionless. "You're welcome." I took my seat.

"Max sounded pretty cool," he said around a mouthful of egg, cheese, bacon, and bagel.

I swallowed. "She is."

A beat of silence. "It was late when you called. Why were you at her place?"

I continued eating. I wasn't sure if he was fishing for conversation, but at this point continuing to be professional would be more helpful to the partnership than drowning him in my personal problems. "I'm staying with her for a while."

"How long?"

"Not sure." I took another bite.

We ate in silence. Everything that needed to be said had been. Now, it was all about the job. Once I finished, I crumpled up my wrapper and threw it out. "You get information from those dealers in New York?" Time to bring the conversation back where it belonged.

He stared at me for a long second. "Not yet. I called this morning, but they don't open until ten. Close at four. Wish I had those hours." He wiped grease from his fingers with a napkin. Guess he was on board with the *back to work* approach, too.

I studied the papers in the case file, which now included background information on Dellafiore. Within two months of starting at Natural Wonders, he'd reported signs of embezzlement. Coincidence? Dellafiore was also the guy who'd turned us on to the paintings. Then, without warning, he'd quit his job, saying he didn't trust Bert Guenther. It all smelled like one of Christopher's diapers.

We read in silence for probably fifteen minutes. Rodney's desk phone rang, a welcome interruption. "Criminal Investigations. Detective Kirke." He paused. "Ms. Cartwright, thanks for returning my call. Yes, a Miller and a MacRae. Yes, I'll hold." He covered the mouthpiece of the phone. "Art gallery."

I'd figured as much, but refrained from saying so. It would not be helpful if I wanted to build a relationship.

"Yes, I'm still here. Yes. Yes. You're sure? Yes. Thank you." He hung up.

I said, "The paintings are still for sale." I knew it. There was no other explanation for Rodney's half of the conversation.

"One of them is. The MacRae. The call was the gallery manager. The painting is listed in their database as available for purchase."

One down. "What about the Miller?"

"They don't have that one in their inventory. I've got a couple more calls out. But if one is a fake—"

"Chances are, they both are. Let's get a warrant." I stood and buttoned my jacket.

"I'm driving. And we're stopping to get you some damn gum. I'm not going to watch you maul perfectly good pens." He walked away without waiting for an answer.

———

We had to do some explaining to a judge to show how forged art could relate to homicide, but we got our warrant. As we were en route, Rodney's cellphone rang. He handed it to me to answer.

"I'm looking for a Detective Rodney Kirke," a woman's voice said. "This is Marlene Xavier from the Daley Art Gallery."

"He's driving. I'm his partner. Is this about the painting?"

"Yes," said Ms. Xavier. "The Miller is still in our possession and is for sale."

"No one has called to express interest in it?" I pulled out a pen and pad.

Next to me, Rodney grunted.

"Not in the last ninety days," Ms. Xavier replied.

I thanked her, hung up, and handed Rodney his phone. "We were right. Both paintings are forgeries."

I stared out the window. A few business types loitered on the sidewalks. The park would be full of people enjoying the spring sunshine, watching it sparkle in the mist. Definitely a more relaxing way to spend the day.

"Why would Guenther get Sylvia to buy fake art? I mean, if it were the other way around, I'd say it was revenge for ending the affair. But he's the one who cut things off," Rodney said.

"Dellafiore says Sylvia was the one who ended it." I unwrapped a piece of gum from the pack I'd purchased. I held out the pack.

Rodney shook his head. "Seems like a lot of the things we *know* come down to Dellafiore's word. I'm beginning to think you've got a point about him. Don't say, *I told you so*."

"Wasn't going to." I cracked my gum.

He sighed. "It always comes down to money and sex, doesn't it?"

———

We arrived at Natural Wonders and spoke to Marcy.

"The paintings? Receipts?" she said. "I don't know if I should let you take them."

"We do," I said. I read her the warrant, then handed her a copy.

Marcy studied it. "Those pictures are valuable."

"We'll be very careful," Rodney said. "We even brought bubble wrap."

"However, we're pretty certain they're fake. So, not all that valuable," I said. I lifted the Miller and slipped it into the padded bag Rodney held open.

Marcy lifted the phone. "I think I should call Mr. Guenther."

I heard her speaking. I removed the MacRae and deposited it in another bag. Then, we taped the bags shut, filled out the chain of evidence sheets, and prepared to leave. There was no reason to wait.

Before we made it to the door, Guenther burst into the lobby. "Marcy says you're taking our paintings," he said, his face red. "I demand to know the meaning of this."

I set down the picture I was holding and took the warrant from Marcy. "It's all here." I read the warrant again.

He didn't say anything, but snatched the paper out of my hand.

"Makes it a little awkward for you, having them hanging in your lobby when they're listed for sale elsewhere," Rodney said. "We know you owned the gallery Sylvia bought these from. Which makes it even worse, doesn't it?"

Some of the red receded from Guenther's face,

making it look like badly mixed cherry ice cream. "If you are insinuating—"

I hefted the picture. "We're not saying anything other than we believe these paintings are forgeries," I said. "As soon as we prove they are, we can move forward." I watched him. Would he put two and two together and figure out trying to keep Sylvia silent on the art fraud was a motive for murder?

More red left Guenther's face. He must have done the math.

"We also have records showing you deposited rather large sums of money into your personal bank account around the same time these paintings were purchased," I said. We didn't. Not until Guenther's subpoenaed bank records came in. Saying we did might prompt a confession. Another trick from Max.

The statement got a reaction. Guenther spluttered. "You said you were Homicide."

Rodney gripped his painting. "We are. Others aren't. Are you offering an explanation?"

Guenther was silent.

While we stared at each other, Helene entered the lobby. "What's all the shouting? Why are they taking Mrs. Bramley's paintings?"

"They think they're forged," Guenther said, trying for a tone of disdain. He failed.

"You sold her *fake art*?" Helene balled her fists. "You lying, scheming, piece of—" It was pretty clear where Helene's loyalties were. She snarled and lunged for Guenther.

I put down my painting and caught her. "Ms. Montgomery, I understand how you're feeling. Don't make us arrest you for assault."

"He took advantage of her," Helene said, her hair falling out of its elegant twist. "He slept with Sylvia, thinking that would get her to buy into his ideas. Now, the art. I'll kill him!" She twisted in my grasp, but I held on.

"Speaking of the affair, we hear Mrs. Bramley ended it. Not you," Rodney said, not missing a beat.

Guenther wiped his forehead. "I have nothing to say to you, gentlemen. Unless you want to put those back and admit you've made a mistake." Like most guilty people, he couldn't stop talking. "Sylvia committed suicide."

Helene screeched in protest.

Guenther drove on. "Maybe she knew the art was forged when she bought it." Yep. Couldn't stop.

"She purposely paid thousands of dollars for fake paintings?" Rodney's skepticism came through loud and clear.

Still holding a struggling Helene, I faced him and shook my head. "No, Mr. Guenther. I don't think so."

"She was in debt because of her gambling." Guenther's chin jutted forward. "The money had to have come from somewhere. Maybe she got into debt to the wrong people and arranged to buy the paintings to disguise repayment of the debt."

The statement elicited another outburst from Helene, this one liberally laced with profanity she must have learned at the construction company.

"Except you brokered the sale." Rodney set down

his painting and pulled out his notepad. "Are you saying *you* were the one she was in debt to?"

Guenther wiped his forehead again, along with his upper lip.

"Marcy, I need those receipts." I spoke to her, but I didn't take my stare off Guenther. "Can I let you go?" I asked Helene, who was breathing hard. She jerked her head. I released her and for a second, I thought she was going to lunge again.

She didn't. "I'm not sure what's going to happen to this company." Her voice dripped venom. "But I'll be damned if you have any say in its future. Even if I have to take out a loan and buy it myself." She stormed back down the executive hallway, and we heard a door slam.

Rodney and I exchanged a look. Those closest to Sylvia hadn't shown much grief thus far, but Helene more than made up for it.

I looked to Marcy. "So, those receipts, please?"

"Mr. Dellafiore might have them, but he's not in. Mr. Guenther..." Marcy's voice trailed off.

I turned my attention to Guenther. "Receipts?"

He blinked. "I don't think we have any."

"You don't have receipts," Rodney said. "A corporate purchase, and you don't have records."

I didn't need to look at him to know my partner found this as unbelievable as I did. "You're making a bad situation look worse. You know that, right? If these were legitimate company purchases, you should have receipts for tax records. It's a simple request."

The silence stretched, getting heavier by the second. I could feel Marcy's tension from across the lobby. Unfortunately, Rodney and I were in a bit of a stalemate. If the paintings were real, the dealers were the ones with the problem. We could detain Guenther for questioning, but if we did, we ran the risk he'd lawyer up. Once lawyers got involved, things got tricky. If we left him free, he might let something slip.

"Mr. Guenther?" Rodney's voice was loud in the silence.

I glanced at him. I couldn't read minds, but I'd buy coffee for a week if Rodney's thoughts weren't in sync with mine.

"I'll look. Wait here." Guenther turned to leave.

"I'll go with you." Rodney set his painting against a chair. "Wouldn't want anything to go missing." He followed Guenther to his office.

After an uncomfortable fifteen minutes, while Marcy stared at me and I didn't speak, Rodney reappeared. "Let's get out of here." He grabbed the painting.

There weren't any receipts.

We reached the car and stowed the paintings. "I went through five file cabinets and the computer records. If that isn't suspicious, I don't know what is." He slid into the driver's seat.

I got in the passenger side and wrapped the chewed gum in a wrapper before depositing it in my empty coffee cup and unwrapping a fresh piece. I stared at the Natural Wonders building. I wondered if Bert Guenther had already called his attorney.

Rodney started the engine. "Think he's only involved in the fraud?"

"Not sure. It's possible Sylvia found out she'd paid big bucks for someone's paint-by-numbers. She got angry, confronted her lover, broke off their affair, and threatened to turn him in." I fastened my seatbelt as Rodney pulled away.

"He hit her over the head and dumped her into Hell's Half Acre, hoping we'd buy the suicide story."

I drummed my fingers on my leg. I pulled a notebook out of my pocket to jot down some thoughts. "Got a pen?"

He snorted. "With your recent habits? No way in hell I'm giving you one of mine."

We dropped the paintings off at the Fraud division with the associated chain of custody sheets. Then, we headed out to grab a quick lunch before going back to the office.

"You bluffed big time on the money." Rodney's warning tone was unmistakable.

He'd learn. "A murder investigation is like a high-stakes poker game. Bluffing is required."

He didn't say anything, but gave a derogatory humph.

"He didn't rush to tell me I was wrong, did he?" I had bluffed, but based on Guenther's reaction, I didn't think I was too far off the mark. "How about a burger?" I pointed at a McDonald's.

Rodney headed for the drive-thru. "Busting him for fraud is a good motive, but it brings us back to how Guenther would know Sylvia would be on Green Island. What do you want?"

We placed our orders and pulled forward. "It wouldn't be hard for him to cotton on to where she was that night. It could be that she argued with her husband and called Guenther for one last fling. Or they'd arranged to meet earlier for some reason. We have to consider the option until we learn otherwise." There were still too many possibilities, too many scenarios in this case to suit me. I would have hoped they'd have started eliminating themselves by now.

"It'll be damn near impossible to prove she met anyone. No traffic cams or CCTV." He pulled forward to the pay window.

I handed him my debit card. "No, there isn't. And we didn't find much at the scene. But something will give."

"You sound sure."

"I have to be." We took our orders from the pickup window and Rodney pulled back out into traffic. The unasked question hung between us. Now what?

"Let's check Sylvia's phone records again, see if there was any communication between her and Guenther after he claims he ended the affair." I sucked on the straw in my milkshake.

"Okay." He shot me a glance. "Thanks for lunch." It was grudgingly given, but gratitude nonetheless.

I unwrapped my burger. "No problem."

I was able to finish most of my lunch in the car. When I saw the fat manila envelope on my desk, I shook out the contents while Rodney unpacked his food. "Not such a bluff after all." I fanned the stack.

"Guenther's financials?" Rodney seated himself and attacked his burger.

I nodded, sat, and scanned the sheets. "No sign of ties to the embezzlement."

"Hidden account?"

"Eh. When was the date of those art sales?"

Rodney wiped his fingers and consulted his notes. "February. Unless he lied."

"Let's assume he didn't." I pulled the statement for February. I highlighted two lines in the statement and handed it to Rodney.

He whistled. "Two cash deposits for ten thousand dollars. Within two weeks."

"Kickback from the art sales?"

"He wouldn't keep the whole amount. Some would have to go to the artist." Rodney crumpled the wrapper and started in on his fries.

I suddenly recognized the lightness I'd been feeling all morning. I was enjoying my work again. What had changed? "What about this? Sylvia ended the affair for whatever reason. She got sick of him, or suspected he was behind the embezzlement. She was the CFO. She might have known about the missing money all along. Guenther swindles her on the art in retribution."

Rodney's mouth was full, but he indicated I should continue.

"She finds out about the fake paintings and threatens to call the police. They argue, he hits her, panics, and dumps the body into Hell's Half Acre, stripping it of the jewelry to make it look like a mugging." The idea held water.

He swallowed. "Sounds plausible except for one thing."

"What?"

He pointed a fry at me. "If that's true, and she really was on the verge of turning him in on the art forgery, what are the chances she'd call him to meet her? It'd be a hell of a coincidence, them meeting on Green Island." No cop liked coincidences.

I didn't have a response.

"Another thing. If Sylvia already knew about the embezzlement, suspected Guenther, and was biding her time, all Dellafiore did was alert Guenther the game was up."

True.

"Then, why isn't Dellafiore dead, too?"

Damn it. "Guenther thought he could bribe Dellafiore into secrecy, but not Sylvia? Remember, when Dellafiore reported the irregularities, he thought Sylvia was responsible. Maybe Guenther figured he could kill Sylvia and make her the scapegoat."

"It's more complicated, but not impossible. Assuming we can believe Dellafiore, which is not a given." Rodney finished the fries, chucked his trash, and shuffled through the papers on his desk.

"If you organized your stuff, it'd be easier to find things."

He flipped me off. "It's my desk. Here." He pulled out a sheaf of papers. "Sylvia's cellphone records. I don't think she'd call a lover from her home or office."

Not if she was smart.

"Guenther ended the affair when?"

I thought back to our conversations with the Natural

Wonders VP. "He said a couple of months ago. March or April. He brokered the paintings in February. I doubt she'd have gone along with the sale if they'd already killed the romance."

He ran a finger down the phone records. "Not much communication in March. A few calls, a few texts. More at the beginning of the month, maybe right after the affair ended and they were still talking."

"Or they hadn't ended it yet."

He handed me the sheets as he finished each scan. "Same in April. Short calls, a few texts. Most were several days, if not weeks, apart." He passed more sheets. "Nothing in May. More importantly, nothing on the night of Sylvia's death." He blew out a breath and tossed the sheet in my direction. "So much for that idea."

"Definitely puts a damper on it." I did my own scan, but Rodney was right. "She could have called from home."

Rodney rummaged around and pulled out another sheaf of paper. After several minutes, he shook his head. "No calls on the home line for those months at all."

I picked up a pen again to start twirling. The motion was soothing, better than a smoke. Certainly healthier. Twirling was less destructive than chewing. "They worked together. It's not out of the realm of possibility they made the arrangements to meet."

"I doubt we're going to find anyone who can confirm. Sylvia and Guenther probably talked privately half a dozen times a day. They could have arranged the meetup at any one of those." He stared at my hand.

"With your mad skills, you should get a baton. With streamers on the end. Sparkly ones. You've got a daughter, right? Don't girls like those?"

I dropped the pen.

"Shit. I'm sorry. I didn't—I'm sorry." Rodney's dark skin reddened. "Just trying to, oh hell, Jackson. I put my foot in it, didn't I?"

"Don't worry about it." The mention of Madeline stung. However, Max and I had engaged in friendly banter all the time. Breakfast and lunch had been my attempt at a peace offering. Maybe ribbing, as opposed to outright criticism, was Rodney's.

He hadn't run to Yannick. We'd put on a pretty good act in front of Guenther. If we kept it up, we'd make a decent team.

Having rejected group therapy at my last appointment, I found myself back in Alverson's office Tuesday afternoon. The thought of baring my soul in front of a bunch of strangers was enough to send me running mentally, if not physically. And we were still waiting on information, so I didn't feel guilty leaving early. Max declined to come, saying she had phone calls to make.

Alverson placed her pad on the table. "Now, how have you been since our last session?"

"What do you mean?"

"How have you been feeling?" She held up a hand. "Don't give me the macho crap. I've heard it all before. You were clearly in a bad spot last time. What about now?"

This was new territory for me. Not only did cops not sit around and discuss emotions, my family never had, either. "I don't know. I mean, I've had my head down, working the case."

Alverson folded her hands. "Have you had any panic attacks since we met?"

"No."

"Why do you think that is?"

This was exactly why I hated psycho-babble. "Doc, I'm not trying to be difficult. I honestly don't know what you want me to say. Things are okay. Even good. I'm sleeping, I'm not all twisted inside. I'm actually enjoying the job again."

She made a note on her pad. "Did you talk to Max and apologize?"

"As a matter of fact, I did." I loosened my tie. "I was right. She didn't need one."

"Hmm." Alverson made a note. "Jackson, have you ever thought it was *you* who needed the apology? It may be true Max didn't require one, but you needed to say the words. More importantly, you needed to hear her response."

"That doesn't make a damn bit of sense."

She leaned forward. "It's called survivor's guilt, and it's common. Plus a touch of PTSD. This thing happened and you survived. Someone you cared about didn't."

I scoffed. "Max didn't die. She survived, too."

"But not in the same way. She's not on the force. She lost her sight. And aside from a couple of burns, you're still on the job. Look me in the eye and tell me you don't feel guilty."

I shifted in my seat.

"You are your own worst enemy, Jackson. In a way, you'd have been better off if Max *had* blamed you. But she wasn't holding you as responsible as you were. And you didn't talk about it with her, which made it worse. Now, it's all out in the open and you can learn to manage your PTSD."

"Whoa. *Manage?* I thought this was about curing the attacks, making them stop."

She shook her head. "It's unlikely they will ever completely disappear. You'll have triggers, things to set it off. What they are or when they happen, I can't say."

I stared at her. "How can I be a detective if I go to pieces on a regular basis? In case you hadn't noticed, my job does require me to be on the ball, even if it's true that I usually get called after the action has happened."

She smiled. "You need to learn what those triggers are, how to recognize an attack, and how to calm yourself down."

What the actual? "You're talking in circles, doc. I can't learn all of that and still be, you know, me."

"Yes you can." She picked up her notepad. "And you're going to start right now."

I called Amy on the drive back to Max's. I left a brief message, telling her I loved her and the kids. Hearing her voice would have been nice, but they were out. Best thing I could do was get a handle on things and get back home.

Then, I called Max to let her know I would pick up Chinese takeout for dinner.

"Hey." I entered the apartment.

"Dining room," Max called. "Where's my kung pao beef?"

"Right here. Sheesh." I pushed over the container.

She sniffed, but not the food. Was she smelling me?

"Checking for cigarette smoke." She sat and pulled out the chopsticks. "How'd the appointment go?"

"It went." I opened my own container. "I'd rather not talk about it."

She paused, chopsticks in hand. "You okay?"

I had spent so much time over the past six months bottling up everything related to the explosion. Wasn't it what Dr. Alverson had been talking about? Why I'd gotten so bad in the first place? "Sorry. Habit. I'm not used to this *share your feelings* thing." I recapped what I'd gone over earlier.

"Well, good." Max dumped her meal in a bowl. "You should see this as progress."

"You call learning I'll have panic attacks for the rest of my life progress?" I picked up my chopsticks, which I quickly dropped on the floor.

"No, but I do say being able to recognize and manage them is." She paused. "It's not any different for me. We're both changed, Jackson. No sense wishing we weren't. That ship has sailed."

I froze. "You have PTSD?"

She picked strips of meat out of her carton. "No, but I was angry. I am angry. Oh, not at you." She set down the food. "At the universe. I'd done the right thing and this was my payment? Talk about a bad joke. I had to learn it was holding me back. I'm allowed to be mad and miss what I had, but it's no good living for yesterday." She picked up a fortune cookie.

"Me being here can't help. I'll pack my things after dinner."

She snorted. "Don't be absurd. It's the best thing possible. It showed me I'm still useful. You need me."

"I'll always need you."

We ate in silence for a while. Max broke it. "You talk to Amy?"

"I left a message on the way here. I should probably stay the week, if you'll have me." Her statement reminded me of a question I'd been meaning to ask. "How much of this did the two of you plan?" I took a sip of Coke.

"All of it."

I choked. They'd planned some, I knew that. But all of it? "So, it *was* you on the phone. Not her mother."

"The night you hit the trike? Yes." She continued to eat, not even looking up.

"Which is why Amy called it an *intervention*. You two planned this."

She looked up and jabbed a chopstick in my direction. "Amy loves you. But she couldn't reach you. She figured if you'd listen to anyone, you'd listen to me. Your wife's a smart woman."

We ate in silence for a few minutes. I examined my emotions. Thankful. Relieved. Annoyed. "You could have told me. Either of you. I'm not stupid."

Max sighed. "She has told you. Multiple times, in multiple ways. You're not stupid, true. But you are a man, a cop, and incredibly stubborn."

"I am not stubborn."

"Yes, you are. Don't be offended. It makes you a good investigator. But it can make you a truly difficult person to live with. Fortunately, Amy understands this.

She loves you, and she wasn't too proud to reach out to the one person she knew you'd listen to. Me."

Max didn't speak for the rest of dinner. She'd always been much better at knowing how to use silence. Sometimes, she'd brandish it as a weapon to force a suspect to cough up information. Sometimes, like now, it was comforting. She'd never been big on whining, but it didn't mean she didn't sympathize with pain. Amy empathized, of course, but it was good to know I wasn't the only one who mourned the loss. Someone else was angry. And while it wasn't an excuse to be a dick, I couldn't pretend I hadn't been one.

Max finished and got up to throw away the container. Then, she faced me. "So, what are you feeling right now?"

I remained at the table, picking over the remains of the Chinese. "Grateful. You're still looking out for the new kid, aren't you?"

"Duh." She walked out of the kitchen, Leroy at her heels.

CHAPTER
THIRTY-ONE

On Wednesday, I made a coffee and food run before heading into the office. Rodney was there when I arrived, going over Sylvia's phone records. "You doing that again?" I asked.

"What the hell else am I going to do? Our suspects all have crap alibis, but we can't put them on the scene. And everything else we have is penny-ante stuff. Shit."

I sat and sipped my coffee. "You're in a mood. I haven't had a chance to piss you off yet. What gives?"

A shadow of guilt crossed his face. "It's not you." He leaned back. "I'm frustrated."

"Something will break." I sipped my coffee and took a peek at the sports section of the paper. I talked a good game, but inside I was just as aggravated.

We spent the morning checking up on outstanding information: the art, calling to see if any of the missing jewelry had turned up. I found it strange that no one had tried to hock it yet. The magical *something* happened around eleven. My phone jangled and I picked it up without lifting my gaze from the papers in front of me. "Criminal Investigation. Davis."

"Detective Davis, this is John Calloway at the Credit Bureau. We've got a hit on one of Sylvia Bramley's credit cards."

Thank you, St. Michael. I snapped my fingers to get Rodney's attention.

Rodney set down the papers he'd been reading. "What?" he mouthed.

I held up a finger. "Where?"

"Someone tried to use her American Express at a 7-11 on Niagara Street this morning. I'm sure it was declined, but the bank alerted us since we'd put a watch on it. Figured you'd want to know it surfaced."

"You got that right. Which 7-11?" Calloway rattled off the address as well as the time of the attempted card use. I committed both to memory and hung up. "I told you something would happen." I stood, grabbed my jacket from the back of my chair, and headed toward the door.

Rodney did the same. "What?" He followed close on my heels.

"Someone tried to use Sylvia's AmEx this morning."

"You said 7-11 on the phone. Any other information?"

"No. But we might be able to get a description or footage from the surveillance camera."

———

The convenience store in question was only a few

blocks away. "Detective Davis, NFPD. I'd like to speak to the manager."

The manager was probably about the same age I was, but with a liberal amount of silver in his dark hair. "Jeremy Farver."

I slipped my badge back into my pocket. "Someone was in here earlier attempting to use a credit card belonging to a murdered woman. American Express. The card would have been declined."

Behind me, Rodney walked up and down the aisles, presumably checking for customers who might be lurking or otherwise able to help.

"I didn't process any rejected cards. Devin?" Farver indicated the clerk beside him, who was probably no older than early twenties.

Devin's forehead puckered. "One. Homeless-looking dude. Smelled and had mismatched clothes. Super dirty. He tried to buy a box of doughnuts and a Yoohoo with an AmEx Platinum card. I thought it was funny, but hey, you never know."

I fixed him with my best investigator's stare. "Not funny enough to make you check the name on the card. Or did you look and run it, anyway?"

Devin flushed. "It was early. Junk food isn't exactly a suspicious purchase. Now, if the guy had tried to buy fifty bucks worth of gas, it would be a different story."

"What did he look like?" I was sure Devin would get an earful from his manager. I didn't need to give him a hard time, too.

"I told you, homeless. He was a white guy, older, gray hair. I didn't get an eye color. He was way shorter than you, maybe even shorter than the guy you came in with. But he walked kind of hunched over, so it's hard to say."

I noted the sparse description as Rodney came back. "Is anyone else in the store?"

"Nope." Rodney looked at Devin. "Unless you're hiding someone in the cooler."

"You two are the only guys here." Devin shrugged. "I don't remember anyone else being here when the guy came in, either. At least, not in the store. If someone was paying at the pump, I'd never see him."

I turned my attention back to the clerk. "If the card was declined, I'm going to say he never got a receipt or gave a signature. He didn't try another card?"

"Purchases less than twenty-five bucks don't need a signature." Devin sounded bored. "I ran the card. It was denied. I told him he needed another form of payment. He grabbed the AmEx back and left. I didn't let him take the goods."

Rodney snorted. I looked at Farver. "I'm sure you have CCTV coverage on the cash register area. We'd like to see the film from this morning when the card was used. Say, between seven-thirty and eight." I knew from Calloway the card had been used at seven forty-two. Maybe we'd get a good look at the guy who'd tried to use it.

"Sure, come on back." Farver motioned us to a door. In the back, he booted up the CCTV footage from earlier, scrolling to the time I'd given him.

Rodney pointed at the screen. "There he is."

I watched as an elderly man, certainly looking enough like a vagrant to pass for one, shuffled around the store. Finally, he approached the register and I got a look at his face. He handed a credit card to Devin, then fumed as he was told the card was no good. He grabbed it, stuffed it in the pocket of his oversized coat, and stomped out. "Stop. Can you print that image?" The guy was in full profile. The best view we had, albeit a bit grainy.

Farver hit a couple of keys and a page whirred out of the printer nearby. "If he comes in again, you want me to call you?"

"Please." I handed over my business card. "Try the office and my cell. If I don't answer, call Detective Kirke." Rodney passed over a business card. "And try to delay him until we arrive. Thanks." Then, we left.

Rodney stopped outside and stared at the storefront. "Too bad they didn't keep him on scene."

I unwrapped another piece of gum. I should have gotten a new pack. "It's a convenience store. They aren't patrol cops. At least we have this." I waved the grainy picture. "Let's hit the drive-thru and go back to compare this to mug shots. Maybe we'll be able to put a name to the face."

He muttered something unintelligible. "Do you think this guy mugged and killed her, or did he pick up the purse somewhere?"

I studied the picture as he pulled away. "We won't know for sure and can't hazard a guess until we find him."

"If we find him." Rodney signaled a turn and went through the light.

I popped the gum. "We will. I've got a lucky feeling today. Haven't felt that way in a while."

We'd gotten one break. Max would have said one

hole in the dam was all we needed to take the entire thing down.

———

We pulled away from the drive-thru and my cellphone rang. Glancing at the caller ID, I knew it was official. I answered. "This is Davis. Go."

"Davis, it's MacMillan. We got a call for you from a guy who works at Niagara Collectibles and Antiques. Someone came in looking to hock some jewelry. The clerk at the shop matched it to the stuff from your victim."

"What time?"

"Call came in two minutes ago. I think he said the guy arrived about fifteen minutes before the employee called. For all I know, the seller is still on the premises."

"Hell, yeah." I looked at Rodney. "Jewelry turned up." I gave my attention back to MacMillan. "Got an address and phone number for me?"

"Yep." MacMillian rattled off the information. I thanked him and hung up.

"We've been waiting for this." Rodney made a left, barely beating the red light. "Where?"

"Niagara Collectibles." I dialed the store. "I'll see if the suspect is still there. If so, maybe they can get him to hang around."

We lucked out. The attempted seller was still in the store. After asking the store manager to keep him there, I told Rodney to head over. "They can drag out the evaluation time for five minutes definitely, but not for longer than ten."

"The address is on Walnut. It won't take five minutes, even without the blue lights." He hung a right on Portage and headed up to Walnut.

No lights, no siren. I didn't want our suspect to bolt. "How in shape are you?"

"I run every morning."

"Then, if he does a rabbit, you'll get a second workout."

"You out of shape?"

"Someone has to stay behind and question the store employees. You wanted to be active. Here's your chance. Unless you'd rather stay put and I'll run."

He muttered a response.

Niagara Collectibles and Antiques was a hole-in-the-wall place between Seventh and Eighth. Fortunately, there was a free spot in front of the shop. I entered, Rodney tailing, and spotted our dirty vagrant arguing with the guy behind the counter.

"It's worth more'n that." The guy's voice was raspy from years of smoking. "Lookit. Those gotta be real diamonds. What's your problem?"

I pulled out my shield. "The problem is those belong to a dead woman in a murder case."

The old man jumped and scampered for the door, dropping a dirty canvas bag, which clanked when it hit the floor. Unless I missed my guess, it was the rest of Sylvia's jewelry. I picked up the bag, knowing Rodney would keep the guy from escaping. I emptied the contents onto the counter. "Still got the list out? The one you used to match the piece he was pawning?" I asked the clerk behind the counter.

"Right here."

I took the list and started comparing it to the items in the bag. I used a pen to push aside the pieces. I doubted there was much left in the way of usable prints, but it was worth a shot. "What was he trying to hock? Don't touch."

The clerk pointed to an earring, the match to the one we'd found near the bridge. "I got suspicious when he didn't have the set. I checked to see if we were on the watch for anything hot and recognized the description off your list."

I hadn't gone through the entire haul, but enough items matched I was sure it was Sylvia's missing stuff. I looked up at the squeak of shoes behind me. Rodney had the guy firmly, but not cruelly, by the arm, holding him in place.

"You can't pin nothing on me." His teeth, what remained of them, were stained and yellow. His breath reeked of smoke and alcohol, enough to give us a contact high. He hadn't had a shower in a long time. The dirt under his nails and caked in the creases of his neck was impressive. "I found it in the garbage. I did. I'm telling the truth. Now, give me back my stuff and I won't lodge no complaints."

Rodney didn't loosen his grip. "We're not giving the jewelry back to you."

He glared at Rodney from under eyebrows that resembled dirty, fuzzy gray caterpillars. "I found it in the garbage. Ain't no one wanted it. Give it back."

"It's evidence in a murder investigation," Rodney looked at me. "Usable prints?"

I looked at the pile of jewelry, most of it with rough edges. We might have gotten something off the necklace, but our vagrant had probably destroyed them. "We'll try. I'm not hopeful." I looked at our suspect. "We should get his prints for elimination."

"Murder?" The man's eyebrows shot up, and panic lit his faded eyes. "I ain't killed no one. I swear. The stuff was in the trash can."

In the meantime, the clerk—who might have also been the store owner—had continued to check the inventory. "Every piece matches, Detective," he said. "The only thing missing is the other earring."

The old man started fighting again, and Rodney pulled out his cuffs. "I didn't do it. I didn't kill no one. I swear to Christ, it was in the garbage. You gotta believe me."

I held up my hand. "Relax. No one is accusing you of murder. Yet."

"Can I let go of you, or will you run?" Rodney fixed the vagrant with a stare worthy of one Max would have given him.

The vagrant shook his head, and Rodney let go of the man's arm. I covered a laugh with a cough when I saw Rodney palm a napkin from a nearby dispenser. The vagrant's shirt couldn't have been pleasant to hold.

I gestured to Rodney, indicating he should take notes. "Let's start at the basics. What's your name?"

"Clarence."

"Last name?"

He shook his head in mute defiance.

"Okay, Clarence. Tell me exactly when and where you found this jewelry."

For a moment, it didn't seem like Clarence was going to talk, but finally he rasped out an answer.

"Maybe two weeks ago. I go through the trash cans in the park. People throw bottles and stuff in the garbage. I take 'em for the recycling money."

I knew what people tossed while visiting. At five cents per bottle, Clarence could get a nice chunk of change. "Which garbage can did you find the bag in?"

"At the end of the foot bridge coming from Green Island." Clarence licked his lips. "I got a good haul that morning. Then I spotted this bag. It didn't look like a fast-food bag or nothing, so I looked in it. There was all this sparkly jewelry. I figured it might be worth something. Since it was in the trash, I took it."

Clarence's lucky garbage can was right by Hell's Half Acre. It appeared my idea was right. Her killer had stripped the body hoping to make it look like a mugging. "When did you find the bag?"

He scratched a stubble-covered chin. "I already told you. Two weeks ago? Yeah, not much more I'd say."

The day or two after Sylvia's death, probably the next morning if the garbage hadn't been emptied yet. Which told me our killer wasn't familiar enough with the area to know when garbage pickup in the park happened.

"You didn't try to pawn it immediately. Why?" Rodney crossed his arms.

Clarence shuffled his feet. "I was scared. Who throws away goods like this? I watched the papers, looking for stories about a jewelry robbery. Or someone offering a reward. After two weeks, I ain't seen nothing. Figured I got lucky. Some damn fool really did throw it away. I need the cash so I came here." He frowned at the counter clerk. "I should have gone somewhere with fewer rules."

"You wouldn't have found a place in the city that would have taken this." I straightened up and pushed the pile of jewelry back in the bag, careful not to touch any of the pieces. "Clarence, I've got good news and bad news."

He squinted. "What's the good news?"

"I believe you when you say you found this in the garbage and didn't take it from the woman it belonged to. I also believe you when you say you didn't kill anyone." I looked at his bent frame and skinny arms. The blow to Sylvia's skull had been delivered with force. I doubted Clarence had enough strength to pick up a full fifth of Jack Daniels.

He scrunched up his face. "What's the bad news?"

"We can't give you the bag back." Rodney's voice gentled. "It's not yours."

"But I found it. You said—"

"I said I believed you." I was not without sympathy. Clarence obviously needed the money. "But as we told you earlier, this belongs to the victim in an open homicide. It's evidence. Plus, I think the dead woman's husband might want his wife's jewelry back." Or not, but it would be Bramley's call. Eventually.

Clarence's shoulders slumped. "Then what the hell do I get out of this? That ain't much good news."

Judging by the look of him, the poor guy probably hadn't eaten a hot meal in days. I pulled out my wallet and gave him a twenty. "Come on. We'll take you to McDonald's so you can get something to eat." I glanced over at the clerk. "Thank you for the tip and the assistance. Detective Kirke, you ready?"

Clarence glared at me, but he didn't refuse the twenty either. "A lousy hamburger?"

"Consider yourself lucky." Rodney clapped him on the shoulder. "If we didn't believe you, you'd get a night in a jail cell."

The look Clarence shot my partner was full of disgust. "Iff'n you'd arrest me, I'd get a square meal and a place to sleep. Now *that'd* be good news."

CHAPTER
THIRTY-TWO

After we left Niagara Collectibles, we called Bramley to inform him Sylvia's jewelry had been recovered. There was no answer at either his home or cell. We left messages, asking him to call us.

I closed Wednesday with another session with Dr. Alverson. The conversations were still uncomfortable but becoming slightly less so. But I avoided saying, or thinking, the letters PTSD. Those letters were for ragged people who couldn't hold a job, not homicide detectives who wore suits and had functional lives.

That's what I told myself, anyway, even if I knew deep down it wasn't the truth.

When I went back to Max's, I'd given her the story about the pawn shop.

"One hole." She nodded in satisfaction. "As always, it's all you need."

I passed out on the couch around eleven. Bramley had still not returned a phone call. If he didn't call in the morning, we'd have to go to his house and see him.

My phone jolted me awake. I jumped, startling Leroy, who had been curled up next to me. I blinked at the phone, which displayed an unknown local number and the time, which was slightly after one in the morning. "Detective Davis speaking."

"Detective? It's Gwyneth Walsh. I'm calling about Keith."

The light behind me came on. Max must have heard the phone ring. I looked over to see her standing at the hall door, tying the belt to her robe. Once a cop, always a cop.

I shook my head. "Ms. Walsh, what's wrong?"

"You've been trying to get in touch with Keith. There were messages from you and Detective Kirke on our home voicemail. Did you talk to him?" The worry in Walsh's voice was palpable.

Our home? She'd made herself comfortable. "He never called me. I didn't hear from Detective Kirke, so I'm assuming Mr. Bramley didn't call him, either. I don't know for sure. This doesn't explain why you're calling me."

"Believe me, I didn't want to. I tried calling the Lockport police, but they won't do anything. They said Keith is an adult and all I can do is file a report. Jackasses."

"They're right. Mr. Bramley could be anywhere. He might be out having a drink, or he might have a flat tire—"

"He would tell me. Something is wrong. I've called his cellphone and it always goes to voicemail. He would answer if he could."

"Maybe he doesn't want to take your call."

"Screw you. I would have figured since you want to arrest him for Sylvia's death, you'd be more interested. Maybe I was wrong."

"Ms. Walsh," I closed my eyes, "we aren't prepared to charge anyone in your sister's death. The person I want is the guilty party." I looked at Leroy's glowing green eyes. "When was the last time you saw Mr. Bramley?"

"He was with me yesterday afternoon. You probably don't believe me, but it's true."

"Why wouldn't I believe you?"

"Because the cops never believe anything. We had lunch at the casino. You can ask them. We paid with a credit card, so you can check, too. Afterward, we went walking by the Falls."

"Then what did you do?"

Gwyneth huffed. "He said he was meeting someone later in the evening." Her voice wavered. "He didn't say where or when."

"You didn't go with him?"

"We had an event at the store last night. I was doing personal color consultations until ten and didn't get home until around eleven."

"Was Mr. Bramley home? I mean, do you know—"

"I've moved in. He wasn't home. I didn't get worried until midnight rolled around."

"Have you called the local hospitals?"

"Nobody will tell me anything. I'm not a relative." The bitterness in her voice was unmistakable.

It was unfair, but it was true. As a girlfriend, even a fiancée, she wouldn't rate unless she was identified by Bramley as an emergency contact in his phone, or if he'd been conscious and able to give information.

"Can you?"

Walsh's voice pulled me out of my thoughts. "I'm sorry, can I what?"

"Can you help me? You're the police. He's a suspect in your investigation. Surely, there's something you can do." Her voice was starting to sound a bit thick, like she was speaking through tears.

"I'll make some calls."

"Will you let me know if you find him?"

I sighed. "I'll do what I can. No promises." I clicked off. Then, I threw aside the blanket and grabbed my rumpled slacks.

Max's voice sounded behind me. "Keith Bramley is missing."

I'd forgotten she was there. "That was Gwyneth Walsh. She hasn't seen him since yesterday afternoon and he's not answering his cell."

"And she called a homicide detective?"

"I've been leaving messages all day about Sylvia's jewelry." I scrolled through my contacts and found Rodney's number.

He answered on the third ring. "Did somebody die, or did we get new information?" The sleep disappeared from his voice the minute I identified myself.

"Walsh called. Bramley's AWOL."

"Shit."

I imagined him sitting up, feeling much the same way I did. If Bramley had skipped town, it was more likely he had killed his wife.

"Now what?"

"Call the area police departments. Whatever happened to him didn't occur in the city limits. Someone would have contacted us because of the connection to Sylvia's case. Check all the surrounding suburbs. Olcott, Newfane, Lockport."

The news of Bramley's disappearance trumped Rodney's desire to be snarky. "He wouldn't be a John Doe." The noises over the line could only mean he was dressing in a hurry. "If he was in an accident, they could run the plates on the car. I'm sure he had a wallet on him, too. In case he wasn't in the vehicle."

"Unless he was mugged and isn't near the car."

Rodney swore.

"I'm going to call hospitals, starting with Niagara Memorial. If we come up empty on those fronts, we can branch out. Maybe call the Niagara Falls, Ontario, police or Ontario Provincial."

"I'm on it." He hung up.

"Your shirt." Max held out the same one I'd worn earlier, along with the tie. I wouldn't look great, but it was better than showing up in boxers. "If he had an accident in Niagara County, Niagara Memorial would be the logical starting point. But if he's not there—"

"I'll branch out to Erie County." I used my phone to look up the number for Niagara Memorial. When the hospital switchboard answered, I asked for Admissions.

"This time of night, Admissions would go through the ER," the woman said.

I thanked her and waited. I heard the brewer whir, and the aroma of coffee filled the apartment seconds later. God bless Max.

"ER, this is Carla Summers."

"Ms. Summers, Detective Jackson Davis, NFPD. I need to know if you've admitted a Keith Bramley this evening."

"Are you a relative?"

"I'm a homicide detective. I need to know if Mr. Bramley is there."

"According to HIPAA regulations, I shouldn't say anything."

HIPAA regulations, my ass. "Mr. Bramley is a suspect in an open homicide. It is urgent I know if he is in your care. If not, I might have to start a manhunt to find him."

"I'm sorry." Carla paused. "I can't give information over the phone."

I took that as she'd tell me in person. My cell beeped and I checked. It was Rodney. "Thank you, Ms. Summers." I switched calls. "Yeah, Rodney. What've you got?"

"Bramley is at—"

"Niagara Memorial."

"How'd you know?"

Max brought out a travel mug with the coffee. "What's happening?"

I held up a finger to her. "I was on the phone with a nurse there when you called. She was being cagey. What do you have?"

"I lucked out," Rodney said. "I figured Grand Island police might have mentioned the accident to Gwyneth, even if they technically weren't supposed to. I hit pay dirt with Olcott on my second call."

Olcott? Who the hell had Bramley been meeting in Olcott? Small town, no major restaurants, and almost an hour's drive from the Bramley home. "They give you any details?"

"Single car accident. He ran off the road and head-on into a tree. They said he was probably traveling at or near the speed limit. No sign there was another vehicle involved. He was unconscious when the EMTs arrived. Did Walsh say anything?"

"Only that he was meeting someone. She didn't know specifics on who, when, or where. But when she got home at eleven, he wasn't there. When she heard our messages and he didn't answer his cell, she panicked."

"You think she's involved?"

Would she have called us if she was? I didn't think she was that devious. "She says she was at work, which is easy enough to check. Was the car damaged? I mean, beyond the accident?" I sipped the coffee. Max must keep the high test stuff, because it was strong and black. Exactly what I needed.

"It's totaled. There are no skid marks or anything on the road to indicate he tried to brake."

"Huh." I sipped again. It was tough to tamper with cars these days. But it wasn't impossible.

"The guys in Olcott said Onstar alerted them to the crash." Rodney paused. "Of course, he or she might have hired someone to help get rid of Bramley."

I blinked. "You're thinking it's Walsh."

"She gets rid of Sylvia to get Bramley, then gets rid of Bramley to get the money. Why not?"

Why not, indeed? Except unless Walsh was lying, she and Bramley had not tied the knot. She might lie to make it look like she didn't have a motive. Obviously, neither Rodney nor I had been invited guests, but I'd seen no announcements in the paper. They'd announced their engagement. There was no reason to think they wouldn't do the same for the wedding. I told him my reasoning.

His response was logical. "They haven't gotten around to it. Or maybe it was a civil ceremony. It could have been done in the last couple of days and they haven't gone public."

"She'd inherit something under intestate marriage rules in New York." I chewed my lip.

"Anywhere from a third to a half. Enough incentive for murder." The sound of liquid being poured into a metal-lined container came through the line. I was sure it wasn't his first cup of coffee.

But Rodney was right. Even a third of an estate as big as Bramley's was a lot of money. *Damn.* "Verify her story. Go to the office and start searching to see if you can find a marriage license."

He grumbled his assent.

"Meanwhile, I'll go to the hospital. Hopefully, they'll be able to tell me something. Maybe I'll luck out and the responding officer is still there." I clicked off.

"Jacket." Max held it out.

"Thanks. Leave the door open?" I shrugged into my jacket. At least I wasn't waking up my wife.

"Take the key." She gave me her ring.

"I'll try not to wake you when I get back."

"You think I'll be able to sleep after this?"

She probably wouldn't. Max might say she wasn't a cop any longer, but not having a badge wouldn't keep her from sitting up and thinking over the case while she waited. "See you later."

I left. We needed to try, but I was pretty sure of one thing. We weren't going to get any answers until and unless Bramley regained consciousness.

———

After a brief debate with the staff at Niagara Memorial where I identified myself and my reason for being there, I proceeded to the ICU. "I'm looking for information on Keith Bramley." Again, I presented my badge. "I understand he was in an automobile accident. Is anyone from the Olcott police still here?"

The nurse shook her head. "No, they left ages ago."

"Is he still unconscious?"

"Yes. We're trying to get in touch with the emergency contact on his cellphone. We assume it's his wife, a Sylvia Bramley. She's not answering."

Bramley hadn't updated his *In Case of Emergencies* information. Not entirely surprising. He'd been burying Sylvia. Since Gwyneth didn't have the same last name, the hospital staff wouldn't think to call her. "Mrs. Bramley is dead. I'm investigating her murder."

"I thought the name sounded familiar. I read about it in the paper." The woman clucked her tongue. "Poor guy."

"Mr. Bramley is a suspect, so any information you can share—"

Walsh's voice echoed down the hallway. "Where is he? Somebody tell me what's going on with my fiancé, damn it!"

She sprinted down the hallway, her face devoid of makeup. She was pretty without it, even with red-rimmed eyes and platinum hair in disarray. An overweight hospital security guard lumbered after her.

I waved him off. "I've got this." I grabbed her shoulders. "Ms. Walsh, stop shouting. It's not helping."

"They won't freaking tell me anything. I'm his fiancée. I have a right to know what's going on." She sobbed and hiccuped, her face streaked with tears.

Up close, I could see her bloodshot eyes. I wondered how long she'd been crying. If it was an act, and she'd been behind Bramley's accident, she deserved an Oscar. "You need to calm down before they escort you out of here. This is a hospital. It's unfair, but under the law you have no rights—"

"I've got every right." She struggled against my grip. "We might not be married yet, but I'm the only one he has. Tell me he's okay, he's alive. At least you can do that much." She stopped wriggling and grabbed my jacket lapels in a death grip.

"You need to calm down." I pried her hands off. She sagged, and I guided her over to a nearby chair. "How did you find out he was here?"

"The hospital called the house. When I answered, they asked for Sylvia. I said she wasn't there. The caller said she was from Niagara Memorial Hospital and Mrs. Bramley needed to call as soon as possible." She buried her face in her hands, then looked at me. "I *told* Keith to update his ICE contact."

I handed her a tissue. "Mr. Bramley is alive but unconscious. His condition is critical. Let me speak to the nursing staff and see what they can do."

I left her sitting there and approached the nurse. I kept my voice low. "The woman at the end of the hall is Mr. Bramley's fiancée. She should be the one you're calling."

"Then, Mr. Bramley should have—"

"I know. Still, can she see him? Just for a few minutes?"

"Absolutely not. She's not his wife or a blood relative. Our ICU policies are very clear. Only relatives are allowed bedside outside of visiting hours." The nurse's face reminded me of a prison matron.

"Can you tell me if there were drugs or alcohol in his system?"

"I'd rather have the charge nurse answer you. Or the Olcott police." Her lips thinned into a prim line. "HIPAA regulations—"

"Yes, so I've been told." I'd hoped for a bit of info when the nurse saw my badge, but she wasn't going to budge. No matter. Rodney would be there soon. He'd have information from Olcott. "If Mr. Bramley regains consciousness, call me." I handed her a business card.

She took it with a sniff. "I'll let the charge nurse and the attending physician know. You'll be called if they decide Mr. Bramley's condition will permit questioning."

It was the best I was going to get. I walked down to Walsh and put my hand under her elbow to lift her to a standing position. "Come on."

"Where are we going? I'm not leaving until I see Keith." Her voice started to rise as I tugged her toward an elevator.

"Yes, you are. They won't tell you anything. Don't

feel too bad. They won't tell me anything, either. You can come back during normal visiting hours, but it's family-only outside those."

"I'm not family?"

"Not yet." The elevator dinged and the doors slid open. I guided her inside. "When *exactly* was the last time you saw Mr. Bramley? You said he told you he was meeting someone. Do you know who or where, or what it was about?"

"Oh my God. Are you deaf or stupid?" Walsh pulled away. "I saw him yesterday. We had lunch at the casino and went to the Falls. I went to work. He said he was meeting someone, but didn't tell me anything. I got home around eleven, and he wasn't there."

She wasn't changing her story. Either she was a very accomplished liar, or it was the truth. Instinct told me it was the latter. "When did you get the call from the hospital?"

"I don't know. After I called you. I didn't look at the clock. I heard the hospital name, threw on some clothes, and left."

I checked my watch. It was ten after two now. I'd give Walsh thirty minutes to get from Grand Island to Niagara Memorial. Assuming she really did leave promptly, her time estimate wasn't off the mark. "I'll make sure you get home. Come back tomorrow morning after eight. They'll probably let you in to see him. But be warned, they aren't going to be generous with information. I know you think it's unfair, but since you aren't married, there isn't too much you can do until he regains consciousness." *If he does.* Best to be positive. I'd talk to Rodney and see what his search had turned up.

"Whatever. But you'd better promise me something." We'd reached the garage, and before she got into her car she poked me in the chest. Her nails were sharp, even through my shirt.

"You need to stop making demands and manhandling me. I understand you're upset. Taking it out on me won't help." I didn't bother reminding her I was a police officer, not her messenger boy. I got the fact she was distraught. Hell, if I'd been in her shoes, I'd feel the same. But building rapport and being sympathetic was not the same as being a doormat.

She scowled, but she let go.

"If you care to phrase your request politely, I'll try my best." I was surprised that blood wasn't welling from my chest.

Walsh looked away, then she wiped her eyes and faced me. "Find who did this. Please. I didn't kill my sister, and neither did Keith. If someone tried to knock him off tonight?" She took a deep breath before continuing. "You need to find out who was responsible."

———

After I followed Walsh home, I called Rodney. "You still at the office?"

He yawned. "I left five minutes ago. Want the highlights?"

I looked at the dashboard clock. It was almost three in the morning. I wanted to go back to sleep. But I also didn't want to delay. "There's a twenty-four hour Tim Hortons on Transit. Meet me there."

"Why can't we meet at Starbucks?" He yawned again.

"Because there aren't any open around here at three in the morning."

With no traffic, I made it to Timmies in short order. I'd ordered coffee and a couple of doughnuts, and grabbed a table by the time Rodney walked in. I waved him over.

He dropped down. "I take back everything bad I ever said about you." He grabbed coffee and a doughnut.

"All it took was the near-death of a suspect." I inhaled the steam off my own coffee and started on my second doughnut.

"If questioned, I will categorically deny it all."

I shook my head. Of course. "What did you find out?"

"Keith Bramley and Gwyneth Walsh aren't married, at least not in Niagara County, NY."

The news didn't surprise me. Once she knew she wouldn't get to see Bramley without a marriage license, she would have provided proof of the ceremony.

"I don't think they've been married in New York State. My search was pretty exhaustive and I turned up zilch. I searched all the surrounding counties and major municipalities. Nothing." He took a gulp of coffee.

"Somehow that fact restores a smidgen of my faith in humanity." At his puzzled look, I continued. "Not everybody lies *all* the time."

"They might have gone across the border." He

finished off his doughnut. "What was she like at the hospital?"

"Pretty upset." I sipped the coffee. The same as I'd have expected Amy to be under similar conditions.

"They tell you anything?"

"Shit, no. They threw HIPAA in my face at every turn. All I learned was he's still unconscious. Hopefully, Olcott was more forthcoming."

"After I buttered them up." Rodney wiped his fingers and pulled out a pad. "Onstar notified Olcott police and EMS of an accident with airbag deployment at ten forty-seven p.m. and said the driver was unresponsive. Emergency personnel arrived on the scene at ten fifty-eight to find Bramley's CTS mashed against a tree. He was bloody and unconscious but alive."

"Then, no on-scene or in-ambulance utterances." What rotten luck.

"He never came to." Despite the infusion of caffeine, Rodney smothered another yawn.

"Stop." I took another gulp of coffee.

"It's three in the morning. I'll yawn if I want to." He took another gulp. "EMS suspected head trauma and internal bleeding."

"What about the scene?"

Rodney flipped a page. "Single car, no sign of another vehicle. No skid marks. They think he passed out and hit the tree. They're still going over the car to see if there's evidence of mechanical failure, but it's unlikely it was tampered with. The car is too new."

"We've got nothing." Damn it.

"Quit your bitching. In a situation like this, they suspect drunk driving. There wasn't a scent of alcohol on Bramley, so they did a quick blood screen for booze and common drugs." He paused to take a sip of coffee.

"And?"

"Keep your pants on." He flipped another page. "Based on his BAC, Bramley had something to drink, but the levels were well within legal limits. Not even close to driving while impaired, much less intoxicated. However, they also found high levels of barbiturates."

I blinked. "Come again?"

"Barbiturates. You know what those are, right?"

I gave him the finger. I was too tired for anything else.

"We'll have to check, but I didn't see prescription bottles when we interviewed him. And there was nothing when we searched the house."

"If he was taking medication like that, you'd think he wouldn't be drinking or driving." I wiped powdered sugar from my hands and took another swallow of coffee. "Unless he's an idiot."

We sat in silence. "Do you think Walsh is involved?" Rodney asked after a few minutes.

"You didn't see her at the hospital. I don't think she was faking. Besides, if she was at work, how would she drug Bramley?"

He swirled his coffee cup. "Put it in something she knew he'd drink?"

"Who takes his own beverage to a restaurant? But we can ask." Unlikely, but not impossible.

"She also could have had an accomplice."

"Too complicated. I hate complicated."

"What are you, lazy? She and Bramley conspire to get rid of Sylvia. He thinks they're going to live happily ever after, but she's got other ideas. What's so complicated?"

I shook my head. "If he'd had a heart attack, or died at home, or—hell, almost anything else—I'd be right there with you. But murder by car wreck? No. It doesn't feel right. And they aren't married yet."

"Whatever." Rodney emptied his cup and looked at his phone. "It's almost four. Is there anything more to be done?"

"Not right now. We'll have to verify Walsh's alibi. We should talk to Olcott first. We don't want to step on their toes. But if these two really did conspire to kill Sylvia, we don't want to sit around and wait, either." I drained my own cup. "I'm going to try and catch a few hours' sleep. I suggest you do the same."

"And we still have the damn paintings." He groaned and followed me to the door.

"And we still have to figure out how the embezzling fits into the picture."

"You know what? I'm tempted to say the hell with detective work and go back to patrol duty." Rodney fumbled for his keys.

"But then, you wouldn't have the pleasure of working with me."

"Yeah. Definitely going back to patrol."

We left and I headed back to Max's, pretty sure sleep wasn't part of my immediate future.

CHAPTER
THIRTY-THREE

I was right. I didn't get to sleep again. Max was waiting up for me. By the time I'd gone over what we'd learned and rehashed our working ideas, I had enough time for a quick shower, to change into a fresh suit, and head out the door. But not before she'd pressed a large travel mug full of extra hot, extra strong coffee into my hands.

"You are a saint." I accepted the travel mug as if it was the Holy Grail.

She grinned. "No, I'm a cop."

"Thought you said you weren't one anymore."

She pushed me toward the door. "I'm not and I am. Don't ask. Now, get the hell out of here."

Rodney had his own oversized mug in hand when I arrived. "You look like shit. Didn't you sleep?"

"Like you look any better. Tell me you went back to bed."

"Hardly. I looked up Walsh's employer, and I have the address. Should we visit now or later?"

I straightened my tie. "Hell, let's go. We both look

like we spent the night on a bus station bench. Time isn't going to help." He started to say something. "Since you're such a smart-ass, you drive. I'll use the time to snooze."

But I didn't sleep in the car. I couldn't stop thinking of Bramley and his accident. Traffic on the Youngmann Expressway sped by, but I barely saw it.

"Who was Bramley meeting?" Rodney asked.

It had to be a rhetorical question. "You didn't mention last night if he was going to or coming from Olcott when he had the accident."

"He was heading out of town." Rodney wove in and out of traffic. "So they said. I guess he might have spun out on the way there."

"There'd be evidence on the road, if so."

"Right. So, we have to find another person. Fantastic. Exactly what we need." His voice betrayed his sarcasm.

"Perhaps, he met his grandmother and it has no bearing on Sylvia's death." I made a note to call the Olcott police to see if they'd found any receipts in Bramley's wallet, or anything else that might tell us where or with whom he'd been last night.

His response was swift and snarky. "His grandmother is dead. Didn't you read his background?"

I pinched the bridge of my nose. "It was an example. Give it a break, will you?"

He humphed and tapped his fingers on the steering wheel. "How's it going with the shrink?" He glanced at me out of the corner of his eye.

"It's going."

"Home yet?"

"No."

"When?"

I stared at the notes from our previous interviews. "When I feel damn good and ready. Are we working a murder or playing Twenty Questions?"

He grumbled and focused on traffic.

The Macy's Walsh worked at was in Amherst. On the way, Rodney and I debated the merits of Walsh as the culprit for both Bramley's accident and Sylvia's murder. He was firmly in the pro category. I straddled the line, unwilling to commit.

"You're impossible." He parked and got out of the car. "I still think you're overcomplicating things. It's all about money. Money and sex. The two constants at the root of man's evil toward other men."

I unwrapped a piece of gum. "I agree it's about money. At least, primarily about money."

"Then, what's the problem? The only person I see making out with Sylvia's death is Walsh. Making out big, I mean."

"Except she's not." I knew half of Rodney's attitude was due to lack of sleep. I wasn't going to psychoanalyze the other half. It might have been me. It might have been the typical hard-charger rookie desire to prove himself on his first case. It didn't matter. "If Walsh and Bramley were married, sure, I'd bite. But they aren't."

He paused by the next row of cars. "Try this. What if she didn't know she'd get squat if Bramley died?"

I thought about it. "I'll make you a deal. I'll agree it's possible Walsh's lack of legal knowledge made her bump off her fiancé prematurely. You agree it's possible someone else is behind this."

"Are those the only two options we have?"

"At this point, standing in a Macy's parking lot? Yes."

He shrugged. "Let's go in."

"After you."

Inside, the makeup displays were crammed with products boasting the ability to reduce wrinkles, lighten skin, and fight acne. All Amy ever used was Almay. I thought she looked fabulous. Thinking of Amy made me think of the kids. Christopher was too young to know what was going on, but what about Madeline? Did she blame herself for my absence?

I cut off my thoughts before I could spiral. If I solved this case and got my head straight, I'd be able to go home. I'd make it up in bedtime stories, Madeline's favorite currency.

We walked up to the Clinique counter. After a few minutes, a heavily made-up woman came over with a bright smile. "Can I help you, gentlemen? Maybe you're looking for a perfect gift for a wife or girlfriend? We have—"

"We're shopping for information, not makeup." I showed the woman my shield.

"Niagara Falls?" The woman wrinkled her nose. "What are you doing in Amherst?"

"It's part of our investigation. Your name is?"

"Lydia Conroy."

"Do you know Gwyneth Walsh?"

Beside me, Rodney removed his notepad and pen. "Are you a manager here?" He looked at Conroy.

"Sort of. Most of our clerks are not Macy's employees. They work on contract. I manage the Clinique contractors." She thought and seemed to make a decision. "Yes, I know Gwyneth."

I noted a sign that had not been removed. "Did you have an event last night, some sort of color consultation?"

"Yes. It was by invitation only. I mean, the store was open, but the event at the counter was for Clinique. For our mailing list customers. The consultations were a part of it."

"When did it start?"

"Seven o'clock." She straightened a display of perfumes.

"Was Ms. Walsh working? If so, was she scheduled for the counter or did she work the event?"

Conroy paused. "Gwyneth worked until closing yesterday. She was at the counter before the event, then did consultations."

Rodney glanced at me. Walsh's alibi was solid.

"Did she leave at any time?" I asked.

Conroy frowned. "She took a dinner break. She was gone around five for an hour, maybe an hour and fifteen minutes. It was a little longer than usual, but she said she'd gotten into a conversation at the food court. We had extra hands, so I didn't give her grief. It's not like she takes a long lunch every day."

The drive to Olcott was about forty-five minutes. That was pure driving time without traffic. At five, she'd be fighting rush hour. How long would it take to spike someone's drink? As Rodney had pointed out, she could have had an accomplice. Or Bramley could have brought his own drink. If the restaurant allowed it. No, it was insane.

"How did she look when she returned?" Rodney didn't say anything on the subject, but his expression told me he'd computed the driving time for himself.

Conroy shrugged. "Okay. She's been a bit tense since her sister died. You do know…" Her mouth dropped open. "Oh my God, that's why you're here. You think she killed her sister."

I shook my head. "This is a separate matter."

"Another death? I didn't see anything on the news last night." Conroy's eyes narrowed. "Gwyneth did call in today, said an urgent personal matter had come up. Is that why you're here?"

"Ms. Walsh's fiancé was in an auto accident last night," Rodney said.

I studied Conroy's face. She was shocked, a look that quickly turned to suspicion. "You think Gwyneth was involved?"

"It's too early to say." I wasn't inclined to share all the gory details with this woman. "Thanks for your time. If you think of anything else, please give me a call at either of those numbers." I slid my business card across the counter.

Conroy picked up the card, put it in a skirt pocket without looking, and walked away. I guess if we weren't paying customers, we didn't warrant such pleasantries as a simple goodbye.

Beside me, Rodney sneezed. "These scents make my nose itch. Should we go to the food court?"

"We're here. I'm getting hungry, anyway."

We strolled down walkways sparsely populated with weekday shoppers. The food court was moderately full, but I found it unlikely we'd find anyone who'd remember Walsh. After a bunch of inquiries over twenty minutes, I concluded I was right. We grabbed sandwiches from Subway and sat.

"As much as I'd like to think I'm brilliant and all, you're right." Rodney sucked Dr. Pepper through his straw. "It's not likely Walsh drove all the way to Olcott and back in an hour, if it was attempted murder and not a true accident. But it's too coincidental. Sylvia gets bumped off and her widower has a near-fatal crash? Puh-leeze."

"Hopefully, the Olcott police found a receipt in his wallet and know where he was. As a house-husband, there aren't any co-workers to question. Let's check for friends, running buddies, anything. Maybe he had an argument with someone."

"Hey, wait a second." Rodney's eyes grew thoughtful. "Maybe it's not only inheritance money at stake here. Who gets the company if Bramley snuffs it?"

"We'd have to pull his will. My guess is either Walsh or it would go up for sale."

"What are the chances Bert Guenther could be the beneficiary?"

We stared at each other. It was an excellent question.

———

On the way back to Niagara Falls, I called Olcott to see if they'd found anything in Bramley's wallet to indicate his whereabouts.

"Lighthouse Grill N Spirit," the officer said. "The receipt was right on top. Burger, fries, and a beer. Date and time stamped for last night at nine forty-three. But that's only when he paid, not when he left."

In other words, he might have left later. In fact, he probably had if the accident wasn't reported until eleven. "He was definitely coming from Olcott when he had the accident?"

"Oh, yeah." Which meant Bramley had been drugged while in Olcott. Who on earth had he met up there to eat with?

We headed to Lighthouse Grill N Spirit. Two of the waitresses remembered seeing Bramley, and both described his companion as a skinny, balding guy with brown hair. "He sat like he's at a desk all day, hunched over," one of them said. "Nervous as a mouse who knows a cat is watching the hole. He ordered a meal, but I don't think he took more than three bites." Neither of them had seen Walsh, but both admitted someone could have slipped in and out without being noticed. It had been a big crowd. They didn't allow patrons to bring their own food or beverages.

Rodney drove back to the station. "You know who the other guy sounds like?"

"Dellafiore." I tapped on the door panel. "Let's get in touch with him. Ask what he and Bramley talked about."

"I'd still like to know what happens to the company now that Sylvia's dead."

"Then, find out."

Rodney muttered something. I ignored him.

On the way back, we stopped at Natural Wonders. Marcy said Guenther wasn't in. "Check the lot," I told Rodney. "Run the plates of any car that looks like his."

But Guenther's reserved spot was empty, and none of the other plates belonged to cars registered to him. Marcy confirmed Dellafiore had tendered his resignation but claimed he hadn't cleaned out his office.

"When will he be back?" Rodney asked.

She shrugged. "I don't know. Unless he intends to abandon his crap. It's generic office supplies."

We left messages for both men with Marcy, as well as on their work, home, and cellphone voicemails.

———

Friday morning, Rodney was waiting for me when I arrived. "They call?" I sat down.

"No such luck." The disappointment in his voice contrasted with the fire in his eyes. "Do we call again or get an arrest warrant?"

I checked my watch. "We don't have sufficient cause. Give it until ten."

Yannick stepped out of his office. "Davis." He beckoned me.

Rodney looked at the captain, then at me. "Why does Yannick want to talk to you?"

I had my suspicions. I walked away, but I heard him muttering as I went.

Yannick closed the door behind me. "Have a seat." He dropped into his own.

"This about the case?" I knew it wasn't, but hey, I'd give it a shot.

"No, but how's it going?"

"Bramley was in a car accident earlier this week. Hoping to get information when he wakes up."

"If he wakes up." Yannick tapped his thumbs together. "This is about you."

"What about me?"

"Don't play dumb."

Damn. "It's a work in progress."

"But you're making headway?"

"I think so, sir." Dr. Alverson seemed to be pleased with my willingness to talk to her, but it was so hard to know what was going on inside her head. She'd be a hell of an interviewee, and a damn good poker player.

"You seem less edgy." He looked me square in the eye. "I trust you would tell me if you needed to go on leave."

I met his gaze. "Yes, sir. Can I go?"

He nodded to the door.

I went back to my desk and sat.

Rodney looked up. "Am I getting a new partner?"

I challenged him with my stare. "Do you still want one?"

We stayed still for several moments. The phone rang and I picked it up without breaking eye contact. "Criminal Investigation, this is Davis."

A woman's voice came over the line. "Detective Davis, Lorraine Atkins."

"Ms. Atkins, what can I do for you?"

Rodney clenched his jaw, got up, and walked away.

I win.

"I've been authenticating the paintings you sent earlier this week."

"Forged?"

"They're very skilled jobs, but when compared to other works by these artists, it's clear they aren't originals. If you want me to, I can describe the details." Atkins sounded prepared to be very precise.

"No. Send a report, please. We suspected they were fake. Knowing we were right is enough. If I have questions, I'll call you." I instructed her to include her phone number and hung up.

Rodney came back holding a can of pop. "Who was that?"

"The art expert who examined the paintings."

"Fake?" He flipped the tab on the can and sat.

"Yes." I studied him as he drank. "You didn't answer my question."

He stared at the top of the can for a good minute, then he looked up. "I don't know. You're…" He paused, swirling the contents of the can. "You're a good detective. Been less of an asshole. I don't know."

"You still have until the end of this investigation to decide." I stood and buttoned my jacket. "Let's get someone from the Newfane police to bring in Guenther on the forgery. Then, we can hit him up on the murder."

"I'd rather pick him up ourselves."

I would, too. "We don't have time. This way, he gets arrested while we're en route. Plus, he's technically in their jurisdiction."

"I suppose you're right. Still don't like it." He shotgunned the rest of his pop. "I guess you can drive this time." He walked away.

I directed my words to his retreating back. "Gee, how swell of you."

I called and had the Newfane police arrest Guenther. It did suck we didn't collar him ourselves, but this way, he could sweat a little before he arrived. It might make him more willing to talk. We needed another break.

After a brief consultation, our counterparts led us to an interrogation room. Guenther was seated at the table, still cuffed. Sweat covered his forehead. He jumped up as soon as we entered. The Newfane officer supervising him grabbed his shoulder and pushed him back down.

"I demand to know the meaning of this." Guenther's voice trembled in contradiction to his angry words. "Art forgery. It's ridiculous. I bought those paintings in good faith."

Rodney and I sat down. "Mr. Guenther." I adjusted my jacket. "We know the works in question are fake. We know you own the gallery where they were purchased. It's only a matter of time before we find who you were working with."

"In other words, you can stop acting." Rodney placed his notebook and pen in front of him.

Guenther deflated like a balloon. "I want a lawyer." He looked at us. "Niagara Falls Homicide isn't here because of art."

"First things first. Your rights." I pulled the card from my wallet and read the Miranda warning. "Do you understand these rights as I have read them?"

"Yes, yes." Guenther's fingers tapped a rapid beat on the table.

"We'll wait for your lawyer, of course." Rodney's voice stayed mild. "You're right. We're not here about the art."

"Then, why are you here?" Guenther looked like a hunted animal.

"Sylvia's death." I waited. Guenther had lawyered up, which meant we had to be careful about what we asked. If he decided to talk, it was on him.

"I didn't kill Sylvia." Guenther's fingers continued their rapid staccato.

Rodney glanced at me, then focused on Guenther. "Are you waiving your right to representation?"

"I won't answer questions about the art, but I didn't kill Sylvia."

Beside me, Rodney opened his notebook. I focused on our suspect. What I really wanted to know was whether Sylvia knew about the forged paintings. But Guenther had made the subject off limits. "The night Mrs. Bramley was killed, did you know she'd be on Green Island?"

"No." Guenther wiped his forehead. "I was watching TV at home. Alone. I even told you which movie."

I leaned on the table and clasped my hands. "Mr. Guenther, with all the ways to watch television these days, it's not a great alibi unless you can provide corroboration."

"I wasn't on Green Island." Guenther's voice was hoarse, barely above a whisper.

"You said you were watching a John Wayne flick." I leaned back. "I love *El Dorado* myself. One of my favorites. Of course, the story is really *Rio Lobo* with different characters. Did you know they even used the same set?"

"No, I didn't." He shot Rodney a look. "The poem is

quite striking. I always make a point to watch it when it's on, just to hear it. Of course, James Caan's performance is excellent."

Rodney flipped back to the record of our original interview with the Natural Wonders VP. "It is. But there's one little problem."

"What?" Guenther appeared genuinely puzzled.

"You told us you were watching *The Searchers*." I held his gaze.

Sweat popped on his brow. "You must be mistaken. I definitely said *El Dorado*."

"Nope, no mistake."

He relaxed. "How can you be sure? You aren't even looking at your notes."

Rodney spoke up. "He's right, Mr. Guenther. I have it right here. You told us you were watching *The Searchers*. 'Not one of my favorites,' you told us. So, which is it?"

He wiped his forehead. "I must have misspoken. We —that is, I usually don't pay much attention. Often, the TV is background noise."

Rodney and I exchanged looks. Guenther had been with a woman. Had to be. Not his wife, and not Sylvia. "Which is it? We or I?"

Guenther's gaze reminded me of a hunted animal.

Rodney sat back. "Infidelity is the least of your worries right now. If someone can alibi you, I suggest you give us a name."

"You can't tell my wife." Guenther's gaze flicked between Rodney and me.

Rodney snorted.

I shook my head. She'd find out. Not from us, though. "Where were you?"

"With a friend." Guenther paused, then gave us a name, phone number, and address. "She'll tell you the same. I didn't kill anyone. I swear." Guenther shook his head. "I want my lawyer now."

Rodney and I got up and left. Guenther would get his lawyer, and someone else would handle the forgery case. We had bigger fish to fry.

———

After we left, we stopped at the address Guenther had given us, which was also in Newfane. The woman there backed up his story. They'd been carrying on for a couple months, since he and Sylvia split. He'd been with her the entire night of the murder.

"Cross him off the list." Rodney scowled. We got back in the car and headed for the office. "We're back to Walsh and Bramley."

"Hmm." I thought this over as we idled at a stop light. "We still don't know for sure who Bramley was meeting the night he had his accident."

"The guy who kind of matches Dellafiore's description?"

"If it was Dellafiore, what'd they talk about?" The light turned green and I pulled ahead. They said everybody had a doppelgänger, but I wasn't willing to go there.

"You really suspect Dellafiore?"

"Yes. He's fed us a convenient mix of lies, truths, and

half-truths. Why? If he really discovered embezzling at Natural Wonders, why not call the police immediately?" I parked in the office lot and we headed toward the door.

"Jackson."

I stopped and turned to see Rodney standing next to the car.

"What I said earlier about not knowing if I wanted a new partner." He paused. "I'm not yanking your chain. I really don't know."

I found myself hoping he didn't. Aside from not wanting the label of being difficult to work with, Rodney was a good guy. The hard-charger attitude would mellow in time and he'd be an excellent partner. "Understood. Can we go inside?" I waved toward the building. "After all, we do have a murder to solve."

We got a call from Marcy immediately after lunch that dragged us back out to Natural Wonders. "Anthony Dellafiore came in to pack his desk."

Rodney wasn't happy to be driving back to Newfane. It was obvious from the edge in his voice. "He couldn't have come in earlier?"

I felt the same, but I wasn't going to let it show. I had another appointment with Dr. Alverson in the afternoon. I didn't need to be driving all over Niagara County.

Marcy waved us through to Dellafiore's office when we arrived. He was throwing things in a cardboard box with abandon. "Mr. Dellafiore, we've been trying to get in touch with you. Didn't you get our messages?"

He jerked his head up, eyes widening a little when he saw us. "Oh, I've been busy. I was going to call you later."

Liar. Dellafiore was going to call us like I was going

to win the lottery. "Marcy saved you the trouble. Let's talk."

Rodney took out his notepad again. "What've you got?" He pointed at an envelope Dellafiore was turning over in his hands.

"I was going to leave it with Marcy. It's for you. I was going through Mrs. Bramley's desk."

"Why?" I couldn't think of a single good reason for Dellafiore to ransack his dead boss's desk.

"I loaned her some things. Since I'm leaving, I wanted them back." He fiddled with the envelope some more.

Bullshit. What could he have given Sylvia, a calculator? I said nothing.

The silence trick worked. "I found this." He held out the envelope. "It wasn't sealed or marked, so I looked inside. It's a suicide note. Who knew?"

I hoped my poker face looked as good as it felt. My internal bullshit meter was pegged in the red. Sylvia's desk had been searched the day we'd found her body. "May I see it?" I donned gloves and tugged the envelope from his hand. The inside note was brief.

To all - I cannot continue this charade. My gambling, Keith's infidelity, my affair, the embezzlement. It's all too much. I find myself too cowardly to face my mistakes, although honesty compels me to admit them. I intend to end life my way. I cannot go to jail. My only regret is that I've caused so much pain to the people I care about. By the time you find this note, I will have taken my final trip to the Falls.

It was signed *Sylvia*. The text was typed, printed by a standard laser printer on regular copy paper, but the signature was in pen. I made a note to have the handwriting folks do a signature comparison with some of the contracts we'd seized. I handed it to Rodney. As he read it, I was impressed he didn't laugh out loud.

"This is quite a find." He replaced the note in the envelope. He handed the envelope back to me and I slipped it inside an evidence bag I carried in my pocket. Any fingerprints would probably be obliterated by now. Had that been part of the plan?

He blinked. "You're taking it?"

"It's evidence." I sealed the bag and wrote up the evidence chain. "You found this in Mrs. Bramley's desk?"

"Yes. I suppose the note clears everyone. I'm sorry you wasted your time." Without something to hold, Dellafiore's hands shook.

I studied him. "We wanted to ask you about something else. A witness stated she thought she saw you at dinner with Keith Bramley last Thursday at the Lighthouse Grill N Spirit in Olcott. Was it you?"

"I barely know Mr. Bramley."

"You didn't answer the question," Rodney said.

He swallowed, his Adam's apple prominent. "It wasn't me."

"Did you know Mr. Bramley had a car accident Thursday night?"

Dellafiore rubbed his chin. "No. Is he okay?" He glanced from Rodney to me. His gaze was searching. For what? "Such a shame. I only met him a couple times, but he seemed like a nice guy. Maybe it's a blessing he'll never find out about Sylvia."

"Oh, he's not dead, just unconscious. He'll be able to give us more information when he wakes up. I'm sure he'll find this note a surprise." It was not my imagination. My words had made Dellafiore turn pale. I held out my hand. "Thank you for bringing this note to our attention. We'll be in touch."

Dellafiore shook my hand with reluctance. "No problem."

I could feel Dellafiore's gaze on my back as we walked away. I knew the suicide note was crap. Had Dellafiore written it, or had someone else planted it for him to find? He'd definitely gotten twitchy when he learned Bramley was alive. I hoped he'd regain consciousness soon so we'd find out why.

———

The gallery that had supplied the paintings, and which would probably lead to the forger, was located in the city limits. I handed off everything we had to the guys in Fraud. They could argue with Newfane about who would take point.

"Thanks for nothing, Davis." Detective Joe Connor grabbed the papers from me.

"Don't be a grump. I've handed you a case, evidence, and a suspect wrapped and tied in a neat package." I spoke in a cheery voice I knew would drive Connor crazy. "All you need to do is cross every *t* and dot every *i*. Merry Christmas, seven months early."

Back at my desk, I handed the evidence bag with the alleged suicide note to Rodney. "What do you think?"

"Dellafiore's story smells worse than my college roommate's socks."

"Too bad we couldn't call him on it right there. The note is undoubtedly forged, but who wrote it?"

"And who signed Sylvia's name?" He picked up the phone. "Speaking of which, we need to get a hand-writing comparison."

"You read my mind." I popped a piece of gum and picked up a pen to twirl in my fingers.

Rodney shook his head. "You're more fidgety than a five-year-old on a sugar high. I wouldn't have thought two cigarettes would cause you such a problem."

"It's like trying to break the habit all over again. It's easier to deal with the urge to smoke if I keep my hands busy."

"And something in your mouth, given the teeth marks. What's it ever done to you?"

"If it's a choice between chewing you out and gnawing on a pen, which would you prefer?"

"Chomp away." He went back to his phone call.

We spent the better part of the rest of the day sifting through our notes after we forwarded the alleged suicide note for handwriting analysis. Guenther was in lockup. Bramley was unconscious. We had nothing new to ask either Walsh or Dellafiore. If we got a call that it wasn't Sylvia's signature, though, things would change.

At three-thirty, I stood. "I've gotta go. Call if anything pops. Even over the weekend. Otherwise, see you Monday." I buttoned my jacket.

"Right." Rodney looked me up and down. "Good luck this afternoon."

"Thanks." I headed out. Max had offered to go with me, but I declined. I appreciated the unspoken moral support. At the same time, I wondered if I'd ever stop feeling like I was approaching the gates of Mordor when I approached the door to Dr. Alverson's building. With my luck, probably not.

———

For the third time in a week, I sat across from Dr. Alverson. Once again, the soft browns of her office utterly failed to calm me. I wasn't as tense as I had been, but I still felt like the time I'd taken a dare and put the terminals of a nine-volt battery on my tongue.

"Have you had any nightmares?" She picked up a pad and pen.

"None." I thought for a moment. "It's been a little weird. I've been sleeping with a furry, portable white noise machine. Maybe that's it."

"A cat, I take it." She jotted a note. "People do say the purr is therapeutic. What about anxiety? Panic attacks?"

I shook my head. "Not outside this office. I've been too busy with this case to think of much else. And I'm concerned about my partner."

"What about him?"

"I was pretty much a dick his first week. He might want out. I'm working on fixing things." I held up a hand. "Yes, I apologized to him. He accepted it, but it doesn't mean he wouldn't rather work with someone else."

"How does doing so make you feel?"

I rubbed my hands on my thighs. "I'd rather he stuck around, to be honest. One, he's a good detective and he'll only get better. I don't want to break in another new guy. Second, I like him. Which surprises the hell out of me, but I do."

"How so?"

"I figured I'd always resent someone who wasn't Max. Nothing against the person, but you know how it is."

"You and Max were very close. It's natural to feel some tension with a new person. I applaud your self-awareness." She set down her pad. "Today, let's talk about situations beyond simple anxiety."

I stared at her. "What else could there be?"

She laughed. "With PTSD, it's not uncommon for certain stimuli to cause what one might call a flashback. You wind up back at the time and place of the original trauma. In your case, the explosion."

"Like the warnings they give about combat vets and fireworks."

"Exactly. I think it's very possible anything resembling the noise, heat, and fire of the incident at Occidental would be a trigger for you. Gunfire may or may not be problematic."

I thought of the grill flare-up. "Doc, if I lose my shit in the middle of a shooting incident, it will be problematic, to say the least. Yeah, I'm a detective. We're usually called in after the action is over. But as a cop, there is always the potential for someone to shoot at me, and I'd need to be able to respond."

"Exactly. Which is why we're going to work on what is called cognitive therapy. As I mentioned, a triggering episode will try to put you back in the original trauma. The techniques we're going to work on will keep you grounded in *this* reality and avoid getting carried away."

Was she honestly saying I could see myself out of the situation? "Sorry, but it sounds like mumbo-jumbo to me."

Her smile was faint. "Take a deep breath."

I closed my eyes and inhaled.

"Keep your eyes open."

"Why?" But I obeyed.

"Your subconscious is going to try and convince your mind you are back at the scene of the accident," she said. "Your body reacts with fight-or-flight. Your heart rate goes up, breathing gets hard, you sweat, get jittery—survival mode. You need to convince your brain you're not in that scenario. Focusing on your surroundings through sight and touch, even through smell, is a good way to start. Feel your current reality as much as you can."

I remained unconvinced. "I'm not sure I buy this."

"Remember, the mind is very powerful. Your subconscious has been winning, bombarding you with all the remembered trauma. What are you going to do if you're in a car? In your backyard? At the mall?"

The grill flare-up came to mind again. *What if Amy hadn't been there?* I took another breath and stared at a vase of flowers. "Okay. Let's do this visualization thing."

———

I left Dr. Alverson's office an hour later feeling like a paper towel that had been soaked and squeezed one too many times. The doc had been pleased with the session. Me, not so much.

Alverson bade me goodbye. "It's good progress. We'll pick it up again next Tuesday." She spoke as if it were something to look forward to.

I didn't share her optimism. I needed comfort. Warmth. Compassion. Max might be my rope, but I needed a warm blanket.

I needed my wife.

I called Amy and she agreed to meet me at a diner we'd gone to often in our dating and pre-kid days. I ordered two milkshakes and waited in a booth until she came in.

She took my breath away. She wasn't wearing anything fancy, a T-shirt with a paint-stained sleeve, jeans, and sneakers. But the way the afternoon sun coming through the windows glinted on her hair and lit the curve of her face was magic. "Amy. Over here."

She turned, smiled, and came over. I rose to meet her. I was going to make it a brief embrace, appropriate for the public, but once I had her in my arms, I couldn't let go. I drank in her warmth and the clean citrus smell of her soap like a man in the desert guzzled water.

After a long minute, she pulled away. "This is a blast from the past." She dropped into the booth seat.

I sat across from her. "I thought it was appropriate. Starting over. I ordered. Hope you don't mind."

We engaged in small talk until our shakes arrived: double chocolate for her, strawberry for me.

"How are you?" She took a sip.

"It's hard, to be honest. I'm trying to take it one day at a time. Make a little progress every day." I tied my straw paper in a knot and yanked, tearing it in two. Then, I repeated the process with one of the halves.

"Want to tell me about it?"

I couldn't help myself. I unloaded everything, including the troubles with Rodney. "Why'd you call Max?"

"Because she's your partner," Amy said.

I blustered.

She held up a hand. "I know the drill. I'm your wife and you love me. You love our kids. But some things you have to hear from another cop." She stabbed the half-melted ice cream with her straw. "When are you coming home?"

I clenched my hand and she squeezed it. "Amy, I've been thinking. This last session, the doc talked about PTSD and triggers and reliving the trauma. What happens if I lose it and hurt you? Or the kids?"

"You wouldn't."

"What if it's an accident?"

She held my hand in both of hers and kissed it.

I wasn't going to let her ignore my concern. "You read stories of people with PTSD lashing out and injuring people during these episodes. Why should I be different?"

"You're not worried about hurting Max?"

"Max would kick my ass."

"Jackson, she's blind."

"Which in no way affects her ability to kick my ass." Max's reflexes were sharp. As she'd learned to use her other senses to compensate, she might have lost half a step, but no more.

Amy sighed. "Why'd you call me?"

"To remind myself what I'm fighting for." My throat was scratchy and my eyes pricked. "I need you, Ame. I don't want to mess it up."

"Jackson, the very fact you're worried tells me you'll do anything to *not* hurt us. But I understand if you need a little more space to convince yourself." She gave my hand another squeeze. "But don't take too much longer. You're racking up one hell of a bedtime story debt. You'll still be paying it off when Madeline goes to college." She looked at the wall clock. "I've got to go. Mom's watching the kids, but it's bridge night."

"Don't want to interfere with bridge night."

"You know it." She stood, and I followed suit.

She grabbed a fistful of my shirt and pulled me down to kiss me. Time stood still. Her scent, the softness of her lips, and the tantalizing promise of more washed every thought from my head. Who cared if we were in public? I cupped her face and responded in kind. The moment might have lasted ten seconds, ten hours, or ten years.

We broke apart and she tugged my chin. "That was a promise, you know."

Fortunately, she stood in front of me, masking any visible effects at the front of my pants. "Can I hold you to it?"

Her answering grin was sly. "I'll be very disappointed if you don't."

Saturday dawned, bright and sunny. I wanted to go into the office and shake the tree again, see if anything fell out. But Max stopped me. "Do you have new information?"

"Not really. I need Bramley to wake up."

"Then, save the aggravation. Besides, I need to buy shoes. You can drive me."

We went to the outlets, where I played baggage mule. It was a role I was familiar with. We were in the Clarks store when my phone rang. "Yeah, Rodney."

"One of the ICU nurses from Niagara Memorial called. Bramley regained consciousness. He wants to see us."

"Oh, sure. The ICU nurse calls the single guy. Was it the cute one, or the one built like the *USS The Sullivans*?"

"Shut up and meet me there." He hung up.

Max looked up, a black flat in her hand. "We're leaving."

"I'm sorry. I can get someone to meet you here and take you home."

"Never mind." She stood up. "Murder is more important than shoes."

I took her home, threw on a suit, and went to the hospital. Rodney was out front. "What took you so long?"

"I had to take Max home. At least my tie isn't crooked."

He muttered, but he straightened his tie as we headed for the ICU. Once there, we showed our badges to the woman at the nurses' station. "We were told Keith Bramley is asking for us."

The nurse, who was rather attractive in a severe kind of way, examined our IDs. "He has. But I remind you, this is the ICU. You get ten minutes." She led us to a room. Before she left, she gave Rodney a long look, the ghost of a smile on her face. I, on the other hand, might as well not have existed.

Bramley was in the far bed, tubes and wires everywhere, the monitor next to him beeping. Walsh was at his bedside.

"What are you two doing here?" The light in her eyes flared. "You arrest people in the hospital? I would have thought that was too far, even for cops."

Clearly, she either didn't remember, or didn't *want* to remember, calling me for help.

"Ms. Walsh." Rodney sounded vaguely irritated despite his polite tone. "Whether you want to believe it or not, we're not on a vendetta against you or Mr. Bramley. He called for us."

"Like hell he did." Walsh's nostrils flared.

"Gwyneth." Bramley's voice was faint. "They're telling the truth." With a grimace, he turned his head. "Sorry, detectives. She's a little sensitive lately."

"Understandable." I moved to his bedside so I could hear him better. "We're likely to get kicked out of here fast." Walsh snorted, and I ignored her. "What did you want to tell us?"

"The accident." Bramley closed his eyes.

I nodded to Rodney, who got ready to take notes. "What about it? The receipt in your wallet was from Lighthouse Grill N Spirit."

His nod was weak. "It was dollar burger night. I had a cheeseburger and a Sam Adams."

"Draft or bottle?" If it was a draft, it'd be easier to drug the glass.

"Draft." Bramley's voice was barely audible.

"You met someone there. Who?"

"The accountant guy. Dellafiore."

I knew it hadn't been a twin. "Why?"

"Got to decide what to do with the company," Bramley whispered. "Sell it or keep it. I was going to keep it and let Gwyneth run things. I don't know anything about makeup. But she does." He paused and his eyelids drooped. I was afraid he was clocking out again, but he opened them. "I got an independent audit. Found discrepancies."

"You called Mr. Dellafiore." I prompted him. Guilt at rushing him gnawed my mind, but ten minutes wasn't a lot of time.

Bramley gave a slight nod. "Wanted an explanation. He accused Sylvia. No way."

"Why didn't you believe him?" Rodney asked.

Walsh tossed her hair. "That company was my sister's life. She loved it more than anything. Even Keith. No way she'd steal from it, even as screwed up as she was with the gambling."

I looked at her. "You knew about the gambling?"

"I told her." Bramley's voice sounded even fainter. "Sylvia wasn't good at hiding it. I wanted her to get help."

I waited. When he didn't continue, I prompted him. "What did Dellafiore say?"

"Got weird. Sly. Said he'd gotten what he wanted and if I kept my mouth shut, he'd show me how to fix it. I could even hire him back. For a price." Bramley laughed, a weak, wet sound.

"What did you say?"

"I told him to go screw himself. I was going to blow the lid off his scheme, call the cops, the SEC, whomever. Then, I went to the bathroom."

If Bramley had left his drink, and Dellafiore had felt threatened, I could completely see him drugging the remainder and hoping a crash solved his problem. He might have brought something in case Bramley wasn't cooperative. "What about your beer?"

The same nurse came into the room. "Time's up, detectives. You need to leave."

"Two more minutes." Rodney stood and went to her. "We're almost finished."

"I don't care. This is a hospital, not an interrogation room. Leave, or I'm calling Security." Considering Rodney an attractive man wasn't going to make her bend the rules.

I leaned in. "Mr. Bramley, was there beer in your

glass when you went to the bathroom?" Behind me, I heard Rodney arguing with the nurse, who stormed out, presumably to make good on her threat.

Rodney confirmed it. "Jackson, we've got a minute. Tops."

I leaned in. "Mr. Bramley?"

It felt like eternity, but Bramley eventually nodded. "Finished it when I got back. It tasted weird."

A hospital security guard entered. Rodney and I left without further incident. Outside, he began cussing a blue streak.

"You couldn't have flirted with her to buy a little more time?"

"Bro, you heard her. She wanted us out."

"You didn't even try."

He shot me a dirty look. "I suppose Walsh and Bramley are still in the frame for Sylvia's murder, especially if he kept the company and she got to run it. But Dellafiore just jumped to the top of my list. Damn it. You were right." His voice held a note of grudging admiration.

I ignored it. "We still have to put him on the scene. How would he have known to go to Green Island? Get a uniform over to Dellafiore's apartment to pick him up for questioning."

Rodney pulled out his phone and stepped away to call.

Dellafiore was behind the embezzlement. Bramley's statement all but confirmed it. But if Rodney was right, Bramley and Walsh still had a powerful motive for killing Sylvia. The two crimes didn't have to be connected. And Bramley had been at or near the murder scene.

I had a fifty percent chance of choosing to follow the right path. The sense I was missing something, something said or done earlier, nagged at me.

Rodney returned. "Uniform is on their way to Dellafiore's. They'll call. You look frustrated."

"I'm missing it. It's there and I'm missing it."

"We might have to guess and go from there." He headed to the car.

I followed. Damn it, I hated guessing.

———

The patrol cop sent to Dellafiore's apartment reported coming up empty. "Neighbors say he left a while ago. He was carrying boxes. Looked like he was in a hurry."

"Thanks." I hung up and reported the results to Rodney.

He cussed under his breath. "Issue the BOLO?"

I nodded. "Notify Immigration and Customs Enforcement at all border crossings. I'll get in touch with Ontario Provincial and Niagara Falls, Canada."

While Rodney put out the "be on the lookout" and contacted ICE, I notified the Canadians. Afterward, it was a matter of *hurry up and wait*.

———

Monday morning, we were still waiting. Dellafiore had proven unusually elusive. We'd spent the weekend calling around. His few family members and friends in the area denied seeing him. A call to Marcy drew another blank.

"Someone's lying," Rodney snarled as he hung up the phone with a little more force than necessary. "A guy doesn't vanish like this."

I tapped a pen on my desk, staring into space. The nagging sense I'd glossed over something hadn't left me alone all weekend. A long walk, a hot shower—nothing had pried it loose.

"Yo, space cadet." Rodney snapped his fingers to get my attention. "What is your problem?"

I shook myself. "We're missing a piece. Something important, and for the life of me, I can't pull it up."

He smirked. "You mean your recorder of a memory isn't perfect?"

"Wiseass. Pass those financials."

The morning had seen the delivery of not only Dellafiore's full history but the analysis from the forensic accountants. We split the stack and read. I took the employment history and Rodney took the financials.

I counted Dellafiore's listed employers. "The guy hopped around."

"Huh?" Engrossed in his reading, Rodney barely looked up, although I knew he was listening.

"In the past six years, he's worked at five different companies, none for longer than eight months, some as little as four."

"Why'd he leave?"

"That's what I'm going to find out." I picked up the phone and connected with four of Dellafiore's past five employers, the fifth being Natural Wonders. In each case, the story was the same. Dellafiore had excellent credentials. He came in, worked hard, identified minor discrepancies, then left. In each case, the parting had been amiable. In fact, all of the employers I spoke to regretted losing him.

My question to each was the same. "Did you ever find the source of these discrepancies?" Every time, the answer was no. They stopped shortly before Dellafiore left. When I scribbled the math on a sheet of paper, it added up to a tidy sum.

"It's not suspicious when taken one at a time, but as a whole?" Rodney said when I told him. We'd ordered pizza for lunch, with a bottle of Coke for each of us.

"Nice little game." I wiped grease from my fingers.

"Here's the proof." Rodney pushed over the papers. "At least, from Natural Wonders. There's the money out, here's the money in. He didn't use a regular bank account. It's some kind of weird online thing in Canada. But it's there."

"He fed Guenther a line of bullshit." I scanned the paper. "Then, he overreached. Instead of giving up and running, he tried to frame someone."

"He got tired of the pattern."

I took a swig of Coke. "Sylvia was the CFO. It was her company. Her baby. She might have been more invested in finding the thief. She had the skills to do it. I bet she'd be able to finger Dellafiore even without knowing about his financial hidey-hole."

"She told him, said she's going to call the cops, and he killed her."

"Why didn't she call someone? Why go away for a week?" If Sylvia knew Dellafiore was her thief, it didn't make sense for her to wait.

Rodney swirled his remaining Coke around. "She wasn't sure." He took another mouthful and swallowed. "Or she wanted a better explanation, but she already had this vacation planned. So, she waited. Deal with her husband's infidelity, then the theft."

I thought about it. "Which brings us back to how Dellafiore knew she was on Green Island. I don't think she would share her vacation plans with him."

He pushed aside the paper. "You remember what's nagging you?"

"No. It's pissing me off." I rubbed my forehead. We were running in circles, getting nowhere. We could do this all night, or I could do something Rodney might hate, but might yield results. I stood and grabbed my coat. "Bring the papers."

"Where are we going?" His forehead was lined in frustration and his voice was aggressive, but he stood, piled everything into a heap, and followed me.

I shoved the door open, inhaling the fresh night air. "I think it's time you met Max in person."

I knocked to announce our arrival, then walked into Max's apartment. "Hey." I beckoned Rodney to follow me. "You here?"

"Where the hell else would I be?" Max came out of the kitchen. "This the new guy?" She waved in Rodney's general direction.

Rodney started. "Hi." If he was a little freaked out, I couldn't tell from his voice.

Two sets of footsteps. I wondered if I'd ever get used to Max appearing to have developed ESP. "Rodney, this is Max."

She didn't move. "Don't stare. It's not polite."

He looked at me and back to her. "How did—"

"Everybody stares. Thanks for admitting it. This way." She crooked her finger, indicating we should follow her to the living room.

I laid my hand on his shoulder. "You'll get used to it."

"She always snappy?" He kept his voice low.

"I am when you talk like I can't hear you," Max's voice carried out to us. "I'm blind, not deaf. And definitely not stupid."

I shot him an apologetic look. "You'll get used to that, too."

We went into the living room, where I settled on the couch. Rodney took the other chair. "Sorry I didn't give you a heads up, but we're in a hurry."

She snorted. "What do you want?"

Rodney tapped his fingers together. "Jackson says we need fresh eyes."

Max lifted an eyebrow.

"In a manner of speaking." He looked at the floor.

I covered my grin with my hand. I knew how Rodney felt. I'd been the same the first couple times I saw Max post accident. However, she'd always had a bite to her personality. Being a woman in a male-dominated field, she had to. "Here's the deal." I laid out all the details Rodney and I had discussed, making a case for both Dellafiore, and Walsh and Bramley. "I'm skipping over a detail. I know it. I just can't *see* it."

"Jackson says the husband/sister solution is *too complicated*." Rodney's voice implied the air quotes.

"No need to complicate things." Max cocked her head. "What does your gut tell you?"

"My gut? I, well…" He trailed off, shooting me a look tinged with guilt.

She trained her gaze on him and he turned brick red under her sightless, but still piercing, look. "Tell me, how long have you been a detective?"

"A few weeks." He gazed at the floor again.

"Jackson was an asshat when you started. I heard about it."

He mumbled something. I glanced at Max, who shot a look at me, then returned to staring at Rodney.

"You don't want to go along with anything he says, even if it makes sense," she continued. "Trying to stake your own claim. Be a hard-charger. Get a little of your own back at his expense."

Rodney said nothing, but his skin flushed. I looked at my hands. I should have seen this coming. I'd gotten my lecture when I showed up on her doorstep an emotional train wreck. It was time for Rodney to get his.

"You passed the exam, so I know you're smart. Dummies don't make detective. Here's something they don't teach you." She leaned forward. "Good partnerships are like good marriages. You have to swallow your pride."

"I have." His mumble was tinged with defiance, like a sullen teenager being taken to task.

"Not enough." She leaned back. "There are days your partner will be a dick. Other days, you'll be the dick. You learn to forgive each other. I did when Jackson was new."

Rodney was smarter than I was at the same stage of my career. He stayed silent.

"You've got a choice, Kirke. You can learn to accept this guy's foibles—and his apologies—or you can leave, right now. Go to Yannick and demand reassignment."

I wanted to chime in, but I didn't. It was not my turn to talk yet.

"Have the decency to make up your damn mind.

For all his faults, Jackson had my six. He'll have yours. Whether you give him the opportunity is up to you." She leaned back. "Now, what does your gut tell you?"

He looked at me and heaved a sigh. "If Walsh and Bramley were married, I could see them working together. But the fact remains Bramley had his accident after meeting Dellafiore. The timing is too tight for Walsh to have been involved. She's smart enough to know that until they're married, she gets squat if Bramley kicks the bucket. The suicide note is crap. My gut says Dellafiore." Rodney's expression said he would rather have chewed glass, but Max had gotten stronger men to face facts.

She leaned back and Leroy jumped into her lap. "I agree. That means you need to put him on Green Island the night of the murder."

I nodded, which I knew she couldn't see, so I spoke. "I feel like I should be able to get there, but there's something I'm not seeing."

"When you questioned Dellafiore, what did he say?"

Rodney consulted his notebook. "Not much. He didn't know Sylvia well, she seemed erratic, blah, blah."

She shook her head. "Skip the notes." She turned to face me. "Jackson, what exactly did Dellafiore say?"

This was why I'd come. What I'd missed. When I was swimming in details, Max could home in on the important ones. I closed my eyes and thought. "He said, 'I'd have no idea why she'd decide to walk back to the hotel. And in that direction, too.'" It hit me. "Shit. If he wasn't there—"

"—how would he know she walked—"

"—and what route she took?"

"So, he was tailing her—"

"—from the casino to Top of the Falls."

"He probably saw her fight with Bramley—"

"—then followed her to Green Island, where he could have found something to hit her with, something easy to get rid of, stripped her jewelry—"

"—and tossed her into the river," Max finished.

Rodney's notebook clattered to the floor.

I picked it up. "What?"

He shook his head. "You two are a freak of nature."

"No, we're partners. It happens when you trust someone deeply." Max's voice sounded satisfied.

He picked up the notebook and turned it over in his hands. "When I was on patrol, I saw guys who had worked together for years. I have never seen something like what you two did. It's like," he paused, "you're in each other's heads, perfectly synchronized. You aren't two good detectives, you're each one half of a freaking awesome detective." He swallowed and looked at me.

I shrugged. "Never thought about it." But I'd described Max as my right hand. Rodney's description fit. No wonder I'd felt incomplete without her.

"I don't know if I can be that."

"I bet you two can be damn good together," Max said. "If you can get over your pride."

He glanced at her and went back to looking at the floor.

"You don't have to do it now." I stood. "First, we need to find ourselves a judge. Then, we need to find Anthony Dellafiore."

CHAPTER
THIRTY-SEVEN

We were able to get the arrest warrant signed Monday night. Bothering a judge after hours was never fun. Losing a suspect was worse.

What we couldn't do was find Dellafiore. He didn't return to his apartment. Calls to area contacts failed to locate him. He hadn't been seen in the casino or places like Top of the Falls. He wasn't in any of the area hospitals. ICE and the Canadian authorities were able to determine he hadn't crossed the border. At least, not using his real name. If he had fake papers under another name, we were hosed.

Tuesday morning, Rodney showed up with two extra-large coffees: one from Starbucks, one from Timmies. "Here. It was a late night."

We'd stayed until almost midnight, hoping something would turn up. We'd called Marcy again. She'd been more polite than we deserved after all our hounding, but she still hadn't seen him. "Thanks." I accepted it. No need to tell him Max had supplied me before I left. It was a two-cup morning, anyway.

He tapped his desk. "About yesterday. At Max's. We haven't talked about it."

"No need." Max's admonition to swallow his pride had hit hard, I could tell. I'd needed time to process the message. So did he. I wasn't going to push him.

He took his seat. "Uniform see anything at Dellafiore's?"

I blew on the coffee and shook my head. We'd gotten a unit to monitor the apartment overnight. Nothing.

Rodney muttered a curse. "Where the hell is he? He can't vanish. Should we check the morgue?"

I'd vented to Max when I got in last night. People did not vanish. Not in real life. They got caught by traffic cams, used credit cards, told the neighbors to feed the fish while they were gone. Dellafiore had done none of that. "Think. Where does he have connections?" I sat and pulled out a piece of paper to make a list.

"Home. Friends. Family. We've checked those." Rodney also sat. "Past jobs? He went to University at Buffalo. Would he go back?"

"Wouldn't be my first guess, but at this point I'll try anything." I made a note to call the faculty at UB.

Our thoughts were interrupted by the ring of my cellphone. I didn't recognize the number. "Detective Davis speaking. How can I help you?"

"Detective Davis? It's Marcy. From Natural Wonders." Her voice was low, but high-pitched at the same time. "You, uh, told me to call you if I saw Mr. Dellafiore."

I reached to tap my pen on Rodney's name plate to get his attention. "You've seen him?"

"He's here now. Just walked in," she said. "I can tell he's upset. I greeted him and he practically bit my head off."

I covered the phone with my hand and talked to Rodney. "Got him. Call Newfane and get a car out to Natural Wonders."

We both stood and prepared to leave.

"Marcy? You still there?" We hurried out, Rodney on the phone with the Newfane police.

"Yeah." She was breathing fast. "What should I do?"

"We're on our way." We had reached the parking lot and slid into a car. A Newfane uniform unit might get there first, but we weren't going to sit by and let another department pick up a murder suspect.

"You want me to keep him here until you arrive?"

"No. Are there other employees there?"

"Production is on spring holiday, but there are a few people around."

"Tell them to get out. Quietly. No need to explain. Say it's police business." I didn't think Dellafiore was armed, but there was no sense having civilians around if we didn't need to. "Then, leave. Do not put yourself in danger and do not let yourself be alone with Mr. Dellafiore."

"Okay." Marcy's voice wavered. "Tell everybody to go. Quietly. Got it." She hung up.

The minute I ended my call, Rodney hit the siren and the blue lights. "He cleared out." He'd ended his phone call first, so he was driving. "Why go back?"

"I don't know." I watched the traffic get out of our

way as we raced by. "Newfane sending backup for the arrest?"

"Yeah. At least two units. I don't get it."

After a while, you stopped expecting criminals to be logical. "He left something behind. He's destroying evidence. Nostalgia. Frankly, I don't care. I want to cuff him."

When we arrived at Natural Wonders, the parking lot was mostly deserted. There were two other cars besides the Newfane black-and-whites and the beater I knew belonged to Dellafiore. We got out and introduced ourselves to the waiting officers.

"We were told you had the warrant," one of them said. "We're supposed to provide support. What do you want us to do?"

"Watch the building." Rodney pointed. "Front entrance and the fire exits. He comes out, grab him. Otherwise, we'll take care of it and holler if we need help."

"What about the other cars?" The patrol cop jerked his thumb toward the vehicles.

I pulled out my gun. "If you see any civilians, get them the hell out of Dodge."

Rodney unholstered his piece. "You ready?"

I nodded. "Let's go."

The lobby was deserted. Soft jazz still played over the PA system. Marcy had probably left it on to maintain the fiction that people were in the building. *Bright girl.* The flowers were fresh, the aroma filling the air. It felt like any other day at the office, except for the lack of people.

"Where do we start?" Rodney asked. "Split up?"

I hesitated. "We don't know if he's armed." *Think. Where would he be?* "The building is essentially a circle. Let's start with the offices. Maybe—"

Dellafiore emerged from the hallway leading to the business areas. He saw us and froze.

"Stay there." I gripped my gun, but I didn't raise it yet. "Police. Anthony Dellafiore. You're under arrest."

Of course, he bolted back down the hallway. Rodney and I took off after him.

Most of the offices were locked. We checked every open door, all of which led to dark conference rooms. The fire exit was alarmed, so Dellafiore hadn't gotten out that way.

Rodney nodded toward the other door. "Think he scuttled around the back?"

"He didn't come back toward us. He has to know he's going in a circle." I pushed the door open. Maybe Dellafiore was hoping he could run around fast enough to get out the front. With any luck, the uniforms outside would foil his plan.

The lab was empty, although the lights were on. Rodney checked the room. "Why do they need this in a makeup company?"

"Don't know." I check the drawers. "Experimentation for new products?"

The closet was empty, at least of people. As we edged down the hallway, I saw one of the uniform officers round the corner. I waved. They must have been circling the building to watch all the exits.

The next door on the hallway was locked.

The third door led to another lab. And Dellafiore.

"Stay where you are." I lifted my gun slightly. The

room was a duplicate of the first, right down to the soapstone counters and Bunsen burners.

"Anthony Dellafiore." Rodney holstered his weapon and pulled out a set of cuffs. "You're under arrest for the murder of Sylvia Bramley. Turn around. Arms out, palms toward the ceiling."

Dellafiore said nothing but took a step back and licked his lips. I could see the sweat on his forehead from where I stood. His hand reached toward a burner.

I tightened my grip. "Don't move."

He jerked his hand and the burner lit. Then, he knocked it into a tray of nearby dishes. What they contained I didn't know, but whatever it was popped into a shower of sparks and smoke. Our target took advantage of the diversion to bolt past us and through the door.

The explosion hadn't been big, but it was enough. I was back at the Occidental Chemical plant. Smoke rolled over me. Sirens wailed. Red flames flickered at the edge of my vision. The heat was at my back. Voices, like a badly-tuned radio station, echoed all around me. I gasped, struggling to breathe.

Rodney's voice sounded like it was coming through a tunnel. "Jackson. Jackson, you okay?"

I couldn't move. My gun clattered to the floor. My heart thudded against my ribs, my breathing rapid and shallow. A back part of my brain told me I was at Natural Wonders. The rest of my mind was convinced I wasn't.

What had the doc said? *Embrace your current reality.* Sure. No problem. Except I didn't quite remember what reality was.

"Bro, talk to me." Rodney's voice was sharp and faint at the same time.

"Go after him." I choked out the words.

"But you—"

"Damn it, go!"

I felt him hesitate. Then, I heard the sound of his footsteps against the ruckus in my head.

Breathe, focus. Use all your senses to pull yourself back. I stared at an outlet at the wall. I gripped the cold, smooth counter. I felt the hard floor under my knees. *This is an electrical outlet. This is stone,* I thought. *This is linoleum. I am not at Occidental Chemical. I am not outside. The smoke is not chemical fumes. I'm in a lab at Natural Wonders and my murder suspect is getting away. Breathe, focus, and get your shit together.*

I didn't know how long it took, but the lab swam back into focus. I gasped. I felt soaked in sweat, but I'd done it. I'd fought my way out and, based on the sounds floating down the hallway, it hadn't taken as long as it felt. I'd come out of the flashback and hadn't hurt myself in the process.

I stood and picked up my gun.

———

I caught up to Rodney in the lobby. He was bent over, coughing. It looked like Madeline's play makeup kit had exploded on his face. Or the time Amy dropped a container of face powder. Dellafiore was nowhere in sight. "What happened?"

"Asshole." Rodney spat. He straightened up, blinking. "I thought I'd cornered him, but he threw some sort of powdery shit in my face. Something from the lab."

Where the hell were the uniforms? Probably still circling. "You okay?"

Rodney nodded, still hacking and spitting.

One of the patrol cops came into sight and I beckoned him to the door. "Has anyone left this building?"

The uniformed officer shook his head. "It's a friggin' circle. There are three exits, two fire doors and this main one. Haven't heard an alarm and we've been trying to keep a close eye on the front. You need help?"

I shook my head. "Concentrate here. We'll hear the fire alarm if he goes out that way. His car is in the parking lot so—"

"Jackson." Rodney's voice was sharp and urgent. "He's down the executive hallway. I hear him."

We re-entered the hall to the offices. This time, Dellafiore was at the fire exit. He pushed on the bar and the alarm went off. The sound froze him in place long enough for us to catch up.

"On the ground." I kept my gun trained on him. "Now."

Once again, Rodney approached with his cuffs out. The fire alarm whooped. If Dellafiore bolted through it, he'd run right into the Newfane patrol cops.

Dellafiore seemed to comply and extended his arms. But as Rodney approached, Dellafiore twisted and kicked. Rodney grunted and doubled over, clutching his groin. Dellafiore tried to run past me, but I blocked him, grabbing his arm and twisting it into an arm bar. "On the ground. Now." I applied slight pressure to his arm. Dellafiore whimpered and dropped to his knees. I turned my head to look at my partner. "You okay?"

"Yeah." Rodney straightened up, his face pinched. "Prick kicked me in the balls."

I felt Dellafiore start to stand up, and I increased the pressure on the arm bar. "I said don't move."

"You're hurting me."

"Then, do what you're told."

He did, and I let up on the pressure again. I looked over to Rodney, who appeared to have recovered. "I'll let you have the honor of cuffing him since you're the guy who took one for the team."

"With pleasure." Rodney made short work of snapping on the cuffs and hauling Dellafiore to his feet.

"Ow." Dellafiore spoke in a whiny voice. "The cuffs are too tight."

Rodney didn't even glance at him. Instead, he focused on me. "No, they're not. Shut up." He looked me up and down. "You okay?"

I re-holstered my weapon. "I feel like I've run a marathon. If we'd done another lap of this place, I'd be on the floor. I need to get back in shape."

"But you're with me."

"Yes. Sorry to leave you hanging. The flash and pop got to me."

"As long as you're solid." Rodney grasped Dellafiore's upper arm, setting off a fresh wave of whining.

I ran my hand through my hair. My breathing and heart rate were returning to normal. "Come on. Let's get this guy booked and finish the paperwork. I'd like to get home for dinner some time tonight." I pulled the fire exit door shut and headed outside.

Rodney followed. "Home for dinner, huh?"

We emerged from the building into the sunshine. I nodded to the uniforms, who had come back around. "We got him. Thanks." Then, I opened the rear of the car and Rodney guided Dellafiore into the back seat. "Great idea."

It was time to go home to my wife and kids.

THIRTY-EIGHT

We got Dellafiore to Booking, then went back to finish the paperwork. "Hey, Davis," Dobrovski called as we walked in. "Where've you been? Making an arrest in a daycare? You two are as shiny as my niece's art projects." He snickered.

I looked at my pants. They glittered in the fluorescent lights from the residue of whatever Dellafiore had thrown in the lab. "Shut it, Dobrovski. You wish you could look this good." I glanced over at Rodney, who was just as sparkly. We looked like we'd taken a roll in a vat of sticky sequins.

We wrote our reports in silence. Eventually, I looked up. Rodney was focused on the paper in front of him. Too focused. The case was over. It was decision time. "Hey, I think Yannick is still here if you want to talk to him." I waved at the captain's office, where the door was open and the lights were on.

"I saw." Rodney didn't move.

Partnership is like marriage, Max had said. Rodney

had seen me at my worst. He'd lived. Breaking in yet another new partner would be a bitch.

"I think I might need another one. Another case." He looked up. "To be sure I'm making the right decision." He glanced at the captain's office and brought his focus back to me. "Consider yourself on extended probation."

"If you say so." I looked at my watch. "You drink beer?"

He grinned. "Depends. Are you buying?"

"I wouldn't have offered otherwise. Let's turn this shit in and go over to Cavanaugh's." I stood, tossed aside the pen, and picked up my report. "But in the interest of partnership, I should tell you something."

He stood and frowned, his eyes narrowed. "What?"

I gestured at his head. "You've got sparkly crap in your hair."

———

I stopped at Max's to collect my things and say goodbye. Surprised to find her not at home, I left a note on the table. I scratched Leroy behind the ears before I left. I'd gotten used to the living white noise machine. Maybe I needed to buy Madeline a kitten.

Next, I stopped at a florist's shop, hoping they had what I wanted. I was willing to drive all over Niagara Falls to find them. If necessary, I'd beg them from a sympathetic homeowner.

I walked through the front door and put my suitcase by the hall table, holding the flowers behind my back. "I'm home."

"Daddy!"

I heard Madeline's joyful squeal and pounding foot-steps, and I braced myself. She jumped up and I caught her with my free arm, hoisting her up so she could wrap her legs around my waist.

"That was a very long biz-nuss trip. I didn't like it."

"I won't leave again. Promise." She looked bigger and felt heavier, but I didn't put her down, clasping her as tightly as I could with one arm. "How about we go out and buy you a bicycle this weekend?"

Her eyes lit up. "A big one?"

"Is there another kind?"

She squealed and hugged me around the neck.

Amy came into the hallway. "Madeline, I told you. Go wash your hands." She eyed me.

I set Madeline down and she scampered off. "Hey."

"Hey yourself." Amy dried her hands with the towel draped over her shoulder.

"Where's Christopher?" I didn't hear him.

"He's being entertained."

Entertained? By whom? I held out the flowers. "I brought you these."

They were calla lilies, white with a blush of pink at the base. The same flowers I'd bought her on our first date, the ones in her wedding bouquet, and the ones I'd bought her after each kid was born. Her favorite. She took them with a trembling hand. "You haven't bought me callas in—"

"Too long." I reached out and pulled her close. "You asked me to come home. Here I am."

"I'm still willing to compromise on dinner and chores." She didn't try to break free of my grasp.

"We'll work something out."

"Last time we talked, you were scared. Has that changed?"

"Yes. I need you. And the kids. I don't know if I'm fixed, for lack of a better word, but I'm better." I tried to calm my heartbeat. "Don't tell me you've changed your mind."

She considered me. The solemn look on her face contrasted with the spark of mischief in her eyes. "I haven't. Besides, I can't let you leave."

I kissed her. "Why? Oh, I know. You want me to deliver on my promise. From the diner."

"I think I promised you." She traced my jawline with her finger.

"I don't really care who promised whom, to be honest. All I care about is the delivery. Do we have time, or is dinner too close to being ready?"

"Dinner is not the issue."

"Oh?" I kissed her neck, down into the opening of her shirt and the hint of cleavage it showed.

She let out a soft gasp. "Stop. We've got company." She broke away. "I'll make good, but you have things to take care of first. By the way, your bedtime story debt is ridiculous."

———

Max was waiting when I went into the dining room. The sight stopped me in my tracks. "What are you doing here?"

"Hi, Jackson. Nice to see you, too. I'm fine. How are you?" She had Christopher on her lap, where he happily babbled away, fascinated by the shiny buttons on her blouse.

I leaned over and kissed his head. "Want me to take him?"

"Not on your life." She pried his fist off a button. "We're getting to know each other."

I sat down across the table from her. "I didn't expect to see you. You weren't home when I stopped to get my stuff. I left a note."

"I know. Thankfully, Mrs. Dockerty across the hall was home to read it to me."

Brilliant, you moron. But Max was laughing at me, so I figured she'd forgiven the lapse. "Where were you? How'd you get here?"

"I took the bus. Niagara Frontier Transit Authority offers discounted rates for the disabled. Therefore, NFTA is my new best friend."

Madeline came back into the room and jumped into my lap.

I shifted her to a more comfortable position. "But where'd you go?"

"Job interview." Max leaned back as Amy brought dinner in and set it on the table.

I blinked. "A job interview? For real?" She had never mentioned anything.

Amy swatted me with the pot holder. "Madeline, sit in your seat."

My daughter hopped off my lap and sat next to me.

"I am employable, you know." Max spread her napkin on her lap. "Blind people get jobs all the time."

"I never said you weren't employable." I helped

myself to potatoes and spooned some onto Madeline's plate. "Amy, help me out. Please."

Amy laughed. "He means great news, Max. Tell him where the interview was."

Max served herself with such fluid dexterity, a stranger would never know she was blind. "Niagara University. I'm throwing my hat in the ring for an adjunct position in their Criminal Justice Program. Got the idea from the receptionist at Dr. Alverson's."

"That's awesome." I meant it. Teaching about police work was the next best thing to doing it. It was the perfect job for her. "I guess this means Rodney and I are on our own. You'll be too busy to consult."

"Not so fast, bub." She took a sip of water. "If you think I'm turning you loose on the world without supervision, think again. You've come a long way. I'll be there to keep you from backsliding."

I paused, unable to find words. I'd been damn lucky and I knew it. "Thanks."

The rapids had carried me right to the edge of the gorge, but I'd fought my way back with more than a little help. All I had to do was refrain from being swept away again. With the people around me, I liked my chances.

ACKNOWLEDGMENTS

When I published my first book, *Root of All Evil*, in 2018, I thought I was ridiculously lucky. It takes hard work, perseverance, skill, and more than a little good fortune to write and publish one novel. A little over six years later, I'm celebrating the release of my first book in a third series and my fourteenth mystery novel.

Talk about ridiculously lucky.

I realize now, even more than then, how many people have helped me get here. To my critique group – Annette Dashofy, Jeff Boarts, and Peter WJ Hayes – I couldn't do it without you. Here's hoping we have as much fun with Jackson and Max as we have with Jim, Sally, Betty, and her friends. To all the police officers, lawyers, and other professionals who answer my unending questions, a million thanks. Any errors are my own. My first piece of advice to new authors is "find your people" and I have mine in Sisters in Crime and Pennwriters, without whom I would not be published.

A special thank-you to the readers who allow me to pursue this madcap adventure called "writing a mystery." Maybe I pull my hair out along the way, but hearing a reader say, "You kept me up past my bedtime" makes it all worthwhile (sorry, not sorry).

I have to offer a special thanks to my first agent, Dawn Dowdle. Dawn loved this series and worked hard to see it in print. Unfortunately, Dawn passed away in 2023, so she'll never see the fruits of her labor. Thanks for taking a chance on me, Dawn. You are missed.

Last, but not least, thank you to my family including my husband, Paul. Through good times and not-so-good ones, you've had my back. I love you.

ABOUT THE AUTHOR

 Liz Milliron is the Shamus-nominated author of the Homefront Mysteries, set in Buffalo, NY in the early years of WWII. The series features Betty Ahern, a Rosie the Riveter turned Sam Spade. She is also the author of the Laurel Highlands mystery series, starring a Pennsylvania State Trooper and a Fayette County public defender in the scenic Laurel Highlands of southwest Pennsylvania. Her short fiction has been published in multiple anthologies including Murder Most International, Blood on the Bayou, and Murder Most Historical. Liz is a past president of the Pittsburgh Chapter of Sisters in Crime and the current Vice President, as well as the Education Liaison for the National Board of Sisters in Crime. She is a member of International Thriller Writers, Pennwriters and the Historical Novel Society. Liz lives in the Laurel Highlands, where she lives with her husband and a very spoiled retired-racer greyhound.

facebook.com / LizMilliron

instagram.com / lizmilliron

threads.net / @lizmilliron

bookbub.com / authors / liz-milliron

ABOUT THE PUBLISHER

Harbor Lane Books, LLC is a US-based independent digital publisher of commercial fiction, non-fiction, and poetry.

Connect with Harbor Lane Books on their website (www.harborlanebooks.com) and social media @harborlanebooks.

facebook.com/harborlanebooks

x.com/harborlanebooks

instagram.com/harborlanebooks

bsky.app/profile/harborlanebooks.bsky.social

tiktok.com/@harborlanebooks

threads.net/harborlanebooks

youtube.com/harborlanebooks

pinterest.com/harborlanebooks

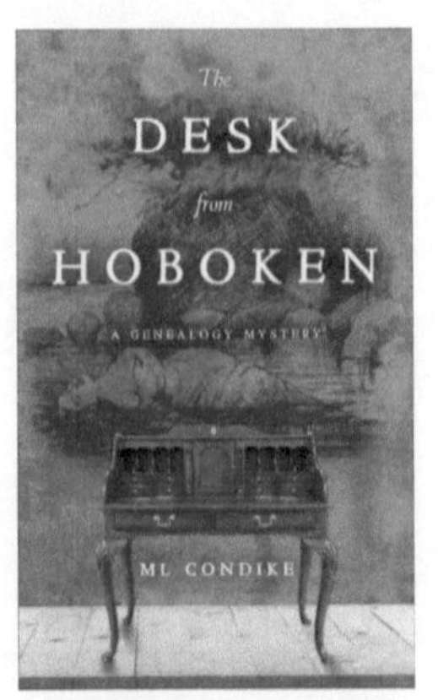
The
DESK
from
HOBOKEN
A GENEALOGY MYSTERY
ML CONDIKE

The
DOLL
from
DUNEDIN
A GENEALOGY MYSTERY
ML CONDIKE
author of The Desk from Hoboken

ESSENTIALS
OF
MURDER
KIM DAVIS

MURDEROUS CONSEQUENCES
USA TODAY BESTSELLING AUTHOR
NICOLE LEIREN